"From the end to the beginning, David Ellis's latest novel delivers a thrilling ride . . . Nothing is what it seems in *In the Company of Liars*, David Ellis's compelling new novel of intrigue, murder, and terrorism."

—*The Philadelphia Inquirer*

"Excellent . . . Ellis keeps us in suspense."

—*Chicago Tribune*

"Ellis took a courageous gamble in using the reverse chronology device. It works . . . [an] inventive, captivating, and eminently satisfying novel."   —*Orlando Sentinel*

"Ellis . . . is bound to find more fans with this thrilling novel that holds your attention from end to beginning. You'll be happy you spent time *In the Company of Liars*."

—*Detroit Free Press*

"Ellis takes some big chances in his fourth book, and he pulls them off in grand style . . . This is another impressive performance from a writer who expands his ambition and artistry from book to book."   —*Publishers Weekly*

"Ellis, 37, can actually write. Oh, and plot like a mo-fo . . . In this tale of murder, terrorism and governmental shadiness, *Liars* unfurls chronologically in reverse, with some purposely bamboozling red herrings tossed in for good measure. Circumstances and characters aren't always what and who they appear to be. Ellis, as those who read him know, digs his twists."   —*Chicago Sun-Times*

continued . . .

"Ellis has put a new twist on thrillers—he's written his latest in reverse chronological order . . . skilled writing and a tricky storyline make it work . . . All these threads are neatly woven into this intricate plot, but nothing is as it seems as the roller-coaster ride keeps coiling backwards, finally hurtling to the starting point. Strongly recommended."   —*Library Journal* (starred review)

"Amply rewarding at the end—which, of course, is the beginning."   —*Kirkus Reviews*

JURY OF ONE

"Smashes through the barriers of coincidence and credulity, leaving readers breathless at the author's audacity."
        —*Chicago Tribune*

"Compelling."   —*Entertainment Weekly*

"[A] terrific legal thriller . . . in the tradition of Scott Turow and even superstar John Grisham . . . The twists and turns are always surprising, the courtroom politics interesting, and the story a grabber from start to finish." —*Toronto Sun*

"Among would-be Grishams and Turows, he's a breakaway talent."   —*The Hollywood Reporter*

"A steady stream of twists and complications . . . a stunning Perry Mason–style courtroom shocker will knock readers right out of their seats. After they pick themselves up off the floor, the ensuing fast and furious revelations will have them flying through the final pages."
        —*Publishers Weekly*

LIFE SENTENCE

LINE OF VISION
Edgar® Award–winner

TITLES BY DAVID ELLIS

In the Company of Liars
Jury of One
Life Sentence
Line of Vision

IN THE COMPANY OF LIARS

DAVID ELLIS

BERKLEY BOOKS, NEW YORK

THE BERKLEY PUBLISHING GROUP
Published by the Penguin Group
Penguin Group (USA) Inc.
375 Hudson Street, New York, New York 10014, USA

Penguin Group (Canada), 90 Eglinton Avenue East, Suite 700, Toronto, Ontario M4P 2Y3, Canada
(a division of Pearson Penguin Canada Inc.)
Penguin Books Ltd., 80 Strand, London WC2R 0RL, England
Penguin Group Ireland, 25 St. Stephen's Green, Dublin 2, Ireland (a division of Penguin Books Ltd.)
Penguin Group (Australia), 250 Camberwell Road, Camberwell, Victoria 3124, Australia
(a division of Pearson Australia Group Pty. Ltd.)
Penguin Books India Pvt. Ltd., 11 Community Centre, Panchsheel Park, New Delhi—110 017, India
Penguin Group (NZ), Cnr. Airborne and Rosedale Roads, Albany, Auckland 1310, New Zealand
(a division of Pearson New Zealand Ltd.)
Penguin Books (South Africa) (Pty.) Ltd., 24 Sturdee Avenue, Rosebank, Johannesburg 2196,
South Africa

Penguin Books Ltd., Registered Offices: 80 Strand, London WC2R 0RL, England

This is a work of fiction. Names, characters, places, and incidents either are the product of the author's imagination or are used fictitiously, and any resemblance to actual persons, living or dead, business establishments, events, or locales is entirely coincidental. The publisher does not have any control over and does not assume any responsibility for author or third-party websites or their content.

IN THE COMPANY OF LIARS

A Berkley Book / published by arrangement with the author

PRINTING HISTORY
G. P. Putnam's Sons hardcover edition / April 2005
Berkley mass-market edition / March 2006

ISBN: 0-425-20429-4

BERKLEY®
Berkley Books are published by The Berkley Publishing Group,
a division of Penguin Group (USA) Inc.,
375 Hudson Street, New York, New York 10014.
BERKLEY is a registered trademark of Penguin Group (USA) Inc.
The "B" design is a trademark belonging to Penguin Group (USA) Inc.

PRINTED IN THE UNITED STATES OF AMERICA

10 9 8 7 6 5 4 3 2 1

For Jennifer, Jim, Jenna, and Ryan Taylor

JUNE

SATURDAY, JUNE 5

McCoy is first through the door. She hears the man running through the house, his bare feet slapping across the hardwood floor. "Back bedroom," she is told via her earpiece by a member of the team at the rear of the house, looking through the kitchen window, blocking an escape route.

They flood in behind her, a team of eight agents, but she is first down the hallway. Her back against the wall, both hands on the Glock at her side, she shuffles up to the bedroom door and listens. Over the sound of her team's shoes on the hardwood, she can hear sobbing. She reaches across the width of the door and tries the knob. The door opens slightly, then McCoy pushes it open wider with her foot and pivots, her Glock trained inside the room, and she sees what she expects.

He is standing at the opposite end of the bedroom, near what appears to be a walk-in closet and then a bathroom. A large bed separates the man and McCoy.

McCoy holds a hand up behind her, freezing the other agents in place, before returning her hand to the Glock trained on the suspect.

"Put the gun down, Doctor," she says.

Doctor Lomas, she knows, is a broken man, nothing like the proud figure she has seen in the company brochures. She stifles the instinct to think of him as a victim, though a victim, in many ways, is precisely what he is. It is hard to look at this man, barefoot in boxer shorts and a rumpled white T-shirt with stained armpits, with flyaway hair and an emaciated frame, and see the promising scientist he once was.

The doctor is crying uncontrollably, his chest heaving and tears flowing. Part of her job is seeing the worst in people, watching them feel, firsthand, the collapse of their lives. But she doesn't often confront a man holding a revolver to his temple.

Behind her, McCoy hears one of the agents on his radio, calling for paramedics. Others are searching the remainder of the house, kicking open doors to rooms and closets.

"I didn't know," Lomas manages through halting breaths, but of course that statement itself means that he did know, or at least suspected. "I didn't. I didn't know, I didn't—"

"I believe you, Doctor," she says calmly. "Put the gun on the bed and let's just talk."

"They'll kill me," he says.

He's not talking about the federal agents swarming outside the bedroom. She knows it. Doctor Lomas seems to assume she knows it.

"There's no 'they' anymore, Doctor. 'They' are all in custody. You're the last one."

He doesn't seem to be listening. Fear of death does not seem to be foremost in his mind. No, what's causing the heaving of his chest, the trembling of the arm that tries to keep the gun pressed against his skull, is not what will happen now but what has already taken place.

The television, resting in a dark oak armoire, is on a cable news station. The headline blaring across the bottom of the screen is "Muhsin al-Bakhari Captured." Reporters are live from northern Sudan, the cameras on the assault that took place last night on a convoy of terrorists resulting in the capture of the Liberation Front's number-two man.

"You know why you're the last one we picked up?" McCoy says to Doctor Lomas, as evenly as she can. "Because we know you're not a threat. We know you're not a bad person. Because we know you were tricked." McCoy motions to the television set. "You see that, Doctor? You see we caught Mushi?"

Doctor Lomas blinks, as if surprised by the change of topic. Suicides, in these instances, often go down a single track on their way to pulling the trigger or slitting their wrists. The key is to pull them away from their tunnel vision, to make them think about anything at all that might sober them up.

"So what?" His voice breaks, trembles. His trigger finger twitches.

She is ten feet from the doctor, but the bed prevents any interception she might attempt. If this guy wants to die, she won't be able to stop him.

"So," McCoy says, "you helped make that happen. This," she says, nodding to him, then gesturing toward the TV set, "was about *that.*"

"That—" Lomas's face contorts, a hideous, trembling snarl of a mouth struggling with the words. "*That's* where it went? To—to *them?* To *terrorists?*"

"We intercepted it," McCoy says quickly. "We have the formula in our possession. It's over, Doctor. No one was hurt."

"Allison Pagone," he whimpers. "She's dead because of

me. I knew she didn't kill herself," he adds, more to himself. "I *knew* they killed her." He starts to quiver again, his
whole body like a shot of electricity has hit him.

"Listen to me, Doctor, Allison Pagone—"

"No closer." Lomas takes another step back and brushes
the wall. With the jerk in his movement, his right elbow
drops, and the gun slides off his temple, pointing upward.

McCoy fires once, into the brachial nerve near the col-
larbone on the doctor's gun side. The doctor's hand immediately releases the gun, which falls to the floor and
bounces into the closet. Two reasons for severing the
brachial nerve—he can't hold the weapon and he can re-
cover, for the most part, from a shoulder injury; had she
gone for his hand, he'd never be able to use it again.

She is on him immediately, as he slides to the floor.
Lomas makes no effort to reach the gun. He doesn't even
seem to notice the wound, a red, widening stain on his
T-shirt, dark at the center.

McCoy finds the nearest piece of laundry, a pair of un-
derwear, balls it up and applies pressure to the wound.
Doctor Lomas stares wide-eyed, a deep, consistent moan
coming from his throat.

McCoy talks to him. She tells him to hang on, everything is going to be okay. She looks up and sees the bullet
mark in the wall, which means it went through cleanly, no
ricochet down to a major organ. He was lucky. Luckier
than some.

The paramedics arrive and take over. In the bathroom
McCoy splashes some water on her face and lets out a
groan. Her partner, Owen Harrick, is behind her, smiling at
her in the mirror.

"It's over, Janey," he says. "This is the end."

"Yeah." She shakes the water off her hands.

"What you have to do," Harrick advises, "is forget about
the beginning."

ONE DAY EARLIER

FRIDAY, JUNE 4

He knows immediately that no one will escape, and that few will survive. He knows it the moment he is blasted out of his drowsiness in the back of the dark truck by a deafening boom, the explosion of what he assumes to be the lead truck in the convoy. He knows it as the truck in which he is traveling screeches to a halt over the uneven terrain, as the men seated on benches on each side of the darkened cargo area fall into each other, and as the truck behind them slams into their rear, sending the men sprawling to the floor.

He knows it as he and the others in the second truck scramble for their weapons. He knows it when he hears, over the sounds of his brothers' cries, the *thwip, thwip, thwip* of rockets cutting through the air—undoubtedly in the direction of the rear truck in the convoy—followed quickly by the explosion upon impact with the gasoline engines.

He knows that the Americans have found them.

And they know who is traveling in this convoy. That is why the obvious security flanks have been eliminated from the outset. In no more than ten seconds, the front and rear trucks have been obliterated, trapping the two middle trucks on a narrow, winding road.

Ram Haroon looks toward the rear of the truck, where the sheath covering the back is flapping open. He sees small flashes from the red-orange gasoline fire two trucks behind.

Haroon races for the exit as the gunfire erupts—the *pop pop, pop pop* from the M4s, the *rat-a-tat-tat* from the stationary machine guns—lead splitting the canvas exterior of the cargo cabin and hitting skulls, torsos, bone. Haroon extends himself horizontally as he dives through the sheath, trying to minimize himself as a target, trying to freeze out the sudden smells of blood, of bowels releasing, of death.

He lands on the hood of the third truck, slamming his head onto the cold surface, and everything goes dark.

First he dreams in smells: the odor of burning gasoline, the copperlike scent of burning flesh. Then he dreams of dust filling his mouth, of wounded cries and urgent prayers before death. He dreams of his mother and sister. He dreams of his leg on fire.

He dreams of a man talking to him in broken Arabic, and Haroon's eyes open. Two sets of boots, two sets of legs, two M4 rifles within inches of his cheek.

"*Irka*," one of them shouts. "On your knees, fuck-face."

U.S. Army Rangers, working in pairs, searching for survivors and confirming the dead. One of them steps back, training the rifle on him, while the other pats Haroon down for explosives. Then he grabs Haroon's shirt and pulls until Haroon is on his knees. His shirt is violently ripped from his body, his hands zip-tied behind his back.

He knows why they attacked and who they wanted. Their high-value target. Muhsin al-Bakhari.

Haroon struggles to gain his bearings, his body limp from the assault and his mind in chaos. He is in northern Sudan. It is early June. It is close to midnight. *"Kiff! Kiff!"* the Ranger says to Haroon, yanking him to his feet. A blindfold is wrapped over his eyes, and he moves forward tentatively, his legs unreliable, assisted by a Ranger's hand cupped under his armpit.

Don't let them take you alive, he has been told. *They will torture you. Corrupt you. Take you to Guantánamo Bay and make you turn on your brothers.*

Die with dignity, they have told him.

But resistance is obviously futile. This whole thing was timed perfectly. The Americans did not plan for a gunfight. They planned for a massacre.

Ram Haroon recalls other instructions as well, outside the presence of the leaders. *Show them your hands and they won't kill you.*

He hears the *thwop, thwop* of the rotors of a Chinook helicopter as he is marched forward, forced into a jog. He feels a wash of air as he approaches the Chinook, and a hand on his head pushes it down, even though Haroon knows the rotors are well overhead.

He is turned around. A hand on his shoulder forces him to sit on a cold aluminum floor. He shivers. The rotors spin faster and louder, the copter shakes—even sitting, he lurches to one side and bumps into the barrel of a rifle pointed at him. The copter shakes again and rises.

He feels a boot pushing against his arm. *"Hal Tatakalm Alingli'ziu?"* an American shouts at him in passable Arabic. *"Ma Ismok?"*

"Zulfikar," he answers wearily. *"Sorirart Biro'aitak."*

A moment passes. The Americans are speaking to each other in excited voices. This is a moment of celebration for the Rangers. Nausea overtakes Ram Haroon, the jerky movements of the helicopter and the smell of burning flesh, still lingering in his nostrils, combining to launch the bile to his throat. They are enjoying themselves, these Americans. A moment for which all Americans have waited for years—the capture of Muhsin al-Bakhari. A story they will share with their grandchildren someday.

Where he will go now, he does not know. They have quickly whisked away the few survivors, including the one whom the Americans prize the most. Left behind is a massacre; over thirty Islamic soldiers dead.

And then it comes to Ram Haroon. He remembers the woman at the airport in America four days ago. *McCoy,* that was her name. Yes. The woman at the airport knew this was going to happen.

Haroon shakes his head, silent. He will probably be sent to Guantánamo Bay, along with the others. He will never see his homeland again. His life will never be the same.

He wonders what has become of his partners in the States. He assumes that they will soon be in U.S. custody as well. And if they have gotten so far as to coordinate this attack, they have probably learned what really happened to Allison Pagone, the American novelist, as well.

TUESDAY, JUNE 1

McCoy knows almost everything about him. She knows his names—his real one and the one he is using. She knows one parent is listed as Pakistani, the other as Egyptian, and that the paperwork all the way back to Islamabad will show that. She knows that the CIA files will show that he is an operative with the Liberation Front, an organization responsible for the death of more than nine hundred civilians in the past five years. She knows he will deny that if asked. She knows that he is studying for a graduate degree in international economics at the state university. She knows when he flew into the United States. She already knew, before receiving the call, that he had booked a flight to Paris. She knew about ten minutes after he bought the ticket.

Jane McCoy stands with her partner, Owen Harrick, and the BICE agent in charge at the airport, a guy named Pete Storino, in a small room with monitors along a high shelf.

McCoy has spent the last ten minutes babysitting Storino, explaining why she couldn't tell him squat, giving him numbers to call to clear all this. Storino doesn't like it and he doesn't like her. The BICE guys aren't the happiest these days. With the reorg under Homeland Security, Storino's agency is now the Bureau of Immigration and Customs Enforcement. They don't like it because people call them "BICE" agents. FBI agents don't like it because they think of their agency as "the Bureau" and don't want another one. The agencies left out of the BICE acronym, like the Coast Guard and Border Patrol, were pissed off because, well, they were left out. Word is, they're going to change it to the Bureau of Investigations and Criminal Enforcement, keeping the acronym but giving it a more general connotation, but McCoy will believe it when she sees it.

"I'm going to make those calls," Storino says to McCoy, sounding like a wounded child who's going to call his mom.

"Great," she says. "I'm going in soon. If that's all right." She winks at her partner with that last comment.

"Do what you're gonna do." Storino closes the door behind him.

McCoy leans forward and watches the monitor covering the small room where the subject is seated. He is cool, his legs crossed, his hands resting on the rectangular table, occasionally checking his watch and shaking his head. He is no dummy, this one. He knows he's being watched. He wants to be a Pakistani student offended by the racial profiling, not a bad guy who's nervous about what the G is going to ask him.

McCoy and Harrick leave the room and walk down a narrow corridor to the door in question. McCoy takes a breath, nods at her partner, and opens the door.

"Mr. Haroon," she says, walking in and taking a seat.

"I'm Special Agent Jane McCoy. This is Special Agent Owen Harrick. FBI."

Ram Haroon is thin but muscular. He has ink-black, kinky hair and a long, coffee-colored face. He looks the age that is on his passport: twenty-six. He studies each of them with coal-black eyes but says nothing.

"Headed to Paris," she says.

He stares at her like the answer is obvious. He has a business-class ticket for a flight that is scheduled to depart in forty-five minutes.

"What's in Paris?" she asks. "And don't say the Eiffel Tower."

He looks away from her, as if amused. Trying to show his resolve. She gets that sometimes, but not very often. Most people hear "FBI" and their knees tremble.

"Is that your final destination, Mr. Haroon?"

The man finally sighs, adjusts himself in his chair, and focuses on her. "I have a round-trip ticket," he says. Of course he does. He's schooled enough to know not to buy a one-way ticket these days. It's like holding up a sign.

Ram Haroon's return trip is in late July. She knows it, and he knows she knows it. He also knows that she wasn't referring to his return leg.

"Is Paris your final destination?" she asks again.

"What does that matter?" He has a heavy Middle Eastern accent but seems quite comfortable with English.

"Do you want to make your flight?"

"I do."

"Then please answer my question."

He stares at Jane's partner for a long moment. "Sight-seeing," he says.

"Sure." She nods and looks at her partner, shrugs, as if this makes perfect sense. "How were classes at the state university this spring? Did you have a good semester?"

He smiles for the first time. He leans forward on the

small table in front of him, drops his elbows. "Trimester," he corrects.

She smiles back at him.

"And it went well, thank you."

"Finals were good?"

He shakes his head.

"What was your favorite class?" she asks.

He thinks for a moment. "Socialism in the twentieth century."

"What was that—a test? A paper?"

He closes his eyes a moment. "A take-home final."

"Who taught it?"

"Rosenthal."

"When was the final?"

"Oh—five days ago."

"Where? What classroom?"

"I just told you it was a take-home final."

Jane McCoy sits back in her chair. She is not at all surprised that he knows the answers. "You were flagged, Mr. Haroon. Did you know that?"

He shrugs.

"Do you know why you were flagged?"

"Because I'm Middle Eastern," he answers. "We're all terrorists. Haven't you heard?"

"I like that." She smiles at her partner, then nods at Haroon. "What was your next-favorite class? After the one about socialism?"

"I liked them all."

"You liked them all equally?"

"I did. But since you have such a—a fascination with my studies, let's say international protection of human rights."

"You liked that one."

"I did."

"Protecting human rights. What'd they teach you—it's a good thing?"

"A good thing," he says. "Maybe you should have taken the course."

This guy is playing this about right. Indignant but not controversially so. Nothing over the top. No hint of a temper, but not icy-cool, either. Right down the middle.

"Name another class," McCoy says.

"Another—? Law of the European Union," he answers.

"Who taught it?"

"Professor Vogler."

"Where was the class held?"

Haroon sighs. His fingers touch his eyes. "In the Smithe Auditorium."

"Are you meeting any friends in Paris?"

"No."

"Flying solo, huh?"

"I will be alone, if that's what you mean. I'm not so familiar with your expressions."

"Oh, you speak better English than I do, Mr. Haroon." McCoy leans back in her chair, as if she is getting comfortable for a long talk. "Let's try some words you might know better. How about the Liberation Front?"

Ram Haroon swallows hard. His face goes cold. You always look at the eyes. A person can keep his mouth straight, his hands still. The eyes always jump.

He should act angry, McCoy thinks to herself. A Pakistani citizen detained at an American airport who is not a Libbie should be terribly offended at the suggestion.

"I am not a member of the Liberation Front," he says evenly.

"Your dad is, though, right?"

"My father was a carpet merchant. He is deceased. And he was not a member of the Liberation Front."

"You Libbies aren't real fond of us Americans, are you?" she asks. "The industrialized nations? You attend our schools and use our computers and cell phones, but you hate us."

He looks at her hard for a moment, but he declines the bait.

"I am not a member of the Liberation Front," he repeats.

Jane McCoy looks at her partner, whose eyebrows arch. "Wait here, please," McCoy says, as if Ram Haroon had any choice.

The federal agents leave the room without saying anything more to the detainee. Agent Harrick whispers to McCoy before they make it back to the monitor room.

"Convincing?" he asks.

"Convincing enough. His grades are top of the class." She looks back at the closed door behind which Ram Haroon is probably wondering what to make of the conversation. "There's absolutely no basis to hold him. There is no proof that he's done anything. And he's leaving, not coming."

"Right," Harrick agrees. "Right."

Pete Storino steps out of the monitor room as they approach. He was watching, no doubt.

"So he's walking," he says to McCoy.

She shrugs. "No basis to hold him."

"Doesn't mean we can't."

No, that's probably true, and she senses that Storino enjoys that fact. There is something intoxicating about power. Serving a warrant, scooping a suspect, holding a Middle Eastern man without cause—all different versions of the same thing, the flexing of muscle, belonging to something important enough that it lets you do things others can't.

"He's not on the no-fly," Agent Harrick says.

McCoy shoots her partner a look. He's debating. Not the time, not the place.

"Well, screw the Bureau, I guess," Storino says, apparently referring to his, not McCoy's. "This guy's walking."

"Sorry about the hush-hush." McCoy shrugs.

"And screw interagency cooperation, too, I guess."

"Not my call, Pete."

"I expect this crap from NSA, even CIA. Not you guys."

"We gotta run, Pete. I appreciate it."

Storino nods once, deliberately, squinting his eyes. "I saw you on the tube. Couple weeks back. It was you, wasn't it?"

"My ten minutes," McCoy admits.

"Allison Pagone. The writer. Killed that guy."

"She wasn't convicted, but—"

"She ate a bullet before it could happen," Storino interrupts. "I made you for Public Corruption. That whole thing was about bribes, right? State lawmakers on the take."

"Something like that."

"Something like that," Storino mimics. "So today I'm making you for CT."

The counterterrorism squad, he means.

"What's the murder of a political guy got to do with this Haroon guy?"

"Hey, I go where they tell me. My day to catch flags."

Storino isn't convinced. "Look, Agent McCoy—"

"Call me Jane."

"—you want to give me the Heisman, give me the Heisman. Do me a favor, though, don't blow smoke up my ass."

McCoy sighs. "Again, Pete, thank you, and I'm sorry about this. I'm just a working gal here."

"You think this guy killed Allison Pagone," he says. "You think she didn't take her own life."

"Pete—"

"I've got a Pakistani national with a flag walking through my airport, I've got someone from Homeland in D.C. telling me to do whatever you say, and I don't know shit about it."

"I owe you one," McCoy says. "Okay? No joke. Any

time." She looks at her watch. "He's going to miss his flight."

"Yeah, I'd hate to see that happen."

McCoy pivots and stands in front of Storino. She jams a finger into his chest. "You *definitely* would hate to see that happen, Agent Storino. Are we clear?"

Storino looks hard at McCoy, then at her partner. Slowly, a smile creeps along his face. "Always nice to see you all from the Bureau," he says.

"Pleasure's been all mine." McCoy turns and walks down the hallway. "Prick," she mumbles out of earshot. "I don't have enough shit to deal with?"

"Janey, the mouth." Harrick chuckles.

The agents leave the airport and begin their trip back to the federal building downtown, where the Special Agent in Charge is eagerly awaiting a report. Jane closes her eyes a moment as the escort drives them back to their car. She has seen death and tried hard to deny responsibility. It does no good to grieve excessively. You mourn the dead but keep fighting to prevent more death. That is what she has been doing, what has propelled her forward. And her job—this op—is not yet done, but it is close. Very close. She'll sleep well tonight for the first time in months. She'll make up for all those nights in May when she paced her small bedroom, thinking everything through, worrying about the number of hurdles that could have clipped her foot.

Does Mr. Ramadaran Ali Haroon have any idea what is about to happen?

Today is the first day of June, the unofficial beginning of summer. It was a hectic February, a chaotic March, an incredibly tense April. And May, the month that just ended, was possibly the hardest thirty-one days of her life.

But it's almost over. They will make their arrests soon, and her part in this operation will be completed. She can't worry about things she can't control. She can only do her part.

Sam Dillon's death started it. Allison Pagone's death ended it.

She shakes her head in resignation, still unable to believe how this began.

MAY

SUNDAY, MAY 16

The crowd is small, which is surprising in a way. The family wanted a small service; it is a tribute to their planning that only two reporters managed to figure out the time and place. The family's success in eluding the media is probably due to their decision to forgo a church service. The media probably had its eye on the church Allison Pagone had attended her entire life. They would have no way of knowing which cemetery had been chosen for her burial.

It's a nice place. Three acres of beautiful land, manicured lawn, well-kept plots. A new two-story granite mausoleum is secluded in a shady area to the northwest. A nicer place than Jane McCoy expects to end up in when her ticket is punched, on her government salary.

From her position in the driver's seat of the limousine, McCoy looks through the one-way tinted windows at her surroundings. First, for the exits. Technically, there is only one. A road that leads from the main gate, snakes through the cemetery, and leads back out.

It's a beautiful day for a service, if there is such a thing, owing primarily to the sun. One of those days when it's hard to keep your eyes open. You won't hear complaints anywhere across the city, though, after the permanent gray sky that prevailed from January through April. With the blinding rays and the temperature close to sixty, people are dressed optimistically, praying that today is a harbinger and not a tease.

It reminds McCoy of the first time she approached her mother's grave after her memorial service. She was thirteen then, hardly able to comprehend the loss, offended at the strong sunlight cast over the headstone, as if someone, somewhere, were trying to make the world beautiful on a day that was anything but.

The limousine is parked on the narrow road only about ten yards from the service. Jane McCoy cracks her window and listens to the pastor.

"Allison Pagone." The minister stops on the words. Jane assumes that the reverend has known Allison over the years.

"Allison Pagone was a woman of substance. A woman of faith." The reverend, an older, pudgy man with a thin beard, looks up at the sky a moment, then collects himself. "Do we judge a woman based on the last year of her life, or on the first thirty-seven? Do we remember only the mistakes she made in a difficult moment, or do we recall all the giving and sacrifice and love she provided for her family and friends? Can we forgive?"

That's a good question. Forgiveness is not something in which an agent of the FBI specializes. Her job is apprehension, sometimes prevention; she is never asked for, and never offers, absolution. She finds the concept overwhelming. She never liked her classes in philosophy—the study

of questions that can't be answered—or religion—the study
of answers that can't be questioned. She preferred her under-
grad classes on criminal justice. *This is right. This is wrong.*
And she never understood how one moment of repentance
can absolve years of sin. One expression of regret erasing
countless misdeeds? It's just not how she's wired.

"I hate these places." A voice through her earpiece; it's
Owen Harrick, who is driving the hearse parked in front of
the limousine.

Jane McCoy looks over at the service. Allison Pagone's
ex-husband, Mateo Pagone, and their twenty-year-old
daughter, Jessica Pagone, are the only ones seated.
Allison's parents are deceased and she was an only child,
so the family is small. The rest of the tiny crowd is mostly
neighbors, some friends from the church, someone from
the publishing house in New York. That woman from the
publishing house is probably mourning the most. Allison
Pagone was a best-selling novelist.

McCoy looks at the ex-husband, Mat Pagone, again. He
is in a well-tailored black suit with a silver tie. He is staring straight ahead in concentration. His right hand is
locked in the hands of his daughter, Jessica, who is also
staring forward with red, numb eyes.

McCoy speaks into the mike on her collar. "See the
hubby?"

Owen Harrick answers back. "Yeah."

"He doesn't do a very good job of looking broken up
about the whole thing. His wife just kicked it?"

"Ex-wife," Owen clarifies.

"That's cold, Harrick," she says, but she chuckles.

"He looks more bored than sad," her partner agrees. "So
what do we do?"

The service is breaking up. The whole thing didn't last
more than fifteen minutes. A closed-casket affair, the coffin already in the ground when the attendees arrived. Mat

Pagone rises with his daughter, holding her hand. Together, they scoop a piece of dirt and drop it onto the coffin.

"We do what we do best," Jane McCoy says into her collar. "We wait."

WEDNESDAY, MAY 12

McCoy is out of the vehicle before her partner has even stopped the sedan in Allison Pagone's driveway. McCoy jogs up the steps to the home, glancing at windows as she passes. She rings the doorbell and knocks urgently on the door.

"Mrs. Pagone," she says. "It's Special Agent McCoy."

She looks at Harrick. He has stepped around to the passenger side of their Mercury, around to the side of Allison's garage.

McCoy knocks again. "Allison," she calls out. She looks at her watch. It is close to seven o'clock in the morning. People are walking their dogs and going for their pre-work jogs. McCoy likes to run in the morning, too, but today she did not have that luxury.

"Her car's here," says Harrick.

They look at each other for a long moment. For this kind of decision, there is no strict protocol.

"Back door," says McCoy.

The back door is an easy decision. There are neighbors outside now—people who have undoubtedly grown curious at the sight of the two serious-looking people in blue coats with the FBI insignia in yellow on their backs who have run up to the front doorstep of the Pagone residence. Better to decelerate the attention by going in the back way. Plus, McCoy knows the back door will be easier to get through.

McCoy pops the trunk of her Mercury Sable and removes her Mag-Lite, a wide, black flashlight. She could call a federal magistrate and get a warrant. That would make some sense. But technically, McCoy has only speculation to support her fears that something bad has happened inside the house. And you have to be careful what you tell a judge in an application for a warrant. To say nothing of the fact that the news could leak and the media could jump on it. It's a small miracle, frankly, that there are no reporters parked along the street right now.

No. No time for legal niceties. This is what is known as an "exigent circumstance," meaning action must be taken immediately to prevent something irreversible from happening, be it destruction of evidence, grave bodily harm, or death. The courts, in their roles as guardians of the constitution and as law-enforcement tutors, have pronounced that warrants are not required in such instances. The *exigent circumstance* is an FBI agent's best friend, right up there with *plain view*.

Anyone listening to the voice mail Allison Pagone left on McCoy's cell phone last night would find these *circumstances* to be plenty *exigent*.

Standing on the back patio, Jane McCoy flicks her Mag-Lite against the glass window of the back door. The glass shatters and falls into the small curtain covering it. McCoy scrapes the edges of the window clean of glass and carefully reaches through to unlock the back door.

She opens it and waits. No alarm. She had noticed an intruder alarm last time she was here. Allison Pagone would be foolish not to have one. McCoy finds the alarm pad on the wall. Nothing. No silent, or audible, alarm. It is disarmed. She walks through the kitchen into the den. She sees the burgundy couch where Allison Pagone was sitting the last time they spoke.

"Allison Pagone!" she calls out. "Federal agents in the house!"

McCoy listens but hears nothing.

"Special Agents McCoy and Harrick, FBI," she calls.

"Maybe she's not home," Harrick offers.

McCoy shakes her head. "No. Her car's here. She's here. You didn't hear that phone message. You didn't—I didn't mean to to—"

"Nothing's even happened yet, Jane. There's nothing to worry about until there's something to worry about." Harrick looks around, calls out Allison Pagone's name.

"I've got a bad feeling." McCoy walks through the downstairs, then meets Harrick back in the den. "I'm going upstairs."

McCoy calls out the name *Allison Pagone* several times as she takes the stairs. *Jane McCoy, FBI. Federal agents in the house.* No response. The lights are on, all the lights you would expect to be on if someone were home.

She walks into the master bedroom. The bed is made. The overhead light is off. The bedside lamp is off. But there is illumination from the master bathroom.

"Allison Pagone." Jane McCoy braces herself. "Special Agent McCoy, FBI," she says with increased urgency. "Are you in there?"

She takes a few steps toward the bathroom and pauses. She looks around. Then she sticks her head into the bathroom. Allison Pagone is lying motionless in the bathtub, her head tucked into her chest, wearing her pajamas. A handgun dangles from Allison's left hand, resting on her chest precariously. Behind Pagone's head the tile on the wall is covered with a splatter of crimson.

"Oh, no." McCoy stumbles several steps back and sits on the bed. "What did I do?"

Her partner, Owen Harrick, makes his way in and makes eye contact with McCoy.

"She's in there." McCoy's voice is lifeless. She nods in the direction of the master bath. She watches Harrick walk up to the bathroom, then in. She hears his reaction, similar to hers. He stays in there a while, presumably checking the body.

McCoy looks around the room, at the bedside table holding an oversized, antique brass telephone, an alarm clock, and a lamp. The room has a ceiling like a cathedral's, about twenty feet high. The walk-in closet is about the size of McCoy's bedroom. She thinks of the voice mail Allison Pagone left on her cell phone last night—about nine hours ago.

Harrick walks back out and looks at McCoy. For a moment he is silent. "She's been dead for hours," he says.

"Yeah."

"Revolver in her hand." Harrick looks back at the bathroom. "No footprints on the tile. Towels are neatly hung. There's a bandage on her right hand but it looks a few days old. Far as I can see, there's no sign of struggle or force—"

"Oh, for God's sake, Owen, she shot herself." McCoy shakes her head. "There's no mystery here." She throws up a hand helplessly. "I screwed up, Owen. I fucked this up."

Harrick blows out a breath, takes a seat on the bed next to McCoy. "She killed a guy," he says. "And she was covering up, too. We know that. She did this to herself."

"Literally, maybe."

"Not just literally. In every way. She put herself in the soup. You were doing your job, Jane. She killed a man. You and I both know it."

McCoy goes to the window opposite the bed, opens it, and takes in some fresh air.

"They were going to convict her and give her the needle," Harrick adds. "Don't make this your fault."

"You didn't hear her message," McCoy says. She looks out through the window at the backyard. For living in the city, Allison has a relatively big lot. This is a neighborhood on the northwest side, which is more residential, more kids running in the streets, lawnmowers and barbecues. More like a suburb. You could probably hit a baseball from her backyard to the nearest suburb. This is where people come who need to stay in the city—teachers, cops, firemen, civil servants with residency requirements. No one would confuse the color of the Pagones' collars for blue, but the ex-husband, Mat, is on a couple of municipal boards that require him to stay within city limits. McCoy has heard that it was Allison who wanted this neighborhood, who simply thought the people were nicer than in some of the trendier parts of the city or than the old money by the lake. The Pagones had purchased two adjacent lots and built a large house, but what they really wanted was the backyard. There's a huge garden, a fancy play area with slides and jungle gyms for their daughter, who probably hasn't touched it for ten years.

You look at someone's possessions, her family, her background, you look at her as a person. Some of McCoy's colleagues don't dig so deep, just focus on the misdeeds and don't judge, don't want to see the human side because it gets in the way. Jane McCoy has never understood that. You focus only on the black, ignore the white, you miss the gray.

"She was going to die one way or the other," she hears Harrick call to her. "She spared herself eight to ten on death row, then a public execution. She did it on her terms."

McCoy moans, turns back from the window. "You find anything else upstairs, Owen?"

"I found the trophy."

"The tro—"

"The murder weapon, Jane. That statuette. It's sitting in her office."

"That statuette—from that association? Dillon's award?"

Harrick nods. "Looks like it had been buried. She went and brought it back. She wanted us to find it. You get it? You see what happened? She wanted it settled. She confessed her sins before she killed herself. She's telling us she killed Sam Dillon."

McCoy sighs. "Call this in, Owen?"

"Sure."

Her team shows up quietly, parking their dark sedans the next street over and coming through the backyard. This kind of crime scene isn't their typical protocol; the feds don't often investigate homicides. But this one doesn't require much detail, anyway. They photograph the scene, dust for prints, gather hairs and fibers, test for residue on Allison's gun hand, finally carry the body out in a covered stretcher. McCoy holds off on calling the locals for an hour, because with the local cops comes the local media. She knows they'll make it here eventually but she wants to give it some time.

She stands outside two hours later, at nine in the morning. The air is cool and crisp; she prefers spring mornings to any other, even under these circumstances. By now the reporters have arrived and are lining the crime-scene tape, shouting questions to anyone who appears to resemble law enforcement. *Was this a suicide? Where was she found? Did she leave a note?*

McCoy peers at them, silent, through her sunglasses. *Something like that,* she does not say to them.

Four sedans are lined up along the curb now. Neighbors have gathered around the home as well. This is not the first news of something amiss at the Pagone residence, but there's been nothing this public, at least not since the search warrant was executed months ago.

Jane McCoy appreciates her anonymity. Like many agents, she is relatively unknown to reporters. She is unaccustomed to scenes like this. Most of what the agents do is under the radar, and here she is, being photographed and taped standing outside the home. It is a matter of courtesy more than anything. She is waiting for someone.

She sees a steel-blue Mercedes pull up quickly to the curb. Roger Ogren, an assistant county attorney, pops out. From what she knows of him, which isn't much, she wouldn't expect the flashy ride. Not his personality and quite the fat price tag for his government salary. But every boy needs a toy.

Ogren uses the remote on his keychain to lock up the car and walks up toward the house. He walks under the tape, stops on the front lawn, looks around, finally focuses on Jane.

"Agent McCoy," he says.

"It's Jane, Roger."

He puts his hands on his hips, wets his lips. "Suicide?"

She nods. "Bullet in the mouth."

He sighs deeply, seems to deflate. Hurry up and stop—he was in the full heat of trial mode, and now the defendant is dead.

"No sign of forced entry," McCoy elaborates. "No sign of foul play at all. GSR on her hand and wrist."

Ogren does not take the news well. The woman he was prosecuting, driven to suicide.

"You were going for the death penalty, anyway," McCoy says

He runs his hands through his hair. "She was a killer. I was about two trial days away from proving that."

"I know. I was following it. You were doing very well."

"Suicide." Roger Ogren stands helplessly a moment. He is in a suit, but his shirt is open at the neck. He got ready in a hurry. He sighs and seems to deflate.

"It's not your fault," McCoy offers, in case he needs to hear it. "If anything, it's mine. This lady was up to some bad stuff. Not just this murder."

"Not just this murder," Ogren repeats. "But you won't tell me what."

"You know I can't."

She tries to read his expression. Really, how upset can he be? Like she said, he was seeking the death penalty, after all. If the defendant killed herself because she couldn't face prison, and ultimately a lethal injection, she just saved everyone the trouble.

He wanted the conviction, she assumes. He's not feeling guilt. He wanted the "w," the pats on the back, the victory lap at the prosecutor's office, the press coverage.

"Everyone knew she was going down," McCoy adds. "Everyone knew you had her."

Ogren stretches, arches his back, extends his arms. Full trial mode, probably hasn't had much sleep. And now this. Like the whole prosecution was just a false start.

"She's not up there anymore," McCoy says. "You want to go see the body?"

Ogren looks over the house wistfully. He is suddenly a man without a place. This is not his crime scene.

"As long as you're sure she's dead," he deadpans, an attempt at dark humor that falls flat.

She smiles at him. "You want to see the statuette?"

Ogren does a double-take, suddenly perks up. "The— what are you talking about?"

"The statuette," she says. "The little trophy. The award from the manufacturers' association. You always thought she used it to kill Sam Dil—"

Ogren steps toward her. "You have it? It was here in her house?"

Jane McCoy gestures behind her. "She had it in her office upstairs."

"That's not possible." The prosecutor squints. "She moved it there, maybe."

"Exactly," Jane agrees. "She had buried it somewhere initially. You can tell because there's some dirt on it. But there's some blood on it, too, and we're getting prints off it. I assume it's the murder weapon. We've inventoried it. We'll make it available to you guys."

Roger Ogren is speechless. It is confirmation that he never had. A murder weapon that had never been found. McCoy wonders if there was any residual doubt in the prosecutor's mind, any lingering question of whether he was accusing the right person. If so, the murder weapon, in the home of the accused, should erase that doubt.

"This was her way of pleading guilty," McCoy tells him. "Before she went, she wanted the record clear, I guess."

Ogren nods aimlessly, his eyes unfocused. "And what about the gun?"

"A revolver. Serial numbers scratched. She must have bought it on the street."

Ogren stares at her. *Weird*, he must be thinking. "Okay. I'll give you a call," he says. "I think we would like that statuette, actually."

"Sure. Call me."

He turns to leave but stops, looks back at the federal agent. "Why did you say it's your fault? Her killing herself?"

She makes a face. "I was squeezing her. Maybe too hard."

Ogren gives her a look of compromise. Squeezing is something any prosecutor can understand. No one ever knows how much pressure is just right.

"You got what you wanted, Roger. Justice was served."

He laughs. A bitter chuckle. "This wouldn't have happened if she weren't out on bail," he says. "She couldn't have gotten a gun and she couldn't have killed herself."

McCoy lifts her shoulders. "Hey, you wanted her dead, she's dead."

The prosecutor glares at McCoy, then turns and walks to his car. He can't deny that he was seeking the death penalty, of course, which means he cannot deny that he wanted death for Allison Pagone. But he doesn't appreciate the bluntness of McCoy's comment. As if Roger Ogren were a killer, too.

"I'll bet *he's* pissed," Harrick says, walking up, watching Ogren leave.

"Something like that."

They walk to their car and drive away. Once in the vehicle, Harrick, driving, casts a look at McCoy. "Something bothering you? Talk to me, Janey."

"It looked too clean," she says. "There's such a thing as looking too much like a suicide."

"Oh, come on." Owen Harrick shrugs. He was a city cop for eight years. He's witnessed a lot more suicide scenes than Jane McCoy.

"A bathtub?" McCoy asks.

"It's private," Harrick answers. "She wanted intimacy. It's also easier to clean up."

"Oh, she didn't want to mess up the house?" McCoy looks at her partner. "She's worried about resale value?"

"It's the house she raised her daughter in. She cares about how it looks. You're thinking way too hard on this. It's a suicide, Jane. She thought about it first, is all. People do plan suicides."

McCoy is silent.

"She killed Sam Dillon," Harrick continues, turning a corner and leaving the sight line of Allison Pagone's home. "She killed him and she felt remorse. That works for me."

"I hope so." McCoy's head falls back against the head cushion. It will be another sleepless night for her.

TUESDAY, MAY 11

*T*he small turn of his head, as if his attention were diverted. The set of his jaw, the clenching of his teeth.
The line of his mouth turned, ever so slightly, from a smile
to something more primitive, almost a snarl but not so
prominent. A stolen moment, an entirely private moment in
public, a stolen glance among a roomful of people, in-
tended for private consumption.

Thursday, February fifth of this year. A cocktail party
thrown by Dillon & Becker, Sam's lobbying firm, an annual party for clients in the city's offices. Hors d'oeuvres
passed by servants in tuxedos, soft classical music playing
from speakers in the corners.

The Look, Allison calls it, though she has never spoken
of such things aloud, except to Sam. A look of pure, unadul-
terated lust, a passion that drives men to do things they
should not do, the most primitive of emotions. She watches
everything about Sam—how he holds his breath, moves his
eyes up and down her body—trying to imagine exactly what

*it is that Sam is imagining, because Allison has no experi-
ence with such things, has never seen this look from her
husband in the twenty years they were married.*

She freezes that image in her mind. She is not sure why.
Maybe because it was one of the last pictures that she has
of Sam—he was dead two days later—or maybe because it
is so staggering to think how far things have fallen.

Allison Pagone sits on the wine-colored couch in the
den. The memories always flood back, no matter how fleetingly, when she sits here. Memories of her childhood. She
remembers when she was fifteen, when she had a party
while her parents were out, a bottle of red wine spilled on
the couch, her enormous relief when the wine blended in
with the color. Another memory: She was six, sleeping on
the couch because she had wet her bed, worrying about her
parents' reaction, then her mother's soothing hand running
through her hair as she woke up the next morning.

She thinks of her daughter, Jessica, and the torment she
must be feeling right now, her mother standing trial for
murder. And she will not be acquitted. Jessica has read the
stories, watched the television coverage, despite the judge's
instructions to the contrary. Regardless of whether she is a
witness, nobody is going to tell a young woman she cannot
read the cold accounts of her mother's crime in the paper.

Allison has watched her daughter age over the last three
months. Twenty years old, she is in many ways still a girl,
but these events have changed that. Allison is to blame, and
she can do nothing about it.

She picks up the phone on the coffee table. She dials
Mat Pagone's office. She checks her watch. It is past nine
o'clock in the evening.

She gets his voice mail. She holds her breath and waits
for the beep. She looks at the piece of paper in front of her.
They spelled his name wrong. It should be Mat with one t,
short for *Mateo*.

"Mat, I know you're not going to get this until tomorrow morning. I'm sorry. For everything. I also want you to listen carefully. Jessica is going to need you now more than ever. You are going to have to love her for both of us. You have to be strong for her. You have to do whatever you can to be there for her. You—you have to—promise—"

She takes a deep breath. "Mat, don't say a word to the FBI. They don't have anything on you. You hear me? They don't have anything. Just keep your mouth shut. You can't help me now so don't make this worse and talk to them. And take—take good care of our—"

Her voice cuts off. She lets out a low wail. She hangs up the phone quietly and puts her face in her hands, ignoring the man seated across from her.

"That was very good, Allison. Now just one more."

Allison looks up at the man, then inhales deeply, composes herself. This is the end now, she knows it. She picks up the phone and dials the numbers, reading them off the business card.

You have reached Special Agent Jane McCoy . . .

She waits for the beep and reads from the paper. "Jane McCoy, this is Allison Pagone. I want you to know that I will not be used. I will not let you rip the last shreds of dignity from my family. You have *me*. It's over for me. If you have a hint of decency in you, you will not deny my daughter both of her parents. I want you to know that you can't toy with people's lives like this. I won't let you turn me against my family. Your little plan didn't work. So live with *that*."

She hangs up the phone and looks up at the man sitting on the ottoman opposite her, training a revolver on her. He is dark in every way—Middle Eastern with jet-black hair, dark eyes, a menacing smile, the way he can look pleasant during all of this.

"Excellent," the man says. "Your flair for drama has paid off."

"You said you'd leave," says Allison. "I did what you wanted."

The man stands but keeps the firearm directed at Allison. "Please stand up," he says.

An hour later. Ram Haroon checks his watch. It is after 11:45 at night. He looks at Allison Pagone, lying in the bathtub, motionless. He looks over the scene. He is reluctant to go back into the bathroom, to step on the tile, so he leans in from his spot in the bedroom. The scene looks entirely clean. Nothing has been disturbed. There is no reason to suspect that this was anything other than a suicide.

He walks to the study and unzips his gym bag. The statuette—it's more like a trophy—is wrapped in plastic. He sets it on the desk near her computer and leaves it in the plastic, still covered with the dirt from behind the grocery store, where it was buried.

Perfect. Better than a suicide note confessing to the murder. This is the proof, the trophy used to bludgeon Sam Dillon in February.

He walks back through the house, careful not to change anything. If the light was on, it stays on; nothing can be altered. If the timing of her death were ever fixed by the authorities, and someone saw a light turn off afterward, it would ruin the impression.

He walks down the basement stairs. He came in through a basement window and returns to it now, jumps back up onto the sill. Once out, he sets the window back into place as if he never were there. He makes it through the backyard, over the fence, into the neighbor's yard. He walks to his car and begins to drive without hitting his headlights.

He looks at his watch. It is exactly two minutes before midnight, before Wednesday. He wonders when she will be found. Some time tomorrow morning, because her trial will resume and she will not show. Someone will rush to

• her door. Maybe the federal agent whom Allison called—
McCoy—panicking.

He picks up his cell phone and hits a speed button.
"Done," he says, and hangs up.

He has to get home now. Final exams start in a couple
of weeks and he's fallen behind.

MONDAY, MAY 10

Ram Haroon already jogged today, so he is annoyed that he has to don the outfit and run again, at the ungodly hour of eleven at night. He is surprised to find that he's not alone out here, that a few other lunatics are running in the cool air. There is a path that winds around a park near the university, a one-mile loop that begins—and ends—at a marker with a couple of benches and a drinking fountain made of stone.

A runner is kneeling near the fountain, tying a shoe. Ram can hardly make the runner out in the darkness but there's no doubt. The runner stands and stretches, then starts down the path, presumably for another mile, though Ram is sure that his contact will veer off to a nearby car.

Left in the runner's wake, on the grass, is an envelope. Ram does not immediately rush over to it, because as long as no other runner approaches, there is no need to act with such swiftness. After a moment of stretching, he makes his way over to the drinking fountain and takes a sip of the icy water. He bends down to tie a shoe that is not untied, and slips the envelope off the grass and into the pocket of his sweatpants.

He is in his student dormitory thirty minutes later. Student housing might not have been the wisest choice, because the courts in America have allowed law enforcement more freedom to search school-subsidized facilities, on the theory that students have a diminished expectation of privacy in government-provided housing. But it made sense, in the end. First, because he lacks the money for a nicer place in the city, but more importantly, because he wants to fit in. He wants nothing out of the ordinary. Besides, there's nothing for them to find in this room.

Except this envelope. He opens it and reads:

Sorry for the short notice. We have had a tremendous break. The FBI is pressing her for information about Operation Public Trust. They want her to provide information that she very much does not want to provide. She is tough but not when it comes to her family. She is at the breaking point. No need to give too many details. The FBI has put her in a corner. I believe she is contemplating this herself. She will do anything to protect her family. I am sure of this. But we cannot assume she will save us the trouble and take her own life.

Do it Tuesday night. The FBI is coming back to her on Wednesday. MUST BE TUESDAY NIGHT. I have included two scripts. She should make these two phone calls. I leave it to you whether you can force her to do this. Your decision. If you can get her to cooperate, you will convince the whole world that she did this to herself. I think she will make these calls willingly, because she will want to say these things, anyway. I leave that to you.

I assume you have the trophy now. It might make sense for you to leave it at her house. People would see her guilt. This has always been your idea, not mine. I still

believe it is too risky. But if you insist on doing this, now
is the time.

I must warn you, if there is the slightest hint that this
has not worked out to our satisfaction, WE will be the
ones who walk away.

Ram Haroon rereads the note, then looks at the other
sheet of paper. It is a script of what Allison Pagone is supposed to say. The first phone call will be to Mateo, her ex-
husband. *Don't say a word to the FBI* and words to that
effect.

The second phone call will be to an FBI agent named
Jane McCoy. Haroon does not know all the details, but he
can gather enough from the script: *Your plan didn't work.
Live with that.* Vague without more context, but Haroon
understands well enough. The FBI is trying to make the ex-
husband talk to save the ex-wife, and the ex-wife, by taking her own life, removes the FBI's leverage.

Excellent. Better than a suicide note, especially the call
to the agent, McCoy—blaming her for placing Allison in
this corner. A plausible explanation for why Allison
Pagone would choose to take her own life.

Yes. This is the perfect cross of the final t, the final
jagged piece of a difficult puzzle. It must be a part of this
plan.

And he has no doubt that he will be able to persuade
Allison Pagone to go along.

SUNDAY, MAY 9

I've never known anyone like you," he told her, and she
  wanted to say the same thing to him. He came up behind
her, cupped a hand around her throat, ran the other hand
lazily up the side of her body, caressed her stomach. She
felt a chill, a welcome chill, closed her eyes and let him un-
button her blouse, bring his lips to the back of her neck,
bring his hands to her breasts.

"There are things you don't know, Allison," he told her
later.

And The Look. The single defining moment, at that
cocktail party only days before his death. The expression of
utter wanting on his face, fixating on her, imagining un-
speakable acts, as he stood among others at the party, unable to move his eyes off her—

"Shit," Allison says, looking down at her hand. The
wineglass has shattered in her grip. She looks at the pieces
before taking note of the two shards stuck into her palm.
Searing pain as she pulls the glass out, unable to look,

wincing, cursing herself. She walks, palm up, to the sink and runs cold water over her hand. It's everywhere, blood on her nightshirt, the floor, but it's all she can do to wrap a towel around her hand. Then she loses her balance and falls to the floor hard.

"Get a grip, Allison," she mumbles. She sits up, rests her head against the cabinet below the sink, and holds her breath.

Bring Sam to me just one more time. Defy logic, the laws of nature, and bring him back to me just this once.

She hears her alarm clock going off upstairs. It automatically resets, and she forgot to deactivate it, for the second day in a row. Her mind has been like that recently, uncannily sharp and focused on the minutiae of her case, even the big picture, but inattentive to many of the general details of everyday living.

She didn't sleep. Only about four hours over the last two days. She's been in the kitchen since midnight, nursing a glass of wine and staring into the emptiness of her backyard. She watched the sky lighten, watched the first rays of the day skitter across the yard, furious at how casually everything was passing her by.

She gets back to her feet and heads outside. She walks through the living room, opens the back door, and the house alarm goes off, blending with the sounds of the clock alarm upstairs.

She finds the alarm pad, deactivates it, and fights a bout of nausea. She heads outside and is unprepared for the cold air but takes it in, embraces the discomfort, wraps her arms around herself and watches the day begin.

"You should see this," she says. "It's beautiful."

Maybe he *can* see it. Maybe he's looking down on her, smiling with that assurance, winking at her, blowing her a kiss. She is religious, but it's been a while. Mat was never much for church so she fell out of practice. She feels hypocritical but she finds herself pleading.

Just let me hear your voice. Just once.
Tell me you forgive me.
Tell me you love me.

Today is Mother's Day, a holiday that will not be celebrated by the Pagone family this year. There are obvious reasons. Having the family to this home is out of the question. The house is like a prison both literally and figuratively. Nor is there any conceivable reason for celebrating anything today.

Good reasons, both of them. But the truth is that Allison can't summon the strength for a façade, anyway. Not another one.

In a little while she finds that the grocery store is not as busy as it typically would be on a Sunday. Before the recent turn of events, Allison had frequented an upscale grocer, not because of its exclusivity, but because it was the only store in this part of the city with some of the exotic ingredients she often sought. And they knew her, because she shopped often, preferring fresh food. But since her arrest, she has noticed the discomfort in virtually every acquaintance. The averted glances, the awkward silences. It's gotten to the point where she avoids them as much as they avoid her. So now she shops at a chain store, where she is relatively unknown. Say that much for the city. One in a million is actually an understatement. It provides her relative freedom.

Very relative. She has to stay within five miles of her home at all times, a condition of her bond. She had to get permission to get a tire changed last week.

She carries a small basket and places a few vegetables in it. She eats meat, used to love it, but these days the idea of being a carnivore seems ironic. She walks past the bakery, past the butcher, toward the drugstore. There is a small coffee shop in the corner, the grocery chain's attempt at modernization. She finds Larry Evans reading a newspaper at a small table. Two steaming paper cups of black coffee sit on the table. He looks over his glasses at her and smiles. She recognizes it for what it is, not a happy-go-lucky grin but an attempt at warmth. Not very many people smile at Allison Pagone these days.

"How you holding up?" he asks.

She puts down the groceries and sits across from him. "How do I look like I'm holding up?"

He sets down the newspaper. "Honestly?"

She sighs. "Don't start lying to me now, Larry. You're the only one I can trust."

"You look tired. Did you sleep at all?"

He's being honest, if not entirely forthcoming; he is omitting a few other adjectives. Allison has forced herself to look in the mirror lately. She has seen the damage.

Larry flicks at his hair. He is dishwater blond, has a rugged, lined face. He has a good-sized frame, not a body-builder but a guy who keeps in shape. He hasn't shaved today; his facial hair is darker than the hair on top of his head. She would probably find him handsome under other circumstances—very, very different circumstances.

She takes a sip of the coffee, steaming hot on her tongue. Something nutty, she assumes. Cinnamon hazelnut, she guesses, then looks over at the small chalkboard next to the counter, where the coffee of the day is revealed in colored chalk: *Cinn-ful Walnut*. Clever.

"You look like someone who's conceding defeat," he says. "And I don't like that. I don't get it, Allison. I just don't get you."

"What's not to get? I'm going to be convicted." She averts her eyes. She looks at the other shoppers, immediately envying their carefree lives. An employee is pushing turkey sausage, pierced with toothpicks, on shoppers. The next aisle down, it's hummus, about ten different kinds offered with pita chips. Little kids hanging on carts, women moving seriously through the aisles. They don't know anything about serious. She would change places with any of them.

"That doesn't have to—"

"Oh, don't deny it, Larry. Please," she adds, more softly.

He reaches for her, then recoils. "What happened to your hand?"

Allison holds up her right hand, wrapped in gauze. "Lost a fight with a wineglass."

Larry peers into her eyes. "You sure you're okay?"

She nods. "I'll be fine as long as you don't tell me I'm going to win my case."

Larry looks away, exhales with disgust. "Did you even show your lawyer what I found?" he asks. "Did you think at all about all that stuff I found? You show that to a judge and you'll be acquitted—"

"Look." Allison scoots her chair from the table, holds her hands up. "Look. I'm not going to debate you, Larry. Okay?"

Larry watches her. She can only imagine the package she's presenting today. She showered before coming but she's still a train wreck in every way. She almost caused an accident on the way to this store. Her eyes are heavy from sleep deprivation and worry. Her stomach is in knots, having been deprived of food for more than twenty-four hours.

"Please don't tell me that things look grand," she says. "They have me all over Sam's house. They have that damn alibi. And they have me, the day before, barging into his office like some deranged maniac—"

She stops herself as Larry's look softens.

"Kind of like now," she says. "I'm sorry."

"It's okay, it's okay." Larry has played the advocate in this relationship. Originally a biographer, now a reporter bent on showing that Allison did not kill Sam Dillon. But he has always been good about this. As much as he has tried to help Allison's defense, shown an unwavering belief in her cause, fought his exasperation at her unwillingness to use his assistance—always, he has deferred to her, the woman on trial for her life.

"You've tried to help me, Larry. I know that. And I hope I've given you enough material back."

"You've been great."

"I don't know about great, but—" She runs her hands over her face. "The book you're writing, Larry? Please go easy on my family. That's what I came here to ask."

Larry's smile is eclipsed, his expression hardening just like that. "You want me to be quiet about what I know."

"Larry, this book is going to sell no matter what. 'By Allison Pagone, as told to Larry Evans.' You'll get a great print run. Just stick to the basics. You don't need the sensationalist stuff."

"So?" He opens his hands. "You want me to back off what I know."

"You don't 'know' anything, Larry."

Larry Evans shifts in his chair, directs a finger at the table. "I know you didn't kill Sam Dillon," he says.

"Stop saying that. You don't know that."

"Then I *believe* it. And I think you're protecting someone."

Allison looks around helplessly. She recognizes her lack of leverage.

"What's happened?" he asks. "Where'd the fighter go? Why are you giving up all of a sudden? What's happened since the last time I talked to you, that now you're acting so resigned to defeat?"

She looks into his eyes briefly. He is challenging her. But she will not tell him.

"Promise me you'll be fair to my family." She recognizes that, from Larry's perspective, she has no bargaining position here. She will not be able to enforce any promise. Allison gets to her feet, takes a moment to gain her equilibrium. She picks up the basket of vegetables, stares at them as if they are hazardous materials, and drops the basket.

"Tell me what happened," Larry pleads. "Something's happened. I can tell. New evidence or something?"

"Something," she says to him. "Look—thanks for everything. For being there."

Larry reaches for her hand. "Allison, tell me. Maybe I can help."

"I can't tell you." She withdraws her hand. "I—I can't."

She goes home, the only place she is allowed to go. The dry cleaner's is a permissible stop as well, but it's closed on Sundays, and she has no cleaning there, anyway. She sits outside on her patio, looking over her garden, at the rusted play-set where Jessica used to swing and slide and climb with such energy and unmitigated delight, and remembers the vicarious enjoyment she derived from her daughter's simplest acts.

She thinks of Sam Dillon. One evening in particular, mid-January of this year. Dinner, his idea, at a little Italian place, a real hole in the wall with the most perfect garlic bread she'd ever tasted. A small room with ten tables, a red-checkered tablecloth, the smells of olive oil and sausage and garlic mingling. She remembers the way he looked at her.

There are things you don't know, he said to her.

She leaves the patio and takes the phone in the living room. She drops onto the couch and dials the numbers.

"Mat, it's me."

"What's going on? How are you?"

"I'll tell you how I am," she says. "I got a visit yesterday from the FBI. That's how I am."

"The FBI? They came to your—"

"Listen to me, Mat. Okay? Just listen, don't talk."

They didn't used to speak to each other like this, but it's one of the few perks of being charged with capital murder, lots of freedom with your emotions.

"Do not talk to them under any circumstances," she says. "If they try to make a deal with you, don't do it. Do not even say hello to them. Don't even let them in. Just yell 'Fifth Amendment' from behind the door."

"With me?" Mat asks. "They're going to talk to *me*?"

"They wanted to talk about you. They wanted to talk about Divalpro. Just let me take care of this. Don't you dare talk to them."

"Ally?" Mat Pagone, her ex-husband, sounds out of breath. "Did you talk to them? About—that?"

"No, and I'm not going to. And neither are you. Just keep your mouth shut and remember one thing, okay?"

"What's that?"

"Your daughter needs at least one parent." She hangs up the phone and holds her breath.

SATURDAY, MAY 8

Allison is awake, in the fetal position, when the alarm surprises her at six in the morning. She probably managed a few fitful hours in there somewhere, but it feels like she hasn't slept at all. It's not the lack of rest but the sense that time has accelerated from last night to this morning. Everything seems to have quickened these last few weeks. Time flies when you want it to stop.

Yes, she did sleep, because she dreamt. She spoke to Sam. They were in his bed. Allison was saying to him, *Can you believe they think I killed you?*

She stretches, considers going for a jog but opts for coffee instead. She makes her own, with an antique percolator she bought a year ago that reminded her of the coffee in Tuscany. There was a time when she waited anxiously for the brew to be ready, when she was eager to move on with her day. These days, there is little to look forward to. She will drink her coffee, listen to classical music, go on the internet later. Sometimes she even reads the stuff about

herself. Sometimes she will check out the website devoted
to her case, *freeallison.com*, not for the support—they have
no reason to think she's innocent, they're simply capitaliz-
ing on a media event—but out of idle curiosity. Much
heavier on the idleness than the curiosity.

They had planned to go to Italy, Sam and Allison. A trip
this spring, before heavy tourism, to less-traveled places
like Poggi del Sasso and Gaiole in Chianti. She had already
made plans for it, already booked romantic rooms in reno-
vated castles with verandas where they could sit with wine
and cheese and watch the sun go down over the breathtak-
ing countryside.

"Oh, God." She wipes the moisture from her cheeks.
"Oh, *shit*." The percolator has been whistling for too long.
She pulls it off the stove, burning herself on the handle,
spilling the entire thing onto the floor, the coffee that she
had burned, anyway. She picks up the percolator and slams
it against the refrigerator, breaking the lid off.

She lets out a loud moan, a deep sound she doesn't recognize, and covers her face with her hands. She is woozy
but unwilling to correct the sensation, unwilling to open
her eyes.

"They think I killed you," she says to him, and actually
laughs, a release of nervous tension. "They actually think
I killed you."

The doorbell rings just after nine in the morning. She
hasn't showered or even brushed her teeth, but she is far
beyond appearances. She goes to the door and stares
through the peephole. She sees a woman, an attractive
woman with a tiny face, expressive brown eyes, cropped
dark hair. A woman who is holding her credentials up for
Allison to see.

"My name is Special Agent Jane McCoy," the woman
says. "I'm with the FBI."

"What do you want?" Allison calls out, her heartbeat
kicking into overdrive.

"A minute of your time, please."

"What does the FBI have to do with me?"

"Let me in and I'll tell you."

Allison takes a breath, opens the door. "What do you want?"

"May I come in?"

Allison leads the federal agent into the den. She takes a seat on the couch. She remembers her father, interrogating her as she sat on this very couch, about her whereabouts the prior evening, when she blew her midnight curfew. She remembers, in fact, that it was Mat Pagone with whom she had spent that evening.

Her parents didn't approve of Mat. She had been quick to accuse them of racism, a strapping Latino boy entering a white, middle-class home to date a younger white girl. Mother said it was a matter of age—Mat was a college freshman at the state university, the starting middle line-backer, and Allison was a high school sophomore. As a freshman a year earlier, she had worshipped Mat, a senior and an all-state player. As a sophomore, she had caught his eye at a postgame party one Saturday night, a party that Allison certainly was not supposed to attend, but which many of her friends did. The kids from both the public and Catholic schools on the northwest side caught all the football games at the state university, only miles away, and managed to get into the parties, too—especially the pretty female students.

Yes, she once was pretty. She had stopped believing that a long time ago.

You're so beautiful, Sam had said to her, *I lose my breath.*

The FBI agent sits across from Allison on the ottoman of a leather recliner. The agent is a petite woman. Soft brown hair cut short, a tiny curved face, the wide innocent eyes of a doe. She is immediately likable, Allison thinks, regardless of the circumstances. That has probably been an asset in her job. The good cop in the routine.

"We can help each other," the agent says to Allison.

"Before you tell me how you plan to *help* me," Allison starts, "why don't you tell me what you're doing here?"

"Well, Mrs. Pagone—or is it Ms. Quincy now?"

Allison chews on her lip. "Is this the part where you tell me that you know all about me?" she asks. "I hate to burst your bubble, Agent Whatever-your-name-is, but you aren't the first to try that stunt. And if you hadn't noticed, my life is hardly a secret these days."

McCoy smiles at Allison. "It's McCoy. Jane McCoy. You've heard of Operation Public Trust. I'm one of the case agents on that investigation."

"Okay," says Allison. "Thank you. Now, please tell me how you intend to 'help' me."

"I think you know, ma'am."

Allison doesn't respond. She thinks of what her lawyer would advise her to do, which is precisely that.

"I've been following your trial," McCoy says. "You know a lot of what we know, quite honestly."

"I'm sure I don't know as much as the federal government."

McCoy watches Allison a moment. She leans forward, her elbows on her knees.

"I think you know *more*," McCoy says.

Allison looks away. "You've got five minutes. You can spend that time baiting me, or you can get to the point."

"Very good." McCoy claps her hands together. "You are out of options, Mrs. Pagone. You're going to lose your case, from what I can see. Maybe you'll beat the death penalty. I don't know. I'm saying, you can help yourself. I can help you. Take some years off that sentence. Keep you close to home so your daughter can visit. But you have to help me first."

Allison steels herself.

You want Mat.

"You have to give me your husband," McCoy concludes.

Allison counts to ten before she answers.

"Ex-husband."

McCoy opens her hands. "Exactly."

"Get out."

"You'd be helping him as well, Mrs. Pagone. Mat was the one. He was the one passing the money to the senators. I know it."

"Mat wasn't even representing Flanagan-Maxx. Not at the time."

"Not on the books," McCoy agrees. "We know he was lobbying for MAAHC. Same difference."

Allison plays with her hands. She inhales deeply.

"Ollie Strickland," McCoy says. "Don't act like you don't know."

"This is ridiculous."

"We'll get Ollie to roll, Allison. In time. He's not there yet. Someone always gives in, and it's usually the one who has less to lose. The ones with mud on their shoes, they're always the last to fall, and they fall farthest."

"Get out, Agent McCoy."

"I know that you know." McCoy fixes on Allison. "I think Sam Dillon knew, too. I think Sam Dillon found out what Flanagan-Maxx was doing, subsidizing a nonprofit group to push their prescription-drug legislation for them. And not just advocating. Bribing lawmakers. That's the illegal part. That's the part your ex-husband was doing."

"You can't prove that."

"No, not yet. But I will."

Allison stands up. "My answer is no."

McCoy rises as well. "Your ex-husband will say yes."

Allison's chin rises; she stares into McCoy's eyes. "What does that mean?"

Drop the 311 if Mat sings.

McCoy stares back with confidence, as if she enjoys having the ball in her court. "It means I'll go to Mat," she says. "I'll make him a deal. I'll get the county attorney to spare you the death penalty if he'll give me the information I need." She raises a hand, as Allison begins to protest. "You two may be divorced, but he's no monster. He'll be more than happy to admit his involvement, if it means sparing the mother of his daughter a death sentence."

"You can't do that," Allison says. "You can't. I have to be part of a plea agreement."

"C'mon, Mrs. Pagone, you were a public defender once." McCoy shrugs. "I'll get the county attorney to drop the 311 request. He doesn't need a plea from you. He'll just tell the court that he no longer wishes to seek the death penalty. He has total discretion on that. He'll give his word to your husband—sorry, your *ex*-husband—and I'm sure Mat will sing like a canary for me."

Allison looks around the room, flaps her arms nervously so they smack against her legs.

Nothing on Mat.

"You don't have any proof against Mat, or you wouldn't be here."

McCoy sighs. "I don't have enough to put him away," she concedes. "And that's only because Sam Dillon is dead. So I figure, Mat owes you one for that. He bribed a bunch of senators and you killed the only person who could put him away. Really, he's getting a pretty good deal here. You kill the guy who was going to roll on him, the least he can do is keep you off death row."

Allison sits back down on the couch. "How can you do this to people?"

"How can I do this to people who commit murder and bribe politicians? It's not that hard, frankly." She claps her hands together again. "I'll give you a couple of days to think about it. Your trial's in recess until Wednesday, right? So how's Wednesday night for you?" she asks, as if she's scheduling a dinner. "Okay. Wednesday. I'll come by after court. But I'm telling you, Allison. If you think you can stonewall me, you're not as smart as you seem to be. Mat will take my deal whether you want him to or not."

McCoy gathers her bag and nods at Allison.

"I have a daughter," Allison says. "She's already going to lose her mother."

McCoy deflates. Allison can imagine what the agent is thinking. *This is what criminals always do. They rob, cheat, steal, maim, and kill, but as soon as the hand of justice grabs the back of their necks, they're begging for mercy.*

"Wednesday night," McCoy repeats, on her way out.

FRIDAY, MAY 7

"They just got this last night," says Special Agent Owen Harrick. He pops a stick of cinnamon gum into his mouth and offers one to Jane McCoy.

McCoy refuses the gum and works on her milkshake. There's fast food all around the federal building downtown, irresistible temptations to Jane. Harrick is more of a health-food nut, but he's also junior to her. Choice of restaurants, when they're working late—which is most of the time—is one of the few arenas in which Jane McCoy pulls rank. Harrick had settled for a chicken sandwich and a side salad. Jane, in a halfhearted nod to dietary considerations, skipped the entrees altogether and just got a large chocolate milkshake.

Harrick lifts the remote and points it at the VCR in the corner of the conference room. "Ready?"

McCoy sucks the last of the shake, then slurps through the empty straw. Harrick looks at her with bemusement.

"Relax," she says. "So I've had my dinner, gimme my movie."

"*Dinner,*" he chides. "Two scoops of ice cream with milk." He points the remote at the screen. "Lights, camera . . . action."

The picture is grainy black-and-white. No surprise there. The Bureau has always focused more on discretion than quality in their surveillance equipment. You want a camcorder that fits into your pocket with a zoom lens that can pick up the wink of an eye from a hundred yards away, no problem. But you want a picture that could compete with the quality of a summer vacation video by grandpa, call Miramax, not the federal government.

"The Countryside Grocery Store," McCoy says. "Corner of Riordan and—what's that?"

"Apple," Harrick says. "Riordan and Apple."

The running time in the corner of the video shows that it was taken last night, just before midnight. The video shows a car parking at a bank, across the street from the grocery store, and the trunk popping. A man emerges from the car, goes to the trunk, then walks up to the store carrying a gym bag. The man on the screen leaves the camera's vision, disappearing into the back of the store.

McCoy blows out a nervous sigh.

Owen Harrick fast-forwards through a good amount of dead space. Jane watches the seconds then minutes fly by in the corner of the screen.

"Here," says Harrick, returning the tape to "play" mode. The tape shows the man reemerging from behind the grocery store with his gym bag and walking quickly back to his car. "That's it. He was out there for less than fifteen minutes."

Jane stares at the empty screen, feels the adrenaline pump through her. She rubs her hands together nervously. "Okay," she murmurs. She tosses the empty milkshake container into the trash. "I'm going to go see Allison Pagone," she says. "Tomorrow morning. A nice, early Saturday-morning meeting."

"You think she's in danger?"

McCoy shrugs. She will no longer give predictions on that subject.

THURSDAY, MAY 6

ountryside. Apple. Riordan. Yellow.
Countryside Grocery Store. Corner of Apple and
Riordan. Delivery entrance in back. Yellow post.

Ram Haroon is vaguely aware of this grocery chain in the Midwest, and he knows Riordan Avenue. But he doesn't know Apple Street. He has to stop and ask for directions. He would prefer not to make a point of asking anyone, but he's out of options. Riordan Avenue extends from the lake to the suburbs. Apple Street could intersect anywhere along that route. The store is probably close to Allison Pagone's home but he simply doesn't know. He thought of going on the internet to find all the Countryside locations, or even to use MapQuest, but that leaves a trail. Sloppy. There is not even a single piece of paper with this information, because he has memorized it.

Countryside. Apple. Riordan. Yellow.

But now, having avoided all paper trails, he is forced to ask a convenience-store clerk for the information. Not ideal, especially when it turns out he's only a couple of blocks away from his destination.

So he finds it, finally. There is a small bank across the street from it. He chooses to park in that empty lot, in a position where he is facing the grocery store. He takes a while, a good five minutes, and looks over the store. The lights are out. The parking lot is empty. It's half past eleven, and the store has presumably long been closed.

After another five minutes have passed, he pops the trunk and gets out of the car. Inside the trunk, in a gym bag, are a small hand-shovel and two plastic freezer bags. He puts on his brown gardening gloves, which will serve a dual purpose here.

Delivery entrance. Yellow.

Haroon goes to the back of the store, the delivery entrance as promised. Large double doors, a metal ramp running up to an elevated dock, level with the back doors. The rear of the building is spacious and well lit, two characteristics that he would prefer were otherwise. An old wire fence runs along the border of the property, propped up by several posts.

One of them, not far from the ramp, is the only one painted yellow.

He walks over to that spot and feels around with his hands to no avail. He places his shovel cautiously into the ground and digs softly until he hits something solid.

And then he smiles.

WEDNESDAY, MAY 5

Ram Haroon sits at the counter of the diner and rotates the coffee cup on its saucer. He steals a look at his watch, sees that it's eight on the dot. By now, most of the families have left the restaurant, most of the little kiddies. There are some couples lining the booths, mostly older folks, one pair of teenagers on a cheap date.

He gets up and heads to the men's room at the back. It's a bigger room than he would have thought. There are two urinals and two stalls with red doors. One of them is occupied. He sees the gym shoes. Normally, one would expect to see pants bunched up at the ankles while someone sits in a bathroom stall. Which means his contact is good, but not that good.

A men's room, he thinks to himself. *Of all places.*

Haroon enters the neighboring stall, puts down the toilet seat, and sits on it. There is probably no point in going through the motions of dropping his pants. It seems a little odd, in fact, given the familiarity with his neighbor.

He hears paper unwrapping in the neighboring stall. A moment later, a single piece of stationery creeps along the floor into his stall. He picks it up and reads it.

Countryside Grocery Store. Corner of Apple Drive and Riordan. Back. Delivery entrance. You will see a yellow post against the fence. Look right there. You are not keeping this so write it down.

Ram doesn't write it down; instead he commits it to memory.

Countryside Grocery Store. Apple and Riordan. Yellow post in back.

Countryside. Apple. Riordan. Yellow.

Ram takes the message and, with his pen, writes a single word on it and hands it back under the stall.

When?

The answer comes back in less than a minute.

Get it now. It will need to happen soon. Wait for my call.

Ram Haroon gets to his feet and flushes an unused toilet. He walks back to the counter of the restaurant, where his dinner awaits him. He keeps his eyes on the Cobb salad before him.

Countryside. Apple. Riordan. Yellow. He says the words over and over in his head, paying no attention to anyone who might happen to pass by on the way out of the restaurant.

TUESDAY, MAY 4

*T*his shouldn't be happening.

"This shouldn't be happening," Allison says, removing her fingernail from her mouth. The nails are reduced to nubs now. She's never had long nails, not since she began writing, but now they have been chewed into nonexistence. "I'm sitting there all day, listening to my lawyer plot strategy, and the whole time, I'm thinking, 'This shouldn't be happening.'"

Mat Pagone drops his briefcase in the living room. He has come in with Allison, after picking her up at her lawyer's office and driving her home—to what was once his home, too.

Allison watches her ex-husband disappear into the kitchen.

What do you mean?

What do you mean, this shouldn't be happening?

Mat returns with two glasses of wine from a bottle already opened. "Drink," he says. "Your head still hurt?"

She accepts the glass. "Only when I think. Did you call Jessica?"

"She's studying, Ally. You know she has that paper. She turned her cell phone off, is all. She's fine."

"She had to testify in a murder trial against her own mother. She is not *fine*."

She doesn't see Mat "off-camera" much these days. He has played the dutiful-supporter part, picking her up for court and taking her home, but that's a public appearance. Up close and personal, he looks tired. Worry and regret have cast a shadow across his face. His career is in tatters, his reputation probably shot. He is lucky but probably can't see that. He never could.

"What I meant before," she says finally, "is I should have pleaded guilty. I should have spared Jessica having to testify."

"Pleading is giving up," Mat says. "That's not you. That would have torn up Jess just as much. She thinks you're innocent, Ally."

"She thinks I'm innocent. Wonderful." Allison rubs her face.

"That's a good thing, I would think. You prefer she thinks you killed Sam?"

"Mat." Allison looks at him directly. "She can't think I'm innocent. Because she's going to blame herself, either way, when I'm convicted."

"You aren't going to be—"

"I am. I am and you know it. Jessica needs to understand that I was convicted because I'm guilty. Not because of her. She has to believe I'm guilty."

Mat opens his arms, the wine bobbing in the glass and almost spilling on the carpet. "You want me to tell her you're guilty? You want me to tell her you confessed to me?"

"That's exactly what I want you to do."

"Won't play, Allison. She'll need more than that."

"Tell her I used that trophy to kill him."

"Ah." Mat says it like a negative, like a grunt.

The police have believed, almost from the outset, that the instrument that delivered the fatal blows to Sam Dillon's head was an award given to him two years earlier by the Midwest Manufacturers' Association for excellency in advocacy. They saw the spot on the mantel of Sam's fireplace, from the pattern of dust, where it had rested for the last two years. The award, they quickly learned, had a solid marble base that would serve nicely as the head of a hammer. On the base, in gold, was a miniaturized version of an old industrial machine with a gear and sprocket. It was determined by looking at other such awards given out by the MMA that this trophy was sufficiently sturdy—indeed, it would be ironic if it were not—to be used as a weapon, bringing the marble base down on someone's head. Assault with a deadly statuette.

Anyone who has followed the suffocating account of this case in the papers, on television, and online would know of this trophy, currently missing and the subject of a rather feverish manhunt by police. Thus, Mat's objection.

"She wouldn't accept that as proof," Mat says.

"No." Allison wets her lips. "I suppose she wouldn't." She goes to the window next to the side table, looks out at the backyard and her neighbors' as well. They built a fence, about four feet high, around the property when Jessica got old enough to wander. She once tried to clear it, like an Olympic high-jumper, using the old Western-roll technique and requiring five stitches on her lip for her trouble.

"Y'know," Mat starts.

She turns to him.

"Never mind." He waves his hand. "Never mind."

"No, tell me," Allison says.

"I was just thinking." Mat averts his eyes, strolls aimlessly through the living room. "There is probably something I could tell Jessica. There is proof."

"What?"

Mat takes a drink of his wine, sets his jaw. "The murder weapon," he says. "You could tell me where it is. I could tell Jessica. If it came to that."

"I haven't even told my lawyer that. Nobody knows that."

But that, clearly, is Mat's point. It would be irrefutable proof to Jessica, a fact unknown to everyone.

"There's no spousal privilege," Allison says. "We're not married. You could be forced to divulge this."

Mat makes a face. The prosecution has already rested its case, and no one is looking at Mateo Pagone to help convict his ex-wife.

"You think so little of me?" he asks.

This again. Always falling back on self-pity. But he has a point. If she can't trust Mat, there is no one left.

She takes a breath as the adrenaline kicks in, her heart races, the memories of that night flood back. She turns again and places her hand on the window. It is colder than she expected.

"The Countryside Grocery Store," she says. "The one on Apple and Riordan?"

"Okay."

"When Jess was five," she continues. "She got away from me at the store. I was beside myself. I was looking everywhere for her. I had the store manager ready to call the police."

She can faintly see Mat in the reflection of the glass. He is captivated, listening intently, but she detects a frown. It only underscores the distance that has always been between them, even then. He doesn't remember this incident. She probably never even told him. He was at the capital, as this happened during the legislative session; this was back when Mat was a legislative aide, before he traded up to lobbying his former employers. It was one of countless episodes in their lives that passed right by him unnoticed.

She returns her eyes to the window. "I found Jessica out back," she continues. "She had wandered through the delivery area in the back of the store. She had gone down that little ramp they have for deliveries and she was standing outside by the fence. She was pointing at this post that was supporting the fence. It was yellow. This was during that 'lemon' thing she had."

Mat, she assumes, again does not get the reference. When Jessica was very young, she had great difficulty pronouncing the word *yellow*, so she used the word *lemon* instead. Even a banana was the color *lemon*. Even after she matured a bit and was able to say the word, she continued for many years to qualify it with the phrase—

"Yellow like lemon," Mat says.

Allison squeezes her eyes shut. It is these little things that always move her. She takes a moment, swallows hard, before continuing.

"That's where I put it." She raises her chin and keeps her voice strong, as she faces the window. "It's still there, that post. The paint has chipped away some but it's still the only yellow post out there. I—I can't say why I went there. I— we hadn't shopped there for years. I didn't think anyone would ever connect me to it."

She takes a deep breath and faces him. His eyes retreat again.

"You buried the trophy from the manufacturers' association next to a yellow post behind the Countryside?" Mat asks. "The one on Apple and Riordan?"

"I did. So if I'm convicted, you tell this to Jessica. But only then."

Mat's gaze moves about the room, anywhere but at her. He is lost in thought for a long moment, blinking rapidly, eyes narrowing. "Okay. If it ever comes to it, I can tell her about that. I'm—let's find something to eat."

Allison takes a step toward him. "You're the only person

who knows this," she says. "I haven't even told my lawyer. If this got out—if anyone found out—"

"Allison." He stops on his way to the kitchen but does not look at her. She senses a tightening in his posture.

"I won't tell a soul," he assures her.

MONDAY, MAY 3

Allison stares at the ghost in the mirror. She wants the judge to see her as she used to be, before the stress started doing its damage three months ago. She wants him to know her as a person, to know her life and background, to understand what she is capable of and what she is not.

But Judge Wilderburth will not know these things. Will not care to know. The facts of the case are the only things of relevance to him. It is a tainted filter, she realizes now more than ever. He will never know the full story. No jury, no judge ever has.

She looks at her watch, expecting Mat to walk in the door any minute to drive her to court, when the phone rings. It's seven-thirty in the morning and the phone is ringing.

She walks out of the master bathroom and finds her phone by the bed. The caller ID is noncommittal; the call is coming from an office.

"Allison, Paul Riley here."

Paul Riley is the first lawyer Allison retained on the case. "How are you, Paul?"

"Great, Allison. I've been following the trial. It looks good."

"Nice of you to say." Allison is sure the comment is insincere.

"The evidence is circumstantial," Paul adds, the classic take from a defense attorney. "They still don't have the murder weapon, do they?"

Allison catches her breath. She grips the phone until it hurts. "The, uh—"

"The murder weapon," Paul repeats. "They don't know for sure what it is, and they surely don't have it, as far as I can tell."

"No—no," Allison manages through the burn in her throat. "They don't have it."

"That will be tough for them, I would think. That's how you really put someone at a crime scene. No murder weapon, it's all speculation."

"I—I hope so."

"I think I've upset you here, Allison. Listen to me, talking about murder weapons. All I really wanted to tell you is I'm rooting for you."

"Thank you, Paul. I should—I should probably—"

"You need to get going. Best of luck, Allison."

She sets the phone down and puts a hand against the wall to support herself. She feels the heat on her face, the perspiration gather on her forehead.

The murder weapon.

The front door opens, Mat calls out to her to come down.

She shakes her head hard. Okay. She collects herself and takes the stairs down.

Jane McCoy sits in the back row, far left corner, a place that has been kept open for her. She's wearing her glasses—first time in years—and a baseball cap. There's no law that says you have to dress up to watch a trial. She's not in hiding, exactly, but she doesn't feel the need to highlight her presence. No one's going to notice her, anyway. All eyes are forward, as the defense begins its case in the trial of *People versus Allison Quincy Pagone.*

McCoy recognizes some of the reporters, who have been given the first two rows on the other side—Andy Karras from the Watch crime beat and Carolyn Pendry from Newscenter Four are sharing notes. You can tell the print media from television by their appearance, clothes and makeup, and by her count most of these people are not going before a camera.

McCoy's left-side seat puts her in the prosecution's half of the courtroom. If this thing lines up like a wedding, this would make her a friend of the prosecutor, Roger Ogren, which amuses McCoy, because she has been anything but.

She sees Allison Pagone leaning in at the defense table as her attorney speaks with her. She looks awfully good for a woman on trial. Her red hair is short now, curling out in the back, and damn, she has nice clothes, a tailored blue suit, white blouse, and colorful scarf. She's probably hoping the seventy-year-old judge will look down on her and think, *How could this cute little gal be a killer?* Maybe this is why the defense waived the right to a jury trial, letting the judge be the sole finder of fact.

Allison's new attorney is Ron McGaffrey. McCoy has never had the pleasure. She has been cross-examined by half the defense attorneys in this town, but not typically the ones on the high end, where McGaffrey apparently falls.

She looked into McGaffrey when Allison made the switch from Paul Riley. Riley, she knew. She liked him. A former federal prosecutor who once ran the county attorney's office as well. Former G-man who could give as well as he got but made it look natural. When Pagone changed lawyers, McCoy was concerned. McGaffrey never prosecuted, and those are always the guys hardest to deal with. The word about McGaffrey is that he never pleads a case, which is probably not a bad marketing device, because every criminal defendant wants a warhorse.

And that's exactly what Ron McGaffrey looks like, as he stands and moves toward the battered wooden lectern between the defense and prosecution tables—a fighter, a tough guy. He has been through the wringer and looks it, a wide, weathered face, bad skin, deep worry lines across his forehead. He is a large man, not tall but a physical presence, a darkness through the eyes, a halt in his stride. He drops a notepad on the lectern, wags a pencil as he leans his considerable frame forward. He took shrapnel above the knee in Vietnam, survived a heart attack a couple years back and quit smoking, which may explain why he's holding the pencil with such reverence.

"Call Walter Benjamin," he says to the judge.

McCoy watches the witness enter the courtroom. She wonders if he will make eye contact with her, but his eyes are forward and down, as he moves his long, thin body along the aisle, trying to maintain his dignity. He takes his seat and is sworn in, spells his last name. He is pushing fifty but looks older. Looks ill, actually, like the last time she saw him. He pushes his small glasses up on his long nose and fixes his hair, chestnut with gray borders.

"I am the director of governmental affairs, Midwest region, for Flanagan-Maxx Pharmaceuticals," he says.

Technically, Walter Benjamin is on paid leave at the moment, but McGaffrey will get to that, no doubt. He doesn't start there. He starts with the company, Flanagan-Maxx, a massive international corporation that "discovers, develops, and markets breakthrough drugs."

McGaffrey takes him through the countries where they have offices and laboratories, the different areas of medicine, the different departments—pharmaceutical, nutritional, and hospital products. The company has billions in revenue worldwide. The point seems to be to cast Flanagan-Maxx as the cold, heartless corporate giant.

"Let's talk about the pharmaceutical products division, sir," McGaffrey suggests.

McCoy moves in her seat. She wants this testimony to be over, and it's just beginning. There is no drama here, this part. F-M makes drugs for virtually anything, from brain disorders to respiratory infections to organ transplants to HIV/AIDS treatment.

"Let's talk about a particular product, sir," says McGaffrey. He has a commanding voice but not as deep as she expected. He compensates for this with high volume. His every word in this courtroom is a controlled shout. "Let's talk about a product called Divalpro."

Walter Benjamin nods without enthusiasm, adjusts his glasses again, and begins to explain it to the judge. Divalpro is a drug marketed to seniors for high blood pressure, one of the most successful products in the Flanagan-Maxx line, one of their cash cows. There is only one problem with Divalpro, a problem that is now known to anyone who follows the news, and certainly to anyone in the state capital.

Divalpro's patent is about to expire. Which means problems for Flanagan-Maxx. It means copycats. Worst of all, it means generic substitutes, drugs with the same active ingredient as Divalpro but cheaper, much cheaper, and therefore more attractive to the state Medicaid system than the expensive name-brand drug.

"Explain, if you would, Mr. Benjamin, the prior-approval list."

This, of course, was the main problem here. The state's department of public aid, always looking to cut costs, installs an immediate preference for cheaper generic alternatives by implementing a "prior approval" system. All generic alternatives receive prior approval from the state

Medicaid system, so a doctor can prescribe them by sign-ing a piece of paper. If the doctor wants to prescribe the more expensive, name-brand drug like Divalpro, he or she is required to go through considerable paperwork for ap-proval. Which one is the doctor going to choose? The pa-tients will ask for Divalpro, given its past monopoly and a considerable advertising campaign through direct mail and television, but the doctor will assure them that the generic alternative is essentially the identical drug. Flanagan-Maxx's profits on this drug will take a nosedive.

This was where Walter Benjamin, director of govern-mental affairs, came in. It was time to hit up the legisla-tures in the seven states he covers, including this one, for legislation to get Divalpro placed on the prior-approval list of medications. If Flanagan-Maxx could pull that off, it would be on the same footing as the generics and would maintain a considerable portion of its client base.

"We weren't asking for preference," Benjamin empha-sizes, ever the company man. "We just wanted to be on the same footing as the generics. We just wanted a level play-ing field."

Sure, and never mind that the state will be spending mil-lions on a drug that could be spent elsewhere in the Medicaid program, when the generic alternative is every bit as effective.

"And Mr. Benjamin, in your capacity as director of gov-ernmental affairs, did you personally, sir, go to our state capital and plead your case?"

"No."

"Who did?"

"We retained the services of Dillon and Becker."

"And who at that firm in particular?"

"Sam Dillon."

"Sam Dillon? The deceased in this case?"

"Yes."

"Why Sam Dillon?"

McCoy studies the witness's face. Walter Benjamin has probably asked himself that very question countless times since February. *Why Sam Dillon? Why did I have to choose Sam?*

"We hired Sam because he knew his way around the capital, so to speak. He was a former state senator. He was a Republican. He was very good."

"And why a Republican?"

"The state House is Republican. By a slim majority, but a majority nonetheless. And the governor is, too."

McGaffrey pauses. McCoy holds her breath.

There is no mention of the state Senate.

McCoy smiles.

"Would it be fair to say that Sam Dillon was one of the most influential lobbyists in the game?"

The prosecutor, Roger Ogren, squirms in his seat.

"Absolutely," Benjamin says.

"Did Sam Dillon lobby on behalf of Flanagan-Maxx in last year's legislative session?"

"Yes. Last year's veto session."

"Can you explain that to the Court?"

The witness looks at the judge. "For two weeks in November, the legislature reconvenes to consider legislation that was vetoed by the governor. They decide whether to override the veto. But technically, they can consider other legislation as well. We had introduced a bill in the House during the regular legislative session last year, but it was carried over to the veto session. It was during veto session that they voted on it."

"Are you familiar with House Bill 1551?"

"I am."

"What is House Bill 1551?"

Anyone with a pulse in this town knows about House Bill 1551, if not by number. Anyone who has read the accounts since the grand jury was convened in February knows the dirty details, which Walter Benjamin will now reluctantly impart. House Bill 1551 was the bill in the state's House of Representatives that put Divalpro on the prior-approval list. Sam Dillon, for all of his considerable talents as a lobbyist, couldn't get the bill passed during the regular legislative session. By all accounts, he had the House and Governor Trotter but was short in the Senate, by three votes to be exact. The problem was Flanagan-Maxx itself, a large drug company that did not have many friends in the legislature, particularly not in the Democratic-controlled Senate. The lobbies for the elderly and the poor, having fought for years for more dollars for the Medicaid program, argued fiercely against a bill that would prevent the savings of millions once the generics came aboard.

Dillon couldn't get it out of the Senate, long and short, and the Speaker of the House wasn't going to call it for a vote, and have his members take the heat, just to see it die in the Senate. So Sam Dillon asked the Speaker of the House to hold the bill over until veto session, hoping that the summer recess might change some minds.

Miracle of miracles, it did. Three senators switched their votes, and in the space of twenty-four hours, both the House and Senate passed House Bill 1551 and sent it to the governor. Why, precisely, these three senators changed their votes over summer recess is the focus of the federal grand jury investigation.

"So it's law right now," McGaffrey concludes. "State law recognizes Divalpro as being on the prior-approval list, once its patent expires this summer."

"Correct." For having accomplished such a feat, Walter Benjamin looks remarkably unhappy about it.

And the judge is about to hear why.

Ron McGaffrey clears his throat, strangles the lectern on each side. "Now, Mr. Benjamin, in the course of your duties as director of intergovernmental affairs, has it come to your attention that Sam Dillon may have used illicit means to gain the support of certain members of the state legislature?"

Roger Ogren stands as the witness begins his answer.

"I am not aware that—"

"Object to the form—"

"—there has been any *proof*—"

"—of the question, Your Honor. Object to form."

"Enough." Judge Wallace Wilderburth holds out his hand. He is heavyset, a sour-faced judge with small eyes, a thick flat nose, and prominent jowls. McCoy can't resist the comparison to a bulldog.

"Rephrase, Counsel," the judge instructs.

"All right." McGaffrey pauses. "Mr. Benjamin, were you subpoenaed before a grand jury in this state?"

"Yes, I was."

"By the United States attorney's office?"

"Yes."

"And you were also questioned by the FBI?"

"I was."

McCoy is on alert now. "Take five," she mumbles.

"Is this an investigation called Operation Public Trust?"

"Yes."

"And as far as you understand it, the federal government is looking into whether lawmakers were bribed to get the Divalpro prior-approval legislation passed in this state."

"Take five," McCoy mumbles again through her teeth.

"That is my understanding," says Benjamin.

"You testified before the grand jury."

"Yes, I did. And I have been advised by my counsel not to answer any questions in relation to that testimony."

"Oh." McGaffrey looks at the judge. "You're invoking the Fifth Amendment."

"I am."

The judge reacts to that. So do the reporters in the audience, scribbling notes furiously and whispering to one another, probably trying to confirm the precise questions Benjamin is refusing to answer. There will be a trial transcript at the day's end, but in today's news-right-now setting, they want to go with this stuff this afternoon. This is the first public discussion of the scandal, and a top executive for Flanagan-Maxx is asserting the Fifth Amendment.

"Well," says McGaffrey, "I wouldn't want you to incriminate yourself."

"Objection."

"Sustained."

"You paid a hundred thousand dollars to Sam Dillon, sir?"

"Yes."

"Do you know how that money was used?"

"I refuse to answer."

"Do you know whether any of that money was used to bribe lawmakers to vote for House Bill 1551?"

"I invoke my rights under the Fifth Amendment."

"Did you talk to Sam Dillon about that? Did you ask him if he ever bribed lawmakers?"

"I won't answer that, sir."

"Did Sam Dillon tell you he bribed lawmakers?"

"Objection," says Roger Ogren. "Calls for hearsay."

"Sustained."

"Did Sam Dillon talk to you in any way, shape, or form about the topic of bribing state officials to get House Bill 1551 passed?"

"I won't answer that."

"Counsel." The judge stares over his reading glasses, frowning at McGaffrey. "He's asserted his rights with regard to this line of questioning. Move on."

McCoy releases her breath. Good.

"Thank you, Your Honor."

McCoy chuckles. She has seen lawyers do this before, when she's testified at a trial or suppression hearing— thank the judge after being admonished, as if to pretend that they had scored something. *Counsel, you're out of order, that question is entirely inappropriate. Thank you, Judge!* What, the jurors are a bunch of idiots? And here, where there's no jury, only a judge as the finder of fact, it's even more moronic.

Ron McGaffrey leafs through his notepad, brings a fist to his mouth and clears his throat, before continuing.

"Did you call Sam Dillon on Tuesday, February third, Mr. Benjamin?"

"I refuse to answer."

"Did *he* call *you*, on that day?"

"I refuse to answer."

"Did that conversation concern the fact that three state senators were bribed to pass the Divalpro legislation?"

"Objection," says Roger Ogren, just as Walter Benjamin repeats his line: "I refuse to answer."

"The objection is sustained," says the judge. "Are we almost done here, Counsel?"

McGaffrey takes a moment, presumably to review his notes, but he undoubtedly wants these final questions to resonate with the court.

"That's all I have, Your Honor."

"No questions," says Roger Ogren.

"We'll recess for lunch," the judge says. "I have some motions at one. Let's reconvene at two. Two o'clock."

"All rise."

McCoy breathes out, stretches her arms. Walter Benjamin's testimony was fine, almost comical, really, especially the discussion of the steps that led to the passage of the Divalpro legislation. Dancing around the Senate like it hardly existed, mentioning the single most important fact—the sudden switch of three votes in the Senate—only as an afterthought. Nary a mention of the fact that Mateo Pagone was the one lobbying the Senate on the bill, the one who spent time with each of the three senators over the summer recess during which they discovered their changes of heart and switched their votes to aye.

She wonders how Ronald McGaffrey must feel about all of this, what steps Allison had to take to keep him reined in, how in the hell Allison Pagone managed to prevent her lawyer from even mentioning the name of the person with the single greatest incentive to make sure Sam Dillon never testified before that federal grand jury probing bribery in the state legislature.

She sees Allison now, touching her lawyer's arm, probably complimenting him. McGaffrey seems resistant to the gesture, which confirms for McCoy the tension that must exist between the two.

She allows herself a brief smile, hoping the physical effort will unwind the anxiety percolating in her stomach. Today went as expected, Benjamin's testimony, but things are far from over. She hasn't decided if she likes Allison, but she knows one thing.

She needs Allison Pagone alive.

That was good," Allison says, under her breath, to Ron McGaffrey when they return from lunch.

"As good as it *could* be." McGaffrey pops a lemon drop into his mouth.

As good as you would let it be, he means. He has felt hog-tied by Allison, she knows, since the day she hired him six weeks ago. Constrained by the lack of time to prepare. Constrained by what he perceived as Allison's unwillingness to fully assist in the defense, if not her outright lies to him. She would feel sorry for him, under other circumstances, but Ronald McGaffrey has a hundred-thousand-dollar retainer resting in his law firm's client fund, and he's first-chairing one of the biggest criminal trials to come along in years. The old saying is, they don't remember whether you won, they just remember you were the lawyer, and McGaffrey's representation of Allison has elevated him a notch in the legal community.

Not that he would ever admit that. He must have felt unbelievably stroked when she dumped her old lawyer, Paul Riley, and came to him. Paul Riley, by all accounts, was the go-to guy these days, at least in the opinions of those who didn't have a personal stake in such things. Yes, Paul was a former prosecutor, and some said that former prosecutors are too chummy with their old colleagues, fall in love with the plea bargain, but Paul showed no aversion to a fight. No, the truth that nobody knows is that Paul dumped Allison, not the other way around. He refused to participate in her defense, said that he couldn't be a part of—what had he called it?

A fraud on the court.

The judge reenters the courtroom and everyone rises. Ron McGaffrey calls his next witness "Call Richard Cook."

Richard Cook—Richie, apparently, everyone calls him—is a junior at Mansbury College in town here, who worked as an intern at Sam's lobbying firm, Dillon & Becker. He's twenty, supposedly, but he looks younger, tight skin, flyaway hair, long sideburns, and skinny neck. He doesn't seem nervous. This is probably exciting for him.

"I ran errands for Mr. Dillon and Mr. Becker. Delivered things. I helped them out with computers, too, when they needed something quick."

"How long did you work there?"

"I worked there about a year. Pretty much three days a week, afternoons."

"You knew Sam Dillon?"

"Yeah. Definitely."

"Let me—let me take you to February third of this year. Do you recall that date?"

This is the same date that McGaffrey raised with the last witness, Walter Benjamin. Benjamin looked like he was going to vomit at the time, as he refused to answer whether he and Sam had had a phone conversation about the bribery of three state senators. Allison wonders how that conversation went. She wonders how much Walter Benjamin knows. She wonders if he blames himself for ever hiring Sam, who was an old friend of his.

"Yeah." The young man nods compliantly. "I remember that date."

He remembers that date because he was working at Sam's office that afternoon, organizing files in drawers right outside Sam's office. Allison knows this because, after Sam's murder, this kid and his father went to the police and reported the very thing about which Richie Cook will now testify, and the prosecutor, Roger Ogren, was duty-bound to disclose this information to the defense.

"All right, son," McGaffrey says, standing at the lectern. "While you were organizing these files, where was Mr. Dillon?"

"In his office. Real close by me. On the phone."

"Do you happen to know who he was talking to?"

Richard Cook shakes his head.

"You have to answer out loud, son."

"No, I didn't know. I was just—I wasn't meaning to listen in or anything. But I heard him. I heard him talking."

"What did you hear him say, son? What did Mr. Dillon say?"

"He says, well—he, like"—the young man works his hands—"he started kind of shouting, like he was reacting to someone. He was like, 'No! Listen! Don't—' Then he got quiet all of a sudden, then he was talking quieter. Like he knew he was shouting and he wanted to be quieter."

"Sure. And Richard, what did Mr. Dillon then say? When he quieted down?"

"He was all, like—he said, 'No one can tie this to Flanagan-Maxx. No one could prove that. Just take the Fifth, if you're so worried.' That was pretty much it."

McGaffrey nods and looks at the judge. His Honor is

taking notes here, and McGaffrey doesn't want to get ahead of him.

"Now, Richard," he says, "when Sam Dillon said, 'No one can tie this to Flanagan-Maxx,' did he explain what he was talking about?"

An old lawyer's tactic, repeat helpful testimony in the question.

"No. He didn't."

"When he said, 'No one could prove that,' did he explain that?"

"No."

"When he said, 'Just take the Fifth,' did he explain *that*?"

"Nope. I told you all I heard."

"But you heard him say 'Flanagan-Maxx,' Richard?"

"Yeah."

"All right. So what happened next?"

"Well, he—I think he got paranoid or something that someone was listening—"

"Objection." Roger Ogren is on his feet. "Foundation. Move to strike."

The judge turns to Richard Cook. "Young man, you'll need to limit what you tell us to what you heard or what you observed. Okay?"

"Okay." The witness shrinks a bit on the stand.

"The answer will be stricken. Mr. McGaffrey?"

"Richard," says McGaffrey, "tell us what you observed, or heard, after you heard Sam Dillon finish by saying, 'Just take the Fifth, if you're so worried.'"

"Well, it was like all quiet for a minute. Then Mr. Dillon came out his door."

"What did he do?"

"He stared at me for a minute. Then he asked me what I was doing."

"What did you say?"

"I said I was filing."

"And then?"

"Then he closed his door pretty hard. He seemed mad that I was out there."

"And what did you do, after hearing all this, Richard? Did you talk to anyone?"

"I talked to my dad later that night."

"And did anything result from that?"

"Well, not until Mr. Dillon was dead. Then my dad and I were thinking that it might have been important, what I heard. So we told the cops."

"Thank you, son. Your witness, Mr. Ogren."

Roger Ogren stands and buttons his coat. He is younger, and not as heavy, as his opposing counsel. Ogren does not have a wedding band on his finger, and Allison makes the assumption that he never has. He seems the type who lives for his work, especially this work.

"My name is Roger Ogren, Richard." The prosecutor glances at a pad of notes on the lectern. "You and I have spoken before, haven't we?"

The witness leans in to the microphone. "Yes."

"Okay. Richard, that phone conversation you were describing? You don't know to whom Mr. Dillon was speaking, do you?"

"No."

No one will ever know to whom Sam Dillon was talking. Sam, and others in his office, made and received several calls from the state capital that afternoon. The phone records did not identify the particular phone lines used from the offices of Dillon & Becker, nor did the phone records at the capital help much. Based on the approximate timing of the calls, they could have been made to any number of politicians or lobbyists or clients, either at the capital or in the city.

But yes, there had been a phone call from Flanagan-Maxx that day, a little after four in the afternoon. The problem is, no one can tie Richard Cook down to a particular time—he can't say four o'clock or two-thirty—so no one can conclusively say that the conversation Richard overheard was between Sam and Walter Benjamin.

"You don't know what Sam Dillon and this other person were talking about, do you?"

"No."

The prosecutor taps on the lectern. "Mr. Dillon was a lawyer, wasn't he?"

"Umm—yeah, I guess so."

"He advised clients on issues."

"You mean like going to the capital and stuff?"

"I mean," says Ogren, "like giving advice to clients. Whether it concerns legislation or other stuff. Mr. Dillon was a lawyer who gave advice to clients."

"I—I guess so. You mean a lawyer like you are? Like, trials and stuff?"

Roger Ogren squirms a moment. He's supposed to be asking the questions. "You don't know if he was or wasn't, is that what you're saying?"

"Yeah. I know he's a lobbyist. Other stuff, I don't know."

"And it's possible that this is exactly what Mr. Dillon was doing on the phone, right? It's possible that he was on the phone with a client, discussing something the *client* had done wrong. He was telling the person on the other end to take the fifth, not himself. Right?"

Richard Cook does not appear to have an agenda here, and Allison can't imagine why he would. He readily concedes the point. He didn't know who Sam Dillon was talking to or what they were discussing.

"Thanks, Richard. No more questions." Roger Ogren takes his seat triumphantly.

"No redirect," says Ron McGaffrey. "But at this time we would submit into evidence, by stipulation, a subpoena for the decedent, Samuel Dillon, to appear before the federal grand jury in the Operation Public Trust investigation."

"It will be admitted," says the judge.

"And if I could simply note, Your Honor, that the date Mr. Dillon was scheduled to appear was Wednesday, February eleventh, which means that Mr. Dillon was found dead only three days before he was scheduled to testify."

"Duly noted, Counsel," says the judge, smirking.

SUNDAY, MAY 2

Do you date immature men?" Sam asked. Not the first time they had met—she had met Sam Dillon on two occasions over the last few years. But this was the first time she had been available. This was after Thanksgiving, last year, after the veto session had been completed.

I always have in the past, *she wanted to answer but didn't. It was odd enough that Sam was a colleague of Mat's, a fellow lobbyist. She didn't need to refer to her ex-husband. That could break the sensation. Or would it? Might it add an element of danger? Intrigue?*

"I haven't dated in twenty-one years," she answered, *referring to Mat anyway. It was unavoidable. Somehow she didn't care, and she felt a breath of liberation in not caring. An even greater lift because the man standing before her at the reception didn't seem to be conflicted, either.*

"I could see where it might be awkward," he said.

She could see that Sam was tipsy. The end of session, even the small veto session, usually prompted small parties,

*and Sam's firm had planned this event as a holiday party.
Allison had only arrived about an hour ago, on Jessica's
invitation, but Sam and some of the others had clearly gotten an earlier start.*

"Because my daughter works for you?" she asked.

*Sam demurred. Shook his scotch, let the ice clink
against the glass. His suit was a soft brown, over a crisply
ironed shirt, bright red tie. He looked like a lobbyist but he
didn't look—what was the word?—slick. Had an ease
about him.*

*Allison glanced over Sam's shoulder at Jessica, who
was standing among other interns her age, laughing at a
joke.*

*"Jessica's very talented," Sam said, avoiding the sub-
ject as Allison had, in a way. She felt a wave of disap-
pointment, wondered if the subject had been forever
changed.*

*Sam followed her eyes, turned his head, then returned
to Allison without looking at her. He raised his glass to his
mouth as he began to utter the words.*

"It's probably not—"

*She cut him off with her own words, surprising herself.
They came out without warning, something she had never
experienced before. She would have to get used to "firsts"
again.*

*"We would need to be discreet," she interrupted. "For
the time being."*

*Sam's glass was suspended at his lips. She saw a flicker
in his eyes, a slight reaction at his mouth, before he shook
the ice and took a drink, eyes fully focused on her.*

They are back. There was a time, after the arrest and the
arraignment, when the press left Allison largely to herself.
It was big news, sensational stuff; then it was nothing until
the trial approached—until then, on to the next salacious
scandal. But since the trial began last week, they have re-

turned with a flourish, the news trucks lining her street, the reporters standing on the curb, hovering over the property line of her house. Cameras filming her whenever she leaves the house, which is hardly ever.

It is, in a way, a very public place to meet, but in truth it's preferable to most spots. Since February, when this started, they have followed her almost everywhere; if she wandered into a coffee shop or café downtown, the pack would be close behind, staring through windows. But for some reason, they have never followed her into a grocery store. Who knows—maybe the store manager would have expelled them. For whatever reason, the media probably found it odd to follow a woman through the aisles of a grocery store as she filled her cart. *Allison, why the scented fabric softener? Have you always used Tide? Why Folgers over Maxwell House?* The breaking news on cable television: *"We are here live at the Countryside Grocery Store on the city's northwest side. Bob, we have just received word that murder suspect Allison Pagone—hold on Bob, I'm getting something"—*the reporter touches her earpiece, then nods triumphantly—*"yes, Bob, we can now confirm that Allison Pagone has decided to go with the sugarless gum Trident as her breath freshener, baffling experts who had predicted cinnamon Altoids."* The newspaper headlines: PAGONE SPLURGES ON FRESH FRUIT. MURDER SUSPECT: "I CAN'T BELIEVE IT'S NOT BUTTER!"

She carries a hand cart with her to the small coffee shop inside the store. She finds him there, as she has every Sunday.

"Hey there," Larry Evans says to her. He is dressed casually as always, a button-down shirt and jeans, baseball cap.

"Hey yourself." There is a cup of coffee, black, awaiting her. She takes a sip and receives a jolt.

Larry Evans gives her the thumbs-up. She isn't sure of the meaning but she can guess.

"Don't tell me the trial's going well," she says to him.

"I think it is." Larry moves in his seat with excitement. "I think you have them right where you want them."

"Like Butch Cassidy had 'em right where he wanted 'em."

"Allison." Larry throws his hands up. "They say you were dumped by Sam and so you killed him? Come on. That's all they can say? That's weak."

"The judge seems persuaded."

"Well, sure—I mean, without any response, it might seem convincing. But you have plenty to say in response." There is a hint of challenge in what he is saying. He has come to learn how stubborn Allison can be. "You start your defense tomorrow, right?"

"Larry." Allison sighs. "They have so much evidence against me. Physical evidence. A motive. An alibi that blew up in my face. I have an answer for all of that? I have smoke and mirrors. My defense is one giant diversion tactic."

The prosecution's case rested on Friday, after three days of damning evidence. It gave the news outlets the weekend to play over all of the proof implicating Allison in Sam Dillon's murder.

Larry doesn't have an answer, of course. He doesn't know how this all played out. Even Larry, the optimist, the one who has rallied to her cause, cannot explain away the evidence placing Allison at the scene of the murder, or her argument with Sam beforehand, to say nothing of the alibi fiasco.

"Testify, Allison," he says. "Tell them what really happened."

She smiles at him. "Larry, I want to win this case as much as you want me to win. I'm just trying to be pragmatic. Their case is solid. And I'm not going to testify, because that could just make things worse."

"How so?"

"I can't—I really can't get into that. Suffice it to say, I can't testify."

"You're protecting someone," he gathers.

"I really—" Allison sighs. "I really can't go there."

"You still haven't shown your lawyer what I wrote up for you, have you?" Larry shakes his head in frustration. "These—the prosecutors don't have a clue, Allison. Either they haven't figured out what I have or they don't want to talk about it because it hurts their case. I'm guessing the former is true. They don't know. Which means you can hammer them."

"You know that what I tell my lawyer is off limits, Larry. That was the deal—"

"Okay, okay. I don't want to know what you tell him." He lets out an exaggerated sigh. "I don't get you, though. You've got a ticket and you won't punch it."

Allison drinks her coffee and looks around at the shoppers, their happy-go-lucky lives and their silly, frivolous concerns.

"So all you're going to say in your defense," he asks, "is that some unnamed, unknown person connected to the bribery scandal killed Sam Dillon because they were afraid he might squeal on them? That's it?"

"I think it could be convincing," she says.

"No, you don't." The heat comes to Larry's face. "No, you don't. You have names and you won't give them." He drills a finger on the table. "I think you know, Allison. I think you know and you won't say. And I don't get that. I have no idea what's going on."

Allison smiles at him weakly.

You certainly don't, she thinks to herself. And she will never tell him.

SATURDAY, MAY 1

Jane McCoy looks over the expansive office of the FBI's special agent-in-charge for the city's field office. The desk is oak, large and polished like a military spit-shine, reflecting the ceiling lights. The carpet is blood-red. The bookshelves along the wall are immaculate, adorned with manuals and a few well-placed photographs. The guy wants to impress, he succeeded.

Irving Shiels has been the SAC for eleven years here in the city, having served overseas before that. She has always gotten along well with Shiels. There is a mystique about him in the office, something unapproachable, the strut in his stride, the cold stare of those dark eyes, but she has been able to reach him on a personal level. A lot of people get tongue-tied around a boss. McCoy, for reasons she cannot explain, is just the opposite. She imagines it's a rather solitary existence, running an office like this, and anyone in Irving Shiels's position would appreciate the occasional joke or informality, provided it doesn't cross the line. A witty comment or personal anecdote can break the ice, and that is her forte. She remembers babbling to him on an internal elevator one day about one of her cases, an international child kidnapping case when she was new to the bureau, and realizing in retrospect that she had been doing all the talking. Shiels probably takes it for confidence, that someone like Jane McCoy could be so freewheeling around him. The truth is, McCoy is just a talker.

"The prosecution's case ended yesterday," McCoy says. "It's everything we expected."

"Right. Read it in the Watch. Looks bad for her." Shiels leans back in his chair, a scowl playing on his face. He rarely lightens up, never seems to err on that side. He's the classic straight shooter. Doesn't drink, doesn't smoke. Doesn't smile, either. "So what's up next?" he asks.

McCoy shifts in her chair. "Walter Benjamin is up next. The Flanagan-Maxx government guy."

"Right. Benjamin."

"I'll be in the courtroom, sir. I'm sure it will be fine."

"I saw where the daughter testified."

"Yes, sir. Jessica was the prosecution's best witness."

Shiels runs a hand over his mouth. "I'll bet she was. Okay." He looks at the ceiling. "Tell me about the doctor."

McCoy sighs. "As far as we can tell—"

"Don't tell me 'as far as we can tell,' Agent. Tell me that we know exactly what is going to happen here." A vein appears prominently in Shiels's forehead. He is quick to heat, at least that's what the other agents say. McCoy has never seen an eruption firsthand. But she can tell just by looking at him. His skin is damaged, broken blood vessels on his cheeks, worry lines on his forehead, a worn mask that ages him beyond his fifty-four years. He wears the authority well, but the skin doesn't lie. Stress will take its pound of flesh one way or the other.

Sure, she understands. This is a career-maker or -breaker for both of them. But Jesus Christ, Shiels knows there are

limits to their surveillance of Doctor Lomas. They can't in-
filtrate the lab and they can't bug his house.

"Sir," McCoy begins again, choosing her words with
care, "Doctor Lomas is going about his business as always.
He has one messed-up life there, but when he's in the lab, he's
going great guns. We're hearing a couple of weeks, he'll
have the formula perfected."

Shiels sighs and raises a hand, as close as he will come
to an apology. "The doctor's still clucking?"

"Yes, sir," McCoy says, her tone indicating that she is as
surprised as her boss. It continues to amaze McCoy that
some cocaine addicts can function indefinitely in society.
They teach their classes, make their deadlines, argue their
cases in court. As long as they have their breaks for the occasional fix, they can go out and do their jobs. Some of
them give in, are overcome by the addiction, but the truth
is, what stops many junkies is the lack of money to continue their habit. And financial resource is one of the few
problems that does not plague Doctor Neil Lomas.

"What about the other problem?"

McCoy shakes her head. "He's not gambling anymore.
He seems steady enough."

Shiels seems okay with that, or maybe the momentary
glazing over of his eyes is due to sleep deprivation. "What
do you get," he poses, "when you cross the murder of a lobbyist with a bribery scandal with a terrorist operation that
could kill hundreds of thousands of people?"

"An ulcer?" she tries.

"Right. Yeah. Exactly." He moves past McCoy and
touches the chair by her shoulder. "And how is the loose
cannon?"

Allison Pagone, he means. "Not loose at all, sir."

"Are we sure we know everything there is to know about
her, Agent?" Shiels is at his window now, looking over the
downtown.

"I'm confident," McCoy says, with a twitch to her gut.

The truth is, she *thinks* she knows all there is to know about Allison Pagone. But she has been around the block. No matter the resources you employ, there is only so much you can know about a person, especially what's inside her head.

Shiels turns and faces McCoy. "And what about the rest of her family?"

"It's covered, sir."

"Covered." He moves his shoe over the carpeting, drawing with his foot, as far as she can tell, a tic-tac-toe pattern. Could be a crucifix. Shiels has seen a lot in his years with the government, and the fact that this thing has him so jumpy doesn't exactly ease McCoy's mind.

"We're watching Allison," McCoy adds.

"You were watching Sam Dillon, too."

McCoy bows her head. A sore point, for all of them. Especially for McCoy. She will not repeat the mistake with Allison Pagone. She can't. It would mean the end of her career, first of all. Maybe not an outright termination but an unspoken demotion, a reassignment, shitty casework. And her career is the least of her concerns. She took it hard when Dillon was murdered, took it personally, even though she had never so much as spoken a word to the man.

"Just what we fucking needed," Shiels moans, pacing the room again. "A celebrity. It's bad enough that all of this is connected. Bad enough we have the county prosecuting a murder case around all of this. Bad enough that Pagone could be telling her lawyer God knows what—"

"She doesn't *know*, sir—"

"—no, that's not enough. No, *this* case has to involve a best-selling novelist. We only have about three hundred media outlets covering this story."

"Don't worry about Allison Pagone, sir," says McCoy.

The special agent-in-charge looks at Jane, then sits on the edge of the desk near her.

"Agent McCoy," he says, "we need Allison Pagone alive."

"Yes, sir." McCoy nods.

"This was your call, Agent."

"Yes, it was."

"And I backed it up to Washington. I told them Jane McCoy's the one they want in charge of this operation. I backed up everything you've done on this. You think I don't get a call from Virginia every single day on this? You know how many people think the Bureau is the wrong agency for this?"

"Sir, I won't let you down. We'll get them."

"Good enough." Shiels moves back to his desk, takes a seat and puts on his reading glasses. This is his way of saying *Get up, get out.*

And don't screw this up.

APRIL

FRIDAY, APRIL 30

work at the city office of Dillon and Becker," says the witness, Veronica Silvers.

Allison remembers her. This woman worked the reception at Sam's firm in the city.

"Let's turn to Friday, February sixth of this year," Roger Ogren begins. The day before Sam Dillon was murdered. Allison remembers this day all too well, remembers storming into Sam's office. It's hard, that memory, the state she was in, and now hearing it aired in public.

"I'd say it was late morning," the witness says. "After eleven."

Allison wishes she could curl up under the table.

"She walked right past me. She was in a mood. She was looking for Mr. Dillon."

"Was Sam Dillon in the offices that day?"

No.

"No. He was at the capital. I tried to tell her."

"What did the defendant say?"

"She didn't seem to believe me. She walked past me and went through the entire suite. She really made quite a scene."

Allison closes her eyes.

"She walked all the way through the offices, opening doors, calling out his name. I was following her, telling her she had to leave. But she wouldn't, not until she was satisfied that Mr. Dillon was not there. I—was about to call security."

"And once she was satisfied that Mr. Dillon was not there, what did she do?"

"She left. She didn't say a word. She just walked out, very quickly."

"Very good, ma'am."

"And the next thing, she goes down to the capital to find Mr. Dillon."

Allison's lawyer objects. This is outside this witness's personal knowledge, but really, what's the point? Everyone knows what Allison did next.

"Thank you, ma'am. No more questions."

Allison chooses not to even look at Troy Thompson as he takes the witness stand. This was the guy down at Sam's office in the state capital who caught Allison on her way in that Friday, after she had come from Sam's city office. She hardly remembers what he looks like and doesn't want to be reminded of anything that happened that day.

Ogren starts with the basics. Thompson is a full-time legislative research assistant for Dillon & Becker who works exclusively at the office in the state capital. On Fridays, when the receptionist doesn't work, Thompson also keeps an eye on the front door.

Roger Ogren takes a breath. "Mr. Thompson, let me take you back to Friday, February sixth of this year. Do you recall working that day, that afternoon?"

"I remember."

"Did your office have any visitors that afternoon?"

"Yes. Jessica's mom," says Thompson. "Mrs. Pagone."

"We'll stipulate to the identification," says Ron McGaffrey.

"Thank you, Counsel." The prosecutor opens a hand to the witness. "Mr. Thompson, what time was this? When the defendant came to the firm."

"It was, oh, just after lunch. A little after one."

"And tell us, Mr. Thompson, if you can. How far a drive is it from the city to the state capital?"

"It runs about ninety minutes, if you avoid rush hour."

Allison sighs. The point here, now clearly made, is that Allison went to Sam's office downtown and then, when he wasn't there, immediately drove straight down to the capital.

And that is exactly how it happened.

"It was just me and Mr. Dillon that day," the witness says. "Y'know, Fridays, there isn't much happening, and Mr. Dillon had been away most of that week so he was catching up."

"That's fine, that's fine. And what happened, sir?"

"I—well, the front door to our office opened, so I stuck my head out. I saw Mrs. Pagone. I started to say hi and she said to me—"

"Where is he?" Allison demanded. "Where's Sam Dillon? Don't lie to me, I know he's here."

"I told her that he was in the back office and I would tell him she was here."

"How did she respond?"

"She didn't. She just started walking back there. Walking very fast."

"Can you describe the defendant's appearance, Mr. Thompson?"

"She was—well, out of breath, I'd say. Her face was all red. Her eye makeup was smeared. She was moving very quickly. She looked—really upset, actually."

"Then what happened?"

"Well, I followed her back there—y'know, so I could tell Mr. Dillon. But by the time I got back there, she was slamming the door behind her."

"She slammed the door," Ogren repeats. "And so what did you do?"

"I—nothing at first. I didn't want to stand outside the door or anything. I heard some yelling. It was her voice but I don't know what she said, exactly. I wasn't standing right by the door or anything. So—the whole thing was kind of awkward. I walked away and went back to what I had been doing."

"What happened next, sir?"

Allison peeks at the witness for the first time. His face is colored slightly, his eyes downcast.

"Then I—I probably shouldn't have, but I went back to the door. Y'know, it was like, part concern and part natural curiosity." He takes a breath. "I stood with my ear next to the door of Mr. Dillon's office and listened." The witness blushes. No one likes admitting such things.

"What did you hear?"

"I heard Mr. Dillon."

"What was he saying?"

"He was saying, 'It isn't going to work out. Mat's a friend. This is crazy. You know that.' That kind of thing. That's the best I remember."

Allison looks forward, trying to remind herself that the judge may be watching her. The witness, surprisingly, got it almost right. Most witnesses think they recall dialogue verbatim and events with a photographic memory, but it isn't so, there have been studies on such things, and Allison's job, when she was a public defender, often consisted of hammering home minor inconsistencies and elevating them to major discrepancies.

But this man on the witness stand came pretty close. Allison will never forget the words awkwardly spilling from Sam Dillon's mouth. His slumped posture in his chair behind the desk, a hand on his forehead, his eyes on Allison.

This isn't going to work out. Mat—Mat's a friend. You know this is crazy. It always was.

"Mr. Thompson, you mentioned the name 'Mat.' 'Mat's a friend,' you said. Let me ask you, do you happen to know the name of the defendant's ex-husband?"

"His name is Mat," he answers. "I know him 'cause he's a lobbyist, too."

"Okay. What did you do next? What happened?"

"I moved away from the door. Because, I mean, it was a personal thing. It was none of my business. What can I say? I eavesdropped. I mean—she seemed so mad, I didn't know. You hear stories, people coming into an office and opening fire or something, irate clients, that sort of thing. But once I realized—it was, like, personal, he was breaking up with her—I moved away." He raises his hands. "I—didn't even know they were dating."

Ronald McGaffrey rises.

"I was there like a few seconds and then went back to my office," the witness concludes.

"Objection," McGaffrey calls out. "Move to strike any characterization that the decedent was 'breaking up' with my client or that they were dating."

"Sustained," the judge says, without bothering to hear Roger Ogren's response. "That comment is stricken from the record."

"What happened next, Mr. Thompson?"

"Mrs. Pagone came out about—gosh—maybe a minute later. She walked straight out of the office."

"Did you speak with Mr. Dillon about it?"

The witness thinks about that a moment, his eyes drifting off. "No. I left about five—maybe a little before five. I went by his office. He was looking out his window. I said I was leaving. He said, 'Have a good weekend,' without turning around. That was—" Troy Thompson swallows on that sentence.

"That was the last time you saw Mr. Dillon alive."

The witness nods.

Detective Czerwonka," asks Roger Ogren, "did you in fact speak with the defendant?"

"Yes, we did. This was Wednesday, the eleventh of February."

"Where did you speak with her?"

"At headquarters. We called her and asked her to come."

"Did she come with a lawyer?"

"No."

"Did you advise her of her rights?"

"We did. She waived her right to counsel in writing."

Roger Ogren admits into evidence Allison's signed waiver.

"What did you ask her?"

"We asked her if she was aware that Sam Dillon was dead. She said that she was. We asked her if she was involved in a romantic relationship with Sam Dillon. She said that she was not."

Roger Ogren looks at Judge Wilderburth. His Honor must be sure, at this point in the trial, that this was a lie.

"She *denied* being romantically involved with Sam Dillon?"

"Yes. In fact, I asked her that question at both interviews. Wednesday the eleventh and Friday the thirteenth. Both times, she denied being involved with Mr. Dillon."

"Okay. Let's stay with the eleventh. Did you follow up with her?"

"We asked her if she had gone to Sam Dillon's offices, looking for him, the previous Friday."

"What did she say?"

"She didn't answer, initially."

"What did *you* say?"

"I told her that there were witnesses. That people had seen her at both the city and capital offices of Dillon and Becker that day, Friday the sixth. And that she had been seen going into Sam Dillon's office at the capital and slamming the door shut, and she'd been heard yelling at him."

"What did she say to that?"

"She didn't speak for a while. I would say about five minutes. Then she said, 'It's complicated.' That's all she said. She got up and left." The detective shrugs. "We had no basis at that time to hold her."

"Was there anything about her personal appearance that struck you as significant?"

"Yes," says Czerwonka, holding up a hand. "She had nails. They weren't particularly long but they were there. But the left-hand index finger—that finger had almost no nail. It was broken down past the fingertip."

Allison curls her left hand into a fist.

"Were her fingernails painted?"

"Not at that time, no."

"All right, Detective. What did you do next? After the defendant left the police station after that brief visit."

"We got a search warrant."

Roger Ogren shows Detective Czerwonka the search warrant and admits it into evidence.

"You searched the defendant's home?"

"Yes. The following day. The twelfth of February."

"Can you tell us what you found, Detective?"

"We looked in her jewelry box. I did it myself."

"What did you find?"

"We found one platinum earring—"

The judge takes notice of this. Chin lifting, mouth parting.

"—with a gold fastener."

"Pure platinum," the jeweler told Allison. "A polished finish. The post is fourteen-karat yellow gold. It's our finest."

They were beautiful. Allison favored platinum, and she wanted to give herself something. Her novel had just been published. Mat had been generous with jewelry over the years, but it was always gold, and no matter how many hints she dropped, he never bought her platinum.

She put them on and looked into the small mirror on the counter. She had never bought herself jewelry before. But something felt right about it. Something about the very fact that she was doing it for herself. She had begun to do such things, as the separation from Mat was becoming more pronounced. It was with a small thrill, mixed with a deepening sadness, that she set down her credit card.

Roger Ogren walks from the evidence table to the witness, holding a bag containing the single earring.

"Is this the earring you found in the defendant's jewelry box, Detective?"

"That's it," he says with assurance. "It obviously stood out."

"And why did it stand out?"

"It stood out," says the detective, "because it is identical to the earring that we found in Sam Dillon's house at the crime scene. It's the second earring of the set."

Ogren shows the detective the other platinum earring, in a separate evidence bag.

"That's the one we found near Sam Dillon's body," Czerwonka confirms.

"And as a reminder to the judge," says Ogren, going back to the evidence desk placed behind the prosecution table, "this is a credit-card receipt for this pair of platinum earrings, purchased by the defendant eighteen months ago?"

"Yes."

"All right. Did you find anything else, Detective, in your search of the home?"

"Yes. We searched the defendant's garbage, of course. We found cotton balls that contained fingernail polish and nail polish remover."

"What color?"

"Red. We ran a check on it." Czerwonka looks at the notepad on his lap. "The actual color is 'Saturday Night Red.' It was made by Evelyn Masters. It's pretty pricey."

"And did you find such a fingernail polish in the defendant's home?"

"Yes. There was a bottle of it in her drawer in the bathroom."

"And remind us, Detective. The broken fingernail you found in Sam Dillon's house after his death." Roger Ogren holds up the evidence bag and approaches the witness. "What was the color of that fingernail?"

"It was the same. 'Saturday Night Red' by Evelyn Masters."

"And yet, by the time you spoke with the defendant at the police station, a few days after the death of Sam Dillon—"

"Her nails had no polish on them," Czerwonka finishes. "She had removed the polish."

"Very good, Detective. Now let me ask, did you find anything else of significance?"

"We did," he answers. "We found, in Mrs. Pagone's laundry, a maroon sweatshirt. A Champion sweatshirt with the name 'Mansbury College' on it."

"All right." Ogren retrieves another evidence bag. "Is this that sweatshirt?"

"It is."

"And did you find anything of significance on it?"

"We found blood."

"Blood that has been matched through DNA testing to Sam Dillon's blood?" Ogren asks. This is a leading question, but these are only foundational questions. Ogren, yesterday, called a forensic scientist to the stand to confirm that the blood on Allison's sweatshirt was Sam Dillon's blood. Technically, the evidence was presented out of order—it had not yet been established that the sweatshirt was found in Allison's house—but this is a trial by judge, not jury, and the judge accommodated the scheduling needs of the witnesses by hearing the evidence out of order.

So now, Detective Czerwonka is confirming that he found the sweatshirt in Allison's laundry during his search of the house.

"Yeah," the detective says, "the sweatshirt we found in the defendant's laundry had Sam Dillon's blood on it."

THURSDAY, APRIL 29

So let's summarize all of this for the Court," says Roger Ogren. He is directing a deputy medical examiner, an elderly man named Ernest McCabe, on the second day of trial. "What was the cause of death?"

"The cause of death was blunt trauma to the skull," says the doctor. "Four independent blows to the head, from two different sources. One of the sources we know about. The clock that was on the mantel. The other source, which was in all likelihood a much heavier and sturdier object, was not recovered."

Yes, it was a much sturdier object. The prosecution knows what the murder weapon is. The award from the Midwest Manufacturers' Association was conspicuously absent from the mantel above Sam's fireplace. It didn't take the police long to discover what had been removed from the mantel. The MMA gives out an award annually, so law enforcement had no trouble finding a replica, had no difficulty seeing how easily it could have been used to kill Sam Dillon.

But they can't find it, not the one used to kill Sam. They dragged the lake near Sam's house. They searched Allison's home and her yard. They searched every waste-disposal facility in the county and dragged every river. They figure Allison killed Sam around seven that night and drove around for hours before returning to Sam's house at close to one in the morning. They assume she has hidden the weapon somewhere. But they couldn't possibly guess where. They would never think to look in the back of a grocery store where Allison shopped before the family moved to their current house.

"The manner of death, Doctor?" Roger Ogren asks.

"The manner of death was unquestionably homicide. The number, angle, and severity of the blows, as well as common sense, rule out any possibility of self-infliction."

"And the time of death?"

"I would estimate time of death at seven in the evening, on Saturday, February seventh of this year. That is based on several things. The rate of decomposition. The contents of the victim's stomach. We know from the receipt that he had food delivered to his house at six-twenty that evening. Assuming that he ate the food relatively soon after receiving it, the digestion of the food was at such a stage that digestion had ceased somewhere around seven o'clock. And we can look at the time that was frozen on the clock that was partially broken over his head. The time on that clock was six minutes after seven p.m. That doesn't conclusively prove that Sam Dillon was murdered at seven-oh-six p.m., but all other evidence would certainly corroborate that point."

"All right, Doctor. Now I would like to take you through all of the details that led to these conclusions."

Okay, Deputy Griggs. Other than the broken fingernail and the platinum earring, did you find anything else at Mr. Dillon's home?"

The witness, Jodie Griggs, is a deputy investigator with the County Attorney Technical Unit. She is a large woman with full red cheeks and curly blond hair.

"We found a follicle of hair belonging to the defendant," she says.

"Objection," says Ron McGaffrey, getting to his feet. "That is assuming facts not in evidence. The DNA testing is the subject of dispute."

A dispute, Allison thinks to herself, *but not much of one*. The defense has not conceded that the DNA tests established that the hair belonged to Allison, but they have come up with no basis for saying it didn't. Allison has told her lawyer, all along, not to even bother contesting it.

"Sustained." The judge nods in the direction of the prosecutor. "The answer is stricken."

"A hair follicle," Roger Ogren tries, "that the County Attorney Technical Unit has determined to be linked by DNA to the defendant?"

"Yes. Our DNA tests have shown that."

"And does the presence of this hair have any significance to you, Deputy?"

"Yes." The technician settles in the witness stand, crosses a leg. "You can only obtain DNA from the bulb of a hair follicle. Hair that simply falls out doesn't have the bulb." She nods to her shoulder. "I probably have a piece of hair on my shoulder right now. But you couldn't get my DNA from it."

"Well, if hair that simply falls out does not contain a bulb, and therefore no DNA," asks Roger Ogren, "then what does that mean for this follicle of hair that you recovered, which contains the bulb?"

"It means it was pulled out," she answers. "It suggests a struggle."

"Very good. Deputy, what else did you find, in the course of your search as an officer with the County Attorney Technical Unit?"

"We searched Mr. Dillon's computer."

"And did you find anything of significance?"

"We did. There was an e-mail—an electronic mail message from Mr. Dillon's computer on Sunday, February eighth, 2004. The very early morning following the night of his death."

"What time was it sent?"

"It was sent at one-eighteen a.m. and forty-two seconds on Sunday, February eighth, 2004."

The prosecutor gets the court's permission to admit a copy of the e-mail into evidence. He hands a copy to the defense and places a slide copy on an overhead projector.

From: "Dillon, Samuel" <sam.dillon@interserver.com>
To: "Pagone, Allison Q." <Allison@allisonpagone.com>
Re: Attorney-Client
Date: Sun, 8 Feb. 2004 1:18:42 AM

A:
NEED TO DISCUSS FURTHER. GETTING WORRIED. MANY WOULD
BE UNHAPPY WITH MY INFO. NEED ADVICE ASAP.
S

"Now, Deputy Griggs, let me ask you." Roger Ogren remains next to the projector. "You are familiar with the prosecution's theory in this case that Mr. Dillon was killed at around seven p.m. on Saturday, February seventh, 2004. Are you familiar with that?"

"I am."

"Now, according to this e-mail"—Ogren points with the tip of a pen to the "Date" line—"this e-mail was sent from Mr. Dillon's computer at one-eighteen in the morning on Sunday, the eighth of February, 2004."

"Correct. One-eighteen and forty-two seconds."

"A little over six hours *after* that timeframe of seven o'clock the previous evening?"

"Yes," she says with confidence.

"One might claim," says Ogren, "that this proves Mr. Dillon was still alive long after the time we argue he died. Notwithstanding the forensic evidence relating to decomposition of the body and of the food in his stomach—notwithstanding all of that evidence and more—one might say this e-mail proves that Sam Dillon was still alive early Sunday morning."

"Object to the form," says Ron McGaffrey.

"Sustained."

"Well, then I'll say it this way. As an investigator into the murder of Sam Dillon, Deputy Griggs, did seeing this e-mail give you pause about the time of death?"

"It did. Until we searched Allison Pagone's home."

"And what did you find in Allison Pagone's home that spoke to this issue?"

"Her computer. Allison Pagone is a novelist. She writes fiction. She writes crime novels."

"I've read them," says Ogren.

"So have I." She smiles briefly. "We looked through her computer. We looked, among other things, at her 'trash' file."

"What is a 'trash' file?"

"It is a file of discarded documents. You do it to clear out space on your hard drive. And then you can 'recycle' the trash, which means you are dumping the files even from that 'trash' bin."

The judge nods. Old-school as he is, he probably has a computer, if not two. He might already understand the concept of a "trash" bin. This judge is probably in his late sixties, which could render him clueless in an information era with exponentially improving technology. Her ex-husband, Mat, can hardly type and only recently learned the wonders of the internet. Her daughter, Jessica, in contrast, who was practically raised online, can do things on a computer that Allison would never dream of understanding.

"Go on, Deputy," says Roger Ogren.

"We found a rather large manuscript in the 'recycle' bin of her trash. Meaning it had been dumped, and then dumped again."

"You have the capability to find such a document, even when it has been completely discarded?"

"We do." The witness proceeds to explain the technicalities of the CAT Unit's data-retrieval methodology. It is not surprising in the least to Allison, and a bit frightening, that the government has the means to retrieve almost anything that ever appeared on a personal laptop computer.

"Tell us about this rather large document you found after it was discarded twice," Roger Ogren requests. "First of all, when it was created, that sort of thing. Were you able to determine that kind of information?"

"Absolutely we were. Once the document is retrieved, you can look at all of the document's properties. It is as simple as clicking on 'properties' on the menu."

"Were you able to print out this 'properties' page, Deputy Griggs?"

"Yes."

Ogren shows her a piece of paper. "Is this a true and accurate slide copy of that page?"

"Yes."

Roger Ogren gets the judge's permission to enter the document into evidence, then places it on the overhead projector:

Location: C:\Documents and Settings\My Documents\Novels\
Best.Served.Cold.Draft.1
Size: 154 KB (158,208 bytes)
Size on Disk: 156 KB (159,744 bytes)
Created: Wednesday, December 03, 2003, 5:19:04 PM
Modified: Thursday, February 05, 2004, 11:04 PM
Deleted: Sunday, February 08, 2004, 3:21 AM
Recycled: Sunday, February 08, 2004, 3:22 AM

"Take us through this, Deputy. What does all this mean?"

"She created the document—meaning she started writing it—on December third of last year. 'Modified' refers to when the document was last modified. She last modified that document on Thursday, February fifth of this year."

"Tell us about the final two rows of information, Deputy."

"As I already explained, 'deleted' is when you remove the document from the hard drive. 'Recycled' is when you remove it from the trash. Dumping it a second time."

"And what does the information here tell us?"

"It tells us that Allison Pagone tried to remove that document from her hard drive on the very early morning hours of Sunday, February eighth of this year."

"And for context, Deputy—"

"Only hours after we believe Sam Dillon had been murdered," she says. "And just over two hours after that e-mail was sent from Sam Dillon's computer."

"Deputy, you work with computers on a daily basis, yes?"

"Yes."

"Can you think of any reason why Allison Pagone would feel compelled, in the middle of the night, to try to eliminate any evidence of a document from her computer?"

"Oh, objection," says Ron McGaffrey. "Move to strike."

"Sustained," says the judge.

"I apologize, Your Honor. Why don't we answer that question another way? Deputy Griggs, did you look at this document that was deleted from the defendant's computer in the early morning of Sunday, February the eighth of this year?"

"Yes, I did. It was fifty-six pages long. It looked, by all accounts, to be a draft of her next novel. The title was *Best Served Cold*."

"Did you read the document?"

"Yes, I did."

"Did you find anything in particular in that manuscript that spoke to the time-of-death issue in this, case?"

"I did. The novel is about a woman who kills her lover after she finds out he is cheating on her. She kills him in the middle of the day. But she knows she can be placed at the scene of the crime at the time of the crime. So later that night, when she's at a party, she excuses herself and goes to the bathroom. She slips out through a window, sneaks back over to the dead man's house, and sends an e-mail from his computer, to make it seem like he was still alive. Then, when she's questioned, she has an alibi for the time when—"

"Your Honor," says Ronald McGaffrey, "I've been patient. This is a rambling narrative. We object."

"Let's keep this question-and-answer, Mr. Ogren," the judge advises.

"Very good." Roger Ogren walks over to the evidence table behind the prosecution and carries a set of papers. He drops off one set for the defense. On the top page is the title BEST SERVED COLD, and beneath that, a NOVEL BY ALLISON QUINCY PAGONE.

"Deputy, is this a true and accurate copy of a printout of the manuscript that was deleted from the defendant's computer at three a.m. on Sunday, February the eighth of this year?"

"Yes. That's it."

Ogren moves the document into evidence. "Take you to page forty-eight, Deputy. Is there a new chapter beginning on that page?"

"Yes, there is. Chapter Five."

"What is the title of Chapter Five?"

"The title is 'Alibi.'"

"Okay. 'Alibi.' Now, if you would, turn to page fifty-one. Are we still on the chapter entitled 'Alibi,' Deputy?"

"Yes."

"And could you read, beginning at the second full paragraph?"

> She sits at the desk and pulls up his e-mail. She is not entirely sure what to write or to whom she should send it. It could be anything at all and serve her purposes. All that really matters is that an e-mail was sent from his computer at nine o'clock in the evening, while she is believed to be at a party, and long after she visited his home at noon today. An alibi. Proof of life.

This manuscript, Allison is sure, hurts her in more ways than one. Bad enough that it contains the identical alibi she created here. The fact that she deleted it from her hard drive only hours after returning from Sam's house speaks volumes. It also shows the judge that Allison can think in diabolical ways. That is not a trait a criminal defendant wants the court to see.

And it hurts her attorney's theory of a frame-up. They will argue that her fingernail and earring and hair follicle were planted at the crime scene by the "real" killer. But even if they could make that case, how do they explain how the killer copy-catted this exact method of manufacturing an alibi? When Allison was notoriously secretive about her novels in process? When Allison never let anyone read them until they were finished? Who could possibly have known that Allison was writing about this particular alibi-creating method?

"Deputy," says Roger Ogren. "You weren't an eyewitness to the murder of Sam Dillon."

"No."

"You can't say from personal knowledge that the defendant killed him."

"No."

"And you can't say from personal knowledge that the defendant went back to Mr. Dillon's home and sent an e-mail, after his death, to provide herself with an alibi."

"No, I can't."

These are all leading questions, but Allison's lawyer will not object, because they sound more like questions that would come from her attorney. They are a setup, of course, to what will follow.

"But what *does* this document you found in the 'trash' bin of the defendant's computer tell us, Deputy?"

The witness nods. "It tells us that whoever committed this crime, and sent this e-mail, followed the exact model of what the protagonist did in Allison Pagone's next novel. A novel that has not yet been published. That hasn't even been finished. A novel that, as far as we know, nobody has ever read with the exception of Allison Pagone. To say nothing of the fact that in the middle of the night following Mr. Dillon's death, she went to the trouble of deleting this document from her laptop."

Allison's lawyer objects, a long-winded eruption, and the judge will sustain the objection, but it doesn't matter. She knows it. The judge will agree, ultimately, with everything the witness just said. Allison copy-catted an alibi from a novel that no one had read, tried to trash the evidence, and got caught.

I live next door to Sam Dillon," says Richard Rothman. He is a scholarly looking man, a former small-business owner in his mid-seventies now, with a long, weathered face and a protruding nose on which his glasses rest.

"Do you recall the evening of Saturday, February the seventh of this year?" asks Roger Ogren. "And if I could direct your attention, sir, to the late hours of the night and the early morning of the following day, Sunday the eighth."

"I do remember that evening."

Of course he does. Under ordinary circumstances, he would have no memory whatsoever of a sleepless night. But when later that Sunday morning, squad cars had pulled up all around his neighbor's home, the memory stuck.

"I often have trouble sleeping," he continues. "Or I should say, my sleep patterns are very irregular. Since my wife died, I just don't sleep like I used to. So, I had slept much of that Saturday evening and by eleven o'clock at night, I was wide awake."

"What were you doing around that time?"

"I was painting. I do watercolors in my sunroom." Mr. Rothman laughs, a throaty chuckle. "Not much of a sunroom in the middle of February."

"Sure." Roger Ogren smiles. "And where does that sunroom face, sir?"

"The room overlooks the road. Oh, I can see across the street to my neighbors. I can also see to the east, to Sam's property. It's a bay window, y'see."

"Sure. So you could see Mr. Dillon's property."

"Can see his driveway, his yard, bit of his house but not much."

"Were you awake at the hour of one in the morning on Sunday, the eighth of February?"

"Yes."

"And could you see outside?"

"Well, yes, I could. I'm a bit hard of hearing. I'm not blind."

"Very good, sir. Can you describe for us what it looked like outside at that time of night?"

"Well, basically it was quiet. But, I'd say a little after one, a truck comes driving down the road and parks outside Sam's."

"A truck. A little after one in the morning. Can you describe that truck?"

"One of those sport-utility jobs. The Lexus. The mini-SUV. It was silver."

The SUV that Allison drives. She has a 2003 model, silver. Roger Ogren has a photograph of Allison's Lexus and shows it to the witness.

"Yeah, it looked just like that," he says. "It was silver. Didn't get a look at the plates, of course." He shakes his head. "It was moving pretty fast down the street, all right. Couldn't really see exactly what happened when it stopped. I just know that it parked by Sam's house. Sam has about an acre of property, so there was some distance. Houses are pretty well set apart out there. That's the point of a cottage on a lake. Privacy."

"That's fine, sir. What do you remember next?"

"I'd say about fifteen minutes passed or so. Say, maybe twenty."

"So this would be about what time?"

"I'd say about twenty, twenty-five past one." He wags a finger. "That time of night, it stood out. Don't see a lot of traffic turning into our subdivision. At least, not in the winter, unless it's the holidays and the young ones are around."

"So a car drove to Sam Dillon's house at just after one in the morning, Sunday morning, and drove away some twenty minutes later?"

"That's right. Yes. It was about twenty minutes later."

Long enough, the prosecutor is saying without saying it, for Allison to return to Sam's house and send an e-mail, at about 1:18 and 42 seconds in the morning.

WEDNESDAY, APRIL 28

A collective pause falls over the courtroom. Opening statements have concluded. The prosecution has called its first witness, the only witness this first afternoon of trial. The media has heard bits and pieces of the anticipated testimony in written filings and at the preliminary hearing, but never in her own words.

It has been a roller coaster, her twenty years. This will be as low as it hits. Allison remembers the moments, all in fleeting flashes, the snapshots that stick. Who knows why certain memories stay with you while others vaporize?

She remembers the nights, when Jessica was a child. Midnight, usually, when Allison would rise from bed and go to her young daughter's bedroom, shake her awake and take her to the bathroom. Jessica always defiant, swinging her arms and moaning, her eyes sunken in sleep, her wispy hair standing on end, mumbling complaints, as she sat on the toilet and tinkled.

Allison was certainly relieved when Jessica's bedwetting ceased around her tenth birthday, but she would always concede a sense of loss as well. These were the times when her love was most tested—casual, everyday moments when her daughter was most annoying and unwieldy, when she was most vulnerable, when Allison herself was incredibly tired. Times like these were when she recognized most palpably the concept of love.

Allison accepts that she cannot judge this young woman with any degree of objectivity, but she finds her captivating. She sees tremendous beauty and cannot imagine how anyone could miss it. Her cinnamon hair, a compromise between Mat's dark brown and Allison's red. Her thin eyebrows arching over liquid brown eyes. Soft, clear skin that most would describe as Caucasian, though the Latin influence is there, too.

Yes, she is beautiful, and that knowledge has always tugged Allison in opposing directions. A mixed blessing. She knows how men think. She knows Jessica will catch their eye, has already done so. There is such a thing, Allison believes, as being too beautiful, so glamorous that things come too easily. So stunning that men will be drawn to her for only one reason. Mat was the first to comment on that. *I was sixteen once*, he said, when Jessica was that age, with the wariness of a man who could read the minds of the young men—boys, really—who called on Jessica.

Allison had tried to keep watch over Jessica the way Allison had wanted it when she herself was that age. She tried to give her space, not appear overly inquisitive, create an atmosphere in which Jessica would feel comfortable sharing.

Look what *that* had gotten her. She had thought it was odd that her daughter, at age seventeen, had no boyfriends at school. Looking at this young woman, Allison couldn't understand how boys could not be interested, and despite Mat's growing suspicion that perhaps Jessica didn't like boys at all, Allison knew better. She asked, and her daughter put her off. *They're so immature*, she would explain.

When the police called, Allison didn't understand, at first. It didn't register. Her daughter and her sophomore geometry teacher, in the parking lot by the school's baseball field. A patrolman had come upon them, late in the evening on a school night. There was nothing automatically incriminating about it. Jessica was fully clothed and the teacher was, too, though the patrolman explained to Allison that the teacher's shirt was pulled out and it wasn't too hard to figure what had been happening before they saw the squad car's headlights.

Did she want to press charges? Request an investigation? Allison didn't know what to say, when she picked up her mortified daughter at the station. They drove silently home. Mat was at the capital, so they had the chance to talk woman-to-woman without the hysteria of an irate father. Allison demanded that Jessica explain herself. So it came out, finally. She admitted it. It had been going on for almost a year, since she was a sophomore and in his class.

"I do," Jessica says, to the court reporter swearing her in.

They didn't press charges. It would be all over the place if they did. An underage girl's name would be kept out of the press, but somehow it would get out. Jessica pleaded with her mother and father, and they ultimately agreed to keep it quiet. The teacher agreed to resign his position immediately and to never teach again. And Allison was left trying to figure out how she missed the whole thing for almost a year.

She never looked at her daughter the same way again. She had expected secrets but not like this. She felt betrayed and inadequate. She explained to Jessica that it was the teacher's fault, that he was the controlling adult, but that Jessica had to take responsibility for her own actions, too. She wanted to teach this responsibility while, at the same

time, she wanted to hover over her daughter's every movement but knew she could not.

Had Jessica known, even then, that her parents' marriage was in trouble? Did that play a part? Allison had
deliberately stayed with Mat until Jessica graduated and
moved on to college. For Jessica's sake. Had her decision
had the opposite effect?

And now there are secrets, again, since the divorce.
Jessica has taken her father's side, and Allison's questions
surrounding Jessica's love life are once more met with de-
rision. She remembers last December, her daughter being
not only evasive but openly hostile to Allison's queries.

There's a guy, she told Allison over dinner, *but you
probably wouldn't approve.*

Jessica gives the appearance of being composed. She is
acting, Allison thinks. She has always been good at that.
Folding her leg, placing her hands in her lap, lifting her
chin and looking over the courtroom. She listens carefully
to the questions and takes a moment before answering. She
has told them that she is a junior at Mansbury College,
with a double major in political science and history. She
has told them that she worked part-time at Dillon & Becker
as a research assistant, that she is considering law school.
She has told them that her parents separated more than a
year ago and were divorced by last Thanksgiving, about
seven months ago.

It's okay to tell them, Allison has assured her daughter
repeatedly, as if Jessica had any choice.

"Tell us about the seventh of February," Roger Ogren
says. "A Saturday evening."

The day Sam was murdered.

"I had been on campus all day," Jessica answers. "About
eight that night, I went home."

"'Home' being your mother's home?"

"Yes." Jessica tucks a hair behind her ear.

"Why did you go to your mother's home, Ms. Pagone?"

"To study. I had a couple of papers due and it's—sometimes it's hard to study at the dorms. So I'll go home and study. I'll do my laundry sometimes, too."

The judge smiles; he must recall when his children did the same thing, took advantage of their time at home for meals and the washer and dryer. Jessica looks at the judge as if she has been left out of the joke. She couldn't smile right now if someone tickled her feet.

"What time did you arrive at the house? You said 'around' eight?"

"I think it was about eight-thirty."

"Was your mother home at eight-thirty on the evening of Saturday, the seventh of February?"

"No."

"When did you see your mother that night?"

Jessica looks into her lap. "I can't say exactly."

"An approximate time, Ms. Pagone?"

Allison, her hand resting on a notepad, catches herself crumpling the sheet.

"I had fallen asleep," Jessica says. "I hadn't been keeping track of time."

She's being difficult. They already know this information. It will have the opposite effect, Allison realizes. The more Jessica fights with the prosecutor, the more it highlights how hurtful her testimony is, how reluctant she is to part with the information.

"Was it before or after midnight that your mother came home?"

"I—I guess it's hard to say," she says quietly.

"Your Honor," says Roger Ogren.

"You can lead, Counsel," says the judge.

"Ms. Pagone, it was after midnight, wasn't it?"

"I—yes, it was after midnight, I believe."

"In fact, it was after one in the morning. Is that right?"

"Yes."

"Closer to two, in fact."

"Yes."

"Where in the house were you when your mother came home?"

Jessica's eyes fill. "On the couch."

"And your mother came in through the garage door?"

Jessica nods.

"Please answer out loud, Ms. Pag—"

"She came in through the garage. Yes."

"Describe her appearance."

"She was probably tired," Jessica says. "It was late. It was two in the morning. Of *course* she would be tired."

"Tell us what she was wearing."

"She was wearing"—Jessica extends a hand—"a jacket. A sweatshirt and jeans."

"A sweatshirt." Roger Ogren retrieves the evidence bag holding the maroon sweatshirt, emblazoned with MANSBURY COLLEGE, and shows it to her. "This sweatshirt."

"Yes, that might be the sweatshirt."

"It *might* be?" Ogren asks. "Jessica, does your mother, to your knowledge, own more than one maroon sweatshirt with the words 'Mansbury College' on it?"

Jessica shakes her head. "I bought it for her. At the campus store."

"So, having the chance to consider it," says Ogren, shaking the evidence bag, "are you confident that this was definitely the—"

"That was the sweatshirt she was wearing. *Okay*?"

"Okay." Ogren replaces the evidence and turns to Jessica again. "Tell us what you saw on your mother's face," he requests. He is clearly trying not to cross-examine his own witness, even though the judge has given him permission to do so. "Did you see something on her face?"

"There might have been some dirt on her face."

Jessica is speaking so quietly that Ogren and the judge lean forward to hear her.

"Dirt on her face." Roger Ogren corrects the problem by

speaking at a high volume himself. "And what about her hands?"

"Yes."

"Yes—she had dirt on her hands, too?"

"Yes."

"She had dirt on her face and on her hands. And what else? Her coloring? Her hair?"

Jessica, with hooded eyes, speaks quickly into the microphone, as if to get the answer over with as quickly as possible. "Her hair was matted down. Like she was sweating. She was pale. She looked sick."

"And did you talk to her about these things, Ms. Pagone? Did you ask your mother about the dirt on her face and hands? Her matted hair? Her pale coloring?"

"Mother—what did you do?" she had cried. "What happened?"

"I asked her."

"Tell me, Mother. Tell me what happened."

"And what did she do or say?"

"She went to the bathroom." Jessica looks away, as if to avoid the entire thing. That is an impossible task now. She is trapped on the witness stand, surrounded on all sides by people very interested in what she has to say.

"What did—"

"She vomited."

"Your mother came into the house, went right to the bathroom and vomited?"

Jessica reaches for the water placed on the witness stand for her. She does not answer the question, but Roger Ogren probably doesn't care. He just wanted to repeat the fact that Allison threw up the moment she walked into the house.

Tell me what happened, Mother. Tell me.

"Did you talk to your mother after that, Jessica? Did your mother tell you where she had been, what she had done, why she had dirt on her hands and face at two in the morning?"

"Objection," Ron McGaffrey says, half out of his chair.

"One question at a time, Counsel," the judge says.

"She didn't say much," Jessica says, before a new question is posed. No one seems inclined to stop her, under the circumstances. "She—I asked her what had happened. She said she didn't want to talk about it. She went upstairs and that was that."

"And what did you do?"

"I—she went to bed. I asked her if she wanted anything. If she was feeling well. She just wanted to go to bed."

"And you didn't talk to her again that night?"

"No. I finally went to my bedroom and went to sleep."

"Then let's go to the following morning, Jessica. The day after Sam Dillon's murder."

Allison's attorney objects. This being the first day of the trial, there has been no testimony fixing the date of Sam's death as Saturday night, February seventh. The judge sustains the objection. Roger Ogren rephrases.

"Sunday morning," Jessica says. "I woke up about ten. I went to get the paper. I made some eggs and started studying."

"When did you see your mother?"

"I went upstairs at about noon. She is—she's usually an early riser, so—I was wondering, I guess, if something—if she was sick or something."

"And when—"

"She was in her room. She said she didn't feel very well. She said she was still feeling sick and wanted to be left alone."

"And what did you do?"

Jessica pauses. She has not looked in Allison's direction yet. She is concentrating on something other than the question, to the point that Roger Ogren steps forward to ask the question again.

"I went into her bedroom. I offered to make her something to eat. Get her some aspirin."

"Where was she at this time?"

"She was—still in bed."

"Did she respond to you?"

"She said—" Jessica clears her throat. "She said that she wanted to tell me something. She said that I might be hearing—"

Allison closes her hands into fists as her daughter breaks down quietly on the witness stand. Her lawyer, Ron McGaffrey, begins to move out of his seat, but Allison takes his hand.

"Let her get it over with," Allison whispers to her lawyer.

An uncommon quiet falls over the courtroom as Jessica struggles to control herself. She finally raises her head again, her eyes dark and wet, a shade of red coloring her face. She inhales deeply and continues.

"She said that I might be hearing things about her. She told me that she had been having an affair with Sam Dillon. She said she was sorry she had done it and she wanted me to hear it from her first."

"Your mother said that she had an affair with Sam Dillon?"

"Yes."

"And how did you respond?"

"I . . . walked out. I was very mad. I . . . had always hoped my parents would reconcile, I guess. I . . . didn't like hearing about another—" Her eyes fall. "I left the house and went back to campus."

Roger Ogren asks Jessica questions about what came next, after Sam Dillon's death. Jessica had read about his death in the papers, like everyone else, she says, the following Monday, one day after Sam was found dead and a day and a half after he was murdered.

"Did you discuss this with your mother, Jessica? The murder of Sam Dillon?"

"I called her. I left a message on her voice mail."

"This was Tuesday, February the tenth."

"Yes."

"Did she call you back?"

"She came to see me," Jessica says. "At my dorm at the college."

Allison stood outside her daughter's dorm room. She had knocked, several times, to no avail. Jessica wasn't there. She didn't know how long she would be gone. Allison didn't know her class schedule, which was unusual. This was the first semester since Jessica had enrolled at Mansbury that Allison couldn't recite the title, professor, and time of each class. She had been like that with her only daughter, twenty questions all the time, trying to involve herself wherever possible in the life of a child who had slowly grown independent of her mother, trying to keep the bird who had flown from the nest on the radar screen, at least.

But that had changed this year. Jessica had blamed Allison for the breakup of the marriage. She had left no room for doubt on that subject. It was terribly unfair, in Allison's eyes; Jessica was focusing only on the result, not the cause. Allison had raised the subject, had wanted the divorce, and that was all that mattered to Jess. Her daughter did not know the details of why, and Allison wouldn't supply them, at least not in a way that placed all the blame on Mat. She didn't want it that way; she didn't want Jessica in the middle of a he-said, she-said. We drifted apart, was all she told her daughter, unsure of what, exactly, Mat had told her.

She didn't know when Jessica would return to her dorm room. She didn't know Jessica's classes, the friends she was making, any boys she might be interested in. She couldn't even be sure she had the right room anymore. She had to ask a young girl who emerged from a neighboring room, who was waking at a little before noon, if this was where Jessica Pagone lived.

She stood in the hallway for more than an hour, watched students return from class, heard them talking on the phones in their rooms. She couldn't entirely relate; she hadn't gone to college like other girls her age. Allison had gotten pregnant as a senior in high school and hadn't started taking classes until Jessica was in grade school. She had desperately wanted Jessica to have this experience, the college life.

Her daughter walked down the hallway just after one o'clock, a backpack slung over her shoulder, her eyes down, frowning. When she saw her mother, she went blank, face turned ghostly white. She became immediately aware of her surroundings, of two other young women walking through the hallway, to whom Jessica offered a perfunctory smile.

She didn't address her mother in any way, simply unlocked her dorm room and let Allison follow her in

"This was Tuesday, the tenth of February," the prosecutor clarifies. "Two days after Sam Dillon was found dead. A little after one in the afternoon."

"Right." Jessica breathes out of her mouth.

"Tell us what happened, Jessica. What you said. What your mother said."

Jessica clears her throat, grimaces. "She told me I shouldn't call her on the phone."

"You never know who might be listening," Allison had told her daughter. "And they can record the fact that you called. They can look at that later."

"She didn't explain why," Jessica continues. "She just said, don't use the phone."

"And what else, Jessica?" Ogren places his hands behind his back.

"She told me that she had been sick yesterday and the night before."

The prosecutor nods along. "She came all the way down to your college campus to emphasize to you that her behavior that weekend could be explained by the fact that she had been feeling ill?"

"Objection," says Ron McGaffrey. "Argumentative."

"Sustained."

"Other than telling you not to call her on the phone, and the fact that she had been ill the previous weekend, what else did your mother say to you, or you to her?"

"It's—" Jessica brings a hand to her face. "It was a while ago."

Roger Ogren looks at the judge. He waits a beat to see if Jessica will continue.

"Did you ask your mother if she had murdered Sam Dillon?" he asks.

Allison stood against the window, overlooking the courtyard surrounded on all sides by the dormitories. Jessica sat on her bed, not looking at her mother, hands on each side of her head.

"You can't say one way or the other whether I killed Sam Dillon," Allison said.

"You didn't kill him, Mother. You couldn't possibly—"

"Jess, they'll expect you to say that." Her delivery was gentle. "They'll expect you to defend your mother. What matters to them are the facts. And the fact is, you couldn't say one way or the other whether I killed him. Right?"

"She said people might be saying a lot of things. She said I shouldn't believe them."

"Saying a lot of things about Sam Dillon's death?" Ogren's tone suggests impatience. He knows the answers to his questions, and Jessica isn't delivering. "Saying things about her involvement in his death?"

"Yes."

"But did you ask your mother if she had murdered Sam—"

"She said that we shouldn't talk about that. That it would be a bad idea to discuss it."

"Okay." Roger Ogren takes a step. "But I want to ask you whether you asked a specific question. Ms. Pagone"— the prosecutor allows for an intake of air; as much as

Jessica has fought him, he has been allowed to repeat this question several times, and her lack of cooperation only helps his cause here—"did you specifically ask your mother whether she killed Sam—"

"*Yes.*" A flash of anger—frustration, probably, and regret—colors Jessica's face.

"And how did your mother react to that specific question? Whether or not she had killed Sam Dillon?"

Jessica swallows hard and lifts her chin. Allison holds her breath. This should be it. This should be the end. In a few moments, Jessica will be allowed to put this behind her. She will not let her attorney cross-examine her daughter.

"She didn't," Jessica answers. "She wouldn't answer that question. We never discussed it again."

Jane McCoy turns down the car radio as Harrick reviews his notes from the trial today. She likes to think of herself as hip to today's music, but she is having difficulty enjoying the violent lyrics and the thrash guitars filling the airwaves these days. That, she figures, is exactly how her parents felt. She is getting old. Forty years old this July and she's a dinosaur. She's got hair clips older than these idiots on the radio, spouting about "bitches" and "forties."

"Okay," says Harrick. "She said she got to Allison's at about eight-thirty that night. She was studying and doing laundry."

"And what time did she say Allison came home?"

"Two in the morning, give or take." Harrick flips through his notes. "She said mom threw up when she walked in. She was a mess. She had dirt all over her."

"Okay."

"Oh, and she said that her mom admitted having an affair with Sam. That's pretty much it, more or less."

McCoy laughs. "Try 'less.' What did Allison's lawyer do with her?"

"Nothing. Didn't ask a single question."

"Interesting. Did she get tripped up at all?"

"No."

"She's lucky," says McCoy.

"Oh, I don't know about 'lucky.' That girl knew exactly what to say."

"Woman," McCoy corrects.

"What?"

"Woman. Jessica Pagone's a woman, not a girl."

"Oh, well pardon me." Harrick chews on his ever-present toothpick. "That 'young woman' knew exactly what to say and how to say it. She may have left the puzzle half-finished, but that's not the same thing as perjury. I didn't hear a single thing in there that could be proven false."

McCoy switches to talk radio, which is buzzing about the Pagone murder trial.

"Yeah, well, the apple doesn't fall far from the tree," McCoy says.

TUESDAY, APRIL 27

The university library is the perfect cover for a graduate student preparing for final exams. Ram Haroon gets very little done in the way of studying. Few do at this place. Most people are surfing the internet in the computer rooms or sitting on couches and talking over steaming cups of coffee.

Haroon heads over to the book stacks on the top floor of the library. West side, third from the end. He pretends to mull over a series of books about northern Africa. He pulls three books down and places two of them on the next shelf below, opens the other one and begins to peruse it.

A moment later, through the space created by removing the books, a note passes through from the other side. Haroon's eyes move about; no one is watching. No one would bother. He takes the note and reads it.

Things are looking bad for her. Trial starts tomorrow and their case is in chaos. Prosecution's case is

strong and she has nothing to point away from her.
She knows she will be convicted.

She doesn't know about us. There's no way. I would
know if she did.

Haroon rolls his head on his neck casually, then removes
a pen from his pocket and scribbles on the sheet of paper,
passes it through.

I still don't like it. She might know but not want to
tell. She might wait to testify at trial to spring it.

The note comes back with new words written beneath
his message.

She won't testify. Too much at stake from her end. She
would rather die. Her words, a direct quote. She's on
edge.

She would rather die. Haroon smiles. He takes the paper
and places it in the book he has open. He waits two minutes
or so before writing his response and sending it through:

A person looking at the death penalty might find it
more appealing to end things on her own terms. I
think it is time for Mrs. Allison Pagone to commit
suicide. I will need your help on timing, of course.
Will she continue to speak freely?

A long moment passes. Probably his partner is just
being careful. In all likelihood not a single person is paying them any attention, standing in the corner stacks as
they are. Still, the notes cannot pass too closely together,
too many times. Finally, the response arrives:

Of course. If you can't trust your ex-husband, who can you trust?

"Exactly," Ram says, as he crumbles the note in his hand and picks up one of the books he has pulled. He will read it for a few minutes, then wander out of the library.

MONDAY, APRIL 26

Allison thinks of her daughter as she sits on a swing in her backyard cradling a glass of wine. Mat Pagone is pacing around the yard, undoubtedly remembering the barbecues on that porch and the games with Jessica in the sandbox. Thinking about things she cannot fathom.

She wonders if there will ever be a time when she can look at this man and not feel cheated. Will she ever get past this? Will she ever look at Mateo Pagone simply as the father of her child, and not as the asshole who took her for granted and cheated on her and, probably, poisoned their daughter's mind against her? Will she ever be able to look back at the decades with him without the words *wasted years* springing to mind?

No, Mateo Pagone is not a bad man. He is old-school, a man who thinks that some of the marital vows do not apply. But not a bad person. Probably doesn't think he has done anything wrong. And they drifted apart. Became less alike the longer they were together. Actually, the better way to say it is that Mat stayed the same, Allison grew up. Developed. From the moment she first indicated she wanted to take night classes toward a college degree, Mat was against it. Wanted to keep Allison the way she had been, dependent, supportive, compliant, and she didn't mean that in a bad way. It was just all Mat knew, what he had seen from his parents, and their parents. The wife stays home, cooks, cleans, raises the child. Mat works and provides for them. She could sense the objection to the classes right away. Not an outright "No," but active discouragement. *Why not join the PTA?* he had suggested. A bridge club. Be a Girl Scout leader. But she did it, anyway, felt that she needed to do it for herself, took college courses part-time, fit them around her daughter and husband, and tingled with anticipation for her future.

Something glorious is going to happen.

She got a college degree in theater, performed in community plays and had no inclination, whatsoever, of making it a career, had no illusions about becoming a star of the stage. In truth, she acted only for herself, not the audience, for the freedom it brought her. But soon she ached for more, and found another way to perform theater. She attended law school part-time, mostly at night. Got a job as a public defender. Wrote a novel and made more money than he did. Their marriage moved farther downhill with each step. At the end Mat wanted to preserve things—she will never know what part of that was appearances and what part was a love for Allison—but even he had seen that the end had come once Jessica moved out to go to college.

The way I am now, I'm no wife for you.

"Jessie's thinking about studying abroad next year," Mat tells her. His hands are stuffed in his pockets. He kicks at a stray weed in the lawn. "Spain. Sevilla, probably."

"Okay." She is disarmed at her response, however appropriate it may be under the circumstances. She has little to say about her daughter's life now, little right to inquire.

Allison had always supported the idea of studying abroad. Jess had been noncommittal. It isn't difficult to discern what change has prompted her daughter's desire for new surroundings. Anywhere, at this point, is better than here.

"I told her you and I would discuss it," he adds, looking at her. The wind kicks a few strands of his thick hair up. He is wearing a light yellow jacket that is probably insufficient for a cold spring day.

"Your call," she says with no emotion. She feels a tug at her heart. She's not sure what Jessica would think of her opinion, anyway. On instinct alone, she'd probably do the opposite of what Allison recommended. Allison hadn't seen it coming, Jessica taking her father's side in the divorce. But Jessica has always adored Mat. It puzzled Allison, always, how the father who spent so little time with his daughter gained such an elevated stature in Jessica's mind. She could probably count on one hand the number of diapers Mat changed. The number of meals Mat cooked. The number of piano recitals and choir concerts he attended. Everything Allison did, all those years, selflessly, yes, and she didn't expect a gold medal for it, but how was it that Mat came away the shining parent?

Well, that wasn't hard to figure. Mat spoiled her. Imposed no discipline. It was Allison who played the bad cop, Allison who pushed her daughter to study and imposed a curfew after that incident with the high-school teacher. And really, she loved the fact that Jess and Mat got along so well. What mother—what wife—wouldn't want that?

But she had expected more when she and Mat split. No, she didn't expect Jessica to accept the news with open arms. But Jess was twenty years old, for God's sake. She had been raised to keep an open mind, to think things through. How could Jessica so easily find fault in one parent and not the other? Allison doesn't know the answer to that question. She doesn't know what Mat said to their daughter. She doesn't know what methods of manipulation Mat employed to subtly cast blame in Allison's direction. All that she knows is that Jessica would do anything for her father and would never blame him for a thing.

Mat drops the subject, looks into the cool air, closes his eyes momentarily.

"Let's go inside," Allison suggests.

Mat follows her into the living room, then heads to the adjacent kitchen. Allison closes the window in the living room, overlooking the backyard.

"My attorney thinks the frame-up theory makes us look desperate," she calls to Mat. She sees, through the window, her neighbor, Mr. Anderson, following his daughter out into his backyard for a game of catch. She remembers when Jennifer Anderson was born, can't believe she's now eight years old, jumping around with a baseball glove, eagerly awaiting warm-weather sports.

"I agree," Mat says from the kitchen. "Who gives a damn about hair and broken fingernails and earrings? You were there at some point, is all it proves."

She looks away from the window toward the kitchen. Mat was probably glad to be in the next room when he said that. He's right, but that's beside the point. He's acknowledging her relationship with Sam, however fleetingly. Mat must be envisioning the spin that Ron McGaffrey will put on this evidence. An earring fell out, a nail was broken, a hair was pulled out during moments of passion. Wild sex on his couch. On the kitchen table. In his swimming pool. On a trapeze over his bed. Men have the capacity to visualize the most painful scenarios in their jealousy.

The truth is that it was incredibly awkward, initially. Allison had been with exactly one man her entire life. Everything had been one way. The first time she and Sam made love and she watched him above her, Allison's heart pounded like never before, one part excitement and three parts utter fear. It was more like her first time than her thousandth.

Sam was taller than Allison by several inches, unlike Mat, so she had to raise her chin to see his face as he rose above her. He had less hair on his chest. A thinner frame. He liked to cup her head with his hand, play with her hair. He liked to kiss her more. Liked to watch her. Made less noise in his climax, clenching his jaw and closing his eyes, little more than a guttural sound from his throat. Liked to stay inside her longer afterward. He was slow and steady.

She realizes that Mat is watching her, standing in the living room with a bottle of wine. She wonders if he can guess what is going through her mind.

Mat had been more like a jackhammer. Quick, powerful thrusts, not a gentle partner. He was a square-framed, strong man, a hunter-gatherer, and he liked to take the lead, needed to. Didn't like it when Allison improvised. He wanted to initiate, wanted to choose the position. Liked to be on top, liked to lie above her, not on her, as if in the middle of a push-up, his triceps bulging, his chest muscles flexing. She often wondered whether he was doing that for her or for himself.

"Forget the frame-up," Mat finally says. "The best witness is you. Say you didn't do it."

Allison looks away, toward the couch. "I can't testify, Mat. You know that."

"We're talking about your life, here, Allison."

"They'll catch me in lies, Mat. I've lied to the police. And they can force me to talk about other things, too. It's not an option."

She walks over to the window again, wants to see the enthusiasm on her young neighbor's face, wants to experience a moment of vicarious joy. The girl flings the baseball over her father's head, and it bangs off the back door.

"I'd rather die," Allison says.

SUNDAY, APRIL 25

Allison finds Larry Evans in the coffee shop at the grocery store. "I got you something," Larry says to her. He slides a small package across the table.

She can tell it's a paperback before she opens it. She can also tell that a man wrapped the present. It's a self-help book, one of those positive-mental-attitude guides she has never read.

"It's about seeing the finish line," he says, and laughs. "I'm guessing you'll choose not to read it."

Allison smiles. "Sometimes I don't know what I'd do without you, Mr. Evans. Sometimes I feel like you're the only—well." She looks at him. "Thank you."

"You have a lot of people supporting you, Allison. You read the websites?"

"Oh, God, not lately." She has appreciated, on some level, the support she has received on her book website, *allison-pagone.com,* as well as several websites seeking to capitalize on the case, including her favorite, *freeallison.com.* But she can't help but feel some distance from these people. They aren't really saying that they believe her to be innocent. They don't know her and they don't know the facts, at least not all of them. They feel a connection to her, presumably because of her novels, and they don't want to confront the real possibility that one of their favorite authors has committed murder.

"No," she says, "I prefer my news from the tabloids. Did you see the *Weekly Inquisitor* up front?"

Larry laughs. "I did. 'Killer Novelist in Love Nest with Ben Affleck.' The photo takes ten years off you, by the way."

"Yeah, I'm really pleased."

"My point is," Larry says, "a lot of people are supporting you."

"Well, I think the list is pretty short." She sighs. "I mean, Mat has really been great. It's a bit odd, under the circumstances, but he's been great. It's just that—I think he wonders about me. I don't think he's convinced of my innocence. I don't think my lawyer thinks I'm innocent, either. And I think you do."

Larry frowns at the mention of Allison's ex-husband. He has been plenty clear, over the last months, about his opinion. "Oh, I think *Mat* knows you're innocent," he says.

She will not engage him. They have done battle on this front more than once. The development in her relationship with Larry Evans over the last few months has been interesting. He came to her initially as an aggressive journalist, unseasoned, which he pitched as an advantage to her. Regardless of his experience or lack thereof, he could be seen as little more than part of the pack of media people who wanted her story, wanted to write a true account of the murder of Sam Dillon and the trial of Allison Pagone. But then, as he began to dig, he took up Allison's cause. He has shared his information with her. And he has slowly shown himself to be someone who is less concerned with getting the behind-the-scenes story of Allison

Pagone's trial than with showing that Allison is, in fact, innocent.

"Hey, it's your life," he says, raising a hand, sensing the objection from Allison and probably not grasping how literal his comment is. "I have something for you. It's probably not much."

Larry has shown an impressive ability to uncover information on this case that is probably more easily found by a journalist than by a defense lawyer or his investigator. Not necessarily cold, hard factual information that could be used at trial, but details, rumors, things that could give her an advantage.

"Still got my nose to the ground," he says. "The prosecutors, they know Sam Dillon called you several times before his death. They're working on the assumption that it was due to your relationship. People who are dating talk on the phone, right? But then they have this other information—someone who worked with Sam—someone is saying that Sam had mentioned something about an 'ethical dilemma.' Which—"

"An 'ethical dilemma,' they said?" Allison feels her stomach tighten.

She could sense it in his voice immediately. Something was different, wrong.

"Is something the matter, Sam?" she asked over the phone.

He didn't respond at first, which wasn't like him. One of the things she had liked most about him was his lack of reservation, his openness to her. Her first response, an insecure response: Sam was unhappy with their relationship. He wanted to end things. She felt a tingle down her spine, a turn in her stomach.

"Something I'm dealing with," he finally said, then tried to change the subject to dinner. Was she in the mood for Thai? Tapas? Greek?

"Sam." It was late January, only a few weeks into the new year. They had been together only six weeks—okay, forty-five days, she had been keeping count—but they had reached levels of intimacy she had never neared with Mat Pagone. And now he was evading her.

Sam sighed. "It's something I'm going to have to—I guess you could say I'm having an ethical dilemma."

Ethical dilemma. Buzzwords used by an attorney, which Allison was, or used to be. She didn't know the rules governing a lobbyist, didn't know how closely they resembled the rules of ethics governing a lawyer. "Something with one of your clients?" she prodded.

"I—I think it's best we not discuss it," he answered. "Not yet, anyway."

Yeah," Larry says, "an 'ethical dilemma.' So the cops, the prosecutors, they're thinking that this probably related to all this Flanagan-Maxx stuff. The idea being that Sam had an 'ethical dilemma' because he represented Flanagan-Maxx and he was becoming aware that this company had bribed legislators. It's like a lawyer hearing that his client committed a crime. A lawyer can't rat out his client, right?"

"Not for a past crime," Allison says. "Not for something like this, at least."

"But then again," Larry says, "Sam's not in business as a lawyer. He's a lobbyist. Does he have to follow the same rules? Who knows? I don't know. But the cop I'm friendly with, he says some people think maybe Sam wasn't calling you to whisper sweet nothings. He was calling you to see if he had to turn in his client, Flanagan-Maxx. He was calling for legal advice."

Allison nods, crosses her legs. Larry looks at her but she will give neither confirmation nor denial. She will simply listen.

"The thinking is that Sam called you because he wanted to know what he should do," Larry continues. "Maybe it was part legal and part, you were someone he trusted. But some people prosecuting this case think that maybe Sam confided in you about that information."

"Yes?"

"Yes. And those same people are thinking that when you got that information, you started to feel threatened. Because Mat Pagone lobbied for Flanagan-Maxx, too. So—Sam tells you that Flanagan-Maxx did some bad things and he wants to tattle on them, and that possibly implicates your ex-husband. So . . ." Larry shrugs.

"So I killed Sam," she finishes. "To protect a man to whom I'm no longer married."

"But who is still your daughter's father."

"And they're going to say that at trial?"

The thing about criminal trials is that, no matter how strictly the prosecution is required to disclose information and evidence, it does not have to turn over its opening statement to the defense. The prosecution does not have to explain to the defense how it intends to tie the evidence together. Sometimes the prosecution's theory comes out in pre-trial motions, but it hasn't in this case. So while the prosecution has told Allison's defense team that it intends to introduce Sam's many phone calls to Allison in the days before his death, her lawyers have assumed that they are doing this to prove a romantic relationship, because Allison has never owned up to it. What she is hearing now is that they might be using the phone calls to show that Sam was talking about turning Flanagan-Maxx—and possibly Mat Pagone—in to the feds.

The trial starts this week, and Allison doesn't know what the prosecution is going to say.

"Some people over there think that," Larry answers. "There's a debate over what course of action to take. Some want to say that Sam jilted you and you were upset."

That is what Allison and her attorneys have always thought the prosecution would say at trial. The scorned lover, seeking revenge.

"But some want to say that Sam told you he was going to take Mat down, and you did what you did to protect him. I thought you should know that."

"Either one gives me a motive to kill," she says flatly. "Either I was a jilted lover or I was protecting Mat."

"Well, sure—but if they say you killed Sam to protect Mat, you have an answer."

"I have an answer?"

"Of course you have an answer, Allison." Larry shakes his head, takes a drink from his coffee, frames a hand. "Let's pretend they're right. Their premise is that Mat was bribing senators, and Sam told you about it, and was maybe going to tell the U.S. attorney as well. If that premise is true, then, sure, arguably you'd have a reason to want to kill Sam. Arguably. But again—if that premise is true, wouldn't there be someone else who had that motive? More strongly than you?"

"That's no answer," she says.

"The hell it isn't. Mat was bribing lawmakers and Sam was going to give him up. And you are the only suspect?"

Allison leans forward on the table. "Thank you for the information," she says. "I appreciate anything you can give me."

"But you're not going to use—"

"Mat didn't bribe anyone, Larry."

"You don't know that. You couldn't."

"I know he wouldn't—"

"Then what was Sam confiding in you, Allison?"

"He didn't confide in me about anything of that sort, Larry. He—" She looks away from him, lowers her voice. "He ended things with me. Okay? He dumped me."

"This isn't going to work out," Sam said, sitting behind

his desk at the capital, a hand on his forehead, looking into Allison's eyes.

"Mat—Mat's a friend. You know this is crazy. It always was."

Larry is quiet. He focuses on his coffee, then looks over Allison's shoulder at the shoppers. Oldies music is piped in over the loudspeakers.

"I know you didn't kill Sam," he says. "And I think I know who did."

"Larry—"

"And I think *you* know, too."

"I have to go. I'm sorry," she adds, because she had promised him some background on her life, some items Larry Evans needed for his book. But his tell-all book is the last thing on her mind right now. She rests a hand briefly on his shoulder and leaves him.

FRIDAY, APRIL 23

Jane McCoy walks into Special Agent-in-Charge Irving Shiels's office. "Sir?"

Shiels is behind his desk, a number of files open before him. He gestures to her to close the door, which she does, her heartbeat escalating.

"I see you got confirmation on Doctor Lomas's debt."

"Yes, sir." But she assumes this is not the reason for her visit. Her little field trip yesterday only confirmed what they already knew about Doctor Neil Lomas.

Shiels takes a breath. "Agent, I just got a call. Muhsin al-Bakhari is making plans to go to Sudan in June. First of June, we're hearing."

"Yes, sir," she says evenly, before the breath leaves her.

Muhsin al-Bakhari. They could not have hoped for anyone better.

"Haroon just booked a flight to Paris for the first of June," he adds.

"So Haroon's going to connect from Paris to Sudan," she gathers.

Shiels nods. "He'll do it when he gets there. He wouldn't be dumb enough to book that flight now. I figure, he'll land on June first. Spend a night in Paris. Book a flight for the third."

Shiels knows whereof he speaks, having worked in the Middle East for years with the CIA. He knows how the Liberation Front operates, as well as anyone *can* know.

The gravity of what McCoy has heard settles upon her. On both of them. Unbeknownst to him, Ramadaran Ali Haroon is going to lead the United States to the Liberation Front's operations commander, its number-two guy, Muhsin al-Bakhari. The brains behind the entire operation.

"When Haroon gets to the airport here," says Shiels, "he's going to be flagged. They'll call us."

"Sure. Of course."

"You have to be the one who answers that call, Agent McCoy. You have to be sure he gets on that flight."

"Yes, sir."

"Work him over. Basic questioning. Quiz him."

"Understood, sir. I'll be on the call that day."

"Good." He nods at McCoy. "That's all, Agent." He turns to a file on his desk, then looks up again at his subordinate, who has not moved. "Something else, McCoy?"

"Only—" McCoy clears her throat. "I was only thinking, sir, that there might be some casualties. Some innocents."

"Lose a few to save a lot." Shiels sighs. "I don't have a better answer than that."

And McCoy didn't expect a better answer. She knows the rules. Anyone playing with fire—whatever team they're playing on—knows the risks. Ram Haroon. Allison Pagone. Sam Dillon. Mat Pagone. Not to mention—

"Needless to say," says Shiels, "let's get this right."

THURSDAY, APRIL 22

It's a small high-rise on the West Side. Ten units, five on each side of the skinny, dilapidated building. McCoy has spent more than her share of time on this side of the city; she worked in controlled substances when she started out with the Bureau. Tough gig. She hated it, especially taking the users into custody. You typically busted the users to get to the dealers, but that didn't mean the addicts walked. It was preferable, no doubt, to take them in and try to rehabilitate them, but she could never shake the unease of putting cuffs on people who were in the grip of addiction.

And now she's back. Back on the grimy sidewalks, back by the small-loan shops, the convenience stores advertising phone cards and cigarettes on the metal fencing that covers their windows, the broken-down automobiles lining the curbs. She sees too many youths running around for a school day. The streets are pocked with deep potholes, the traffic signs are painted with graffiti. A car alarm is going off the next street over. She hears two women yelling at each other in a low-rise above her, through a closed window.

So many problems, it's suffocating to even consider where to begin.

"I'm going," McCoy says, turning her face toward the collar of her leather jacket. She doesn't work undercover, but this is hardly a stretch for her—jeans and a baseball cap—and she wants to have the conversation personally. She's not as out-of-place on this particular block; many parts of the West Side, contrary to popular opinion, are racially heterogeneous. The whites around these parts are heavily ethnic, first-generation Eastern Europeans, mostly, along with Koreans, Latinos, and African Americans. So she doesn't fit in precisely, but she's not off by much.

McCoy takes the length of the street, then turns at the crosswalk and moves to the east side of the avenue. An Asian grocer is sweeping the sidewalk outside his place. A young, very pregnant woman in a wool cap is waddling toward her.

McCoy blows a bubble with her gum. The heels are a bit uncomfortable but it fits the scene, so she works it as best she can. She gets the attention of one boy, an African American kid sitting on a stoop, playing with a deck of cards that rests on the step below him. It's not much of an ego boost; the kid looks about thirteen.

Still, she winks at him for a response.

"Lookin' good, my woman," he says in a squeaky, preadolescent voice.

Good. She has just about passed him and continues on a step or two, before turning back and facing the boy. "Hey, handsome," she says, working the gum some more. A little flirtation does wonders on a kid this age. "Shouldn't you be in school?"

"Oh, man," he squeaks. He lifts the deck of cards, then proceeds to drop three of them on the step between his feet. He shows her one card—the three of clubs—and starts shuffling the three cards around with rather amazing speed and agility. "Tell me where it lands, pretty lady."

McCoy chuckles for his benefit and takes the opportunity, while he works his trick, to inventory the boy. A flashy Starter jacket with hood, gloves sticking out of his pockets, leather high-tops, an open cigar box by his feet that holds a few dollars and some change. He's keeping a little in the box—singles and a few quarters—to make the game look low-stakes. The rest is probably in his sock, but that's of no concern to her.

Of concern to her is the gym bag to his immediate right.

The boy stops, shows his palms, and looks up at McCoy triumphantly. The three cards are lined up next to each other between his feet. There is no money involved here. He's just showing off.

She leans into him. "What's your name, kid?"

The boy smiles at her, showing thick gums, white teeth. "Jackson," he says. "Tell me which card's the three of clubs, pretty lady."

McCoy leans in, still closer. "I don't gamble, Jackson," she says quietly, evenly, no longer smiling. "I'm an FBI agent. You're not in any trouble," she adds, raising her hand preemptively, as she sees the boy begin to adjust his position, angling himself to the right. "But you will be if you reach for that bag."

McCoy gestures over her shoulder. "See that guy turning the corner right now? Two o'clock."

The boy looks over, undoubtedly seeing Harrick emerging from around the corner.

"He's my partner. If he sees you try to signal Jimmy in any way, we'll lock you up."

The reference to Jimmy, she figures, is as meaningful to the boy as her threats. She is telling him that she already knows what is going on upstairs.

"Put your hands on your face, Jackson," McCoy says. "Do it now."

The boy complies eventually, slapping a hand on each cheek. He doesn't seem particularly worried. Closer to sulking.

McCoy takes his gym bag and opens it. She doesn't find a weapon and didn't expect to. She lifts a hand-held radio out of his bag and puts it in her jacket pocket. "What's he paying you, out of curiosity?"

"Twenty bucks a pop."

"What's a pop? Half a day?"

"Seven to one, lady. Damn." The boy shakes his head. He has just lost one of his day jobs. The other one, which apparently starts at one, involves the card hustle, but not here. Jackson probably hits the train station, the bus terminal, somewhere downtown where the white folks don't so much mind being hustled by such a cute little guy.

"I'm taking the radio with me, Jackson. But all the same, keep those hands on those cute cheeks of yours. Don't make a move now, okay? My partner has a short fuse."

"I ain't movin', lady," he answers in his disappointed voice.

McCoy pats Jackson's shoulder and moves up the stairs. She uses a key that was copied from an upstairs neighbor, last week. Harrick followed the woman to the store, showed her his credentials, and persuaded her to let him make a copy.

McCoy speaks into her collar. "Am I clean?"

"Clean," Harrick's voice crackles back in her earpiece. What he means is that Jimmy, upstairs, has not looked out his window, down at McCoy talking to the boy, nor has Jackson made any attempt to signal his boss from the stoop.

Once inside, McCoy removes her heels, takes one of the two flights of stairs and stops on the landing. She tosses her leather jacket, leaving a pajama top—nothing frilly, just a light-blue top. She takes off her cap and musses her hair.

"I'm going black," she says, removing the earpiece.

She takes the next flight of stairs and walks up to the door. There is loud music coming from the apartment, as they had been told. But it's not as loud as she had been led to believe, and she realizes she should have considered the source, an eighty-one-year-old woman.

Still, it's her excuse, so she'll use it.

She bangs on the door and shouts. "Hey!" She gets no response so she tries again, slamming the door hard, getting a good feel for its sturdiness. It's thin, cheap wood, which is no surprise, but there's at least a chain lock, also predictable. She hopes like hell she will not have to break down a closed door.

"You wanna turn that music down?" she shouts.

The voice comes from inside the apartment. "What's your problem?"

"My problem is you, jerk-off!"

She hears him moving inside, toward the door, possibly approaching the peephole.

She takes a step back before he gets too close.

"Take a pill, sweetheart," the voice says through the door.

"It's eight-thirty in the morning!" she hollers, watching the door.

"Christ, lady—"

McCoy lets her weight transfer to her toes. She sees the door crack open and comes forward with full force, before the keychain has even stretched taut against the space, while the man is still in the midst of positioning his weight backward to open the door. That's the key. It would probably take her several attempts to get through this door if it were shut, assuming she could do it at all. It's all about surprise and balance.

She leads with her shoulder. She wants to keep her feet but it's been a while, and anyway, this guy will be on his back, too. She hits the door and feels a pop in her shoulder, nothing permanent, but something she'll remember for a while. Something this guy, Jimmy, will remember for a while, too.

The chain lock pops from the force. McCoy manages her balance as she stumbles on the hardwood floor of the apartment. Jimmy is on the floor behind the door.

"I'm a federal agent," she says quickly, lest Jimmy get any ideas. Under these circumstances, this might be good news for Jimmy. But she will take no chances. She removes her weapon, tucked in the back of her jeans, her credentials quickly following, a badge on a leather base. She kicks the door shut and keeps the weapon trained on Jimmy, before he even knows what has happened.

Jimmy is mid-thirties, with stringy blond hair and darker facial hair. Why do these idiots think goatees look good?

"FBI," she says. She motions with her weapon. "Get up. Sit down on that disgusting couch." McCoy backs up and kicks at the stereo until it shuts up. "Sit, Jimmy. Sit. This might work out okay for you."

"Don't know what you're talking about," Jimmy answers, making his way to the couch and falling on it.

McCoy gives him a crosswise look, lets her eyes move about the room. There are betting slips in piles on a desk, next to a ledger with numbers in three vertical columns—one for the bettor, one for the game, one for the amount, all in code. Four—no, five different cell phones—ghost phones, stealing signals from legitimate phones, making them untraceable. A bowl of Cheerios, half-finished, sits on the desk as well. "This wouldn't be your first offense," she says, deliberate in her choice of the conditional tense. "You probably know the sentencing guidelines better than I do."

"This ain't right."

"That's what you get for chincing on your sentries, Jimmy. A ten-year-old kid?"

Jimmy's jaw clenches. He's probably got some ideas about that kid in his head.

"Wasn't his fault," she says. "We've been watching you. It wouldn't have mattered."

"What the hell is this?" Jimmy asks.

A fair enough question. A federal agent, dressed in a pajama top and jeans, comes in solo and doesn't seem all that interested in busting his chops. McCoy felt she had no choice. She wants to involve as few people as possible in this operation. And okay, maybe she wanted a little physical exercise.

"I have a couple of questions for you, Jimmy. If you answer them, I'm gone in thirty seconds. If you lie, we're not friends anymore."

Her new amigo squirms in his seat, folds his arms. "So ask me," he says.

"Doctor Neil Lomas," she says. "And if you tell me you don't know him, I'm cleaning up this apartment."

Jimmy ponders this, and that confirms her suspicion. Giving up the name of one of the people who places bets with him is not asking too much, considering the alternative. But this one is giving him pause.

She wonders what he knows about Doctor Neil Lomas. Does he know why he started gambling? Probably not. Does he have any idea that Doctor Lomas is in the process of producing a deadly drug that will be indistinguishable from baby aspirin?

Definitely not. No, Jimmy's hesitation has nothing to do with Agent McCoy's interest in the doctor.

"I got no business with that guy," Jimmy says.

Actually, as phrased, Jimmy is probably telling the truth.

"Doctor Lomas was into you for fifteen grand," she tells him. "You were getting impatient. Stomp your foot twice if I'm wrong."

"What the fuck."

"Now, just like that," McCoy adds, "you're leaving him alone. You haven't sent anyone after him for months. That's because he's all paid up now. Right, Jimmy?"

Jimmy shakes his head.

"Just give me a name," she says, sensing his obvious reluctance. "I know Doctor Lomas didn't pay you himself."

Jimmy's mouth parts. He is probably weighing jail time versus incurring the wrath of the person who purchased Doctor Neil Lomas's debt.

Besides, he probably couldn't give McCoy a name.

This guy is scared. She could brace him a lot harder, but she's not particularly interested in spending the entire morning with Jimmy, and she most certainly does not want to haul him in.

She pulls a photograph, folded in half, from her back jeans pocket and shows it to him. She watches his eyes.

Jimmy's eyes go cold as winter, mesmerized, seemingly, by the photograph. He loses what little color he had in his face.

No question. She never really had any doubt.

"Lady," says Jimmy, "you *definitely* didn't hear me say yes."

"No, I didn't," she agrees. He didn't need to say the words. "I was never here, Jimmy, right?" she asks, but she knows that the last thing that Jimmy wants to do is discuss this conversation.

"Fuck *yeah*, you were never here. Keep me outta this shit."

"You're out of it." She considers telling him to fold up shop, but that would be another unnecessary request. This place is burned now. Jimmy will be out of here in a matter of hours.

"And listen to me," she says, on her way out. "You lay a hand on Jackson out there and I'll find you. We understand each other?"

"I got you, lady. Just go."

She heads back down the stairs and re-dresses, her jacket, heels, and baseball cap. She emerges from the apartment to find little Jackson, wearing a soulful expression with his hands still plastered to his cheeks. She removes two twenties from her pocket and puts them in his hand. Call it severance pay.

"We're all good, Jackson," she says to him. "Take off now. Stay out of trouble."

Jackson lets out a moan.

"And the three of clubs is the middle card," she says to him.

SUNDAY, APRIL 18

So the question is," Larry Evans says, "why did Flanagan-Maxx hire only Sam Dillon to get the Divalpro legislation passed? Dillon was a Republican, so he was the natural to work the House and the governor. But what about the Senate? Why didn't they hire anyone to work the Senate?"

"That's an easy question," Allison says. "The Senate Dems don't like Flanagan-Maxx. They won't like this legislation. So they use someone else to push the Senate."

Larry sips his coffee, clearly unsatisfied with the answer. "They funnel money to the Midwestern Alliance for Affordable Health Care? Their arch-enemy, suddenly their best friend." Larry points at his notes. "A quarter of a million dollars to MAAHC last year? That's how much F-M paid to MAAHC, last year. Did you know that?"

Larry has been reading the reports filed with the state board of elections, as well as Flanagan-Maxx's financial statements for the previous year.

"And, lo and behold," he continues, "MAAHC turns around and gives a hundred grand to Mat Pagone to lobby the Senate for the Divalpro legislation. House Bill 1551."

"So?" Allison shrugs. "Seniors want Divalpro."

"Bullshit. Every seniors' group except MAAHC was opposed. The generics would be every bit as good, and everyone knows it."

"Okay, fine." Allison tucks a hair behind her ear. "So, Flanagan-Maxx knows they have no friends in the Senate, they want a different face supporting it. They kick some money to MAAHC to support the legislation. MAAHC uses some of that money to hire Mat, they keep the rest of it. I still haven't heard anything illegal."

Larry works his jaw, drums his fingers on the table. He disagrees with Allison, clearly, and she senses more. She also senses that Larry knows Allison knows more than she is saying.

"Flanagan-Maxx didn't want its fingerprints on the Senate," he says. "They knew what Mat would have to do, and they wanted a wall between themselves and Mat. That's why they didn't hire Mat to begin with, straight up. They used MAAHC as that wall."

The grocery store is busy today. So is the café. This has become a place to socialize, where women catch up with each other while keeping one eye on their wandering kids.

"Tell your lawyer," Larry says. "Tell him what I found out."

"What I do with my lawyer is my business. We agreed on that. You don't talk to my lawyer. You talk to me."

Larry reaches for his jacket, a light one hanging over the back of his chair. "You aren't going to tell him," he gathers.

"I didn't say that."

"Why won't you tell him? Here." Larry pushes the documents in front of Allison, printouts from the state board of elections' website and financial documents on Flanagan-Maxx. He points at the documents as he hikes his laptop bag over his shoulder.

"That's all you need, right there, for an acquittal," he says. "And you won't use it."

SATURDAY, APRIL 17

This is McCoy."

"Agent McCoy? Roger Ogren. I see weekends are no better for you than me."

"They might be a little better for me, Roger. You're on trial in a couple of weeks. And call me Jane."

McCoy tucks the phone into her shoulder and reaches for the cheeseburger on her desk. She is losing weight and can't afford to. A little midday fast-food is the ticket. Only one she knows.

"Yes, that's right," Ogren says, "I'm on trial in less than two weeks. I'm wondering if you're aware of any surprises in store for me."

McCoy almost coughs up her sandwich.

"Nothing I know of," she says.

"You're being coy, Jane."

"I'm not, really."

"Unless my memory fails me," he says, "you have Allison

Pagone's home bugged. You can hear everything she says in there with that fancy eavesdropping equipment."

McCoy squeezes her burger, causing a dollop of mustard to fall on her jeans.

"Shit," she says, not to Ogren.

McCoy didn't want to talk to Roger Ogren, or any state or county official, for that matter, about the fact that Allison Pagone's house was wired for sound. But the subject had to be broached. Not long after getting Allison Pagone in their sights for Sam Dillon's murder, the prosecutors and police executed a warrant to search her house. McCoy's best guess was that they wouldn't even notice the eavesdropping equipment. But she couldn't be sure. She and Irv Shiels debated it. They most certainly couldn't have loose lips discussing the fact that Allison Pagone's house was miked up. That, obviously, would defeat the purpose of eavesdropping. So the two of them went to the county attorney himself, Elliot Raycroft, and told him. They also threatened, cajoled, and ultimately stroked him into understanding that they couldn't tell his office a damn thing about what they were doing, and in return, he had to keep quiet about the bug. The conversation was about as enjoyable as eating sand.

She doesn't like the fact that Ogren's even raising the topic, but she's not surprised.

"Surely she must be saying something, Jane. Something I can use."

"She doesn't talk about the case in her home," McCoy says. "Not anything substantive, at least. Not anything that concerns you."

"Anything that concerns *you*?" he ventures.

"Maybe." McCoy wipes at her jeans but it's pointless. She'll have to do a load of wash tonight, because these are her only good pair of jeans.

"Look, she talks in her house, obviously," McCoy

elaborates. "But she seems to limit her discussions about the case to her lawyer's office. She doesn't have many visitors, and she's certainly not going to start talking about her case to anyone. If there was something there, I'd tell you, Roger. I've told you before, haven't I?"

"That's why I called."

"Well, there's nothing new to report. I'm looking at her for something unrelated to this murder. I haven't heard anything from her in that house that is remotely of interest to you. Scout's honor."

"You were a Scout?"

"I was a Brownie for about two days. I hated it. Hey, Roger?"

"Yes?"

"You're still keeping quiet about this? No one else in your office knows that we have her place miked up, right?"

"Yes, Jane," Ogren replies with no shortage of condescension. "I'm keeping quiet."

ave a seat, Allison, please. Get you anything?"

"I'm fine, thanks."

Ron McGaffrey sets his considerable frame behind his desk and dons his reading glasses. He lifts a document and reads from it. *"Best Served Cold?"* he asks.

Allison starts. "What—what did you say?"

"Were you writing a new book with that title?"

"Well, yes," she says, the heat coming to her face. "That was the working title. How do you know about that?"

"Roger Ogren sent it over this morning," he says. "Seems it was deleted from your computer? Removed from your hard drive?"

"Yes, that's right, it was." She crosses her legs. "I didn't like it."

"Okay." McGaffrey slides it across the desk. "Well, *they* liked it. Especially page fifty-one. They marked the passage."

She sits at the desk and pulls up his e-mail. She is not
entirely sure what to write or to whom she should send it.
It could be anything at all and serve her purposes. All
that really matters is that an e-mail was sent from his
computer at nine o'clock in the evening, while she is believed to be at a party, and long after she visited his
home at noon today. An alibi. Proof of life.

"This was in a chapter entitled 'Alibi,' by the way," he
adds sourly.

"That's right." She throws the document down on the
desk. "So?"

"So?" he asks sarcastically. "*So*? The story's about a
woman who kills the man she was sleeping with. She kills
him during the day but she doesn't have an alibi for that
time. So she goes to his house at night—when she does
have an alibi; she's at a party but she's snuck out—and she
sends an e-mail from his computer. To show he was alive
and well when she left him that day."

"Yes. That's right." Allison makes no attempt to hide the
anger.

"This novel was deleted at"—McGaffrey looks down at
another document—"three twenty-one a.m. on the morning after Sam Dillon died. A little over an hour after you
got home, found your daughter at your house. With dirt on
your hands, according to Jessica."

"I don't remember when I deleted it, Ron. I work in the
middle of the night all the time."

Ron opens his hands. "I have a client who isn't telling
me everything."

"I didn't mimic my own book, Ron."

"I don't care if you did or you didn't. I need to know
these things."

"Well, I guess it never occurred to me."

"It never occurred to you." Now her lawyer is doing the
mimicking. "That e-mail was a big help to us, Allison. It

put time-of-death in play for us. It leaves room for the possibility that Dillon was still alive past one in the morning.
We know, from Jessica, that you were home at two. If Sam
Dillon was murdered later that morning, you have an alibi.
Jessica spent the night and saw you the next morning. But
now"—he points to the page of the novel—"*now*, everything I just said is what your character did in your book."

Allison pinches the bridge of her nose, tries to stay
even. "Ron, nobody thinks Sam died the next morning. Not
even our own pathologist. The partial digestion of his dinner, the broken clock fixed at 7:06. He died around seven
on Saturday night. Everyone knows that."

"Who knew about this—this *Best Served Cold* book?"

"Nobody." She shrugs. "I was notorious at my publisher
about keeping my work secret until it was finished."

"I'm not talking about your publisher. Friends?
Neighbors? Your ex-husband?"

"No, no, and no. Nobody."

"Your daughter?"

"I said nobody. Nobody knew, Ron."

McGaffrey's face is crimson. He throws his hands up. "I
need time to work with this."

"If you're talking about moving the trial date, Ron,
we've discussed that already. That was the first thing I told
you. I'm not moving it."

"That's the most ridiculous thing I've ever heard." He
holds out his hands, as if beseeching her. "Give me a couple
of months and maybe I can give you the rest of your life."

Allison leaves the chair and walks to the window.
McGaffrey's law firm shares a floor of a downtown high-
rise. McGaffrey got one of the two corner offices. She can
see a glimpse of the lake to the east, the rest of downtown
and the pricey lakefront housing to the north. Mat had
wanted to move into one of those lakefront condos. He
cited proximity to work, avoiding the expressway traffic
downtown, but she always assumed it was the cachet of

near-north housing that Mat coveted. She preferred their home on the northwest side, the quiet neighborhoods. She liked seeing little kids on tricycles; the streets with trimmed lawns; neighbors talking over the fence; the annual block parties. Something like suburbia, but without giving up the coffee shop, a deli, a couple of restaurants within a short walk.

"We can't say someone framed you if nobody knew about the alibi in that book," Ron says. "But I can work on time-of-death. Give me some time here—"

"No, Ron."

"Why in the world—"

"Because we give them time, they might find the murder weapon." She turns to him. "And we don't want that. We definitely do not want that. Okay?"

Moments like this must come often in the life of a criminal defense attorney. How often do clients come out and say, Yeah, it was me. Rarely, in his own limited experience. Clients don't want to tell, lawyers don't want to ask. It usually happens like this, in some kind of code. *We don't want them to find the murder weapon.*

"I see," McGaffrey says, as if disappointed. Surely, he didn't think Allison was innocent. If he banks his practice on defending the wrongly accused, he will have no career. Surely, he has adopted the mantra of any defense attorney, the same mode of thinking Allison developed in her few years as a public defender. Put the government to its proof. Make it hard for the government to rob someone of his or her liberty. It's not about freeing murderers. It's about keeping the government in check.

It's more than that, she realizes, for most defense attorneys. It's more of a game. More about winning. It almost has to be that way.

"We're not moving the trial," she says. "And I'd rather not discuss it again."

THURSDAY, APRIL 15

Jane McCoy looks at the envelope on the conference table. It was removed from a larger package that was addressed to Tashkent, Uzbekistan. The envelope has been scanned for fingerprints and revealed a thumb, index, and ring print. The prints have been checked against every fingerprint database in the federal government, as if they didn't already know. The prints are a clear match for Ramadaran Ali Haroon.

On the back of the envelope Ram Haroon's signature is scribbled across the sealed fold, so that if anyone were to open it, it would be obvious. The FBI has opened the envelope, of course, and the note inside has been translated. Which means that the FBI has had to purchase the exact kind of envelope used—not a difficult chore—and they have their best man practicing Haroon's signature so that they can seal this back up and send it to its destination with an "authentic" signature. Their man will have to sign Haroon's name adequately and also imitate his handwriting on the front, where the lone word "Mushi" is scribbled.

She looks at the message, translated to English:

My dearest Mushi:
    Much progress has been made. Anticipated date is middle of May. Arriving in Paris on June 1. Will deliver in person.
    I am honored to have been chosen.

"Mushi" refers to Muhsin al-Bakhari, the top lieutenant for the Liberation Front. One of only four people who speaks to their leader, whom they call the Great One.

"Haroon's speaking straight to the *shura majlis*," says Special Agent-in-Charge Irv Shiels. Shiels knows these people, having spent more than a decade in the Middle East with Central Intelligence. That, presumably, is why the Bureau is handling this. The CIA is no fan of the Bureau— the feeling is mutual—but Shiels knows the Liberation Front as well as any of them, so the CIA is largely deferring to Shiels and the counterterrorism squad in the field office here, at least for the part of this operation that involves Ram Haroon. The story goes, Shiels fell in love with a field officer over there and wanted to settle down back in the states, back in this city, where he grew up. So he switched to the Bureau and quickly became special agent-in-charge.

McCoy understands the nerves in Shiels's voice. The *shura majlis* is the four-person consultative council that advises the Liberation Front's leader on matters of religion, finance, war operations, and the like. Muhsin al-Bakhari is the head of the council, making him the CEO, so to speak, of the Liberation Front. Haroon is communicating directly with al-Bakhari, meaning the mission is one that the Libbies are taking seriously.

The Liberation Front does not like layers of bureaucracy. It is not a small, tightly wound group with a firm organizational structure. Rather, it is a series of loosely banded clusters throughout the world, many of them lying dormant while they await their instructions. Most disturbingly, the Liberation Front has focused recruitment on youth—rebellious, impressionable, idealistic children and young adults—both because they are the future of any rebellion and because they escape detection more easily. College kids protesting on campuses will not draw as much attention, because they have always protested. The best estimates are that the average age of suicide bombers and perpetrators of violence is twenty-one. The Libbies' strategy, as far as the U.S. government can tell, is to recruit and indoctrinate these young people and then leave them to their own devices until the time comes. Then, in quick succession, they are given their instructions and execute the plan. The less time between formulation and execution, the less chance for mistakes or second thoughts.

For something like what the Liberation Front has in mind here, the fewer people in the loop, the better. At this point, before they even have the formula, the general thinking is that only a handful of people in the Liberation Front even know what is happening. That, McCoy assumes, is why Haroon signed his name over the seal on the envelope. It is not so much that they fear the U.S. government reading the letter; they don't want whoever will receive this letter and deliver it to al-Bakhari to read it.

"Sir," McCoy asks, "how is this going to play out?"

Shiels's lips sink into his mouth, his eyes narrow. "We don't need to know," he says, smiling at her as if they have a mutual complaint. Beyond the scope of the local FBI office's job, he means. "My guess? If he's really delivering this to al-Bakhari, they'll follow him there. And all bets are off. It'll be Rangers, I assume. They'll ambush the lot of them and hope to get al-Bakhari alive."

"Sure." If their surveillance of Ram Haroon leads them

to Muhsin al-Bakhari, the U.S. government—Army Rangers, Shiels is predicting—will proceed with full force. The United States has been searching for al-Bakhari for years. It wouldn't be a place for bystanders. "And what if he doesn't deliver to al-Bakhari?" she asks.

"Then, we may not catch the big fishes. Haroon will perform his faithful service and the Libbies will probably kill him."

"They'll kill him?"

"He's of no use to them, Agent. Not for intel, at least. He's been to the States. He's documented. Maybe not with his real name, but nevertheless." Shiels gets out of his chair. "However this turns out, Ram Haroon's days as an undercover operative for the Liberation Front are almost over. And I'm sure he knows that."

WEDNESDAY, APRIL 14

*H*e recalls when life was simpler, or at least when it seemed simpler. Certainly that was all it was, a mere illusion, the innocence of childhood. He prefers to think of his earliest memories, before the move to Peshawar. His family was happy. More accurately, he remembers being happy and either made the assumption that his parents were, too, or was too engulfed in the self-centeredness of early childhood to know one way or the other.

That is one thing that bothers Ram Haroon about his mother. He doesn't know if she was happy. Father said she was. Father said she was beautiful and intelligent and forceful and loving.

Ram believes that. But after almost twenty years, he remembers little of his mother and his sister. Memories fade and are replaced with some combination of reality and fantasy. Probably his mother has grown more beautiful, his little sister more adorable, with time.

And his memories, such as they are, are grounded far

less in the visual and more in the senses of smell and touch and hearing. He can remember the basics—clothes his mother and sister wore, the color of their hair—but he cannot recall the intricacies of their faces purely from memory; he can place them, but what he is remembering, he realizes with pain, are the few photographs that remain of them.

He remembers the sand near their home, where Mother would make the bunda pala—*stuffed fish that she would bury for hours in the hot sand to let it bake. He remembers the succulent aroma of the* sajii, *the spiced leg of lamb impaled on a branch and cooked near, not over, an open fire, and licking his fingers with delight when the meal was over. He remembers his mother's voice, her confidence and the change in inflection when she addressed her dear son.*

Zulfi, she called him.

He remembers her English as well, the language spoken only by Pakistan's elite, from which Mother came. She taught poetry and English at the university in Quetta, in the Baluchistan province. He remembers her English as much as Urdu, the language the government was trying to push as the only official language, the language Ram's father spoke almost exclusively. Ram's father, Ghulam, tried to converse with his wife in English but could rarely keep up; Mother often referred laughingly to his attempts as "Urdlish."

He remembers that Mother read. He remembers that she debated with Father, not in intemperate tones, about politics and society. "You have one parent who is brilliant and one who is clearly the inferior," Ram's father would say, as Mother smiled. Neither would confirm which was which. Ram—Zulfi—would direct his finger from one to the other intermittently and guess, leaving them laughing uproariously.

He remembers when his sister, Benazir, was born, the earliest memory he has. He cannot recall specifics except for his mother's singing sepad *when Beni was born, the neighbors coming to the house and singing poems late into the evening. He remembers holding Beni in his arms awk-wardly, her tiny, splotchy, contorted face, under the watch-ful eyes of his parents.*

He remembers the day, four years later, when his mother and Beni did not come home. He remembers play-ing with other children in the streets, returning home ex-pecting to find his mother and baby sister, instead seeing only his father sitting on a carpet, his hands over his face. He recalls the paralysis he felt, never having seen his fa-ther as vulnerable, not making a sound until his father fi-nally became aware of him.

"Sit down here, Zulfi," Father said, extending his arms, revealing a face wracked with pain, wet with tears.

R am Haroon brings a hand to his face and sighs. It is painful but helpful to remember his mother and Beni. That's what his father did, he said, and so will Ram. He will do this for them.

Ram takes a final look at the letter, handwritten in Arabic.

My dearest Mushi:

Much progress has been made. Anticipated date is middle of May. Arriving in Paris on June 1. Will deliver in person.

I am honored to have been chosen.

Ram folds the letter carefully and places it in an enve-lope. He licks the flap, seals the envelope, signs his name over the seal with the ornate pen his mother once used to write her poetry. He takes a bus to the post office about a mile from the university campus.

The wait in line is excruciating. Not the time that it takes; a Pakistani is accustomed to longer lines than this for such things. He simply wants this out of his hands. He removes his notepad and checks the address against the one he has written on the envelope, checking and rechecking. He realizes he is being ridiculous—he has been educated at the finest universities and now he is worried that he has not accurately copied a single address in Tashkent, Uzbekistan onto an envelope.

He makes it to the front of the line and walks up to a postal agent.

"I'd like to speak to Raoul," he says.

*S*he sees Sam's eyes, notices him because he was talking to some clients before his attention was suddenly diverted. His client's perceptions of him are paramount, it is the whole reason for the cocktail party, but he is overtaken by her, by pure lust, his gaze running up and down her body, his imagination running wild. It is, she is sure, the most memorable expression she has ever seen on a man's face.

"Mother, you're blushing." Jessica Pagone drops her backpack on the opposite side of the table in the restaurant where they have agreed to meet, on the northwest side, within the distance permitted by the terms of her bond.

And then Allison thinks of Sam's fateful words. *This isn't going to work out. Mat—Mat's a friend. You know this is crazy. It always was.*

Jessica remains standing and watches her mother, almost accusingly.

"Jess, c'mon." Allison lifts a bang off her forehead. "Sit."

"You cut your hair," Jessica says, taking the seat across from her mother and not elaborating on the observation.

And Allison will not ask for elaboration. She will not seek a compliment from her daughter. If pressed, Jess would probably comment favorably. But the whole thing would be so forced, so unlike them now, so awkward. As if things aren't awkward enough.

There is a truce. They are not fighting. They have not so much as bickered since Sam's murder. It is not as if things are openly hostile. Things are simply tense.

Allison divorced Jessica's father and, not long afterward, began an affair with her father's colleague in the lobbying business—a man for whom Jessica worked. That is all, apparently, that Jessica needs to know to choose sides. The murder of Sam Dillon has complicated things, makes it harder for Jessica to hold her grudge; she no doubt realizes that her mother has more urgent things on her mind right now. And so she has reacted with all the right words. She has shown concern. Given words of encouragement. But it is all still there, simmering beneath the surface, Jessica's intense resentment, even if she tries to mask it with a comforting expression.

"You're losing weight," Jess says. "You have to eat."

True enough. With the nerves keeping her stomach in knots and all of her exercise to still those nerves, Allison has lost close to fifteen pounds in a little over two months.

"The trial starts soon," Allison says.

"I know."

A waiter takes their order for drinks—just water for Allison, iced tea for Jessica. The server is cute, Allison thinks, probably a college boy, and she sizes him up as she has sized up every man of his approximate age—Jessica's age—wondering, however improbably, whether this will be the man Jessica finds. She has envisioned the perfect man for her daughter. Caring, passionate, strong. She wants a man who makes Jessica feel loved, who challenges Jess to be a better person, supports her unequivocally. This, she supposes, is what every mother wants for her child.

"It's okay to tell them," Allison says.

"I don't have a choice."

No, Jessica doesn't have a choice. She did once. She had a number of options the first time the police paid her a visit. She probably could have gotten away with it, too. The police probably wouldn't have charged a young woman who failed to give incriminating information about her own mother. But Jessica didn't know that, and it probably wouldn't have mattered, anyway. By then, the police were pretty sure who they liked for the murder. And that is all history. The prosecution has subpoenaed Jessica Pagone and she will have to testify against her mother. However hard she may try to equivocate, they will make her answer the questions the same way she answered them in the police station.

"Mother?" Jessica asked, when Allison came home at close to two in the morning, her hands and face dirty. "What have you done?"

Allison wants to hold her daughter. She wants to caress her, kiss her, talk to her intimately again. She wants to ask her about boys, about school, about her hopes and ambitions.

But they don't talk about such things anymore. They haven't for some time. Because the marriage didn't break up overnight. The descent began—oh, it's so difficult to pick a starting point, but what Allison means by this is the first time that the problems were on the surface—about three solid years ago, their anniversary dinner, after a bit too much champagne, when Allison openly wondered what, exactly, they were celebrating. Or that same year, when Allison paid an unannounced visit to Mat's firm and found Mat in his office with a young associate, a female associate, a very attractive young female associate with shiny brown hair and a cute figure. It was nothing inherently incriminating; they were not locked in an embrace or straddling each other on the desk. Mat was sitting in his chair, turned away from the desk, in a way that Allison could only describe as unusually informal, the young associate—Carla was her name—half-sitting, half-leaning on the desk on the same side as Mat. Only separated by about three feet, speaking in quiet but comfortable tones. No, nothing on its face incriminating per se, with the exception of their reactions, Mat leaping to his feet and stuttering out a greeting to Allison, the young associate Carla jumping off the desk so quickly that she almost hit the wall behind her. Mat's suddenly reddened face, his struggle to collect himself, finally getting to the point where he could ask Allison what she was doing here. Allison had wanted to ask Mat the same question. But she didn't. She even shook Carla's hand, took it lightly but then solidified her grip, and she imagines—probably exaggerates this, she admits—that Carla squeezed back, as if for that single moment they were locked in a territorial battle that Carla, apparently, was winning. Yes, that is probably the point where Allison first let the feelings that had been boiling below for so long finally surface, when she finally questioned what the hell she was doing with this man. And Mat knew it, on some level.

And so Jessica did, too. What the two of them, Mat and Jess, said to each other, Allison will never know. She did not ever—would not ever—share this incident with her daughter. She will not be that kind of person. But after that, Jessica and Mat grew closer, spent more time together away from home, away from Allison, had lunches together, probably got together in places that Allison never knew. *I don't know what's wrong with her,* Mat probably told Jessica. *I'm trying to keep this marriage together but your mother seems to want something else. I'm doing all I can, Jess. She's shutting me out.* And the vacation they took together, Mat and Jessica, after the divorce was finalizing, spending this past Christmas in Florida together while Allison spent the holiday alone. Just one quick phone call was all the notice Allison had. She had been preparing to make dinner and spend Christmas Eve with her daughter, even considered having Mat join them. Then the phone call, two days before: *Mother, I'm going with Daddy to Sanibel for the holiday. Talk to you when I get back.* Just one voice mail on her phone and she would spend Christmas alone.

Allison tried. Since the breakup, she tried to engage her daughter about school—*Same old, same old*, Jessica would say. About her friends—*My friends are my friends. Some are fair-weather, some you can count on.* About her love life, a topic from which Allison was now shut out. *There's a guy*, she told Allison last December, *but you probably wouldn't approve.* She remained mum, initially, wouldn't elaborate, despite Allison's claim of an open mind.

There's a guy, but you probably wouldn't approve. She thinks of her daughter's words now with a rush to her heart. She thinks of her daughter's elaboration, finally, after Allison's prompting moved from delicate insistence to pleading.

And so here they are, not talking like mothers and daughters are supposed to talk. Instead, they stare at each other and hunt for topics of small talk. Jessica is in a turtleneck and jeans, little makeup as usual, her hair in a ponytail. She is prettier every time Allison sees her, which is far less often these days. The distance, however, has allowed Allison to witness the developments in her daughter more clearly than when she saw her every day. She sees it in the curve to her chin, the cheekbones high on her face, the way she carries herself. Jessica is becoming a woman. But there is something else there, too, and Allison feels it in her fear. Allison is afraid, not that she is losing contact with her daughter, but that she no longer knows who Jessica is, or what has happened to her since the divorce and their estrangement.

"You doing okay?" Jess asks, making an effort at cordiality. No, it is more than that. Jessica still cares. Liking and loving someone are two different things. Allison will always be her mother. Jessica is letting her stubbornness hold her back, but it can only go so far.

"I'm doing fine," Allison assures her. "I told you, everything will turn out fine."

Her daughter nods without enthusiasm. "Are you still working on that new book?"

"Not—not really."

"I liked it, what you had so far. A vengeful woman. It had more edge than the first two. More passion, y'know? But the title could use some work. *Best Served*—"

"Jess, I really don't want to discuss that. You know that." The waiter brings Allison her water, the iced tea for Jessica. "Listen, I just want you to know that—you need to understand, if you try to testify differently than what you told the police, they'll prosecute you for that."

"I know that."

"I know you know, sweetheart, but—"

"'Sweetheart?' I think we're past 'sweetheart,' Mother."

Allison recoils. How cruel children can be, with the slightest comment. Her daughter has had to cope with more than the divorce and what she undoubtedly perceives as Allison's infidelity; she has had to live with endless media reports on a murder trial in which her mother stands accused. She imagines that Jess has a small support group of friends, but Mansbury College is a small school. There must be talk. She must sense it over her shoulder, as she passes. *That's Allison Pagone's daughter. Her mom killed that guy.* Allison has had to endure the same experience, but then again, she is not twenty years old, still trying to find her place in the world. At least Allison is responsible for her own infamy; Jessica is an innocent victim.

Or a victim, at least.

Jessica seems to sense that she has crossed the line, regardless. "You're going to win the case?" she asks. "You're sure?"

Allison inhales deeply, stifles a number of emotions. "This is going to turn out fine, Jess. I promise. Just make sure that you're clear on your testimony. If you make a misstep—"

"I won't make a 'misstep,' Mother. I've gone over this with Paul Riley a hundred times. And your lawyer, too. I'm not a kid anymore."

Jessica has certainly inherited her mother's strong will, her father's snappy temperament. She will do great things, this young lady, if she can get past all of this.

Jessica stirs her iced tea, keeps her eyes focused on the table. "They have a really good Caesar salad here," she offers. She seems to notice something, then reaches into her glass and pulls out the lemon from her iced tea.

"Yellow like lemon," Jessica says.

Allison hangs on tight to her emotions. Her daughter is trying to change the subject. Trying to lighten the mood. This is the most she can hope for, now, these generic questions about her book or how she's doing or the quality of a particular salad at a local restaurant or a fond memory. Any attempt at warmth is so welcome that these innocuous comments almost reduce Allison to tears.

She thinks of the things her daughter doesn't know about her and, necessarily, the things she doesn't know about her daughter.

MONDAY, APRIL 12

The meeting takes place five floors below Jane McCoy's office in the federal building. Assistant United States Attorney Wayman Teller, from the Public Integrity Division, starts the meeting as soon as McCoy and Harrick enter the room.

Wayman Teller is African American, middle-aged, and graying, dressed like most of the federal prosecutors she knows, which is to say presentable but forgettable. AUSAs make decent cash for public officials, more than McCoy, but they don't spend it on clothes. Teller is in a suit with a tie pulled down. It's casual attire around the office nowadays, which means the assistant U.S. attorneys can dress down when they're not in court, but she hasn't noticed much of a change in their wardrobe. Convincing a federal prosecutor to loosen up is like convincing the Pope to slam-dance. It's just not in their nature.

Three FBI case agents are in the room, McCoy's colleagues, as well as two other federal prosecutors. But this is Teller's show. Teller has been running Operation Public Trust since its inception approximately three months ago. The case is still in its infancy, but things have moved quickly.

"Agent McCoy," Teller says.

"Call me Jane."

"Thanks for coming," Teller says. "I think you know the basics, but let me be sure."

"Great."

"Flanagan-Maxx Pharmaceuticals has a product called Divalpro," he begins.

"Right," McCoy says. "Controls high blood pressure. The patent was about to expire. So F-M wanted Divalpro on Public Aid's prior-approval list. They needed legislation. That's House Bill 1551."

"Okay, good." Teller smiles. "You know more than I thought."

"I know that F-M hired Sam Dillon, and they had MAAHC hire Mat Pagone to work on the Senate. And I know that Dillon had the votes in the House and the preliminary approval of Governor Trotter. Neither of whom would publicly acknowledge this unless and until Mat Pagone delivered the votes in the Senate."

Teller pushes a piece of paper in front of McCoy. "This is a memorandum from the chief of staff to the Senate majority leader, Grant Tully. This was during last year's legislative session. It's a roll call of perceived votes on House Bill 1551."

McCoy looks at the memo. "They didn't have the votes," she says. "It was three votes short of passage in the Senate."

Teller nods. "So the Speaker of the House, wanting to help out and realizing that the bill won't pass during the regular session, put House Bill 1551 on what's called 'postponed consideration.' It gives them until the end of the year to pass it."

"It gives them veto session," McCoy says, "in November. But between May and November, somebody needs to convince three senators to change their votes."

"Exactly. Which, of course, is exactly what happened." Teller grimaces. "Senators Blake, Strauss, and Almundo flipped. In one day in November, House Bill 1551 was called for a vote in the House, passed by two votes, then was called in the Senate and passed by a single vote. Governor Trotter signed it on Christmas Eve."

When no one would be paying attention. McCoy chuckles. "So the question," McCoy says, "is what happened between May and November of last year to make three senators change their minds."

"That's right. Senator Almundo is a member of the Latino caucus and a pretty close friend of Mat Pagone. Blake is in the city, too, also an ally of Pagone's. Senator Strauss is downstate, just south of the interstate. All three have constituencies that are poor and have a high elderly population. Which is why they were opposed to the legislation in the first place."

McCoy takes this in. Most of this she already knew. Most of what will follow, she assumes, will be new information.

"Mateo Pagone withdrew large amounts of money from his personal account on four separate occasions in June, July, August, and September of last year," says Teller, opening a file. "Nine thousand in June. Eighty-five hundred in July. Eight thousand in August. Forty-five hundred in September."

Mat Pagone was no dummy. Every withdrawal was short of the ten-thousand-dollar withdrawal amount that triggers automatic reporting by the bank to the federal government.

"That's thirty thousand dollars," she says.

Teller opens another file. "Senator Blake spent several

weeks in Sanibel Island, Florida, from mid-December last year to mid-January. A nice place on the water, a boat for his use. He paid for it by check, a check for seven thousand dollars. Blake was down there almost three weeks and there's not a single transaction that appears on his credit card. He didn't write any other checks, either. We know he went to the restaurants—one in particular—and we know he paid cash and, apparently, tipped well."

McCoy can see that. Mat Pagone sent Senator Blake on a nice Florida vacation. Blake wrote a check for seven thousand for his lodging and the boat—smart move—but got something like ten thousand in cash under the table from Mateo Pagone. He blew all of it, probably, or most of it, in Florida so that he wouldn't have to explain the sudden appearance of ten thousand dollars in his checking or savings account. He never deposited a dime of the bribe money. He just lived it up on an extended getaway.

"Mat Pagone spent a few days down there himself over Christmas," Teller continues. "He took his daughter, Jessica."

McCoy nods, as if she didn't know that.

"Blake and Mat Pagone had dinner together one evening, we're relatively sure. But that's it. That's the only record of them being together down there, and it's just an eyewitness. We imagine that Pagone popped for a whole lot more than a dinner, but we can't prove it, because everything was in cash."

"Okay," McCoy says. "And what about Senator Strauss?"

"Senator Strauss just bought a new SUV," Teller continues. "He put twelve thousand down. Emptied a savings account to do it. This was three days after we have him eating lunch with Mat Pagone at the Maritime Club downtown, in October. We can find no other reason for why Strauss was in town—he lives about sixty miles from the city—other than having this lunch. That weekend, he's buying a new

car. We figure Mat Pagone helped him replenish that savings account, only that account is probably a jar in his backyard."

"You have the lunch receipt?" McCoy asks.

"Yeah." Teller hands her a photocopy of the bill,
charged to Mat Pagone's membership at the Maritime
Club. Glazed chicken, roast beef, Cobb salad. The salad
was eight dollars, so unless they really overcharged, this
was an entrée. The drinks were two bourbons and soda, one
gin and tonic, and one iced tea.

Lunch for three, not two.

"Okay," McCoy says, sliding the photocopy back to
Teller. "Go on."

"Senator Almundo is renovating the basement in his
home on the West Side. On the books, the contractor is
charging him ten grand. Looks to us"—Teller looks around
the room at the federal agents—"like the job is more like a
twenty-thousand-dollar effort, give or take. We're thinking
ten thousand was passed in cash."

It wouldn't be the first time a home contractor took
cash. McCoy sighs. She is ready for the punch line.

Teller opens his hands. "We know Mat Pagone, or
someone working with him, put money in their hands. All
three of them. But the principals aren't talking. Strauss,
Almundo, Blake—they're all taking five. Blake can point to
a check that he wrote for the Sanibel home and boat, and
we don't have much to work on otherwise. Almundo will
say the renovation was for ten grand, not twenty. And
Strauss will just plain deny the whole thing. These guys
were well coached. They didn't put a single penny in the
bank."

Teller needs an eyewitness to the payments, he is saying,
or stronger circumstantial evidence. As long as these senators kept the money in a jar behind their house, or blew it
on dinners or the ponies, there is little the federal government can do. They can't even get these guys on tax evasion,

because they can't prove that they received this income, much less failed to report it.

"Are you sure it wasn't *Dillon* who handed over the money?" McCoy asks.

"No, we're not. Mat Pagone could have withdrawn the cash, and Sam Dillon could have paid it out. Or they could have had someone else do it. Someone who wouldn't draw any suspicion whatsoever." Teller smiles without emotion. "We were about to find that out."

They were going to find out, Teller means, because Sam Dillon was about to testify before the grand jury, until he was murdered only days before.

"Dillon came to *us*," says Teller. "He called us and told us he wanted to talk about Flanagan-Maxx. We had just convened the grand jury. He said he wanted us to subpoena him, so we did."

Sure, that makes sense. Dillon wanted to give the appearance that he was being compelled to testify, when in fact he wanted to talk.

"So there we are," Teller concludes. "The people at Flanagan-Maxx are playing see-no-evil, hear-no-evil. The senators won't talk. We can't even say for sure who put the money into their hands. Probably it was Pagone, or someone he trusted." Teller shrugs his shoulders. "But we don't know, Jane. We're at a dead end."

"So you want Mat Pagone," McCoy gathers. "That's the problem."

"Our problem, Jane," Teller replies, "is you."

McCoy raises her hands.

"We need Mat Pagone," he says. "We flip him and the whole house of cards comes down."

"I need him more." She shakes her head. "That's a boat we can't rock."

Teller nods, as if he understands, but he doesn't. He doesn't know. Only a handful of agents, and the SAC, Irv Shiels, know what they are doing.

"What is CT looking at him for?" Teller asks her. "Can you tell me that much?"

"I can't. Sorry."

It can't be the first the time the gang in Counter-Terrorism refused to talk shop.

"Then let us talk to the daughter. Jessica. She was there in Sanibel."

"Absolutely not," McCoy says. "Off-limits."

"Then his wife," Teller requests. "Ex-wife. Allison."

"No way," she says firmly. "Can't do it."

Teller doesn't respond to her comment but opens another file. "Dillon had mentioned to someone in his office that he was grappling with an 'ethical dilemma.' He wouldn't elaborate, but it seems obvious enough to us. He was thinking about turning in his client. He told this guy in his office that he was talking to a lawyer."

"Okay," McCoy says, like she doesn't get the point.

"Allison Pagone was not just his girlfriend," Teller adds. "She was a lawyer. A former PD."

"She was only a public defender for two years," McCoy says. "She's been writing books the last few years."

"That's two different reasons for Dillon to confide in her, Jane. Girlfriend or lawyer. Hey, look, if she has nothing to tell us, fine. But let's ask her."

"No one talks to Allison Pagone, Wayman. Or Mat. Or Jessica. I'm sorry, but there's no give there. We're watching them and they need to think everything is perfectly normal."

The prosecutor looks at the case agents, his fellow lawyers.

"Did Allison Pagone kill Sam Dillon?" he asks Jane.

McCoy laughs. "Guys, if there's some way I can get some of this information for you, I'll do it. Otherwise, please keep me posted on this, okay?" McCoy gets out of the chair. "And keep your hands off my suspects."

SUNDAY, APRIL 11

McCoy sets a steaming cup of coffee on her desk and drops down in her chair. She hasn't had a weekend off this entire year, but no one has told her to come in. This operation does not know weekends from weekdays. The bad guys don't take days off, so neither will she.

Her office is nothing short of disastrous. She didn't inherit the typical female gene for neatness or cleanliness. Stacks of paper line her floors, force her to walk an obstacle course just to reach her desk. She has received countless comments on this from her colleagues, and no, she doesn't prefer it this way, but it is what it is. Maybe they should have taught a course at Quantico on this.

She has made an exception, however, for this operation. She had a new set of cabinets brought in, devoted to the files on this case. It has helped dramatically, being able to call up a file on a moment's notice. She has had her setbacks, falling into her typical practice of setting down a piece of paper somewhere and forgetting where, but she even planned for that inevitability, making an extra copy of everything in her file and placing it somewhere else—her master files.

Owen Harrick walks into her office, dressed informally—a sweater and jeans—like McCoy. "Haroon sent this e-mail yesterday," he says.

With the assistance of a warrant signed by a federal magistrate, the FBI is monitoring Ram Haroon's e-mail, not only the address assigned to him by the university but also another address Haroon uses, *pakistudent@interserver.com*. It is from this address that Haroon has been communicating on sensitive issues. Haroon rarely uses this address, which makes any correspondence he sends from it raise flags all the more quickly with the Bureau.

The e-mail that Harrick places on McCoy's desk is one sentence:

Please inform MAB that communication will be sent early next week by mail.

She reads the initials—*MAB*—and feels a shudder, a knot seizing her stomach.

"Let's watch the post office, then," she says easily to Harrick, because she wants to show calm to her partner. He is undoubtedly feeling the pressure as well. Neither of them has ever worked on anything nearly so consequential.

"He's talking about Muhsin al-Bakhari, isn't he?" Harrick asks.

"Who knows, Owen? Let's just do our job." McCoy takes a piece of paper and writes out a quick to-do list. They will put people at the post offices around the state university. They will have to be ready, starting tomorrow, for a package that Ramadaran Ali Haroon will be sending to his partners overseas.

SATURDAY, APRIL 10

*T*he Pakistani government attributed the bombing at Baluchistan University to an aerial assault by the Soviet Union. The communist-controlled Afghan security service, the KHAD—Khedamat-i-Ettela'at-i-Daulati—had instituted countless air and ground attacks in Pakistan since the country had become the focal point for Afghan resistance to the Soviet invasion. The Afghan refugees had pooled in various parts of Pakistan, including the Baluchistan province. Ram Haroon had seen some of the Afghani Pathans in Quetta; they were generally confined to the refugee camps, but they were sometimes seen in the markets. He remembers their bruised, creased faces, their defeated postures. People who had lost their homes, sometimes their families, clinging to little more than life itself.

Ram's mother, a university professor, and his four-year-old sister accompanying her mother to class were two of the nineteen casualties of the attack. Ram recalls the moment that he heard the news in utter darkness, his eyes *squeezed shut as he and his father sat on the floor of their home.*

Mother was gone. Beni was gone.

It was the Americans, they said.

Ram listened to them only because he was looking for magic healing words, and it was only afterward that their words registered in any meaningful way.

Three weeks passed. His mother and sister were buried. Ram's father did not work, could not work. Father would leave at night and not speak to his son about where he went. Ram saw a change in his father but attributed it to grief, when a part of him knew all along it was something else.

Five weeks after the death of his mother and sister, Ram's father moved Ram and himself from Baluchistan to Peshawar, ground zero in the arming of the mujahedin against the Soviet aggression. "We must put this behind us," Ram's father told him. Ram was hardly able to comprehend, still reeling from the loss of his mother and sister. Now Father wanted to leave the only home he had known?

"Some day I will explain it to you," Father promised.

Ram Haroon wipes the sweat from his face and focuses on his computer in his student dormitory. He types in the name on the e-mail and thinks hard about the words to write.

Please inform MAB that communication will be sent early next week by mail.

Ram types in the web address—*pakistudent@interserver. com*—hits the "send" button, and the document disappears. He looks at the photographs by his bed: his father, mother, and sister. Beni would be twenty-two years old if she had survived the bombing. She would be a student, like Mother was, probably a future professor, or a doctor, or lawyer. Everything would be different. They never would have moved to Peshawar.

Ram moves over to his small bed and cradles the photographs in his hand. "My time may be coming, too," he says to them. At least in his case, it will be his choice.

THURSDAY, APRIL 8

*T*here's a guy, but you probably wouldn't approve."
Jessica's evasive comment to Allison, last December,
over dinner.

"Tell me," Allison prodded.

"You'll just tell me no."

Allison drew back. It was true, she had never failed to
give her opinion on her daughter's choice of boyfriends.
But she had never forbade her daughter from acting on
her own instincts, and certainly had no place doing so
now, when Jessica was twenty and living at her college
dorm.

She knew Jess, however distant they had grown. Jessica
could have avoided the subject, or lied about it. She did
neither. She had broached the topic and left it dangling.
Jessica wanted her to inquire, Allison figured.

"Tell me," Allison said again.

Paul Riley shows Allison in to his office. It has a gor-
geous view, this corner office, and Paul has plenty of mem-

orabilia to decorate the two walls without windows. Artists' etchings of his trial work, photos of Paul with prominent officials. Paul Riley, after all, is the lawyer who prosecuted Terry Burgos, the man who killed six girls on a college campus about twenty years ago. Paul was the guy Allison wanted, when suspicion first gathered around her after Sam's death. Since he begged off representing her, she persuaded him to represent Jessica.

"How are you holding up?" he asks her, and he knows the question is loaded.

"I'm fine, Paul, thanks. You?"

Paul defers as he always does. "Twenty balls in the air," he says.

"I'm concerned with one particular ball."

"Sure." Paul plays with a cufflink on his starched shirt. His shirt is soft blue, matching his eyes.

"She needs to understand the importance of not straying from her testimony, Paul."

"She knows that, Allison. I know that. There's only so much I can share with you now, obviously." He smiles. His loyalty, of course, is now to his client, Jessica.

"She came to my house about eight-thirty that night, the night Sam was killed," Allison says. "She had been at school all day. I got home close to two in the morning. Jess was asleep on the couch."

Paul nods but doesn't speak. He will not share his conversations with Jessica to anyone, not even Jessica's mother.

"My worry is that she'll try to protect me," Allison explains. "That she might say something crazy."

Paul's eyes narrow, divert from Allison. She knows he will not elaborate. For all she knows, Jessica has spoken poorly of her mother to Paul. Paul might be thinking, *Oh, Allison, I don't think you have to worry about Jessica trying to protect you.*

But she cannot take the chance. Perjury, obstruction of

justice, and perhaps worse could await her daughter. This case is all over the press. If the prosecutors are embarrassed in so public a forum, they might look wherever necessary, including at Jessica, to make things right.

"Was there something in particular you had in mind?" Paul asks. He has chosen this question carefully. Nothing from his end, but if Allison has something to say, this is the way.

"What I have in mind," Allison answers, "is that Jessica might say she was at Sam's house that night."

Paul Riley's unflappable expression shows the first sign of a break.

"She might say that she killed Sam," Allison predicts.

Allison remembers it well, that cocktail party two days before Sam was murdered, Thursday, the fifth of February. The Look, she calls it. She remembers Sam, standing across the room, a cocktail in his hand, the look of pure longing as his eyes passed over her, an utter lust that temporarily took hold of him, captivated him as if there were no other person in the room but her.

"Tell me, Jess," Allison had requested of her daughter, six weeks before that time, last December over lunch. "Tell me about this guy I 'wouldn't approve of.'"

Paul Riley stares intently at Allison. "And, if I may ask hypothetically," he tries, "what would be the reason for Jessica being at Sam's house on that Saturday night?"

"It's someone at work, Mother, okay? And I'm not going to discuss this."

She remembers the primitive look in Sam's eyes at the cocktail party.

She remembers her own position by the bar, having just gotten a drink, seeing the expression on Sam's face and stopping short, following Sam's line of vision to a young intern at Dillon & Becker by the name of Jessica Pagone.

Allison takes Paul's hand. "I'm counting on you to protect her, Paul," she tells him.

MARCH

WEDNESDAY, MARCH 31

She left that cocktail party immediately, without a word to Sam, without a word to Jessica. She went home and paced her house, did not sleep, as night blurred into early morning. There was no mistaking it. "Someone at work," her daughter had told her in mid-December, and now she had seen who the "someone at work" was, firsthand. She had seen The Look on Sam's face.

She showered early Friday morning, February sixth, and drove to his office in the city.

"Where is he?" she demanded. She bypassed the receptionist and hunted him through the halls, looking into each office, calling out his name. But he wasn't there, they explained. Mr. Dillon was downstate, flew down to the capital this morning for some meetings.

So she went to her Lexus SUV and drove to the capital. He could be at his office or he could be anywhere at the capital, any number of rooms, most of which would be *closed to her. No matter. She wouldn't stop. She would wait, if necessary. She would find his car and sit on it. She would see him today.*

First, the office. After two wrong turns, her knuckles white, her eyes clouded by tears, she found the building.

"Where is he?" *She ignored the young man who popped out of an office to assist her.*

The boy trailed after her, alarmed, no doubt, but she found Sam Dillon in his office and slammed the door behind her.

Sam was on the phone. He was disarmed by Allison's appearance, the fact that she had traveled down here, the haggard, agitated, hurt expression that Allison knew she couldn't hide.

Sam made quick work of the phone call and stood up. His lips parted but he didn't speak. Allison grabbed the first thing she could find—a small pillow, embroidered with the crest of the state Senate, resting on a small love seat in the corner—and hurled it at Sam.

"You prick," *she hissed.* "You prick."

"What *are you talking—*"

"My daughter?" *Allison took a step closer. Her throat caught. She tried to calm herself but she couldn't control the wave of adrenaline.* "You're the guy at work? The one I 'wouldn't approve of'?"

"Allison." *Sam came around the desk.* "What the hell?"

"This is your 'ethical dilemma,' Sam? You can't decide whether you want to fuck me or my daughter?"

Sam's face froze, but he quickly recovered. "Now calm down a minute—"

"How could you make me believe that what we had—"

"Allison, I'm not sleeping with Jessica." *Sam dared to approach her, tentatively reached out and took her shoulders.* "I'm not sleeping with your daughter. Not now, not ever."

Her heart skipped a beat. She was perspiring. She

wanted, more than anything in this world, to hear these words, to believe them, but his reaction— including his guilty expression—told her that she hadn't been far off.

She had seen that same look of guilt on Mat's face when she had paid him that surprise visit years ago at his office and found the young intern sitting on his desk.

History was repeating itself.

"You tell me everything," she said calmly, through gritted teeth, removing his hands from her, "and you tell me right now. I saw that look on your face last night. And now I know why my daughter wouldn't tell me about the 'guy' she was interested in at work."

"Sit." Sam gestured to a chair, sat on the edge of his desk facing her.

"I'm fine standing," she said.

"That's all it was," Sam explained, followed by an exaggerated sigh. "Jessica was interested in me, yes. Yes, she made overtures. Before I met you, Allison. Before that. She's been working here for a year. I just met you a couple months ago."

Allison found that she was holding her breath.

"Nothing happened, Allison. Nothing. But yes, she—she showed interest. And I was flattered. Okay? I'm a middle-aged, divorced man and a beautiful twenty-year-old is interested in me. Sure, it boosted my ego. Sure, I probably didn't discourage it. It was the kind of harmless, flirtatious stuff that happens. But then one night—this is probably, I don't know, I didn't exactly mark my calendar—maybe November of last year, she said she wanted to see me outside the office. So I make a joke, right—how about I go into the parking lot?—but she's serious, she wants to start dating me. I said no, Ally. I said it was inappropriate for more than one reason, and it had nothing to do with you—I didn't even know you yet. It was inappropriate because she was Mat's daughter, because I'm almost thirty years older than her, and because she worked for me."

"And what did she say?" Allison asked, her voice trembling.

"She said—" Sam raised his head, as if to recount the events. "Oh, she said, she couldn't control two of those three, but she could quit her internship."

Allison raised her eyebrows, to show she was not finished listening.

"I said no, Allison. Christ Almighty, I said no."

Allison sat down in her chair, feeling her physical exhaustion for the first time.

"And what's this," Sam asked, "about the 'look on my face' last night?"

Allison chewed on her lips, cast her eyes downward. "I saw you looking at her at the party," she answered. "I saw that look on your face."

Allison types on her laptop, a present from Mat, since the county prosecutors seized her last computer and seem to be in no hurry to return it.

She always loved the theater best. *A Doll's House*, Ibsen's play, was her favorite. She played the lead, Nora Helmer, the underappreciated mother, the wife to Torvald, in an amateur production one time. She remembers moving about the house in the final scene, when Nora left Torvald, left him devastated and confused, Nora finally empowered and taking control.

Plays are so hard, though, because so much of it is language. Dialogue can be so trying, so difficult to write exactly how people talk. But at least she knows the subjects well.

ALLISON: I don't want Jessica to think I'm innocent.

MAT: Why not?

ALLISON: Because if she thinks I'm innocent, she'll

think that her testimony put me in jail. If she knows I'm guilty, it will be easier for her to accept.

(Mat seems uneasy with this. It is putting a lot on him, forcing him into a difficult conversation about their daughter.)

MAT (sheepishly): What—what should I tell her? How could I possibly convince her that you're guilty of murdering Sam?

ALLISON (pondering): Tell her that I buried the trophy at the base of a fence, near a yellow post, behind the Countryside Grocery Store on Apple and Riordan.

Allison reads it over and frowns. She hits the backspace button on the laptop and watches the cursor gobble up word after word, until this passage is wiped out.

"Needs more work, Ally," she says to herself. She has time.

TUESDAY, MARCH 30

*P*eshawar was like another country. The terrain was not dissimilar but the people were. Other than the Afghan refugees, Ram had met very few people who were not natives in Baluchistan. Peshawar was different, a dusty town on the western border. Dozens of languages spoken on the street, different accents speaking each language. The contrasts were staggering. Exquisite Islamic architecture in one direction, an Afghani refugee camp teeming with women and children, sick and deprived, in the other. Men of all ages moved through the streets with assault rifles slung over their shoulders.

Father had said that he would sell carpets in Peshawar, that commerce was good there, better than in Quetta, and Ram knew that this was owing to the overflow of refugees and freedom fighters, and Americans and British there to help them fight the Soviets. Peshawar, near the Khyber Pass, was the principal gateway for the mujahedin *into*

Afghanistan, and this had made Peshawar an international city in the most notorious sense of that word.

They lived with Father's cousin in a small house. Ram and his father shared a bedroom, slept nestled together every night. Father would always wait for Ram to fall asleep, caressing his hair, singing to him. They clung to each other, Ram believed, out of utter fear of losing the last remnant of their family.

But sometimes Father would leave the bed after he thought his son was asleep. Ram, as he was now called— he would never again be addressed as Zulfikar or Zulfi— would sometimes rise from the bed and listen in on conversations taking place between his father and the men who would come to visit.

They would talk about weapons. They would talk about jihad.

Ram saw changes. There had been enough upheaval already for him, the loss of his mother and sister, the move to a new village, but the single constant in his life, his father, began to change as well. There was something to the look in his eyes, something Ram had never seen previously—a sadness, an anger, a sense of purpose. And soon enough, in less than a year from the time they landed in Peshawar, they moved again, to their own home. Father was doing well in the carpet business, he told Ram; things were better financially than they had ever been before, and they would stay that way. Ram was glad, for his father more than himself. Ram just wanted what he had in Quetta. But there was no turning back, of course. So he did what his father told him to do, did not discuss politics and concentrated on schoolwork, which his mother would have wanted.

It was not until Ram was thirteen, after the Soviets had been repelled from Afghanistan, after the American CIA largely left Peshawar behind along with thousands of armed militants, after the United States reimposed economic and *military sanctions on Pakistan for its development of nuclear technology, that Ram's father finally told him.*

Ram Haroon walks into the foyer of the Wickard Building on campus and removes his gloves and hat. Even the short trip from the dorms to this building, in this weather, requires full gear. He has spent the better part of two years in America's Midwest, and still he remains shocked by the extremes in the climate.

Out of the corner of his eye he sees his contact, sitting in the lounge area in the open foyer, wearing headphones, face buried in a textbook. Haroon readjusts his backpack, and his contact, at the opposite end of the foyer, gets up and leaves through the south entrance of the building. Haroon makes his way into the lounge area and mills around a moment, as if to choose a seat in the rather populated site, then decides to take the seat where his contact was sitting only moments ago.

It is a chair in the corner of the lounge area, really two panels forming an L. Haroon takes off his coat and sits on it, then sets his backpack on the other chair and makes a point of sifting through its contents, while his other hand reaches under the cushion and quickly finds the note. He does not immediately read it, naturally. With one casual maneuver, he drops the note—a piece of stationery folded in half—into the pack.

Haroon kills twenty minutes until his class on socialism in the twentieth century is to begin. As he reads the textbook for the class, he reaches into his bag, removes the note, and drops it into the textbook.

Things are proceeding as planned. The testing is coming along very well. There is a high degree of confidence. Finalization should coincide with final exams.

As for her: Things are as good as could be expected. She is more concerned with protecting family than winning case. No indication whatsoever that she has any idea, regardless. This was probably all about nothing. But the doctor is insisting we keep watch, so we will.

The doctor. Ram Haroon smiles. His contact is keeping the reference vague, but Haroon knows. He can do his homework, too. Doctor Neil Lomas is his name, and he is good. Unsteady, but good. Nervous about nothing, but good. He can be as neurotic and dependent as he wants to be, as long as he delivers the formula.

But all in all, good news here. His contact has gone to great lengths to assure Haroon that things are proceeding appropriately. He expects to hear such things, of course; they want Haroon to feel safe and secure. They want this job to go through as much as Haroon's people do. Yet Haroon realizes that his partners are sharing the risk, in their minds probably taking greater chances than he is. Haroon, after all, is doing this for a cause, something he is willing to place himself in harm's way to achieve. His partners are Americans, doing this for money. A jail cell or notoriety would be far more horrifying to them than to Ram Haroon. So he must assume that these assurances are sincere, that his partners truly believe the coast to be clear. They will hope for the best, which is to say they will hope that Allison Pagone does not know what they fear she knows. They will hope for a trial that proceeds without incident, and then they can move forward with their plan. What they do not realize is that Haroon could never agree to let Allison Pagone live. If she were convicted, she could make a deal at any time, trade information for leniency or even clemency. The only way to guarantee Allison Pagone's silence, he recognizes, is to silence her.

MONDAY, MARCH 29

Allison closes the door in the small, sparsely furnished room in the public library. This is an unexpected place to meet but, in a way, that's the point. This library is about three miles to the south of Allison's home, which makes it a bit closer to Mansbury College, from which Jessica had to travel to meet her.

Allison turns from the door. Jessica is wearing an oversized sweatshirt and jeans, her hair back in a ponytail. Her expression is a combination of concern and antagonism; Jess has never been able to reconcile the two over the last few months. She resents her mother but she loves her, too, and she is desperately concerned about this criminal prosecution.

Allison hasn't seen Jessica for several weeks, so despite the urgency of this meeting, she cannot help but first take measure of her daughter. She is truly a beauty, a natural one, not relying on makeup or an extravagant hairstyle or anorexic dieting. She has a strong, intelligent face, a complexion reflecting her father's Latino heritage and her mother's pale skin, wide dark eyes, a full mouth. Allison has always felt that Jessica could have her selection of guys, though she no longer enjoys that notion.

There's a guy, but you wouldn't approve.

It's someone at work, Mother, okay?

"Is everything okay?" Jessica asks, touching her mother's arm. Oh, that look on her face. Jess is trying to hold everything together, something she has recently found not to be easy at all.

"It's going to be fine, Jess. I'm sorry to be so insistent like this. And I don't have long to talk. We—we probably shouldn't talk very much about this."

They shouldn't talk, Allison means, because Jessica will be a witness at trial. Anything that the two of them say could be discovered by the prosecution.

"You went straight from campus to my house that night," Allison says. "You were studying on campus, then you came home to get away from the noise. You got to my house at eight-thirty. You studied, fell asleep, then I came home sometime before two in the morning."

Jessica frowns. This, almost verbatim, is what she told the police. "Did something happen?" she asks.

"I think it might be better," Allison says, "if you simply testify that you got to my house at eight-thirty. There's no real reason to elaborate on what you were doing before that. It's not relevant."

"It's not relevant," Jessica responds warily, "but you're pulling me out of class in the middle of the day to have me meet you here."

Allison drops her head.

"Did something happen, Mother?"

"Jess." Allison raises a hand, looks her daughter in the eye. "I want you to remember what you told the police. You went into some detail about the fact that you were at the student center studying, then you went back to your dorm room, then you came to my house."

"That's right."

"There's no need to volunteer that information, but have it ready." Allison sighs. "The best thing would be not to talk about it at all. Just to say, 'I got to my mother's house at eight-thirty.' The less said on the subject, the better."

There is a small circular table with two chairs in the room, and Jessica carefully settles into one of them. She tucks a stray hair behind her ear and stares at the table, runs her hand over the surface slowly, as if she were cleaning it with a cloth.

"Talk to Paul Riley about this," Allison pleads. "Whatever he thinks you should do, trust him. You always have the right to invoke the Fifth Amendment, too."

The mention of taking the Fifth, Allison realizes, is explosive, and has the effect she feared. In what passes for only an instant, Jessica is in tears, covering her face with her hands.

Allison rushes to Jessica, folds her into her arms. The intimacy is welcome to Allison, circumstances notwithstanding. She cannot remember the last time she held her daughter.

"This is my fault," she whispers to Jessica. "Nothing is going to happen to you. Nothing is going to happen to me. Nothing is going to happen to your father. Believe that, Jess. Believe it. This is all going to be over soon, and you can get on with your life."

Her daughter sobs uncontrollably, a complete meltdown. Allison did not want this, but this was important enough. The subject had to be raised. She has to be sure.

"This is my fault," she repeats, resting her chin on her daughter's head, caressing her hair. "I won't let anything happen to you or your father."

SUNDAY, MARCH 28

Larry Evans scribbles on his notepad. "And why do you think it was so successful?" he asks. "*April Showers*?"

"Oh." Allison looks over Larry's head at the shoppers in the grocery store. "I think women readers liked a strong female character. A character with warts, bumps, flaws, just like any other person. Yet, April wasn't threatening to men, I don't think. They liked her, too. She was funny. She was feminine. She didn't mind having a door opened for her."

"I liked her. I loved that book." Larry smiles. "By the way, what's your favorite book?" he asks. "Best thing you ever read?"

Allison shrugs, as if there were so many from which to choose. In fact, she has an answer at the ready, but it's not a book. She remembers the character, because Allison herself played the role in college theater. Nora Helmer, wife of Torvald, identified principally in her life as such—the flighty wife, the mother, when in fact it was her strength that held everything together, her courage that saved

Torvald's life, his lack of courage that finally propelled her to leave him. *I have been performing tricks for you, Torvald. That's how I've survived. You wanted it like that.*

The way I am now, I'm no wife for you.

Larry seems to be observing her, probably notes the change in her expression. He makes a point of glancing at his watch. "I don't mean to monopolize your time here with background."

"No, that's fine." Allison waves a hand. "These subjects are far more enjoyable than what most people want to talk about these days."

Larry puts down his pen. "I'll tell you something, Allison, if I may." Larry bites his lip. He has a way about him, a low-key approach. She imagines his rugged looks and easy demeanor play well with the female population.

"You may," she says.

"I think you're innocent."

"Oh." Allison laughs, an outburst closer to dismay than joy.

"No, I mean—I wouldn't say that if I didn't mean it. I just don't see it in you."

Allison smiles. "Larry, we met about—what—six weeks ago? We've spent all of maybe twenty hours together. You don't know me."

"I'm a good judge of people. Plus, I'm no lawyer, but—well." He shrugs his shoulders.

"But what?"

Larry shakes his head. "I was going to say, the evidence looks pretty thin to me. Like it just doesn't say very much. They have evidence that you were there. Your hair, the earring, the broken nail. Sure. And yes, Sam's blood was found on your sweatshirt. But if you and Sam were seeing each other—"

Larry looks at Allison, as if he were a ten-year-old who just cussed in front of his mother.

"I'm not saying you were or you weren't," he quickly qualifies.

Allison, of course, has denied having a romantic relationship with Sam to the police, and she has made no public statement on this subject. The police got it out of Jessica when they questioned her, which puts Allison in a bit of a pinch. Larry Evans, ever the diplomat, has tried to keep away from the sensitive topics in their discussions. He doesn't want to poke the bear.

"This is all I'm saying, Allison. That stuff—the hair and fingernail and earring and blood—just means you were there at some time. It doesn't mean you were there on the night he was murdered."

"His blood just happened to be on my sweatshirt?"

"Oh, it wasn't like a significant blood spatter or anything," Larry says. "So yes. People bleed sometimes. I had a girlfriend once, cut her lip and I ended up with her blood all over my shirt." He shrugs. "I'm just saying. All of these things could happen in a different setting. Not when he was murdered."

"They say I went back to the house at one in the morning the night he was murdered," Allison replies.

"They say a *car* that looks like yours—a Lexus SUV—drove to his house then."

"Who else would be driving my car?"

"Assuming it was your car."

"Yes, assuming it was my car."

"Who else would be driving—" Larry grunts a laugh. "Do I have to spell it out?"

Allison shakes her head in frustration. "I'm the only one with keys to my car, first of all. And they have me barging into Sam's office the day before, shouting at him. And the office aide overheard Sam dumping me. *And*"—she raises a finger—"they have me returning home at two in the morning, with dirt on my face and hands."

"You mean *Jessica* has you returning home at two in the morning with dirt on your face and hands."

Allison draws back. "I'm not enjoying this conversation."

Larry Evans leans forward, his eyes narrow. "You know what I think about this conversation, Allison, if I may say so?"

She waves a hand, still fuming.

"I think you're trying very hard to convince me that you're guilty."

Allison looks away, not ready with a response, but something hot and creepy invades her chest. "Why all this talk about Jessica?" she asks.

Larry equivocates, raising his hands, cocking his head.

"Is this coming from your source in the department?" she demands. This has been Larry Evans's primary chit in their deal, the source in the police department, from whom he would feed Allison nuggets of information.

"They're wondering about the chronology of events that night," Larry admits. "It's standard procedure, from what I'm told. They do a timeline. And they fit their witnesses on that timeline. What can they say about Jessica? She says she was at your house at—what was it—eight?"

"Eight-thirty," Allison whispers.

"Okay, but what about before that? She says she was studying back at Mansbury College, but there's no corroboration for that."

Allison takes Larry's hand. "Tell me everything, every single thing, they're saying about Jessica."

"That's it, Allison. I'm not saying she's a suspect. They're just trying to tie everything up, and Jessica is a big piece. *She's* the one who says you were away from the house on the evening Sam Dillon was murdered, *she's* the one who says you had dirt on your hands and your face, *she's* the one who says you were wearing that sweatshirt with Sam's blood on it, and *she's* the one who says you admitted having an affair with Dillon when you denied that fact to the police. So she matters to them a great deal. It's a circumstantial case, we all know that, and she's the biggest link. So my guy there, he was just saying, when your best witness against a suspect is her daughter, there's going to be some concern."

Allison cringes. "But they're not saying she was a suspect."

"No, *they're* not."

Allison glares at Larry.

"Hey." He raises his hands. "I'm just a reporter. But my job is to look at facts. So I'm supposed to believe that you went to his house, bludgeoned him, an earring fell out, a nail broke, a hair fell out, and you got a little blood on your sweatshirt."

Allison doesn't answer.

"A sweatshirt that says 'Mansbury College,' by the way."

"She gave me the sweatshirt," Allison insists. "It was mine. Just because she's a student at Mansbury, that means no one else could wear a sweatshirt with the school name?"

Larry Evans smiles. His eyes drift from hers. "No," he concedes. "Of course, it could have been your sweatshirt. That doesn't mean the story washes."

"This is ridiculous."

"This *is* ridiculous," Larry agrees. "What is ridiculous is whatever it is you're doing. She's close with her father, you've told me. Her father was in trouble. He was being investigated by the feds. Maybe Sam Dillon knew something. He was a threat to your ex-husband. Which made him a threat to someone who loved your ex-husband." Larry takes a breath. "Look, I don't know your daughter, Allison. But it makes sense. She worked at Sam Dillon's office, right? She was close to all of this."

"Jessica didn't murder Sam," Allison says.

"Oh, okay." Larry falls back in his seat, waves a hand at

her. "*You* did, right? You beat him over the head, accidentally left some evidence behind, and some evidence on you."

"Why is that so hard to believe?"

"Why is that—" Larry Evans messes with his hair, shakes his head absently. "Allison," he says, leaning close now, his hand trembling, "who wears expensive platinum earrings with a sweatshirt?"

Allison jumps out of her chair, spilling the remnants of her cup of coffee, knocking Larry's notepad to the floor. She moves quickly from a walk to a run out of the grocery store.

FRIDAY, MARCH 26

Allison climbs into Mat's Mercedes outside the building that houses the law offices of Ronald McGaffrey. Today is the second time she has met with McGaffrey, after her original lawyer, Paul Riley, dropped out of the case.

"Everything go okay?" he asks.

"Yeah. It was fine. Ron's good. He's not Paul Riley but he's good."

"I've always heard that," Mat agrees.

The sun is setting, casting the commercial district in shadows. Mat maneuvers his vehicle through the heavy rush-hour traffic on the way to the interstate to take Allison home. The windshield is dirty and the water fluid is frozen. The car is filthy from the salt and slush that has splashed up recently. It is that wet, cold season when you'd just rather be inside.

And now she has to drive home with Mat. Mat is one of those drivers who curses at others on the road, has a running commentary on the lane changes, the poor acceleration, the general timidity of other drivers. He is a different person when he gets behind the wheel.

But in fairness, Mat is better about that now, primarily, she assumes, because of everything that's happened. He has treated Allison gingerly since her arrest, more respectfully than ever before. Say what you will about him, he has tried to make this easier for his ex-wife.

"The case is circumstantial," Allison says. "They have plenty of bad stuff but none of it can be tied directly to me. That, more than anything, is our defense."

"But 'more than anything' does not mean everything," Mat says.

She doesn't respond to that. She knows what Mat's thinking, and he's right. Ron McGaffrey immediately focused on the one potential opening. Things were amiss with Sam Dillon. Word trickled out, not long after Allison's arrest, that federal prosecutors were probing a potential bribery scandal in the state legislature. Opponents of House Bill 1551, placing Flanagan-Maxx's product Divalpro on the state's list of prior-approved Medicaid drugs, had cried foul when three senators—Strauss, Almundo, and Blake—suddenly flipped their positions during veto session last November, and the bill quickly made its way to the governor's desk.

Of course it raised red flags. The local paper, the *Daily Watch*, ran articles and editorials critical of the hasty, back-room shenanigans. Opponents of the bill, who had felt completely ambushed by the maneuver, began to take a closer look at the fact that one of the proponents of the bill—a very curious one at that, the Midwestern Alliance for Affordable Health Care—had for the first time in its history hired an independent lobbyist, Mateo Pagone, and had paid Pagone a hundred thousand dollars to help get the bill passed out of only one chamber, the Senate. That, combined with everything else, including the sudden changes of heart of three senators, led to a cry for an investigation.

No one knows when, precisely, the U.S. attorney's office began its probe, but the papers reported that federal prosecutors were presenting evidence to a grand jury as early as this past February, only about six weeks ago.

And in the midst of all this, the man principally responsible for the passage of House Bill 1551, lobbyist Samuel Dillon, was found murdered in his lake home just outside the city.

"Ron isn't going to point at you, Mat." She says it bluntly, to get it over with.

"I was stupid," Mat says, perhaps only to himself. "Really stupid." Mat has a tendency toward self-flagellation when things are rough. He is a tough man but his self-esteem is thin.

"You got away with it." What he did *was* stupid. There is no rationalization, in the end, though Allison has created some. Every politician takes bribes, in some form or another, except they are usually countenanced by the law. No one will ever convince her that a state representative who takes $10,000 in perfectly legal contributions from a company, then supports legislation on that company's behalf, has not been "bribed" in some sense of the word. There is, in some twisted way, at least some element of forthrightness in simply stuffing the money in a legislator's pocket. The only difference, in her mind, is disclosure. Legal contributions go on the books, are reported publicly, but who really cares? Who really pays attention to disclosures from the state board of elections?

Which is not to say that what Mat did was okay. But given the murky land of political contributions, and knowing this flawed man for over two decades in a way probably no one else ever has, Allison can at least give some context to what he did. She believes, in her heart, that no good would come from putting Mat in prison for this crime. She can forgive him this transgression. It is not the bribery of three senators that really bothers her, anyway.

It's the fact that he was too cowardly to do it himself.

THURSDAY, MARCH 25

McCoy reads over the message sent yesterday, Wednesday the twenty-fourth, by Ram Haroon to the web address *pakistudent@interserver.com*. She sees now what she always suspected, that this operation will not be ending as soon as she would like:

> The work is nearing completion. It should be ready within six weeks. However, transfer cannot be made until the legal proceeding is completed, or the matter is terminated in other ways. Target of mid-May, at the latest.

She feels a chill down her spine. Haroon is referring to Allison's trial, the "legal proceeding," which has a trial date in late April. He is saying that they will not be confident enough to make their move until they are sure that Allison Pagone has said nothing, or knows nothing.

Or until the matter is "terminated in other ways," meaning, she assumes, the termination of Allison Pagone.

WEDNESDAY, MARCH 24

I am thirteen," Ram said to his father. "I am old enough to understand whatever it is you are doing."

His father didn't respond at first, looked at his son suspiciously.

"I am a carpet merchant," he insisted.

"You talk about weapons," Ram said, accusingly. "You talk about the Americans. You talk about bombs and jihad and the Liberation—"

"Enough!" his father exclaimed. And so it went for three weeks. Ram hardly spoke to his father. Ram's bitterness was not directed at what he was sure his father was doing, but at the fact that he had been shut out. He still missed his mother and Beni desperately, even several years later, and now he was beginning to feel as if he did not know his father, either.

And that, finally—after Ram explained this very thing to Father—was what led to their conversation.

"I will tell you," Father began. "Because you are right.

You are old enough. But I want you to understand one thing, Zulfi."

Ram recoiled. It was the first time in years that Father had called him by his given name.

"I want you to understand," he said, "that just because I am doing this does not mean that you should as well." And then he carefully placed his hand on Ram's shoulder and sat him down in a chair. When he finished explaining it to Ram hours later, he left him, again, with this same qualification. And then he told him one more thing.

"There are many people who would kill us if they knew," he warned his son.

Ram Haroon types in the web address *pakistudent@-interserver.com* and sends off his message:

> The work is nearing completion. It should be ready within six weeks. However, transfer cannot be made until the legal proceeding is completed, or the matter is terminated in other ways. Target of mid-May, at the latest.

Ram stretches his neck and decides to go for a run in the cool winter air. Is it late winter or early spring? He doesn't even know. He pays little attention to such things. Between schoolwork and this mission, he scarcely has had time to enjoy his stay in the United States. He has found the country to be a nice place to live, on the whole. The people are relatively friendly and generous. Yes, there are those who look at him askance based purely on his racial makeup. But that is the small minority of people. The pace is astonishingly quicker here than back home, with considerably more emphasis on material possessions, but Ram has come to the conclusion that the Americans and his people, generally speaking, are not very different at all. He was surprised to learn this upon arriving in the Midwest two years ago.

His friends overseas do not see the U.S. as he does, just as the Americans do not see his homeland the way he does. To the Americans, he assumes, his people are camel-riding, gun-toting extremists. The problem with the Americans is that they simply don't understand the fundamental concept that people—his people and any others—aren't born to hate. They are bred to hate.

And that is a problem that Ram Haroon simply cannot control. He is just a small part of a greater machine, trying to reconcile competing interests. To some he is evil. To others he is heroic. He will leave the labels to others. He will focus on his task and complete it, like a good soldier. And the only thing he hopes for, after all of this is over, is that he will be alive.

Another thing he cannot control.

TUESDAY, MARCH 23

Roger Ogren greets McCoy when she gets off the elevator at the county building.

"Agent McCoy," he says. "Thanks for coming to me. I could have made the trip."

The trip being a walk of three blocks from the federal building, where McCoy works.

"No problem. And call me Jane." She follows him into his office. The fact that he has an office separates him from several of the prosecutors on the floor, who are gathered in two large rooms she passes, each assigned a chair.

Roger Ogren's office is uncommonly neat. There is a tray for incoming mail that has only two pieces of paper in it, folded neatly. Law books—the local court rules, attorney indices, the criminal statutes—are lined up precisely on a row of low, black metallic shelves on the back wall. *One of that kind*, she thinks to herself. She never trusts someone who cleans up every day. If he says *pardon the mess*, she's leaving. On principle.

Ogren takes his seat behind the desk. Behind him, McCoy sees family photographs that she assumes do not include a wife. Lack of a wedding ring confirms it. It's her instinct. Look at the finger. She has been hit on by more married men than she can count.

She could see him as single. He's overweight, not ridiculously so but enough to add a second chin, a puffiness beneath his eyes, a stomach that covers the front of his belt. She can see it in the way he carries himself, too, not the typical authority she sees in most law-enforcement types. This guy has a chip on his shoulder, a wariness to his eyes, like he's wondering what everyone's thinking about him. This is not a personality trait she would expect from the man who has been handed this highly publicized prosecution.

But there are explanations for that. One of them is seniority. He has the word *lifer* all over him. He has probably never held another job and probably would not care to. So he's up there on the chain, regardless of merit. But she senses another reason, and she knows these types, too. He's a pit bull. Put him on someone and he doesn't let up until they're bloody and lifeless.

"We're aware that you're looking at the Senate," Ogren says. "Aware from the newspapers, that is."

Oh, a rebuke, right out of the gate. The feds have not been sharing, he is saying.

"I assume," he continues, "that this is the reason for your sophisticated eavesdropping device in her house."

McCoy smiles at him, not pleasantly. Roger Ogren has been sworn to silence on this point, yet he raises the subject every chance he gets.

"I've done my homework," Ogren says. "And if I'm right, you can hear absolutely everything that goes on in her house."

"Not quite everything," McCoy answers. "But yes, it's been a good device."

The Infinity transmitter allows the eavesdropper to not only listen in on and record phone conversations; it also serves as a microphone that permits the recording of all room sounds. Ogren has read up on it, apparently, and he's thinking that McCoy must have some solid information from hearing every conversation that Allison Pagone has been having in her house—in person or on the phone.

"We didn't bug her house to learn about your case," she says, not for the first time. "And I can tell you, based on what I've heard, that she doesn't talk about your case in her house. I assume she limits those conversations to her attorney's office. There hasn't been a word about whether she killed Sam Dillon, or anything like that. Really, Roger."

"But you can confirm for me," he tries, "that you're investigating this bribery. This pharmaceutical drug bill."

"I can't confirm anything." She smiles, not warmly. "And you're not supposed to ask."

Surely, Ogren knows there is more to it than that. If this were just about a public corruption scandal, the feds wouldn't be so hush-hush.

"Well." Ogren opens his hands, smiles plaintively. "Sam Dillon was killed just before he was going to testify in Operation Public Trust. Am I wrong about that?"

"No, you're not wrong."

Ogren pauses a beat, blinks his eyes and looks away, makes a face. Finally he leans forward, laces his hands. "Sam Dillon was expressing concern to people in his office. There was a problem. An 'ethical dilemma,' he called it. The obvious thought is that Sam Dillon discovered something, and we're thinking that this 'something' is this bribery thing you're investigating. And if we think that, the defense is going to think that. We need to be ready. So I was hoping that you might give us a look-see at what you have."

"Our operation," McCoy says, "has nothing to do with Dillon's murder."

"I don't think that it does, either. I know my story and I like it. But the defense is going to make hay."

"The defense can't look at what we're doing," she says. "It's sealed information."

"I know that, Agent." *Agent*, he is emphasizing, not lawyer. That is his point here. Don't *you* tell *me* about the law governing grand-jury secrecy.

Ogren hands her a sheet of paper, a printout of the e-mail that was sent from Sam Dillon's computer at one-eighteen in the morning, early on the Sunday following Sam Dillon's murder. "I wonder if you can make sense of this for me," he requests.

"I've heard about it, sure," McCoy says. "Everyone has."

"She must have sent this." The prosecutor points at the document. "We have her returning to Dillon's house around one. She came back and sent that e-mail. Why?"

"To throw off time of death," McCoy says, like it's obvious. "She killed him at seven, but she wants people to think he was alive well after that time. Just in case anyone saw her there at seven."

"That's a big risk to take. That's hard to believe."

"That's what makes it smart." McCoy stares at Ogren a moment, to see if this is registering with him. Apparently not. He doesn't know. She picks up the paper and flaps it. "This doesn't look familiar to you, Roger?"

"Familiar." That stops Ogren. His eyes move to the ceiling, then back at her. "No."

"You guys have her laptop, right?"

"Yes."

"And you've searched it—"

"We've looked at it, sure." Ogren's eyes zero in on her. "Help me out."

"You haven't read it."

"Read *what*?"

"That story she was writing," she says easily. "A new

novel. Something called 'Revenge Is a Dish Best Served Cold' or something like that. There's a part in there about an alibi."

"And it will look familiar to me." He reaches for a pen and paper.

"Very." McCoy opens her hands. "You guys don't check the documents that are deleted from the hard drive? That's the best place to look."

"She deleted it."

"Yeah, hell, yeah. Wouldn't *you* to try to get rid of it? You kill someone and try to manufacture an alibi, something you're taking right out of a novel you're writing? First thing you do is get rid of any trace of that novel. The only problem being, these days, we can find anything."

"Jesus. 'Revenge Is a Dish—'"

"I can't remember exactly. I think the chapter was literally called 'Alibi,' though."

"I don't know how that was missed," he murmurs, his jaw clenching.

"Oh, in fairness, it's buried in there. You'd have to read the entire manuscript. Or maybe your techies haven't gotten to it yet."

Ogren, who has been writing notes, stops suddenly, his head slowly rising to meet her stare. "How do you know about this?" he asks. "You know the contents of her computer?"

"We were at her house, Roger. Remember? When we planted the bug."

"Yeah, but that was without her knowledge. Obviously."

"Obviously."

"You can't conduct a *search* without her knowledge," he says. "At least after the fact."

McCoy shrugs. He has her there, or so he thinks. He is assuming that the federal agents broke the law, because he isn't thinking it through. It's not his area.

"Oh. Oh, shit," he says. "You went in under the Patriot Act."

Under the Patriot Act, the federal government can search certain suspects without their knowledge, even after the fact. This is confirming something Ogren probably already suspected, that this operation involves terrorism on some level.

"Sam Dillon wasn't murdered because of anything related to terrorism," McCoy says with confidence. "I like your story. The jilted lover."

"I have to take your word for that."

"Listen, Roger, if terrorists murdered Sam Dillon, we would be all over you to take a pass on this prosecution, for now. Think about it. We would have been in your office, the day after Dillon's murder, begging you to hold off. Or we would have assumed jurisdiction." She opens her hands. "We're not doing that. The two aren't related. The only reason I ever came to you is because we were afraid you would detect the bug in Allison's home, and word would get out."

That makes sense, and the explanation seems to sit well enough with the county prosecutor. He sees that he doesn't have a choice, in any event. The only thing he could possibly do is drop the charges against Allison, and he won't do that.

"If Allison Pagone is a terrorist of some sort," Ogren says, wincing at how ridiculous it sounds, "I have to know that. She could ambush me at trial."

McCoy shakes her head. "It's not like that. You won't hear her say a thing like that at trial. If she discloses a single witness that makes your hair stand up, let me know. But she won't, Roger. She won't do that."

"She won't," he says, "because she wouldn't be dumb enough to admit to something like that at trial?"

McCoy doesn't answer.

"Or she won't," Ogren continues, "because she doesn't *know*?"

McCoy smiles. A quick study, this one. "She won't, period." She gathers her bag and heads for the door. "You're on the right track with your case," she says. "The rest of this is way out there, totally peripheral. It has nothing to do with your prosecution. Okay?"

Ogren seems to be temporarily placated, but overall, he is still probably feeling very much in the dark.

"Pull that deleted document off her hard drive," she says. "You'll like what you find." She shows herself out. It is a bit troubling to her that she is getting good at this.

MONDAY, MARCH 22

Ron McGaffrey sits in Allison's home, on her burgundy couch in the living room. He just received the files from the case—a case he had undoubtedly read about, a case about which he has probably foamed at the mouth for the chance to defend. So enamored was he with the prospect of being Allison's lawyer, he has paid her a call at her home. He read over the file this past weekend, he has told her, and she listens to him complete his assessment of the case.

"The case is a classic circumstantial prosecution," McGaffrey summarizes. He is leaning back on the couch, an ankle crossed over the other knee, waxing eloquent as lawyers often do.

"You were there, at some point," he says. "You broke a nail. You lost a strand of hair. Lost an earring. You were there. It doesn't mean you were there on the *night he was murdered.*"

But it *does* mean she was there, at some point. She told

the police that she was not romantically involved with Sam Dillon. She has no other explanation for why she would have visited Sam Dillon's home by the lake.

"The blood on your sweatshirt is a bit troubling," McGaffrey concedes. "But it's not consistent with a spatter. It's not very much blood. It could have come at other times, too." He looks at Allison. "A nosebleed, perhaps. Something that just trickled on your sweatshirt."

Allison nods.

"If you had a friendship with Dillon, or some other kind of relationship," McGaffrey says, "that is an explanation for all of this. It doesn't put you at his house on the night of the murder. The last time you saw him was when you went to his office at the state capital."

Allison winces. It is hard not to think about the last time she saw Sam Dillon.

At that moment, she was sure that she loved him. At the moment that he was gone, her feelings for Sam crystallized, moved from an intense passion, from her reawakening of feelings dormant for so many years, to love.

"I love you," she said to him. She reached for him but it seemed inappropriate. Her hand was only inches from his head, from the blood that caked the back of his beaten skull. She wanted him to see her one more time, even if he couldn't see her. She wanted to look into his eyes, but she would not move him. His face was peaceful, defeated, his eyes closed but his mouth open ever so slightly.

She picked up the trophy from the manufacturers' association and placed it in a plastic freezer bag from Sam's kitchen.

"You weren't there," McGaffrey repeats, as if to convince himself. "And then there's the issue of your meeting with Sam at the state capital the day before he died. Friday. They're saying he ended your relationship and you were furious. This is based only on your appearance—you seemed upset—and a few words from Dillon to you that were overheard. This is based on one person's brief overhearing of a part of a conversation that he knew he wasn't supposed to be overhearing. Reliability is a question."

Allison nods, as if she is on board. But the staff aide heard it accurately, more or less.

"This isn't going to work out," Sam said, sitting behind his desk at the capital, a hand on his forehead, looking into Allison's eyes.

"Mat—Mat's a friend. You know this is crazy. It always was."

McGaffrey puts on his reading glasses and looks over some notes on a pad, undoubtedly notes from the transcript of the preliminary hearing, the testimony of the aide who overheard part of their conversation. "'It isn't going to work out. Mat's a friend. This is crazy. You know that.'" McGaffrey looks at Allison. "These are words susceptible to more than one meaning."

"Okay," Allison says. "Good."

"A silver Lexus sport utility vehicle drove to Dillon's house after one in the morning," he continues. "The witness didn't see the plates. I would expect that Lexus sells quite a lot of those in these parts."

"I would think so."

"Who has keys to your car, Allison?"

"Just me."

"Not your ex-husband?"

Allison shakes her head. "I bought it after we separated."

"What about your daughter?"

"No, Ron. Just me. But like you said, there are lots of Lexus SUVs out there."

He nods, but he was hoping for something better. "And that's their case." The lawyer tosses the transcript on the couch. "At least so far. They have no murder weapon. They have no eyewitness. And there's some question about time of death."

"Not in the state's opinion, there isn't."

"No, that's right. They have him getting food delivery at six-twenty or so, and partial digestion suggests he died about forty-five minutes later. Assuming he ate the food when it arrived, that means seven o'clock, more or less. They have the clock used to hit Dillon over the head that broke, that was frozen at 7:06 p.m. And the rate of decomp suggests around seven, too."

"I can say I was home at seven," she says.

"Right. And then there's this whole thing about the trip to Dillon's house at one in the morning. The e-mail sent from his computer. An e-mail sent to you, by the way. That's a wild card."

"What do you mean by that?" she asks.

"Well." He opens his sizable hands. "If Dillon sends an e-mail at one in the morning, it means he's alive. That doesn't square with time of death, six hours earlier. They've got to be wondering about that. If they have you as the suspect, then they figure you went back there, too, and you sent the e-mail. But why? It doesn't make sense. You have an alibi for seven. You were home. Not that anyone can corroborate that."

"No."

"But still. It's not a bad alibi. So why go back? And why send the e-mail to *yourself*? You're putting up a red flag. You're saying, 'Hey, look at me.' If you're smart enough—diabolical enough—to make a premeditated trip back to his house, why leave a calling card?"

She was lucky, she thought, though lucky hardly seemed the word, that Sam did not use a password to protect his screen saver, because she certainly couldn't ask him for the password now. The screen was black with asteroids and stars moving about, probably the standard screen saver— Sam barely had learned how to use his computer, he surely hadn't formatted his own screen saver—but with one push of the computer mouse, the screen returned to his e-mail in-box. She hit the "compose" icon and pulled up a blank mail message. She typed in the words and addressed the message to her own web address, allison@allison-pagone.com:

Need to discuss further. Getting worried. Many would be un-happy with my info. Need advice ASAP.

She sent the e-mail and checked her watch. It was close to twenty after one. Having sat down for even a minute, she felt intense exhaustion sweep over her. But she resisted. Now was no time to get weary. She only had to get back home now—yes, that included having to pass Sam's body downstairs one more time—and she would be safe.

"The problem, of course," McGaffrey says, "is that your daughter was home when you arrived back at your house from wherever you had been."

Allison nods along.

"Mother—what did you do?" Jessica had cried. "What happened?"

"Tell me, Mother. Tell me what happened."

"So some time after seven," her lawyer says, "certainly before eight-thirty, when Jessica arrived, until about two in the morning—let's call it from eight to two, those six hours—the question is where you were. A question for another time," he adds.

He is merely going over everything. He won't spend his first meeting with her interrogating her on details. He'll probably suggest something later. She could have been at a movie, perhaps, or two movies, something that started at eight o'clock that evening and went into the early morning. This thought has already occurred to Allison. You pay for a movie in cash, usually, and then you sit in a dark theater where no one sees you. Two movies, almost back-to-back, could take over five hours. How she had managed to get dirt all over her hands and face, of course, would be another matter altogether.

"All of this is circumstantial," he summarizes. "And the one-in-the-morning e-mail, quite honestly, is weird. I can't think of a rational reason. Neither can they."

"Criminals make mistakes," Allison says. "That's why they get caught."

McGaffrey smiles. He takes her statement as a general proposition, not a specific indictment of Allison herself. "Do you mind my asking, Allison, why the change in lawyers?"

"You're the best," she says quickly. "I have a lot of respect for Paul Riley—"

"Oh, yes."

"—but I think his forte these days is more of the white-collar variety. You're the best at what you do."

Her words could not have been more soothing, Allison is sure, if she had uttered them naked, rubbing his body with lotion on a Hawaiian beach. She has never known a profession that breeds more self-importance and egotism than the practice of law.

Except maybe politics.

"Paul Riley wanted me to cut a deal," she adds. "I'm not cutting a deal. I want a fighter, and that's your reputation."

"You know, I like and respect Paul a great deal," he says, though Allison senses this is the kind of prelude you typically hear before the knife goes in the back. "But I've always felt that people who used to prosecute—they like their adversaries. They sympathize with them. They usually seek compromise."

"And you?" she asks.

"I don't cut deals with prosecutors," he says, his chest heaving a bit. "I don't like them. Oh, don't get me wrong," he adds, leaning forward in his chair. "Personally, they may be the nicest people on the planet. But they are too absolute. Once they make the decision to prosecute, they don't let anything get in their way. Then they overcharge the crime to scare the shit out of people and force them to plead out. They forget that their job is to be fair, to seek justice. They just want to win. They stop looking around, as soon as they decide to indict. They get tunnel vision. Anything that suggests a defendant's innocence, at that point, must be discredited. They're never wrong."

Allison smiles. This is the kind of outrage you want in an attorney, or at least most people would want.

"This case, perfect example," McGaffrey says. "I can see how this happened. They have circumstantial evidence that is decent, but not great. Maybe you're their suspect, maybe not. But then they think you're lying to them about being romantically involved with Sam Dillon. They put circumstantial evidence together with a lie, and they charge you. They give almost no thought to the fact that Sam Dillon has this big federal bribery probe swirling around him."

McGaffrey needs to check his dates. The prosecutors didn't even know about the bribery scandal until after they arrested her.

McGaffrey continues, undeterred. "Sam Dillon, a guy who might have some very incriminating information about this bribery, suddenly turns up dead, but they charge *you* because they can put you at his house at some point and you lied—in their opinion—about being Dillon's girlfriend. I'll tell you what, Allison. We're going to show them a thing or two about due diligence. We're going to turn this bribery thing upside down. Sam Dillon had skeletons, or someone else did and he was going to give them up. That's who killed him. And then they send an e-mail to your address to give the cops a suspect on a silver platter."

"I was framed?" Allison asks.

"Could be. Could be. Who knows? I'm just getting started. Give me a few months and we'll pull this thing apart like a turkey leg at a—"

"No," Allison says. "No, no."

"What's that?" McGaffrey frowns.

"I'm not moving the trial date, Ron. This thing is crushing me. Crushing my family. I want it done."

"Allison, this is—we're talking about six weeks away."

"I know that. And I understand it makes your job tougher. But Ron, this is a deal-breaker."

"I can't try this case in six weeks. I just got this."

"A deal-breaker, Ron. I want you. Everyone says you're the best, and that's what I need. I can afford you. I can afford you and as many associates or partners as you need to get up to speed. I'll give you a retainer today. How is fifty thousand?"

McGaffrey deflates, mulls it over. She can imagine what he's thinking. He has a thriving practice, sure, but he's not the best—he may think so but Allison puts him a step below Paul Riley—and this is a case that will give him national publicity. The change of attorneys, alone, will be news. His picture will be everywhere. Bios about him, profiles in the newspaper. Catching this case will give him instant credibility.

To say nothing of the fact that Allison has put fifty thousand dollars on the table without blinking. Lawyers in private practice relish retainers because they don't have to chase the client to collect the fee. It's already there, in a client trust account. McGaffrey will blow through this number by the time the trial is over; her defense will probably run a couple hundred thousand dollars, if not more.

"That's one condition," she says. "The trial date."

"There are *conditions*." McGaffrey pronounces the word with distaste. "And more than one." He gives her the floor, her condition number two.

"Leave my family out of this," she says. "My ex-husband is one of those lobbyists they're looking at. You start pointing fingers all around the state capital, one of them will land on him. And that's a bad thing."

"That's a bad thing—because he's part of your family."

"That's a bad thing," she answers, "because pointing at him would be pointing at me."

"What are you saying to me, Allison?"

Allison takes a moment. This is a privileged conversation. Nothing that she says to Ron McGaffrey can be repeated, under any circumstances.

She clears her throat.

"The theory goes that a certain 'someone' bribed those senators, and Sam found out, and that certain 'someone' knew that Sam knew, and killed him before he could talk."

"That's the theory, yes."

"What if I were the one who bribed those senators?" she asks.

Her new lawyer frowns.

She smiles sheepishly at him. "The theory in general sounds pretty good, Ron. But let's not get too specific. And let's *definitely* not start accusing my ex-husband."

SUNDAY, MARCH 21

They trained him. They taught him about weapons, about explosives. They taught him English—not the basics, which Ram already knew, but slang and common phraseology. About American culture. About American security procedures in airports and government buildings. How to walk into a room without being noticed, how to extract information from an asset without giving up any of his own.

He was smart, they told him. He was not physically strong, not big, but he was highly intelligent. He would be an undercover operative.

Ram Haroon peeks around the end of the aisle, toward the café in the corner of the grocery store. He sees her there, Allison Pagone, talking to Larry Evans, the man who has asked her for the opportunity to write an account of her murder trial.

He knows plenty about Allison Pagone. He knows she has told Larry Evans things that she hasn't told anyone else. He knows that in Larry Evans's apartment are stacks of notes and research on Allison Pagone and Flanagan-Maxx Pharmaceuticals and members of the Senate and the prescription drug Divalpro.

They are finishing up. Haroon pulls his baseball cap low on his face.

Larry Evans walks out of the grocery store to his car, a low-end import, and drives away. Haroon knows where he is going. He knows where Larry Evans lives, where he parks his car. He knows that the underground garage does not have a security camera.

He also knows a quicker route to Evans's apartment than the one Evans is taking.

The apartment building is on the north side, four stories of brick. A key card is required to activate the small lot beneath, but there is a back entrance that requires only a key.

That won't be a problem. Picking a lock was one of the first things they taught him.

Haroon parks his car on the street—illegally, out of necessity, but this won't take long. He enters through the back and stands in the shadows by a parked truck. The garage is dingy and dark, holds about forty vehicles. This is rental property, not well kept. The garage smells like one, oil and gas and exhaust fumes. He hears the hydraulic door lift a moment later. Larry Evans's car rolls down the ramp and toward Haroon, and he steps back into the shadows.

The car turns into the spot two down from the truck and the engine dies with a small gurgle. Haroon steps out from the shadows. There is a small window on the hydraulic door that, combined with a weak overhead light, provides faint illumination down here. But it's still dark enough, and the lack of the cameras is reassuring, in any event.

Evans emerges from the car, slams the door shut, slings his backpack over his shoulder, and begins a casual walk until Haroon makes himself visible.

"Mr. Evans," Haroon says.

"What—" Evans does a double-take, instinctively drops his backpack and gets his hands free.

Ram Haroon laughs.

Evans looks around him quickly. "What—what are you doing here?" He regards Haroon warily for a moment, then walks up to him, lowers his voice. "What the fuck?"

"I want to talk," Haroon says.

Evans's eyes move to the corners of the garage.

"There are no cameras down here," Haroon says. "I suppose you already know that."

Evans frowns, then lets out a nervous release. "In the car," he says.

Haroon takes the passenger seat. Evans slams the door shut and looks at Haroon, impatient.

"Don't do that again," Evans warns. "You're gonna give me a frickin' heart attack."

"She likes you," Haroon says. "She trusts you. I can see that."

"You were—" Evans leans into him. "You were at the grocery store?"

"I was. Not close enough to hear, of course, but I can see from her expression that she's at ease around you. She believes you are the trusted journalist you claim to be."

Evans shrugs, falling back in his seat. "The fuck did I tell you?"

"You are still confident that Allison Pagone knows nothing?"

"Yeah." He looks at Haroon. "Yeah. This 'ethical dilemma' that Dillon had? At this point, she's assuming it had something to do with that bribery thing. The prescription drug."

"Divalpro," Haroon says.

"Right. She figures that Dillon was on to this bribery thing but didn't want to involve Allison in it. Probably because her ex-husband was in on it. That was his dilemma.

He knew if he turned in Mat Pagone, he'd be hurting Allison."

"So Dillon *wasn't* talking about our operation." Haroon trains a scolding look on Evans. "When he told Ms. Pagone he had an 'ethical dilemma,' he wasn't talking about us."

"Hard to say," Evans says. "Likely, no. But how can we be sure?"

"So Sam Dillon was killed for nothing. Without my authorization, and for nothing."

Larry Evans wets his lips. He does not like the topic.

"I never said I killed Sam Dillon," he says. "I never said that."

No, of course he didn't. He's too smart to reveal such things to Haroon. It's part of his training, no doubt. Haroon's training was no different. Admit nothing unless you have no choice. Co-conspirators can be caught and made to turn on each other. The less known, the better. Yes, there is a trust here, between Haroon and Evans, but it only goes so far. From Evans's perspective, why admit he killed Sam Dillon? Dillon is dead. Whether he knew about their operation or not, he is dead, and now Allison Pagone may know something.

"When is this formula going to be ready?" Haroon asks.

"April, May," Evans says. "We lost some time after Dillon died. The doctor flipped out. But he's back in line now. He's working on it. You understand, he can only develop it when no one's looking. But he's close, he said."

"How hard can it be?" Haroon asks.

"The hard part is the detection. Anyone could taint children's aspirin. The hard part is getting it past the regulators."

"Fine. Well, I promised this formula in April or May. Am I going to be wrong about that?"

Evans raises a hand. "You know, as well as I, that the doctor is worried about Pagone. Her trial. He wants her situation resolved first."

"Her 'situation resolved.'" Haroon chuckles. "I like that."

"She's going to be convicted," Evans continues. "She seems to want it. She's protecting someone. Her ex-husband, I think, or maybe her daughter, or both. I don't really get it. But she's going to let them convict her, Mr. Haroon."

"And she thinks you believe in her innocence."

"Oh, yeah." Evans lightens up. "She thinks I'm a crusader. I'm doing like we said. I'm piling fact upon fact against her ex-husband and her daughter. The more I push, the more she resists. By the time I'm done with her, she'll be *begging* them to convict her."

"Fine." Haroon thinks things over, clears his throat. "This other thing. About Mrs. Pagone's 'situation' being 'resolved.' We are clear that I will handle that. Not you."

"Crystal," Evans says.

Haroon looks at him.

"We're clear, Mr. Haroon."

"All right. Good. It's not time yet. It will be soon. With any luck, we can make the transfer before the trial. Then, by the time anything happens to Mrs. Pagone, you and the doctor will be on a beach somewhere."

"Okay." Evans looks like he has something more to say. Haroon raises his eyebrows.

"Mr. Haroon," he says, "I really don't think Allison Pagone knows anything. I really don't think she needs to die. It's too risky. She's high-profile. And the doctor will have a coronary if someone else dies. He's not in our business. We need him to keep working for us."

Haroon waits out the impassioned plea, then immediately says, "It's my decision. It's my money and my decision."

Evans raises his hands.

"You will let me know when things are looking darkest for her," Haroon says. "That will be when we do it."

SATURDAY, MARCH 20

I killed Sam.

You want to protect me, but you can't.

Pointing at you is pointing at Jessica.

Mat parks his Mercedes in Allison's driveway. It's like old times, a tradition for them. The city is crawling with great weekend breakfast spots, and Allison needed the time out. The place where they went is well within the confines of her conditional bond. It's a place they've been many times, in fact. Mat, true to his nature, stuck with his favorites, in this case an omelet with chorizo and goat cheese. She could make a short list of his favorite foods and would bet her mortgage that Mat would not stray from those few items, regardless of the restaurant. Veal piccata. New York strip, medium-rare with crumbled blue cheese. Cheese ravioli. *Carne asada*. Omelette with chorizo and goat cheese. Or a good old cheeseburger.

"Thanks," she says, and this part is new. Thanking him

for breakfast. It's one of those subtle changes that comes with divorce. Nothing is taken for granted now.

"It was fun," he responds without looking at her. He has that same sensation, she imagines. It's still weird, their relationship since the divorce last year.

"We should go in." Allison looks at Mat. Neither of them is particularly excited.

I killed him. I killed Sam.

We have to protect Jessica. Pointing at you is pointing at her.

Inside, she offers Mat coffee but he declines. He sits on the burgundy couch that is no longer his, although if anything in this house should go to Allison, it is this old piece. Mat never really cared for the couch, anyway. Objectively, Allison wouldn't disagree. A dark purple couch in a room that was otherwise black-and-white. But it was the only piece of furniture from her old house where she grew up, and she would never consider getting rid of it.

"So—what we were saying at brunch." Mat is calling to Allison, who is in the kitchen. "I want you to think hard about this."

Allison comes into the living room and sits across from him in the leather chair. Mat looks at her briefly but his eyes wander. This is not his strong suit here, his attempts to help her. She will have to carry the ball, a phrase he often used.

"You want me to think hard," Allison says, "about my lawyer claiming that you killed Sam? And framed me? And he puts you on the stand, and you refuse to answer? So that you look guilty, not me?"

"Yes," Mat says. "It could be enough."

"The judge wouldn't buy it." Allison shakes her head.

It's worth a shot.

"We should at least consider it," Mat says.

"It would ruin your career."

I don't have a career. Not anymore.

"My career." Mat has already suffered considerably from the allegations surrounding the Divalpro legislation. There are at least three state senators who would never speak to him again, would feel threatened if they did. That kind of thing spreads like cancer in the capital. Mat's career as a lobbyist is effectively over. "Tell me that's not the only reason."

"It's not the only reason."

Mat is silent. He is working this through in his head, trying to keep everything straight.

He is older now in so many ways. He has lost so much in so short a time. He has maintained his composure publicly but she can see it all over him. He has lost his wife's love. He has lost much of his career. And he must know, he must have some sense of self-incrimination for all of this.

I killed Sam.

"I killed Sam, Mat," Allison says. "I suppose you already know that."

Allison rubs her hands together. She is feeling a chill. Mat cannot look at her at all now.

"That's not the point," he says.

"No, here's the point." Allison walks over to the mantel and takes a photograph of Jessica. *"She* is the point, Mat. Jessica."

Mat looks again at the mantel, past the photo of Jessica. Their wedding candle, their unity candle, used to sit here. It is now in a box in the basement. The pictures of Mat are gone, as well, which surely has not escaped his notice. The mantel is now little more than a shrine to their daughter.

"If they start looking at you," Allison says, "they might start looking at Jess, too."

He turns his head to the side, not facing her but acknowledging her. There is no answer to that comment. If they have nothing else, they have the love of their daughter in common.

Mat looks at his watch. "You're going to be late for your little 'meeting.'"

He's talking about her weekly visit with Larry Evans at the grocery store. "Larry's been a help," Allison says. "He believes in me."

"He's really going to write the book?"

Mat is being shut out from her writing career, is the point of all this. He's playing the jealous ex-husband.

"He's a good writer," she says. "He's shown me some stuff. And he has sources. It's been very helpful."

Mat shakes his head. "Fine."

"I need someone on my side," she says. "I need *someone* I can count on."

Mat shoots her a look.

"You can go now, Mat. Thanks for breakfast." Allison walks into the kitchen and places a hand, for balance, on the sink, before she runs the water and splashes it on her face.

I killed Sam. I won't point at you because it would point at Jessica.

Okay.

Allison looks at her watch. Time to meet Larry.

WEDNESDAY, MARCH 17

Paul Riley sits with Allison in a conference room at Paul's office. It's jut the two of them, yet an assistant has brought in pastry and pots of coffee. It has been standard fare at the law firm of Shaker, Riley & Flemming. They make an impressive show for clientele. An oak-finished courtroom stands to the side of the reception on the main floor, for mock trials and training for associates, lest anyone doubt that this is a preeminent trial law firm. And Paul, himself, is very good at what he does.

"I think I know why you want to talk," Allison says.

Paul smiles. He has an incredible ease about him. She can see how he comforts people. No matter how much they may want to deny it, defense attorneys have to play some kind of psychiatric role. Allison, in the few years she worked as a public defender, did not have the same polish.

"I can't try this case, Allison. I can't represent you. I want you to understand." Paul places a hand down on the table, a smooth green marble. "I don't suggest—I understand what you're doing. But I'm an attorney. I can't be a part of it."

He *could* be a part of it, Allison thinks. He doesn't want to be. And that is understandable.

"I want you to think about this, Paul. I can't do this without you."

"I think you're underestimating yourself, Allison." Paul struggles with this a bit. "Look. I realize there is more than one way to look at this. But frankly, I look at this as a fraud on the court. And I don't want to be a part of it. It's that simple."

A fraud on the court. Well, sure, in a general sense. Surely, Paul has represented people who have lied to him. A lot of defenses are lies, themselves, although the difference is that the defense attorney doesn't actually know it, not for certain.

Yes, that is the difference. In this case, Paul Riley knows it's a lie. For certain.

"Any new lawyer I get is going to have the same problem," she notes.

Paul stares at her, traces of amusement supplying his answer.

"Unless I don't tell him," Allison concludes.

Paul shrugs. He is not going to give an answer. He can't advise her to do something unethical, though the ethics, in this instance, are a bit muddy.

"Any new lawyer I get," Allison says, "is going to ask you why you quit."

"Is that what I did?" Paul's look is something between cocky and happy.

Oh. Okay. Allison chuckles. "Paul?" she says. "You're fired."

Paul snaps his fingers. "Darn the luck."

"Then do this for me," she says. "I'd like you to represent my daughter, Jessica. She, obviously, is a witness. She's going to need guidance."

"There could be the issue of a conflict," he says cautiously.

"I waive it, Paul. She will, too."

The waiver of any conflict of interest does not appear to mollify Paul. "Allison, I know things that you don't want Jessica to know. If I'm her lawyer, I'm going to be withholding information from my own client."

"Not relevant information, Paul. You know that. You know that."

"But that doesn't—"

"Listen, just talk to Jessica. Tell her that you're keeping information from her. If she demands that you tell her things, then she can get another lawyer. Just talk to her. I'm only talking about her testimony in my trial. All that matters is that she sticks to what she told the police. I just don't want her falling into a perjury trap."

Paul thinks it over. He shoots a cuff, works on his tie.

"Double your fee," Allison says. "I'll pay anything."

"It's not that, obviously—"

"Just talk to her, Paul. If the arrangement doesn't work to your satisfaction, I won't say another word."

Paul sighs, finally nods. "I'll meet with her," he agrees.

"Thank you. Thank you, Paul. I'll tell her to call you." She gets up and offers a hand. "I understand your position, by the way. I might do the same thing, if I were you."

Paul takes her hand and looks into her eyes. "Allison, promise me one thing," he asks. "Promise me you will be very careful."

SUNDAY, MARCH 14

This isn't going to work out, Sam said, sitting behind his desk at the capital, a hand on his forehead, looking into Allison's eyes.

Mat—Mat's a friend. You know this is crazy. It always was.

Allison stops her run a half-mile from her house. She can't shake Sam from her thoughts. When she goes blank during the runs, he visits her. When she tries to sleep, he comes to her in dreams, leaving her breathless with hope before she awakens and crashes even harder.

She ran nine miles today, give or take. She doesn't time herself or measure the mileage specifically. She doesn't want to be caught in the trap of wanting to run faster or farther. She wants the freedom of just running for its own sake, releasing the nervous energy that threatens to consume her.

She grabs a large water and Sunday paper and sits outside at a small café. She reads quickly through a story on the front page about Flanagan-Maxx. The *Watch* has been trickling information about it for around a week now. House Bill 1551, the controversial Divalpro legislation, which garnered plenty of attention and criticism when it was passed last November, is now the focus of a federal investigation. The news first leaked a few days ago, when the clerks of the state House and Senate confirmed that federal agents had subpoenaed the roll calls on the legislation— the lists of who voted how. Once the reporters sunk their teeth in that, it was obvious what the feds were looking at—the three senators who suddenly changed their votes to "aye," allowing the bill to squeak by and pass to the desk of a supportive governor.

Now, today, the *Watch* is finally beginning to connect the dots. The principal lobbyist behind the bill was Sam Dillon, and another lobbyist pushing the bill was the ex-husband of Allison Pagone, accused of murdering Sam.

So it's out now. Her heartbeat kicks up, as much as she tells herself that she knew this was going to happen, sooner or later. It's going to be tougher now, for Mat and for Jessica.

She looks out at the street, at the cars passing by, the people walking arm-in-arm to brunch. An old man with two schnauzers pretends not to notice when one of his dogs urinates on a parking meter.

Jessica used to beg for a dog, but they never got one. Maybe they should have. Maybe Allison should have been stricter with Jess, should have watched her more closely in high school. Or maybe they should have been more like buddies than mother-daughter. She can't shake the feeling that she should have known that a high school teacher was preying on her daughter. And more recently, she should have known that Jessica was carrying a torch for Sam Dillon, even if nothing came of that but a girlish crush.

"Allison, I'm not sleeping with Jessica," Sam swore to her.

She leafs through the newspaper, scanning the headlines, her mind filled with regret. She wishes, so desperately, that she could turn back time and change what happened.

Her eye catches on a headline in the editorial section. An article by Monica Madley, something of a fire-breathing liberal feminist to most, but Allison enjoys her columns. She assumes that Madley puts on her overly provocative persona for its own sake.

THE "WOMAN SCORNED"?
OLD THEORIES DIE HARD
IN PAGONE MURDER CASE

Oh, I can see it now. County Attorney Elliot Raycroft and his assistants, sitting in a posh office rich with cigar smoke, pondering the theories surrounding the death of Sam Dillon. "Oh, I know!" Raycroft says, snapping his fingers. "I know why Allison Pagone killed Sam Dillon. She was a 'woman scorned.'"

Now, for those of you living in a cave, Allison Pagone is a best-selling novelist indicted last week for the murder of capital big-shot Samuel Dillon. Anyone watching the preliminary hearing last week was treated to the picture of Allison Pagone as a hysterical woman bent on killing a man who had recently rejected her advances. He dumped her, so she killed him.

Or maybe not. Remember last year, when our legislative leaders ramrodded a bill through both chambers in a single day, allowing pharmaceutical giant Flanagan-Maxx to market its blood-pressure drug Divalpro along with the generics? Well, turns out that the architect of that legislation was none other than Sam Dillon, who was assisted in his efforts by none other than Mateo Pagone, who until recently was Allison Pagone's husband.

Maybe the woman isn't so hysterical? It gets better.

Allison rubs her eyes. The point here, obviously, is an attack on typical male perceptions, but in the process Madley is writing an opening statement for the prosecution. Mat bribed some senators, Sam Dillon discovered it and was going to tattle to the feds, and Allison killed him.

Allison held her breath as Sam explained.

"Nothing happened, Allison. Nothing. Okay?"

She listened to him with her mind. But her heart was being ripped apart. Her body had gone cold.

She wanted desperately to believe him. But it didn't erase the feelings. She was threatened by her own daughter?

"I said no, Allison."

Allison sat down in her chair, feeling exhausted for the first time.

"And what's this," Sam asked, "about the 'look on my face' last night?"

Allison chewed on her lips, her eyes down. "I saw you looking at her at the party," she answered.

"You saw—what did you see? I looked at your daughter? I thought she was attractive? Okay, guilty as charged." He opened his hands. "She looks like you."

She shook her head.

"Allison, don't you get it?" he said. He moved to her, knelt down at her knees. "I'm in love with you. How do I begin to convince you of that?"

She was in a fog. She couldn't see him, couldn't see Jessica.

"You begin to convince me of that," she said to Sam, "by firing Jessica."

Allison turns her head away from the newspaper, but

she has nowhere else to go. The picture is becoming clearer now, for the prosecutors and the media, and she has work to do. It's time to snap out of the self-pity and keep her eyes open.

"Now," she heard herself saying.

Sam paused. Allison looked away from him, closed her eyes, and heard him rise, lift the phone.

"Jody, hi, it's Sam," he said. "Is Jessica Pagone there? Great. Put it—put it into my office up there, would you? Tell her to take it in there."

Allison became aware that her face had fallen into her hands, her body was trembling. This was not right. She knew that. But she had just regained something, in these last few months, and she was attributing it to Sam Dillon.

And she would not let it go.

She heard him talking. It was important. Close the door, Jessica. We have to talk. I've made a decision about something.

"Jessica," she heard Sam say, "I've been thinking about things. You and I had a couple of personal conversations at the end of last year. I—no, it's okay," he said, his voice soothing. "I understand. It's not that. It's just that, well—I've been thinking. And under the circumstances, I think it's best that we find you another place to work."

Allison felt the moisture on her hands, felt a shiver run through her body.

"It just makes me uncomfortable, Jessica. I—probably should have done this before. I would never repeat this to anyone. I'll give you a great recommend—"

Allison opened her eyes, looked up at Sam, an elbow on his desk, his slumped posture.

"This isn't going to work," he told Jessica, bringing his hand to his forehead and looking into Allison's eyes. "Mat—Mat's a friend. You know this is crazy. It always was."

A long pause. Allison could hear her daughter's

protesting voice through the phone. Sam said nothing as Jessica spoke, his face locked in a grimace.

No, she felt sure. This was not right. This was not the way to handle this. Yet she did nothing to stop it.

"Jessica, I'm a lobbyist. It's the appearance of impropriety. It's not about being mad at you. I'm not mad at you. I'm—this is just the way it has to be, okay?"

There were more protests, more defensive responses. And then it was over. Sam hung up the phone, looked at her with a wounded expression.

Allison got to her feet and left the office.

Allison's eyes return to Monica Madley's newspaper column, her diatribe against the cliché of the hysterical woman who lashes out at the man who scorns her. Maybe the prosecutors will read this column and come away convinced that they made a mistake and bought into a stereotype.

Or maybe, she fears, they'll decide that they have the right stereotype, but the wrong woman.

FRIDAY, MARCH 5

Jane McCoy opens the file on her desk:

Zulfikar Ali Haroon was born in a small village outside of Quetta, in the Baluchistan province of Pakistan, in 1978. His father, Ghulam Zia Haroon, was a shoemaker. His mother, Jamila Khan Haroon, was an English professor at Baluchistan University.

In March of 1985, an aerial bomb destroyed a wing of Baluchistan University. Among the casualties were Professor Jamila Haroon and her four-year-old daughter, Benazir. The blast was widely accredited to the Soviets, as one of many attacks against Pakistan since that country became the focal point for resistance to the Soviet invasion of Afghanistan.

Less than two months after the deaths of his wife and daughter, Ghulam Haroon was recruited. Ghulam joined the *Hizb-i-Islami,* the most fundamentalist of the Afghan resistance groups that formed the Central Alliance, and the group that received the bulk of CIA arms supplied to the *mujahedin*.

Ghulam Haroon was dispatched to Peshawar to assist in the flow of arms to the *mujahedin*. From the moment that he arrived in Peshawar, he introduced and registered his son as Ramadaran Ali Haroon, changing his first name from Zulfikar. Ghulam Haroon purported to work as a carpet merchant, but his principal work consisted in training and supplying freedom fighters on behalf of *Hizb-i-Islami*.

"Jane, Mr. Benjamin's here," Harrick says. "In the conference room."

They take a stroll down the hall.

"Hello, Mr. Benjamin," she says when she enters the conference room. "Mr. Salters."

Walter Benjamin is the director of governmental affairs, Midwest region, for Flanagan-Maxx Pharmaceuticals. Gerald Salters is his lawyer, an aging veteran of the criminal courts.

"Appreciate you coming back down," she says. "You came in through the underground entrance?"

"Of course," says Gerry Salters.

"Okay. Good." McCoy opens a file folder. Her notes from their last meeting were typed by an office assistant. A wonder, that the typist could comprehend her lousy penmanship. "First, I'd like to go back over what we originally talked about. Then I'd like to cover something new."

"If you have a specific question, my client can certainly answer it," says Salters. "But I don't see why we need to cover old ground."

"Call it a favor," she requests. You always learn at least one new thing when someone tells a story a second time. Which is precisely why defense attorneys don't like to let their clients have more than one conversation with law-enforcement types.

"That's fine," Benjamin says to his lawyer. The

Flanagan-Maxx executive is painfully thin, but not in a way that she would attribute to exercise. He doesn't look fit. He looks ill, actually. But you don't see a lot of happy, healthy faces sitting across from you in this job. Not two years ago, she recalls putting the squeeze on an executive who was borrowing a little here, a little there from some corporate accounts, when suddenly he vomited all over the conference-room table. She ended up with no information from him that day except what he had eaten for breakfast.

Benjamin starts his narrative—hiring Sam Dillon to pass the Divalpro legislation, paying MAAHC to hire Mat, and the sudden switch of three votes in the Senate that allowed it to pass.

"How did Mat Pagone prevail on Senators Strauss, Almundo, and Blake to change their minds? Agent McCoy, I have no personal knowledge of that. You think I have time to micro-manage like that? I've got seven state legislatures I'm dealing with, I've got seven sets of statutory and regulatory compliance issues to deal with. I don't have time to ask those questions."

"Understood," she says, because she believes him.

"But then Sam calls me one day, January of this year. Couple months ago. About two months after veto session. He says he has some concerns about what may have transpired in the Senate. He tells me, he's hearing whispers in the corridors of the capital. He says he heard Senator Blake talking about a trip to Sanibel Island, and he knows Mat took the same trip at the same time. So now, Sam says, he's thinking about those three new votes for our bill. Strauss. Almundo. Blake. He tells me, flat-out, what that concern is." Walter Benjamin shrugs. "We didn't know what to do. Neither of us. We're not sure. We don't have the power to subpoena or immunize people. We can *ask*, but how exactly do you do that? Approach a sitting senator who just voted for your bill and accuse him of being on the take? We have to have a continuing relationship with these people. That's political suicide.

"We asked Mat, did he bribe those senators? He said no. Were we totally convinced? Maybe not. But I didn't know. Sam didn't know. What more, in God's name, are we supposed to do? We have nothing but suspicions."

"Okay, Mr. Benjamin," McCoy prods. "Keep going."

"So Mat comes to Sam, late January of this year. He's panicked. He says federal agents want to talk to him. He says they've seized his bank records. They're looking at money withdrawals Mat made over several months. It looks bad. It smells. Sam says to Mat, come clean. Tell me what happened. And that's when Mat drops it on Sam."

McCoy nods. This is her favorite part, or least favorite, depending on the perspective.

"Mat denies the whole thing, right? But he says it to Sam hypothetically. Mat says to Sam, 'If I were to have done something wrong, the same could be said of you.' He says to Sam, 'If money were handed to Senator Strauss, it wasn't handed to him by me. It would have been handed to him by you, Sam. So we're in this together.'"

Benjamin sighs. "See, Strauss apparently had lunch at the Maritime Club with Sam and Mat, last—I guess it was October."

"Right."

"And that was after they played racquetball at the club. Sam and Strauss. But before that, apparently, Mat saw Sam and handed him a bag. A gym bag. He told Sam it was Strauss's clothes from another time they had played— sweats, in a gym bag that Strauss had left in a locker. Turns out, I guess, that gym bag had some money in it, too. Sam swears he never looked. I'm sure if he had, he would have found some dirty clothes in there. But somewhere in there was, I assume, about a hundred one-hundred-dollar bills. About ten thousand dollars."

"So Sam unknowingly handed the money to Strauss," McCoy says. "In the locker room before racquetball, before all three of them had lunch."

"Exactly," Benjamin says. "And Sam's no dummy. He gets it. Mat Pagone's telling him, if he has any inclination to squeal, Sam will go down with him.

"So Sam meets with me and tells me all about this. We don't know what to do. So he calls you guys, the FBI. You know he called you. He wanted you to subpoena him before the grand jury."

"Understood," McCoy says. "But let's back up. Back to what happened after Sam confronted Mat, and Mat threatened Sam."

Walter Benjamin frowns. McCoy, after hearing all this, wants to focus on conversations between Benjamin and Sam Dillon.

"You're not a target, Mr. Benjamin. You know that. Sam came to see you, you said. Start with that."

"Okay." The executive sighs. "Sam comes to my office and tells me that his worst suspicions have been, more or less, confirmed. Mat Pagone all but admitted to bribing these senators and threatened Sam if he cooperated with the feds. Sam swore to me that he didn't know what was in that bag that he handed to Strauss. And I believed him. I'll go to my grave believing that. Sam's a trusting sort of guy. Yeah, he's political, but—Mat hands him a gym bag and says, 'Strauss left this in the locker room, last time we played,' Sam's going to believe Mat. He's not going to assume there's bribe money in there."

"I believe you, Mr. Benjamin. I do. Sam Dillon was a good guy. What happened next? Next thing you remember, after meeting with Sam?"

McCoy sees Owen Harrick, in her peripheral vision, his pen poised. McCoy asked for Benjamin to repeat the entire story for cover; this is the only part she needs to hear again.

"The next thing I remember?" Benjamin looks at his lawyer. "Like, going home or whatever?"

"Like," she elaborates, "did you speak with anyone about this conversation?"

"Not in any detail, no."

"At all," she insists.

"At—" Benjamin's focus strays to the ceiling. "Well, right. I think I told you this before. The scientist who came to my office. We were going to have lunch together. This was right after Sam left my office."

"Okay. What was his name again?" she asks, another attempt at cover.

"Doctor Neil Lomas," Benjamin says.

"Right. That's right. Okay. Tell me about that again."

"Well, he could probably see the look on my face. He told me I looked upset. We were supposed to have lunch in the cafeteria—we did that once a week. I said I needed some fresh air. We went across the street to this Italian place. Neil—Neil and I—Doctor Neil Lomas," he explains. "He's one of our top researchers. Works in pediatric drugs."

Oh, yes. McCoy knows all about Doctor Neil Lomas, one of the chief pediatric researchers for Flanagan-Maxx Pharmaceuticals.

"We've been pretty close, recently. Neil's wife left him, just like that, about a year ago."

Fourteen months ago, to be exact.

"And he'd gotten into some problems. He'd been—well, I don't know if I—Neil came pretty unwound when his wife left. It was out of the blue. He was a train wreck. So— he'd been having some problems."

Some problems. McCoy would react, visibly, under other circumstances. Yes, Doctor Neil Lomas has been having some problems. Cocaine for starters, a habit that set him back about twenty thousand dollars over the last year. McCoy doesn't know if this was the result, or cause, of his wife's rather hasty departure. Now he gambles, too, and he's not very good at it. Self-destructive habits, both of them, and McCoy has always wondered whether addictive gamblers, deep inside, *want* to lose. Lomas has a second mortgage on his house and tough alimony payments to boot. Yeah, a few problems. He was into a bookie for over fifteen thousand before his debt was purchased by someone with another agenda, and he's not off the cocaine yet.

A drug-addicted, distraught gambler. The perfect scientist to compromise. Buy his debt, supply him cocaine, whisper whatever bullshit into his ear that he needs to hear, and he's yours.

Benjamin, given his audience, doesn't want to mention Lomas's narcotics use or gambling problems, and McCoy won't force the issue. She won't tell Benjamin that she knows the identity of the person who purchased Lomas's gambling debts from the bookie Jimmy, that she knows that this is the same person who is supplying Lomas with cocaine on a daily basis, after work. McCoy wants, in fact, to give the impression that she is entirely unconcerned with Doctor Neil Lomas. But that may be difficult.

"So there was a history of confiding in each other," Benjamin explains. "But I swear to you, I didn't go into detail. I just told Neil there were some problems. That there was some possibility that someone had been doing something they shouldn't, and that there would be a federal investigation."

"And how did Doctor Lomas respond to that?"

"He was concerned. Like a friend should be."

"Be specific, please, Mr. Benjamin. Word-for-word, if you could."

"Word-for—okay. Well, he asked me questions. He wanted to know what *kind* of investigation. He wanted to know what department was being investigated. He asked me who was interested. He wanted to know who had initiated this investigation. He wanted details."

"Word-for-word, Mr. Benjamin."

Benjamin closes his eyes a moment. "God. Okay. I said there might be a problem with something. I said someone outside our company had raised a very disturbing concern. He wanted to know who had raised the concern, he wanted to know what kind of concern. Well, he could pretty much figure out the *who* part."

"He could?"

"Well, he had seen Sam walk out of my office. In fact, out of common courtesy, I had introduced them."

Jesus. McCoy's stomach reels. This is new information, a seemingly innocuous detail from Walter Benjamin's perspective. Benjamin had given Doctor Lomas a name, a name that Doctor Lomas had passed on.

"So," McCoy says, with all the casualness she can muster, "Doctor Lomas knew that it was *Sam Dillon* who had some disturbing information."

"Yeah. I mean, the name 'Sam Dillon' meant nothing to him. I just said, Sam had raised some questions."

"And what did Doctor Lomas ask about that?"

"Well, he wanted to know *what* questions. I said I didn't know."

"You lied?"

"Yes. I said I didn't know, because if I told Neil I *did* know, he'd keep pressing me. You have to understand Neil. You have to understand our relationship. I've been his confidant. The guy he talks to. He needs someone like that. So he would expect the same from me. He would expect me to be open with him. So I lied."

"Tell me, Mr. Benjamin, exactly what you said."

Walter Benjamin pauses. "I said, 'I don't know the details. All I know is that Sam told me something illegal was taking place, and he was going to report it to the U.S. attorney, and he wanted me to know in advance because the feds might be paying us a visit soon.'"

McCoy looks at her partner.

"And I told Neil, that was all I knew. I said I didn't know any details. Sam had just paid me a courtesy call, I told him, so I wouldn't have my pants down when the FBI showed up."

"And this was Tuesday, February third?"

"Umm—right. Yeah. I remember that day mostly because it was the last time Sam and I spoke. It was, what, less than a week before he was mur—"

Benjamin's face goes cold. The room is silent. McCoy tries to avoid his stare but she can't; her eyes involuntarily move to the Flanagan-Maxx executive, staring at her, his mouth open.

"Oh my God," he mumbles.

"Hold up." McCoy waves her hand furiously. "Hold up. I'm only asking about Doctor Lomas because I need to know who you spoke to. That's it, Mr. Benjamin. Don't connect him with Sam Dillon's death. Really. There's no connection there."

There is such a thing as protesting too much, and McCoy wants to dance that fine line. This is what she feared when she brought up the topic, but it was too important not to address. She cannot let Walter Benjamin blame himself for this. She cannot ask him to bear that kind of a burden.

She will bear it herself. The death of Sam Dillon was her fault.

"Who have you spoken to in the company since this investigation began?" she asks.

Walter Benjamin's face is flushed. He is still grappling with the thought he has just had.

"Did I get Sam ki—" His throat closes. He places a hand on his chest, as if struggling for breath. "Did I—"

"No, you most certainly did not. Really, Mr. Benjamin. This had nothing to do with you. Now, could you answer my question?"

"Who—have I spoken to at the company? Well, our CEO. Our chief counsel. That's it."

"Doctor Lomas?"

"No. I haven't spoken to Neil. Should I—what do you want me to do?"

"Don't go out of your way to initiate conversation. What I would like for you to say is, 'There's something going on in my department. I've been instructed not to discuss it.' Just something like that. To anyone who asks, not just Doctor Lomas. I'm sure Mr. Salters here has already given you that advice."

"Okay." He nods. "Okay."

"You've been put on a paid leave, correct?"

"Yes, I have."

"You'll be back soon, Mr. Benjamin. No one thinks you had anything to do with the bribing of those senators, and we'll make that clear when the investigation is over."

Benjamin brings a trembling hand to his face. "That's—very nice to hear."

"But you will comply with what I've asked?"

At this point, Walter Benjamin looks like he just completed a marathon. He would probably agree to stand on his head if she asked. "I will repeat what you said. 'It has something to do with my department. I've been instructed not to discuss it.' I'm not talking to anyone, Agent McCoy. Believe me."

"Thank you, sir. Thanks, Mr. Salters. I think that's all I have for you."

Benjamin and his attorney stand up, the former with some difficulty. He looks at McCoy as she gathers her things.

"Neil?" he asks.

"Doctor Lomas has nothing to do with this," she assures him. "Forget about Neil."

She hopes that he will take her advice. She has thought

enough about Doctor Neil Lomas for every man, woman, and child in this city.

Harrick shows them out, then returns a moment later. McCoy has not left her spot at the table. He places a hand on her shoulder.

"He's been a good boy," Harrick says. He's referring to the wiretap of Walter Benjamin's phone. They are taking no chances.

"Walter Benjamin is a decent enough guy caught up in something ugly." McCoy tries to get out of her chair but stops. She is weary, emotionally and physically exhausted, and this thing has hardly begun.

"I didn't mean to put that bug in his ear," she says. "Now he thinks that what he told Doctor Lomas might have gotten Sam Dillon killed."

"You had no choice, Jane. We had to be thorough."

"You see the look on his face?" She shakes her head. "On the mere suggestion that he might be responsible for what happened to Dillon? I've never seen anyone so tortured."

Harrick takes the seat next to her. "I have," he says. "I've seen it on your face every single day for the last month."

WEDNESDAY, MARCH 3

The firm's party after veto session: Sam was a bit drunk but shy, nevertheless, as he broached the idea of dating me. It felt weird but exciting. Even feeling weird, itself, was exciting. It made me realize how boring my life had become.

Meet for a drink at Roy's: Our first date! Sam had a Jack and coke. I had a glass of wine. We approached it up front, the issue with Mat. Sam brought it up. We lost track of time and missed our dinner reservation. We ended up going to a diner, The Mad Hatter, for a late-night dinner. I wanted to invite him home but didn't.

The lake: The next day, I had done so much talking about jogging, he invited me to his place and we ran around his lake. It was freezing but beautiful. He made me breakfast afterward and really screwed it up. The eggs were runny and the bacon soggy. It was the best breakfast I ever had.

I wanted to sleep with him so badly but I left in the afternoon.

Allison pulls away from the desk and leaves the room. She feels dizzy. She lowers herself to a crouch and takes a moment. "Do you remember that?" she mumbles to him. "Do you remember that moment, after breakfast, and we were all sweaty from the run, and you mentioned the shower? Do you have any idea how much I wanted to get in there with you?"

She feels the pain in her stomach. She needs to eat today, or it will be forty-eight hours without food. She also needs to get back to her original purpose for coming upstairs and working on the computer, not the memories she was composing, and certainly not whispering sweet nothings to a man who is dead.

He is dead. She needs that fact to penetrate her skull.

The problem is, she has no pictures of Sam. Not a single photo. It's probably because they were so covert, initially, not wanting to flaunt a relationship in Mat's face, and photography was a form of documentation. She has nothing to look at but what's in her mind's eye, and that will fade like everything else.

So this is her scrapbook, her reminder of every day they spent together. But now she needs to get back to it. She switches screens, from the memorial she is composing to her dialogue.

MAT: You know what you should do. You should blame me. You should say I killed Sam. Blame the empty chair.

ALLISON: Don't be silly.

MAT: I mean, at trial. Your lawyer should point at me. Put me on the stand. I'll refuse to answer. Take the Fifth.

ALLISON: It would never work, Mat. The judge would never buy it.

MAT: It's worth a shot.

ALLISON: What about your career? Your reputation?

MAT: I don't have a career anymore.

ALLISON (pondering, troubled): We can't do it. Pointing at you would be pointing at Jessica.

Allison arches her back, stretches her arms. This is too forced. Not natural enough. That's what dialogue is all about, right? Writing how people talk.

She goes back to the other screen, but she can't get Sam out of her head.

"There are things you don't know, Allison," Sam had told her. This was—what?—maybe two weeks before he died. Yes. Two weeks. The following week was the phone call. She had pushed him to elaborate. Things had been going so well, and now—now they seemed different.

"It's something I'm going to have to—I guess you could say I'm having an ethical dilemma," he told her, sighing through the phone.

And the next week—a Wednesday, she remembers. The Wednesday before he died. Another phone call, even though Sam was in the city.

"I—I can't explain what's going on, Allison."

"This is that 'ethical dilemma' you were talking about?"

"I really—I can't talk to you about it."

"Something's going on," she said.

"Yes. You're right. And when the time comes, I'll tell you. Not now."

"I'm worried about you," she told him.

"Oh, Jesus." Allison wipes the sweat from her forehead. She can't keep doing this, torturing herself like this. However difficult it may be, she must focus.

TUESDAY, MARCH 2

I promise not to make a habit out of having you come to my house," Allison says to Paul Riley. She stretches, after two hours of preparation for the preliminary hearing this coming Thursday, March 4.

"Not a problem," Paul says. They are in the living room. Allison told Paul that she didn't want to spread out at the kitchen or dining-room tables. She wanted something more comfortable, she told him. For the most part, they just talked, anyway, didn't cover many documents, so the living room worked just fine.

The state will call a forensic pathologist to confirm death by homicide and to fix the time of death near seven p.m. on the night of February seventh of this year. Roger Ogren will call the two detectives who interrogated her and searched her house—the first time, not just recently—to authenticate the physical evidence and to testify that she lied to them about being linked romantically to Sam Dillon. There will be testimony linking the hair follicle, the fingernail, and the single platinum earring to Allison and the blood on her sweatshirt to Sam. The judge will hear about Allison storming into Sam's office in the capital the day before his death.

The state's second search of Allison's home, which took place over this past weekend, was directed at looking for what the prosecutors believe to be the murder weapon, a small gold statuette with a marble base, presented to Sam Dillon by the Midwest Manufacturers' Association only two years ago. An award, authorities have finally figured out, that has been missing from Sam Dillon's mantel since the night of the murder.

It was a sufficiently small item that it could have been hidden anywhere, which meant that the prosecutors had leave to literally take her house apart looking for it.

"They find that trophy," she tells Paul, "and I'm finished."

"Well, then, let's hope they don't." Paul is not looking at her as he says this. It must be difficult to hear a client acknowledge such things. Even someone who has spent his entire adult life in criminal law must find some revulsion in representing people who have done wrong. It is harder to focus on your important role in the system of criminal justice when your client all but tells you that she bludgeoned a man to death.

"Paul," she says, "I've been in your shoes. I want you to know, I don't expect the impossible. At the end of the day, I did what I did. If I can't beat this, it won't be for lack of having a good lawyer."

"I appreciate that, Allison. But obviously, it won't stop me one beat from doing everything I can."

"Oh, I know that. I have no doubt. But doing everything you can is different from being able to sleep at night. I killed him, Paul. I wish I could take it back but I can't. The truth is, I loved him, and I'd do anything to bring him back. But without him"—she takes a breath—"this may sound like an odd thing to say, but life just isn't the same without him. I've had almost a month to think about this. I am more or less resigned to whatever happens. I want to fight this with everything I have, and I will. I don't want to go to prison. It's just—if things go badly, I don't want you losing sleep over this. I don't want you thinking an innocent person is rotting in jail. Because that wouldn't be the case."

"You are something else, Allison Pagone." He closes up his briefcase. "I appreciate you trying to put me at ease, but believe me, I'm a professional. I'll tell you what would keep me from sleeping at night," he adds.

"Not doing the best you can."

"Exactly."

She gets up to see him out. "The judge is going to find probable cause, isn't she?"

Paul nods. "Yes, she is," he says.

MONDAY, MARCH 1

Allison sits in her living room, stirring a cup of tea aimlessly, as the workers go through each of her rooms. There are actually companies that specialize in cleanups of crime scenes. This doesn't qualify, exactly; there is no blood or guts here, but the place has been tossed to the state of being almost unrecognizable since the county sheriff's deputies searched her house Saturday.

Men and women in blue uniforms are restoring everything to where it was, leaving the obvious question of how they would *know* where everything was. She imagines that when they are finished, she will have to improve on their work. But it's still preferable to give them the first shot, picking up everything off the floor and putting things back in drawers.

Okay, to be fair: The cops tried not to obliterate the place when they came through. The sheriff's deputies didn't whip clothes out of drawers but just felt around. A marble statuette hidden in a lingerie drawer could be detected without having to pull out all of her bras. But they pulled the drawers out, moved furniture, pulled up the edges of some of the carpeting, even took a loose floorboard in her hallway and yanked it out. Plus, they didn't wipe their shoes very well when they came in. The place was a mess. At the end of it all, they walked away empty-handed.

What, she's dumb enough to hide that trophy in her house?

She hears two vacuum cleaners shut off, almost in sync, upstairs. There must be ten of them, which makes their work go quickly. It's not yet noon, and the leader—foreman?—approaches her with an invoice. He doesn't look her directly in the face. He knows who she is. It's hard to live in this city right now and not recognize the name *Allison Pagone*.

"All done, ma'am," the man says.

"Please don't call me 'ma'am.' It makes me feel old."

"You don't look old—Ms. Pagone." He smiles at her as he hands her the invoice on a clipboard. "Five hundred even."

"Can I pay with a credit card?"

"Oh—yeah, okay. We prefer checks."

"I prefer credit."

"It's out in my truck."

"I'll go with you. Anything to be out of the house for two minutes."

She goes without a coat and instantly regrets it. She walks up to the white van, with the name AAA-AFTERMATH emblazoned on the side, and smiles to herself. These guys will do anything to be first in the phone book.

"Door's unlocked," he says. She gets into the passenger seat, he takes the driver's side.

Once inside, the man leans in to her. "It's what's called an Infinity transmitter," he says to her. "Very, very high-tech stuff. There's one in your bedroom and one in your living room. Right where you were sitting just now, on that purple couch."

Allison's mother, God rest her soul, would hate to hear that couch described as purple. "What does that mean?" Allison asks, gathering her arms around herself. "What's an Infinity transmitter?"

"Well, for your purposes—think of it two ways. First, anything you say on your phone will be overheard. But it's a dual-purpose—think of it as a microphone, too. They can hear anything you say in the house, pretty much. It can probably cover about three, four hundred feet. So I'd say"—the man raises his chin, purses his lips—"the living room and the kitchen. Anything you say in either of those rooms, and obviously anything you say on the phone in there, will be heard and probably recorded. Then, your bedroom. Anything you say in the bedroom or the master bath, they can hear. I can't give you a guarantee beyond that. The hallways, the foyer, I don't know. But they've got both phones covered. And they've got the main places in your house where they'd expect you to have conversations. You really want to talk in private, go outside, and even then, keep your voice down." The man nods. "These guys know what they're doing."

"So let me make sure I understand this." Allison stares at her house as if it's a prison. "If I talk on either phone, or talk in my living room, or kitchen, or master bedroom— they will hear everything I say."

"Yes. And record it, no doubt. They can listen to it contemporaneously or later, at their convenience."

"Okay," Allison says, a chill coursing through her. "They can't *see* me, though, right?"

"Correct. It's only audio."

"Super."

"The bad news is, you have a serious loss of privacy

here. But the good news is, you know about it. You can work it to your advantage. They're wearing a blindfold, Ms. Pagone. And they can only hear what you *let* them hear."

"Okay." Allison sighs, braces herself for the cold outside. "Only what I let them hear," she repeats.

SATURDAY, FEBRUARY 28

Allison puts on her coat and goes outside, to avoid having to watch them scour her house. The warrant is limited to a search for a gold statuette with a marble base, an award given to Samuel Dillon by the Midwest Manufacturers' Association two years ago.

At least they were specific, she thinks.

They've been in there almost three hours. She sat in the kitchen but finally couldn't bare it. She's second-guessing herself, given the weather today. It's teeth-chatteringly cold outside, single digits. She wishes to God they could have had the decency to conduct this search last week, when the temps were north of freezing. She can see them turning over chair cushions, going through all the cabinets in the kitchen, removing all the china—God, she hopes they don't break anything—even looking through the freezer.

Someone finally got a good look at the empty spot on Sam's mantel and had the sense to ask, *What used to be here?*

She wonders what other surprises lay in store for her. She senses that Roger Ogren is not to be underestimated. He suffered a rather embarrassing loss in a big trial a few years back, a trial in which Paul represented the accused. She assumes Ogren will be especially teed-up to have another shot at one of Paul Riley's clients.

She remembers the trophy—the *award*, Sam called it. The MMA puts more money into lobbyists' coffers than any single contributor. It was an award that said that Sam Dillon was the best at what he does. She remembers reaching for it on the mantel, commenting on it, Sam's nonchalance, but she knew that he was appreciative. Sam didn't advertise his success like others in his business—like Mat, for one. He had more of an aw-shucks demeanor, confident but humble, which Allison assumed played well with politicians. Let them be the center of attention, Sam will stay behind the scenes. Sam had already had his time in the spotlight as a three-term state senator. Now he was making four times as much and working less.

Sam was almost awkward with her at first. Maybe that was because she had been married to a colleague. Maybe. But she sensed a gentle quality in Sam in matters personal, and she liked it. Preferred it. She'll take shy and sincere over smooth any day of the week.

This is when it hurts the most. When things move slowly, when she's not working on her case or worrying about her family. It's just sinking in. It's only now, three weeks after his death, that she is beginning to truly comprehend that she will never see him again.

It's awkward, the whole thing. She only really dated him for two, two-and-a-half months, and it was a covert courtship, at her insistence. She has never met Sam's daughter, Julia, a television producer in Los Angeles. She didn't even attend his funeral.

So she has been forced to mourn in secret. In a perverse way, that almost makes it easier, as if the whole thing never happened because it hasn't been publicly acknowledged. But that's just mind games. The rush of adrenaline is gone. The searing, utter joy as his image played through her mind, the hope that he brought to her life are washed away now as she struggles to hold the pieces together.

If he had just told her. Oh, if he had just said the words in those phone calls.

She could sense it in his voice immediately. Something was different, wrong.

Sam sighed through the phone. "It's something I'm going to have to—I guess you could say I'm having an ethical dilemma." That was all he would say, and she let him keep that distance.

A week passed. Sam had told her he would be down at the capital most of that week and might not even have time to call. It was agony to Allison, not even speaking to this man who had swept into her life; she felt like a schoolgirl with a crush, waiting by the phone just on the chance he might call. She was filled with insecurity, despite Sam's mention of an ethical problem. Sam was distant for the first time in their admittedly short relationship, and it burned inside her.

He called, that Wednesday, the Wednesday before his death, the day before the cocktail party at his firm. Her caller identification told her that he was calling from the city.

"You're in town," she said to him.

"I'm—what?"

"I have caller ID, Sam. You're in the city."

She heard him sigh. She felt her heart drum. Why was he being secretive? Why hide the fact that he was in the city?

Was there someone else? Had this relationship been more one-sided than she had imagined? Had she pushed him too hard, too fast?

"Okay, I'm in town."

It didn't make sense. The legislature was in session. Why wasn't he down there?

"I just wanted to say hi," he said. "I—I can't explain what's going on, Allison."

"This is that 'ethical dilemma' you were talking about?"

"I really—I can't talk to you about it."

"Something's going on," she said.

"Yes. You're right. And when the time comes, I'll tell you. Not now."

"I'm worried about you."

"Listen, I—we can't talk about this now. I just wanted to hear your voice. I'm not up for twenty questions."

It was like a kick to her stomach. She didn't know what to make of this.

"I'll see you tomorrow at the cocktail party?" she asked.

"Yeah. But we can't—y'know—Jessica'll be there. All the staff will be."

"Right." She could hardly protest. It had been her idea, not his, to travel below the radar for the time being.

"I'll be here when you need me," she told him.

THURSDAY, FEBRUARY 26

Roger, it's Jane McCoy."

"Well, Agent McCoy!" Roger Ogren's voice, over the phone, is heavy on the sarcasm. He has a thing for that sing-song voice, like it's endearing or something, and McCoy doesn't have to struggle for reasons why this guy strikes out with the ladies.

"It's Jane, Roger."

"To what do I owe this wonderful surprise?"

McCoy rolls her eyes at Harrick, who smiles.

"I think I know what your murder weapon is," she says.

Through the phone, McCoy hears feet coming off a table. She has gotten his attention. "I'm all ears, Jane."

"I was looking at the crime-scene photos you sent over," she explains. "I see something missing."

"Missing," Ogren repeats. "You've been to Dillon's house."

"Just once." McCoy looks at Harrick. "There was something—"

"Something on the mantel," Ogren interrupts. "There's a dust pattern. Front and center. Something's missing. You know what it is?"

McCoy takes a breath. "About two years ago, Sam Dillon received an award from the Midwest Manufacturers' Association. It's an annual award for representing their interests or whatever. Sam was their lobbyist. It looks like some Academy Award or something—it's a long, gold thing shaped like some old-fashioned machinery. The base is square, and marble."

"That's our murder weapon," he says, an accusatory tone to his voice.

"I don't know if it is or it isn't, Roger, but it's not in the pictures you sent me."

"It's not in our inventory at all." Ogren is leafing through some papers. "It wasn't anywhere in the house. She must have taken it with her."

"Could be."

"Was his name on it?" Ogren asks.

"Don't know. Don't remember. Why?"

"Because if the award didn't say 'Sam Dillon' on it, we might not have noticed it in our search. When we flipped her house. We could have gone right past it."

"You think Pagone has it at her home?" McCoy asks.

"Don't know, but I'm not taking any chances."

"You're going to search her house again."

"Damn straight."

"Roger?" McCoy says, her voice turned up a notch. "Not a word about our bug, right?"

Roger Ogren sighs with disgust. "I'm not going to mess with your device," he promises. "Hell, don't take *my* word for it—you'll be able to listen in the whole time we're there."

McCoy laughs.

"Thanks, Agent McCoy. You've been a real princess."

"It's Jane, Roger." She hangs up the phone and looks at her partner.

Owen Harrick is watching her. "Remind me never to cross you, Jane," he says.

WEDNESDAY, FEBRUARY 25

*T*hey wanted him to go to America. Not Washington, D.C., or New York, the obvious spots, but to a large city in the Midwest. It was Ram Haroon who had suggested this city. One of the biggest in the Midwest, two solid universities in town with international-economics programs, good highway access to other cities, if that was where the mission took him.

The mission. They were vague, as Haroon would expect. If put under interrogation, he would not be able to say anything concrete. He did not know how long he would be in the States, though he suspected that the matter would be completed within two years, the time it would take him to complete his degree.

His first year in the States was uneventful. He enjoyed his classes. Liked most of the people he met. Met a couple of women, one of whom was American. It was not until November, last year, that he was approached.

"There will be an American," they told him. They

showed him a picture, told Ram the man would go by the name of "Larry Evans." They gave Ram no background on Evans. He was working with a scientist at a company called Flanagan-Maxx Pharmaceuticals with its principal headquarters just outside the city. He was working on obtaining a formula for a drug. When the assignment was completed, Larry Evans would hand Ram a piece of paper and maybe a couple of samples of the product. They told Ram nothing more.

But Larry Evans told Ram much more, because he assumed Ram already knew. The drug, Ram learned, would appear to be baby aspirin but would, in fact, contain a deadly ingredient that would ultimately kill—ultimately, not immediately, and that was the point. If children all over Western Europe began falling simultaneously, there would be an outcry. This drug, Larry promised, would kill slowly over months, attacking children's immune systems, while other children were taking it as well.

The drug could be made rather quickly. Anyone could make a poison. What would take time, Evans explained, was masking the product so that the chemical could not be detected by regulatory agencies.

Ram listened to Evans, noted the lack of any emotional reaction as he described the devastation that these drugs would cause. He was clearly not Islamic, and Ram didn't know if Evans was anti-Western at all. This was not about idealism. This was about twenty-five million dollars.

For some reason, Evans wanted to explain the details to Ram. From the outset, he wanted Ram's approval. "This guy, he's one of their top scientists. He's got a problem, though. More than one. He likes cocaine and he likes to gamble. He was into a bookie for over fifteen thousand dollars. Now he's into me for it. I bought the book. I bought this doctor's debt. Now he owes me. And I'm cutting him in on the prize money, too."

"You're sure he can be trusted?" Ram asked.

"I'm sure. He needs me. I'm supplying him cocaine. I give it to him, in moderation. He'll never get caught, because I won't let him. And the pharmaceutical company—he's a top scientist. They have no idea. This guy is testing this stuff, developing this formula, without anyone's knowledge."

"And this is not a matter of conscience for this scientist?"

"He doesn't think we're killing anyone," Evans said, laughing. "He thinks this is for preventive research. It's illegal, yeah, he knows that. He thinks I'm working for a foreign government. But he doesn't think I'm selling it to you." Larry tapped Ram's arm. "I'm telling him what he wants to hear," he said. "He's so caught up in drugs and trying to keep his head above water, he'll believe what I tell him."

"I am not entirely satisfied," Ram said.

"Look—this guy's life got turned upside down. His wife left him, he got in a bad way with drugs. I'm telling him to develop something for me that won't be used to kill anyone—it will be used to save lives—and he'll get a couple million dollars in a foreign bank account when it's over. He can retire, move somewhere, start a new life. This guy's not going anywhere. And you know what he really wants? He wants me to bring him more free cocaine. Every day."

Ram shook his head.

"You think I want to get caught?" Larry Evans asked. "If I get the first inkling that this guy is turning, I'll be out of the country before you are. Believe me."

Class dismissed. The twelve students in his seminar on international human rights rise almost simultaneously. Two of them go to chat with the professor, which Ram Haroon has done as well from time to time, in line with his instructions to be in the middle of the pack in everything he does.

Ram walks out of the classroom and heads upstairs to the school's library. He walks over to a set of carrels reserved for audio recordings. Most of the lectures are recorded now, and many research materials—especially many from foreign sources—are on audio only. Ram walks past the carrels and fakes a cough. He sees Larry Evans, sitting in one of the carrels with headphones on. Ram walks to a water fountain and takes a quick drink, then turns around and walks to the carrel where Larry Evans sat only moments ago.

Evans is gone. Ram pulls the chair out and finds a scribbled note taped under the seat.

Everything looks good. It seems clear that Dillon knew nothing about this. There was something else going on at the company, something not even remotely close to this. It was related to the company bribing state lawmakers to get a prescription-drug bill passed. No one will ever connect it to us. The good doctor has been assured. He is back at work. We are back in business.

I will still keep an eye out. I'll let you know, but the bottom line is, don't worry. If she knows something, I'll find out.

Ram Haroon looks around. There have been unexpected, unwelcome developments. A man named Dillon is dead, a man who might have known. *How* he could have known about this is anyone's guess. It's hard to believe, and Ram does not believe, in his heart, that Sam Dillon knew anything. Which means that Allison Pagone does not, either. But he must be clear with Evans. He will have to insist, at some point, on his terms, that Allison Pagone be eliminated. He must insist that no chances be taken. No more mistakes can be made.

SUNDAY, FEBRUARY 22

Allison has shopped at a different Countryside Grocery Store before, where she and Mat used to live, but this is her first time setting foot in one for years. She likes the anonymity, from the outset, not knowing the butcher and deli clerks, not having to look at the expressions on their faces when she approaches.

No one seems to take notice of her as she plucks granola, a jar of jalapeño-stuffed olives off the shelves.

No one seems to take notice, that is, except for one man. A man in a heavy coat, a flannel shirt, a baseball cap. Not a bad-looking guy, a big frame. He smiles at her and holds up his hands cautiously. She realizes that she is standing alone in this particular aisle with the man.

"I'm not a vulture, Mrs. Pagone," he says, showing her his palms and maintaining a respectful distance. "I'm a journalist but not one of *those* kind. I have a proposition for you, and all I ask—all I ask is that when you're done shopping, you let me buy you a cup of coffee in the café in the corner." He waves his hands. "That's it. I think you'll be very happy you did. And their coffee's surprisingly good."

Allison looks down at her cart. "I *am* done shopping," she says.

"One cup of coffee. I'm going over there now, you can forget you ever met me if you want. But I think you'll be glad you heard me out. I think I can be of some assistance. I *know* I can be."

Allison chews on her lip. The man passes her without another word.

She takes her time, going through another couple of aisles. She peeks at the corner café and sees the man sitting, reading a newspaper, joking with the woman who served him.

She pushes her cart over to the area and parks. "Okay," she says. "Five minutes."

The man pushes a cup of steaming coffee in front of her.

"I know I'm not the first journalist to approach you, Mrs. Pagone."

"You're about the twentieth. I had to change my phone number."

He extends his hand. "My name's Larry Evans," he says.

WEDNESDAY, FEBRUARY 18

Allison leaves Paul Riley's office downtown and takes the elevator to the lobby, then transfers over to the parking elevator and takes it down to the bottom level. When the doors open, she sees Mat Pagone's Mercedes double-parked nearby.

"How are you, Ally?" Mat asks, as Allison jumps into the passenger seat.

She opens her mouth, allowing for the possibility of about three hundred different answers to that question. "Well," she says, "looks like *you're* in the clear."

Mat nods slowly. "I'm not sure how I feel about this."

"Oh." She laughs quietly. "Well, it doesn't really matter how you feel about it. Maybe you should have thought about how you 'felt about it' before you paid off those senators. And made Sam an unwilling participant."

Mat blinks his eyes in surprise, wets his lips. Never, she assumes, has he had the facts put to him so harshly.

"It's done," she says. "No one can lay a finger on you now."

"I—" Mat touches his forehead. "Thank you doesn't seem enough."

She is being hard on him, she can see. This is how you hurt a man like Mateo Pagone. He is, in many ways, utterly broken now. But that seems to drive Allison away from sympathy. Because Mat Pagone is the luckiest man in the world right now.

"I'll need your help, of course," she says. "You think you can handle that?"

Mat turns to her. "Allison," he says softly, "you really think so little of me?"

She pauses a moment, looks at him, then leaves the car.

TUESDAY, FEBRUARY 17

don't approve." Paul Riley paces the conference room near his office. "I'd advise you not to go this way, Allison. This is insane. It's not too late to change your mind."

"I'm not changing my mind."

Paul sighs, runs a hand over his mouth.

"I have no choice," she adds.

"Plead it out, Allison. Let me call Ogren. Let's get in a room and hammer this out."

"No. For the reason you said, Paul."

"I know what I said. But you're playing a serious game here. With grownups. Allison." He opens his hands. "Motion to reconsider."

Allison stands and stretches. It's nice to be free again, however free that may be.

"I'm going to do it," she says.

"Against my advice."

"Against your advice." Allison walks over and touches Paul's arm. "I can make this work," she assures him.

MONDAY, FEBRUARY 16

The gate opens, and Allison walks out of the detention center. Paul Riley is waiting for her, leaning against his car, his arms crossed.

Allison breathes in the fresh air, however cold it may be. A weekend in a holding cell does wonders for appreciation.

"They agreed?" she asks, referring to the prosecution.

"They agreed," he says. "One million dollars bond, and you can't go outside a five-mile radius of your house."

"I can live with that." She walks around to Paul's side of the car. "Mat put it up?"

"Mat put it up." Her ex-husband put up a hundred thousand dollars in bond, one-tenth of the million, as the law requires. He knows she's good for it. And she's not going to flee, regardless.

They drive in silence. With Paul's blessing, not his approval, Allison rolls down the window and lets the frigid air lick her face. The sun is setting, coloring the clouds a pale orange. The city isn't known for its sunsets, but she finds it beautiful. One weekend is all she needs to know that she does not want to do even harder time in a maximum-security prison.

Allison is beyond exhaustion. She hardly slept the entire weekend, any momentary drifts into unconsciousness clouded by the image of Sam lying still and bludgeoned on the floor of his living room.

In the relative solitude of Paul's car, Allison closes her eyes and thinks of Sam. The smell of his hair, the touch of his lips, the warmth of his smile. It is all so staggering. She does not look forward to what will come next because she will have, for the first time since his murder, the chance to mourn, and that will be harder than everything else she must do.

They drive to an underground garage, where Paul gives his name to an attendant and shows his driver's license. They head down the ramp, park, and take the elevators up. When the doors open, they are met by a young man, who escorts them down a long hallway.

The office door is closed. As the young man reaches for the knob, Paul whispers into Allison's ear. "Remember, I do the talking."

When they walk in, a man and a woman, seated on a couch, get to their feet.

"Hello, Agent McCoy," Allison says. "Agent Harrick."

"It's Jane. Nice being out?" McCoy asks.

"Very. Thank you." She looks at Paul. She has already violated his command. She is sure that he isn't surprised by this.

Harrick moves the two chairs by the desk so they face the couch. It looks like a talk show in the office.

"We have a deal?" McCoy asks.

"We haven't seen the final documents," Paul says.

"You have. We'll have the signatures tomorrow."

"It seems like my client is taking all the risks," Paul says. "And getting very little in return."

McCoy recoils. "'Very little in return'? I think absolute, complete immunity for her ex-husband is quite a lot, Counselor."

"More than just immunity," Allison says. "He doesn't even have to talk to you about it."

"That's right, Mrs. Pagone, which means, in effect, that we can't investigate this bribery at all." McCoy frowns. "We're not exactly happy about that. There are three state senators who are going to walk away from this. Your husband—your ex-husband—doled out thirty grand to them, and they're going to walk."

"You can still go after them in other ways."

"With what?" McCoy asks. "Sam Dillon is dead, Mrs. Pagone. And your husband doesn't have to so much as smile at us. The senators aren't dumb enough to talk. We can't prove anything."

"Then leak your investigation," Allison suggests. "Name them. Give someone some ammo to run against them. That'll hurt them more than a jail term."

"It's not our problem, obviously," Paul says, trying to re-assert himself.

"So"—McCoy opens her hands—"we have a deal?"

"We'll give you an affirmative response after everything's signed," Paul says. "The agreement, the affidavits, everything."

"That will be tomorrow," McCoy promises. "This is warp-speed for Washington."

Paul laughs.

"We have a deal," Allison says.

A look of relief washes over Jane McCoy's face. She puts her hand out to her partner, who hands her a photograph. "Have you ever seen this man?"

Allison looks at the picture. "No," she says.

"You will soon, I'd expect. He will introduce himself to you."

"This is Larry Evans, I assume?" Allison asks.

"Yes." McCoy smiles. "That's the name he'll use, I expect."

"And what is Larry Evans going to do?" Paul asks.

McCoy shrugs. "He's not going to hurt you," she says to Allison, anticipating the obvious concern. "He's going to watch you. He might try to strike up a friendship. We're not sure, exactly. We assume he'll approach you but we don't know how. The point is—"

"The point is," Paul says, "you can't guarantee that he won't try to hurt her."

"No, I can't. I can't guarantee that." McCoy stops on that point. *She's being straightforward, at least,* Allison thinks to herself. "But this much I can say to you: He has no reason to hurt you. You're a celebrity now. It would be a big deal. He'd have to be desperate to do that. And you can put him at ease about that. You can make him feel safe."

"How does she do that?" Paul asks. "Make him feel safe?"

"She—" McCoy turns from Paul to Allison. "Mrs. Pagone, let him know that the only thing you know about is the bribery. That's what the 'ethical dilemma' was. That's what Sam was talking about to you on the phone. Or this thing about Sam dumping you, which the cops seem to be buying. Whichever. It could be either of those, as long as it's not the thing *he's* worried about."

*S*he remembers her conversations with Sam, remembers the quiver in his voice immediately. Something was different, wrong.

Sam sighed through the phone. "It's something I'm going to have to—I guess you could say I'm having an eth-ical dilemma."

And the next call, a week later, the Wednesday before his death, the day before the cocktail party his firm threw. Her caller identification told her that he was calling from the city.

"I—I can't explain what's going on, Allison."

"This is that 'ethical dilemma' you were talking about?" she asked.

"I really—I can't talk to you about it."

"Something's going on," she said.

"Yes. You're right. And when the time comes, I'll tell you. Not now."

"I'm worried about you," she told him.

What *is* the thing Larry Evans is worried about?" Allison asks. "What is this all about? What was the 'ethical dilemma' Sam was talking about?"

"I don't think Sam Dillon knew anything," McCoy answers. "I don't see how he *could* have known. I think Sam Dillon was talking about the bribes."

Allison doesn't comment, but she agrees with that assessment.

"Okay," Allison says, "but what is Larry Evans worried about? What was he afraid that Sam knew about?"

"That, I can't tell you, Mrs. Pagone. And if you think about it, it's in your best interest that you not know. It removes any possibility that you could slip up."

Allison has to concede the logic. It's something big, she knows that much—big enough that the federal government will guarantee immunity for Mat Pagone if she helps them. Whatever it is, it can't be what Sam was referring to over the phone. If a crime of that proportion—whatever it is— were going on, it wouldn't cause Sam any 'dilemma' whatsoever. He would report it. Sam was talking about the bribes, about his unconfirmed suspicions about Mat and his prize client, Flanagan-Maxx. Now, *that* would be an ethical dilemma.

But Larry Evans didn't know about bribes or House Bill 1551 or the prescription drug Divalpro. All he knew was that, some way, somehow, Sam Dillon appeared to have some damaging information that threatened Evans.

This thing must be a high priority, to receive this kind of treatment from the feds. *National security*, she assumes with a shudder. The kind of thing where the government would be willing to bend all sorts of rules to get a job accomplished. Neither she nor Paul has ever heard of the federal government promising not to prosecute, or even interrogate, a suspect in exchange for someone else—in this case, his ex-wife—doing something for them in an unrelated case. Nor is it technically enforceable, as a legal matter, but the feds would have a hard time going forward against Mateo Pagone when the attorney general of the United States and the local U.S. attorney have signed letters agreeing to this plan.

"Mrs. Pagone," McCoy says again, "if it helps you to know this, I don't think Sam knew anything about what's going on. It wouldn't fit."

"It has something to do with Flanagan-Maxx," Allison guesses. "Sam was worried about this information he had just discovered about bribery. That's what the 'ethical dilemma' was."

"We think so, yes—"

"But they were taping his conversations. They thought maybe he was talking about this other thing, this crime you're investigating. They thought the 'ethical dilemma' referred to whatever this is, when really he was talking about bribery."

"Yes. Exactly," McCoy says. "Someone—someone—" McCoy freezes. She seems to be pondering what she can reveal. "Listen, Mrs. Pagone, we are confident that what you just said is correct. Sam was seen with people at Flanagan-Maxx at a time when other people were doing things they shouldn't be doing. Okay? And they got nervous, bugged Sam's phone, and they heard him talking to you about an 'ethical dilemma' and going to the U.S. attorney. Which made them even more nervous."

"And so Larry Evans killed Sam," Allison says, "just in case he did know. Before he could talk to the feds."

McCoy sighs. She will let the empty air fill her response.

Say it, Allison silently pleads. *Say that Larry Evans killed Sam.*

But McCoy just stares at Allison.

"So," Allison says, "you want me to lead this guy—Larry Evans—to believe that this is all related to the bribery scandal? You want me to make him think that the 'ethical dilemma' was that Sam had found out about the bribes."

"Yes," says McCoy. "Which we think is true. But what's true is beside the point. What matters is what this guy Larry Evans believes."

Allison nods. "And he needs to believe that I know nothing about his crime. Which happens to be true."

"Make sure he believes that." McCoy frames her hands. "If you start talking about bribery, or Sam breaking up with you—well, Larry Evans will be very relieved to hear either one of those scenarios. I don't think Sam Dillon knew what Evans was involved in. I don't think Evans thinks he did, either. He's inclined to believe that you know nothing. He's just not sure, and the people he's working with aren't sure, either. So, *make* him sure. If he believes you know nothing, he'll have no reason to hurt you. My guess is, he'll just wait around, making sure, until this is all over. Until he gets what he wants. And then you'll never see him again."

Allison sighs. "Maybe I can satisfy him up front, and he'll just go away."

"That would be great," says Harrick. "But I wouldn't expect it. You've made some people nervous, Mrs. Pagone. And we understand that they're insistent that you be watched, just to be sure. No, I think Larry Evans will stick around until this thing is over."

"When the topic of Mat or Jessica is raised," McCoy adds, "be very defensive. Be protective. I suppose, Mrs. Pagone, that that will not be very difficult for you."

Allison glares at McCoy.

"And you will swear," Allison says, "that Larry Evans is the one who killed Sam."

"Yes. We will swear to that. You saw our affidavits. Your daughter's in the clear, Mrs. Pagone. And so are you."

"My daughter didn't kill Sam."

"And our affidavits agree with you," McCoy says, which is not the same thing as agreeing with Allison's statement.

Allison looks at her lawyer, Paul Riley. Paul does not seem satisfied, and she can sympathize, from his perspective. He is representing Allison, not the rest of her family. Worrying about the fate of Mat or Jessica Pagone is not in his job description. But it *is* in the job description of a mother and ex-wife. The FBI clearly understands that. Allison is not getting much for herself in this deal. Yes, the affidavits from several agents of the FBI, identifying Larry Evans as the killer of Sam Dillon, will clear Allison as well as Jessica. But they also have figured, correctly so, that Allison could beat this charge if she were so inclined. There are two people at whom Allison could point to establish reasonable doubt. They just happen to be Mat and Jessica.

"My problem here," Paul says, "is there's little guarantee of safety for my client. You can't predict what this man, Larry Evans, will do. You can tell us he *probably* wouldn't want to kill Allison. You can give us odds. Odds aren't a guarantee. This guy Evans will never be sure about Allison."

"What do you want us to say, Counselor?" McCoy asks. "I acknowledge that your client is taking a risk here. She's doing it for her country. And," she adds, "to keep her family out of jail."

Paul shakes his head.

"Look," McCoy says to Allison. "You studied to be an actress, right?"

"I was a theater major, yes," Allison confirms with embarrassment.

"So—this is the role of a lifetime."

It is, Allison realizes, a role that she has played before. *Nora Helmer*, she thinks to herself, a prisoner in her own home, underappreciated even after she saves her husband. A role that, in many ways, Allison has played her entire married life.

"Be protective of Mat and Jessica," McCoy advises. "If anyone brings either of them up, mentions their potential involvement—whether it's this guy Evans, or Mat, or Mr. Riley here—be defensive. Insist on their innocence. Say you'll 'never let anything happen to them.' Stuff like that. Just be sure you say it in the parts of the home where Larry Evans can hear you."

"And you're sure he'll be listening?" Allison asks.

"As sure as I'm sitting here," McCoy says. "Your place is bugged, Mrs. Pagone. We'll confirm that for you."

"How are you going to confirm it? You can't very well waltz in."

McCoy looks at her partner. Allison senses that Harrick has a thing for McCoy.

"Did you clean up your house after they searched it?" McCoy asks.

"Of course I did. Right away."

"Okay. Here's what we'll do. I've been talking to the county prosecutors. I'll give them a reason to want to search your house again."

"What reason?"

"I'll mention the statuette," McCoy says. "The murder weapon. I'll tell them it was on Sam's mantel, which is true, and now it's missing, which is also true. They'll want to do another search. They'll take your place apart and you'll need it cleaned up afterward. This time, you'll call one of those companies that specializes in that sort of thing. I'll give a name and number to Mr. Riley here, and a specific time for you to call, and it will be our guys who take that call and do the cleanup. FBI technicians. They know what they're doing. They'll confirm it. And they'll tell you where, in the house, he can hear you best."

"Sounds like you already know," Paul Riley says.

McCoy shrugs. "I would imagine it's the area around your telephones. Where are your phones?"

"One in my bedroom," Allison says, "and one in my living room."

"Okay. He'll have your phones tapped and he'll have the ability to hear around there as well. So if you want him to hear something, sit in the living room. Or the bedroom."

"Will the FBI be eavesdropping, too?" Paul asks.

McCoy shakes her head. "We can't bug Allison's home. We can't run the risk that Evans would detect it. He's good, this guy. He has top-of-the-line industrial espionage equipment. We put something inside her house, we can't be sure he won't know about it. That would blow everything. So no, we just have to rely on our other surveillance."

"And if they become the wiser?" Paul asks.

"They won't." McCoy deflects her eyes.

"You mean you *hope* they won't."

"That's what I mean, yes." McCoy opens her hands. "I'll say it for the tenth time. She's taking a risk. We're grateful. You'll probably know what this is about someday, and you'll be a hero, Mrs. Pagone."

"Until then," she says, "I'm a black sheep."

"Mrs. Pagone," Owen Harrick chimes in, "you're only a black sheep because you wanted to be. We'd be more than happy to put this bribery scandal front and center. We'd be more than happy to feed all kinds of information on Operation Public Trust to the county attorney. Roger Ogren would definitely take that bait, because it's an obvious motive. He might even drop the charges against you, eventually."

"No—"

"He charged you because you fell into his lap, Mrs. Pagone. And you fell into his lap because you *wanted* to."

"We could tell him about your daughter, too," McCoy adds, squeezing the pressure point. "We're doing what you want us to do here."

"No, you're right, I understand that," Allison says. "I don't want you mentioning this to the county attorney. Nothing about Mat, nothing about Jessica. That's"—she looks at Paul, then at McCoy—"that's part of this deal, I thought."

"It is," McCoy assures her. "We won't say a word about Jessica. I'll handle those conversations personally with Roger Ogren. We'll keep the AUSAs off of your ex-husband, too. That won't be fun, but we'll do it."

That won't be fun. What McCoy means, Allison assumes, is that this thing is so top-secret that even other federal prosecutors are being kept in the dark.

A chill creeps up her spine.

"Right. Okay." Allison takes a deep breath. "That's what I want. I'll do what you ask. I'll—I'll work with this man. Larry Evans. I'll put him at ease. But the federal government doesn't go near Mat or Jess. And if something—*happens* to me, the deal still holds."

"Of course," says McCoy. "That's in there, too."

"We can't guarantee that Roger Ogren won't approach Mat on his own," Harrick says to Paul. "There's going to be a leak or two to the papers—we agreed on that. The bribery thing is going to come out, in small amounts. Just so we're clear on all of that."

Allison nods. It was a negotiation, over the last several days. Of paramount importance to the federal government, apparently, is that Larry Evans accomplish whatever his

plan is. And that means Larry Evans has to feel comfortable
about Allison. The feds wanted to splash the bribery scandal everywhere; Allison, for Mat's sake, wanted just the
opposite. They reached a middle ground. The story would
leak, a little, to the papers. But there would be no hard evidence turned over to the county attorney prosecuting
Allison's case. No names of specific senators. No phone
records. And Special Agent Jane McCoy gave her word
that she would block Roger Ogren if he got too close.

Roger Ogren probably will approach Mat at some point.
But Mat will do fine on an alibi. And he can refuse to answer questions about House Bill 1551 under the Fifth
Amendment. He can dummy up just like everyone else
around him will do.

"Roger Ogren's going to stick with his theory," McCoy
predicts. "You were a wounded ex-lover looking for revenge. It's not a bad story, you certainly made sure that he
has evidence to support it, and—look—this guy's going to
have a tight trial date. He can't start chasing new theories
when he's short on time. Plus, I'm going to be telling
Ogren, every other day, that the bribery scandal has nothing to do with Sam's death."

"We're clear on the trial date, right?" Harrick asks.
"You'll demand a speedy trial?"

"Yes," she says.

"That will put the trial in May, probably," Paul Riley says.

"That would be perfect," McCoy says. "The timing
would be good."

So whatever it is the FBI is worried about, Allison assumes, *it should be over by May or so.* This was a matter
on which McCoy has been adamant, a quick trial date.

"We can talk to Mat a little more easily than you can,"
McCoy says. "We'll let him know what he's to do. You can
help him, too, Mrs. Pagone, but just be careful about talking to him."

Allison understands. Mat will not have too much difficulty. His job is not very complicated. More than anything, he will simply be a foil, a sounding board in Allison's house, prompting Allison on certain subjects for the benefit of Larry Evans. He will offer to confess, will talk about how dumb he was to bribe state officials, things like that. Allison will rise to his defense, helping to convince Evans that this murder was connected to the bribery scandal, when Allison knows very well that it was not.

"I'll write some things out for him," she says. "Dialogue is what I do."

"Fine." McCoy looks at her partner for confirmation. "Yeah, you can write some stuff out for him, if you like. As long as it doesn't sound like it's being read over the mike. I mean, Mat's a lobbyist and a lawyer, I assume he can pull this off."

"He can pull it off," she assures them.

"But listen, Mrs. Pagone. If you want to type up some dialogue, fine, but you can only hand it to him. No e-mail, no regular mail. Only hand-to-hand exchanges."

Allison nods. "Mat's going to pick me up from the law firm when I go down, and drive me home at night. We might have brunch on weekends, things like that. I'll have plenty of chances to invite him in."

"Mat's car won't be miked up, will it?" Paul asks.

"No." Owen Harrick shakes his head. "We'll be watching his house. And we'll have someone at his parking garage downtown. No one's getting to his car. Consider it safe."

McCoy raises her eyebrows, lifts her hand tentatively off her knees. "I think that's it. I think this is the last time we're going to speak together, Mrs. Pagone, until we're in motion. We'll get the papers to you through Mr. Riley here. We'll talk to you through Mr. Riley or Mat. You talk to Paul in his office, or to Mat in his car. Otherwise, assume someone is listening."

"What about my daughter?"

"Your daughter can't know about this at all," McCoy says, simply.

Allison could not agree more. This is dangerous enough. "My daughter's not in danger, though? Right?"

"I—I can't imagine why, Mrs. Pagone. If you're under the spotlight, then so is your family. Anything that happens to you or your family right now would be national news. Listen. Let me make this clear to you, okay?"

Allison sits back. She wants, needs, this reassurance.

"If I'm Larry Evans right now, I'm thinking, odds are you don't know anything. I just need to keep an eye on you. Any violent act against your daughter or Mat, or you, will only make things worse. Evan is hoping that this is going to play out as a non-issue, and you're going to help him believe that."

"He's not going to touch your daughter," Harrick says. "He has no reason to. This guy is calculating. He won't take a risk that isn't worth taking."

"*Allison* is a risk, at the end of the day." Paul Riley puts an arm over Allison's chair. "She's a risk, and if this man can find a convenient way to kill her, he's going to take it. This guy is a pro, you already said. He can find a way to make it look believable."

McCoy grimaces. Allison knows what she's thinking. She can't deny the possibility.

"I'll do it," Allison says. "We'll be ready." She looks at Paul. "I'll do it."

M cCoy collapses into a chair in Harrick's office. "You look like shit, Jane."

"I feel like it. You see Allison?"

"Yeah. That lady's torn up," Harrick agrees. "I think she loved Dillon."

"She's so motivated right now—she's got the adrenaline

pumping. She's trying to keep her family protected. She hasn't had a chance to feel pain yet."

"She's smart," Harrick says. "She spends almost her whole time talking about Mat and his immunity—"

"When what she's really worried about," McCoy finishes, "is Jessica." She points to the file containing the agreement. "This is all about those affidavits naming Larry Evans as the killer. This is all about keeping Jessica away from a murder charge."

"Right." Harrick puts his hands on his knees. "Shiels is going to want us."

"I know, I know." McCoy brings a hand to her face.

"For the hundredth time, Jane," Harrick tells her. "It wasn't your fault."

"Okay." McCoy pushes herself out of her chair. "Allison Pagone can't die," she says, as Harrick steers her down the hallway. "Even if everything else goes as planned, if I let another civilian die, I—it can't happen."

"She won't die," Harrick promises.

"You think she's up for this, Owen?" McCoy hates this feeling of vulnerability but she can't help it. She needs the reassurance. "You think she can handle this?"

"I think she has no choice." Owen puts a hand on her back. "She's a mother," he says simply.

FRIDAY, FEBRUARY 13

Allison takes the chair that is offered and sits. She declines a drink but thinks better of it, says she'll have some water.

Detective Joseph Czerwonka returns to the interrogation room with a bottle of Evian and sets it in front of her. He takes the seat across from her. "I'm going to tape this conversation," he tells her.

She nods. The detective reaches for the tape recorder, in the center of the small desk that separates them, and hits the "Record" button.

"My name is Detective Joseph Czerwonka," he says. "The date is February the thirteenth. Time is three-thirteen p.m. I am speaking with Allison Quincy Pagone. Mrs. Pagone, I am going to advise you of your rights. You have the right to remain silent. Anything that you do say to me can and will be used against you in a court of law. You have the right to counsel. If you cannot afford an attorney, an attorney will be provided for you. Do you understand these rights, Mrs. Pagone?"

"I do."

"Would you like to have an attorney present?"

"No," she says. "I waive counsel."

"Do you understand that I am recording this conversation?"

"Yes."

"Okay. I'd like to go over a few things since we spoke two days ago. First, do you have anything you'd like to say?"

"No."

"Okay." Czerwonka is dressed better today than two days ago. He's wearing a crisp blue shirt and a nice silver silk tie. She figures he's expecting to be on camera today.

"Mrs. Pagone." The detective reaches into a bag at his feet. He sets a large plastic bag on the table. In it is a single platinum earring. "We recovered this earring from your jewelry box yesterday. Do you acknowledge that this is your earring?"

"I won't answer that."

He nods. "Can you explain to me why I found only one earring, and not two, at your house?"

"No comment."

"Mrs. Pagone, I'm giving you the chance to explain this for me. We found the second of these two earrings at Sam Dillon's house."

She stares at him. "That's not a question."

"Do you have any explanation for that, ma'am? How one of those earrings found its way to Sam Dillon's house?"

"No comment."

"No comment," he repeats. "You won't provide us any explanation?"

"I have nothing to say."

"Are you familiar with a brand of fingernail polish called 'Saturday Evening Red'? Made by Evelyn Masters?"

"I have nothing to say."

"That was the brand of polish found on the broken fingernail at Mr. Dillon's house."

Allison nods. Again, no question pending.

"We also found that polish in your home," he says. "And we found cotton balls in your garbage that contain that polish, along with traces of nail-polish remover."

She stares at him.

"Did you recently remove that nail polish from your fingers?"

"No comment."

"Were you romantically involved with Sam Dillon?"

"I already answered that, last time, Detective."

"You said 'no,' last time. Is that still your answer?"

"I have nothing more to say."

Czerwonka is not deterred. "Are you refusing to answer any questions at all, Mrs. Pagone?"

"It looks that way."

"Let me—let me be candid with you, Mrs. Pagone. We have a hair follicle that looks a lot like yours, recovered from Sam Dillon's home. It has the bulb still attached, which means there's DNA. We now have a sample of your DNA and I think there's going to be a match. What do *you* think?"

She shakes her head.

"And you know we're going to do a DNA test on that sweatshirt," he adds. "You think that's going to be your blood we find on there? Or Sam Dillon's?"

"You'll find what you find."

"We've got your fingernail, we've got your earring, and we have a silver Lexus SUV—like the one you drive—seen at Sam Dillon's home around one in the morning, and we've got you returning to your house with mud all over you, a little before two. We've got you going to Dillon's office in the capital the day before he was murdered. You were shouting at him. By all accounts, it sounds like he was dumping you. Ending your relationship."

Allison folds her arms.

"I'm giving you this chance to explain this to me, Mrs. Pagone. Look." Czerwonka makes a face, leans on his elbows. "I could see why you don't want to admit being involved with Dillon. He works alongside your ex. You two probably wanted to keep it quiet. I get that. I'd probably do the same thing, if it were me. And then the thing gets complicated. He says some awful things to you. Breaks your heart. I've been there. You—you've had a tough go of it. A divorce, then a rebound, then that guy dumps you, too. Your head, it's not where it should be. You're not doing anything like a cold, calculated murder. It's like the heat of the moment, you just snap. That's not Murder One, Mrs. Pagone. You've been a lawyer. You lawyers call it diminished capacity, right? Manslaughter, maybe. Maybe—who knows? Temporary insanity."

Allison rolls her neck. She'd like to reach over and smack this guy.

"That's not life in prison. That's not a needle in your arm. But see, you don't help me out here, I have to see this thing the way it looks. Premeditated murder. I have all I need, right now, Mrs. Pagone. How we charge you is up to you now, not me."

"I have nothing to say, Detective," she says. "Do what you're going to do."

"Just—" He raises a hand. "Just talk to me about Sam. We know you two were an item. You told your daughter, Mrs. Pagone. Just tell me what you told her."

"Do what you're going to do, Detective. I'm not saying another word."

Joe Czerwonka's lips move into a grim smile. He shakes his head, as if to say, *you had your chance.* "I'm going to place you under arrest, Mrs. Pagone," he says, rising to his feet. "For the murder of Samuel Dillon."

THURSDAY, FEBRUARY 12

Special Agents Shiels and McCoy for Mr. Raycroft."
Irv Shiels places his hands behind his back and
slowly paces the county attorney's suite. Raycroft has cut
himself a nice piece of the floor in the county building,
separated himself and his assistant from the rest of the
masses and spent a decent sum on redecorating. McCoy,
having spent a career in public service, can only imagine
how that one played with the rest of the office.

"Shiels and McCoy." An office assistant, organizing
books on a shelf to their right, looks at them. "Weren't they
a music group?"

Shiels stares at the young man blankly, then looks at
McCoy.

"Please come in, Agents," Raycroft's secretary says,
holding a door open for them.

County Attorney Elliot Raycroft comes out from behind
a mahogany desk. Another man, on the dumpy side and
younger, stands as well.

Introductions all around. The guy with Raycroft is Roger Ogren, the lead prosecutor working the Sam Dillon homicide. Ogren oversaw the search of Allison Pagone's home by the County Attorney Technical Unit today. The CAT unit handles all crime-scene work these days, with the police serving only as an assist.

"This is of interest to you?" Raycroft asks as he sits at his desk. The man is mid-fifties, on the slender side, a little creepy in McCoy's opinion. The way he looks at you, sizing you up, looking for the angle. His hair seems to have come from a bottle, trailer-hitch rust, she's thinking.

Shiels nods. "We are looking at Allison Pagone for something. It's something that we cannot discuss at this time. It's something, let me be clear, that I'm under orders not to discuss."

Raycroft looks at his sidekick, Ogren, and smiles. His teeth are too perfect. He must use those whitening products they have now. Must come in handy, only a month before the March primary. Raycroft is unique because he's a Republican in a city that has been controlled by Democrats since the days of stagecoaches. The Democrats messed up, got into a racial thing and split their vote in a runoff, allowing this guy to sneak in with the heavy backing of the state GOP, which has been dying for a candidate who can do something in this city. Thanks to the power of incumbency, Raycroft was reelected, but it's far from a lock this time. He even has a challenger in the primary, which is forcing him to spend money when he should be fortifying his war chest.

"You came over here to tell me that you're not going to tell me anything?" he asks.

"We came by," says Shiels, playing the straight guy here, "because we know you searched her home today."

Raycroft looks at his watch. "Agent Shiels, can we get to it?"

"We planted a bug in Allison Pagone's house. It's a

sophisticated model, an Infinity transmitter. We don't know if your people found it."

Raycroft looks at Roger Ogren, who makes a face. The answer, apparently, is no.

Shit. They didn't know. They had no idea about Larry Evans's bug, and now Shiels has told them. But they couldn't be sure. They couldn't take the chance that the CAT unit would find the transmitter and start talking to the media. They had no choice but to front the issue and claim the transmitter as their own.

"First we've heard of it," says Raycroft.

"Well—obviously, Mr. Raycroft, it's paramount that this information not leave this room. It would defeat the purpose."

"Obviously."

McCoy catches Roger Ogren scoping her out. She doesn't really mind, but she likes to catch them in the act.

"You can't discuss why you're looking at Allison Pagone?" he asks.

"No, sir. I'm sorry—like I said, orders."

"Is this related to Sam Dillon's murder?" First time Ogren jumps in, and he's a little too eager to participate. A confidence thing, she figures. "Do you have information about that?"

"We don't." Shiels shakes his head. "If we did, we'd tell you."

From the looks on their faces, the county guys aren't exactly getting in line to agree with that statement.

"Mr. Raycroft, Agent McCoy here is my point on this operation. If we pull anything from the bug, you'll be the first to know. She'll contact Mr. Ogren here. We want to assist in any way we can. But we need to be clear on the confidentiality. Nobody can know what we're doing, sir."

"I heard you the first time, Agent Shiels." The county attorney is making a point to show he's unimpressed. "If we leak this to the press, you'll shake your fist at me."

"I'll put you in handcuffs."

Raycroft comes forward in his chair. Probably isn't spoken to like *that* every day. But he's reading Shiels, who is not budging an inch, and his air seems to deflate. He's imagining his perp walk before the cameras on the eve of the general election.

"If you'd like to speak with the attorney general of the United States, I can arrange that call," Shiels adds.

McCoy pipes up. She wouldn't, normally, but the game of who's-got-the-biggest-dick-in-the-room is getting a little heated. "We should be clear, gentlemen," she says. "What we are looking at with Allison Pagone is unrelated to the reason you are looking at her. We don't know who murdered Sam Dillon and it's not a part of our case. We bugged Pagone's house after Sam Dillon's murder, and we had no idea that she was going to be implicated for that murder."

A silence now. Wounds being licked. The feds have come to the county office and pissed all over it.

"And you won't tell us what's going on," Raycroft manages.

"We can tell you this much," says Irv Shiels, who raises a hand and adjusts the volume of his voice. "We can tell you that it's big enough that I overreacted at the slightest hint of this leaking out. It's big enough that our policy of cooperation with your office has to be a one-way street this time. It's big enough that the attorney general really is expecting your call, to personally thank you for your cooperation."

Good recovery. A slip-up with the handcuffs comment, she thought, but he reeled him back.

Shiels sighs. "We'd never ask you to pass on the prosecution. In fact, we'll help you, if we get anything from the wire."

This is a point worth making. A high-profile murder trial before the general election in November could be a significant advantage for Raycroft. If they told him not to prosecute, he'd hit the ceiling and demand more information.

"When this is over, Mr. County Attorney," Shiels adds, "we'd be grateful if you'd join us at the press conference. We'll be explaining that this was a multi-jurisdictional effort between a number of federal agencies and, of course, your office."

Oh, and he nailed the landing. Talk about finding Raycroft's G-spot.

"Well." The tone in Raycroft's voice has grown merrier. "It sounds like your investigation is exceptionally important, so of course my office will respect that. Roger will be more than happy to cooperate. When do you think this operation is going to be completed?" he throws in, like an afterthought.

What he's really asking, she realizes, is, *When can I have that press conference?*

"Summer," says Shiels, who realizes as much as anyone that this is a good answer.

"Fine. Very good." Raycroft nods.

"And we'd like to ask a favor, sir," Shiels adds. "Assuming that you're going to indict Pagone, which it sounds like you are—"

"A fair assumption."

"—we'd like you to agree to bail."

"Bail?" Ogren cries. "For a capital murder? *Agree* to it?"

"We need her out. She goes inside and we can't use her."

"Oh." Ogren clams up, looks at his boss.

"I think," Raycroft says, "that there are shades of gray here. 'Agreeing,' I'm afraid, is out of the question. But 'not opposing' is a different matter. Not opposing very vigorously is still another approach."

"Put restrictions on it," McCoy suggests.

"She's not going to flee," Shiels adds. "We're on her. And if by some chance she does, I take the heat. I'll make a point of it."

"But she won't flee," McCoy repeats. "She'd never get past us. Never."

They rub and stroke the county attorney a little longer and he agrees to "not oppose" the request for bail. This is so out of Shiels's character, this coddling, that McCoy considers razzing him about it when they reach the elevators. She considers, also, being out of a job five minutes later.

"Thanks," he says to her, as they walk back to the federal plaza. "I dropped the ball there." He grunts. "'Handcuffs.' Anyway, nice save."

A compliment. She wishes she had a witness. Harrick will never believe it.

"Keep those boys in line, McCoy," he adds.

WEDNESDAY, FEBRUARY 11

Y ou were home all night," Detective Czerwonka confirms.

"Yes," Allison says. "I was home all night."

"And to be clear, here. We're talking about last Saturday,
the seventh of February."

"Yes. I was home all night." Allison gives an exaggerated sigh. "Are we going to be much longer?"

"We've told you all along, you're free to go if you want,"
says Czerwonka's partner, Jack Aiken. He looks to be a little younger, and fitter, than Czerwonka, and he's let his
partner take the lead.

Yes, they have repeatedly informed her of her right to
leave, because if she is free to leave, then this conversation
cannot technically constitute an "interrogation," and therefore no Miranda warnings are required. What, they forgot
she practiced criminal law for almost three years?

"I'll answer whatever you'd like," she says.

Joe Czerwonka is a large, weathered man who seems to

have a gentle side, too, which makes her think he's a grand-father. Or maybe it's just dealing with females. If she were a man, this guy might be breathing down her neck. Instead, he turns away from Allison, talks to his partner as if she weren't in the room. "It's just—confusing to me," he says. "See, Mrs. Pagone's daughter, Jessica, told us that Allison came home about two in the morning on Sunday."

"Yeah," Detective Aiken confirms, referring to his notes. "Yep, she said, 'Two in the morning.' She said she got to Mrs. Pagone's house at about eight-thirty, Saturday night, and her mom wasn't there. She said Mom didn't get home until two."

"That's almost six hours unaccounted for," Czerwonka says to Aiken.

"You talked to Jessica?" Allison looks at them sharply. "You didn't notify us."

"She's twenty years old, Mrs. Pagone. She doesn't need parental notification."

"What did Jessica tell you?" Allison pounds the table. "Tell me what she said."

Aiken looks at his partner. This is Czerwonka's call. "Well," the senior detective says, "your daughter seems to remember you coming home and not looking so hot. Upset. And dirty, I guess. Mud on you. And she says you threw up when you got home."

"Jessica said *that*?" Allison asks, feigning surprise.

"Yeah, she did. And she said the next day, you told her you'd been dating Mr. Dillon. The two of you were having a romantic, shall we say, relationship."

"That *is* confusing," Aiken says to Czerwonka. "Mrs. Pagone here says she was home all night and she wasn't sleeping with Mr. Dillon. Her daughter says just the op-posite."

"Maybe it's a mixup," Czerwonka says to his partner. "Maybe we misunderstood what Mrs. Pagone here has been telling us."

Allison says nothing.

"Well," Czerwonka continues with Aiken, "when you talked to Jessica, did she give any indication she was confused?"

"No," Aiken says. "No, she was crystal clear on it. We went over that point over and over again. Mom came home about two, looking all out of sorts. And then she spilled it—that she was having an affair with Sam Dillon."

"Well, did she know it's a crime to lie to a police detective?" Czerwonka asks.

"That's enough," Allison says.

"Yeah," says Aiken. "She knew she had to tell the truth. Otherwise, it's obstruction of justice. Yeah, Jessica understood that she could get in all kinds of trouble for lying to me."

"I want you to stop this." Allison stands up.

"It's no act, Mrs. Pagone." Czerwonka laces his hands together. "One of you is lying about this. You or Jessica. Should we pick her up for lying to a police officer?"

"Leave her out of this. She has nothing to do—" Allison looks away.

"Nothing to do with what?" Aiken asks.

"Nothing."

"Look, Mrs. Pagone. Take your seat if you would," Czerwonka says. "Let me make this easier for you. We know you went to Sam Dillon's office downstate last Friday—the day before he was murdered. We know you were upset."

Allison holds her breath. Something she can't control, what happened at Sam's office.

"You went to his offices up here, first, then you drove all the way down to the capital to find Sam Dillon. You already told us, when we started this interview, that you didn't have business with Dillon. You said that already. So why the rush to go down there? It's personal. Of course, it's personal. Okay."

Allison sits down, as previously requested.

"You rush into Sam's office and close the door. Okay, you want privacy. But you didn't quite *get* privacy, Mrs. Pagone."

The words pierce her heart. Her body accelerates. She is ready to say it right now, if necessary. Something in her— caution, perhaps, or simply the inability to speak—forces her to keep quiet for the moment.

Somebody *heard* her conversation with Sam?

"There was an aide at the office," Czerwonka continues. "You may not have noticed him in your haste. He heard what was going on in there."

"You don't understand," she says.

"Then help me out here."

No. No. Let him take the lead. She closes her eyes. *They know*, she thinks with a mounting horror. *They know I made Sam fire Jessica. They know Jessica had a thing for Sam and he rebuffed her. They probably know Jessica was upset, upset enough to—*

"'This isn't working out.' 'Mat's a friend.' 'This is crazy.'"

Allison opens her eyes to a satisfied Detective Czerwonka.

"Sound familiar, Mrs. Pagone?"

Something's not right. Those were the words Sam used, on the phone with Jessica, but the look on the detective's face tells her he is misreading it.

"He dumped you, Mrs. Pagone," Czerwonka concludes. "You're not the first. I can say that from personal experience."

He dumped—me. Me, *not Jessica*. Allison's heart leaps. The office aide heard the words but didn't know the context. He didn't know Sam was on the phone, talking to Jessica.

Sam dumped me. Yes!

"But then you deny you were involved with Sam," the detective says. "And it looks bad for you. Because it's so obvious to us that you two *were* an item."

"And that means, score one for Jessica," Aiken adds. "She was telling the truth. Which means she was probably also telling the truth about you coming home at two in the morning on the night Sam Dillon was murdered."

"We need you to explain this to us, Mrs. Pagone. You've lied to us twice. There's an innocent explanation for that? Great. I'm ready to believe it. But you've given me nothing to believe, so far."

Allison brings her hand to her forehead. "It's—complicated," she says.

"Life is complicated," Czerwonka responds. "Explain this to us."

Allison gets back to her feet. "You said I'm free to leave."

Czerwonka freezes. His partner looks at him.

"Yes," Czerwonka says, to keep the record clear on this point. A good detective is always thinking about keeping a confession legal. "But this is not the time. Right now, you should be putting our minds at ease."

"I'm leaving, then."

"Mrs. Pagone." Czerwonka stands, along with his partner. "I'd advise you not to leave town any time soon."

"I'd advise you to get a law degree, Detective." Allison hikes her purse over her shoulder. "You can't make me do anything."

*T*here will be a time," Father said, "when they will want you to risk your life. That," he added, "is when your true dedication shows."

Ram Haroon drinks his beer slowly. He is the only non-Caucasian at this place on the west side. It is close to midnight. The dozen or so people inside are getting louder, growing more boisterous in their inebriation. This was an asinine choice, this spot. Haroon sticks out, as the Americans say, like a sore thumb. And it could well be only a matter of time before one of these drunken idiots decides to tap him on the shoulder and tell him to go back to his own fucking country.

Ram drains his beer at ten to midnight. He walks toward the bathroom, ignoring any stares that might be coming his way. He turns down the small corridor where the restrooms are located but passes them, goes to the exit door and pushes it, steps out into the alley.

Larry Evans is standing there, awaiting him.

"I assume there is an excellent explanation," Haroon says, "for what I have been reading in the newspapers and seeing on television."

"Everything's fine," Evans says.

Haroon approaches him, partly so he can keep his voice down but more to make his point clearly. "Last week, you tell me there is a man, Sam Dillon. You tell me your scientist is nervous. You tell me you're going to keep an eye on this man Dillon."

"And I did." Larry Evans is immediately defensive. "I listened to him. Watched him."

"'Keep an eye on him,' you said. You said nothing about *killing* him."

Larry Evans takes a moment with that. He will neither admit nor deny killing Sam Dillon, obviously. "I think all the worry was for nothing," he says instead. "I don't think Dillon knew and so I don't think she knows, either. The woman. Allison Pagone."

"And how does your scientist feel about this?"

"He's upset. He wants me to watch Pagone, so I will. But I think we're okay."

"You *think*." Haroon runs a hand over his mouth, paces in a small circle. "Her home is still bugged?"

"Yes. And it's been interesting. She looks like she's going down for the murder."

Haroon nods. "I saw on television. She was questioned today."

"She's going to be arrested." Evans stuffs his hands in his pockets. "She thinks so. It's like she *wants* to go down for it."

"Why would she want to be arrested for murder?" Haroon turns to Evans.

He shrugs in response. "I think she's protecting her daughter."

"But why?"

"Here's the thing." Evans steps closer. "They were both there that night. The night he was murdered."

"Allison Pagone and her daughter?"

Evans nods. "Both of them. And Allison *told* her daughter she killed Sam. She confessed, that night."

"That doesn't make sense. Why would she do that? Confess to a murder she did not commit?"

Larry Evans laughs.

"You killed Sam Dillon," Haroon says. "Correct?"

"I never said that, Mr. Haroon. I never said that. All you need to know is that I would never be connected to it."

A man stumbles by, a drunk, singing to himself, oblivious to the two men standing in the darkness of the alley.

"We've been out here too long," Haroon says. "The police won't find your surveillance equipment in Allison Pagone's house?"

"No. City cops? They'll have no idea. I promise you. And worst case, they'd never be able to trace it to me or anyone else."

"All right. And what, exactly, do you propose we do?"

"We sit tight, for now. I'll keep an eye on Allison Pagone. I promised the scientist I would, anyway. We watch her. We do nothing for a couple of weeks. You and I don't speak. My scientist does nothing. I'll listen and watch and see what happens."

"All right. Now listen to me carefully." Haroon stands

within inches of Larry Evans. "Nobody else dies unless I say so. I will decide when and how, and I will do it. There will be no more mistakes."

The perceived criticism does not seem to sit well with Larry Evans, but it is clear who has the upper hand here. Haroon could abort this operation at any time, and Evans says good-bye to twenty-five million dollars.

"That's the way the doctor wants it, too," Evans says. "Nobody else dies. So don't worry. No one's killing her."

"Unless and until I say so." Ram Haroon straightens his coat and walks down the alley.

TUESDAY, FEBRUARY 10

Allison stands outside her daughter's dorm room, or what she believes to be Jessica's dorm room. The divorce has separated Allison more fully from her daughter than from Mat. This spring semester, she knows virtually nothing about what classes her daughter is taking, or even where she lives.

"Yeah, that's Jessica's room," says a student.

Allison looks at her watch. She has been loitering in the hallway for over an hour. Jess must be at class. Hopefully, she'll come back here soon. Allison has other engagements.

Just after one in the afternoon, Jessica walks down the hall, a backpack slung over her shoulder, her eyes down. Her daughter is wearing a deep frown. She looks up and sees Allison, turns ghostly white. She is immediately aware of her surroundings, manages a perfunctory smile to two students who pass her. When they're gone, she lowers her head and moves quickly toward her mother. She unlocks the door to her dormitory room and walks in first. Allison follows.

Jessica closes the door and locks it.

"What are you doing here?" she asks.

Allison takes her daughter by the shoulders. "I wanted to be sure you're okay."

"I'm okay," she says, though she does not look it. Her hair is flat, her eyes bloodshot and weary.

"Everything is going to be fine, Jessica. This is all going to work out."

This statement, naturally, is of little comfort to Jessica. She looks at her mother with a combination of distrust, fear, and resentment. "What did you do?" she asks. She wiggles out of her mother's grasp, takes a step back, so that now her back is to the door.

"I can't tell you, Jess. For your own protection. I can't." She puts her hands together as in prayer. "But you have to believe me. Something is going on. Something bigger than all of this, bigger than all of us. All you have to know is that, whatever happens, I'm going to be fine. And so is your father. You have to believe—"

"I have to believe *you*?"

"I'm going to be charged with Sam's murder," she says.

"*You're* going to be charged." Jessica's face contorts; she angles her head to get a different look at her mother, as if it could change reality.

"Yes," Allison says simply. "It was *my* earring, Jess. Not yours. You've never borrowed my earrings. Never. Do you understand?"

She does, eventually, taking in her mother's statement with a mounting horror.

"No one is ever going to know you were there that night," Allison says.

Jessica looks around the room, claustrophobic, though she knows she can't leave. This conversation cannot take place in the open.

"Sit," Allison says.

Jessica moves to her bed, unmade, with three pillows scattered. She was always that way, her beautiful daughter. Always loved to bury herself in the pillows.

"Now listen to me." Allison clears her throat. "The police will have reason to believe that I was at his house that night."

Jessica looks up at her mother.

Allison raises a hand. "They will probably think I killed him. That's a pretty safe bet. And it's okay with me that they think that. It's okay because nothing's going to happen to me."

"No," Jessica whispers, her voice failing, tears coming fast.

"Jessica, I don't have time for this," Allison says. She needs to stay above her emotions so that Jessica will follow her lead. "And I'm not going to tell you why. But I'm covered. I am not going to be convicted. That's a one-hundred-percent guarantee. Now look at me."

It is a moment before Jessica manages to comply, her body quivering, her eyes unrecognizable.

"I'm not going to tell you anything more than that," Allison continues. "It will be tough for you but you're going to have to deal with it. You'll understand, one day. For now, you have to listen to me. Okay?"

She can hardly expect a warm response from her daughter, and she does not receive one. Jessica, it seems, can't decide whether she resents or appreciates her mother's strength.

"Fine," she says.

"Okay, good. The police will be investigating me, and they'll come to you, no doubt. They will interview you. You need to be ready with some answers. So we have to make sure that you and I are clear on this."

"You want me to tell them things that will make you look guilty."

"Let's get started, Jessica," she says. "Do what I ask and this will turn out okay for everyone."

Ram Haroon sits in the passenger seat of the car, staring into a wall in the underground parking garage downtown. It's cold inside the car, in a parking area that is not well insulated. They couldn't very well leave the vehicle running for the last half-hour, while Ram Haroon received his instructions.

"Let me be sure I understand this correctly," he says. "This woman, Allison Pagone, must be dead, but it must appear that she took her own life. That she committed suicide out of guilt, remorse over her crime, and that she preferred death by her own hand to execution."

"Yes," the driver says.

"And you feel quite strongly that *I* should be the one who makes this happen."

"Yes," the driver says. "It must be you. Larry Evans, obviously, can't be used."

"Larry Evans is an idiot," Haroon says.

"But effective. He has the scientist in his pocket."

They sit in silence, the windows fogging while the temperatures plummet. Ram Haroon rubs his hands together.

"You miss Pakistan?" the driver asks.

Haroon looks at him. "Don't you? Why you'd want to return to this city is beyond me."

Special Agent-in-Charge Irving Shiels purses his lips. "*Na'am,*" he says. "*Ohebbo tughuyor al mawassom.*"

"Yes?" Haroon laughs. "You like snow and ice and freezing temperatures?"

"Damn right I do. This is home for me." Shiels looks Ram over. It's been years for the two of them. Shiels, if memory serves, was never much for sentimentality, doesn't seem comfortable with it. "*Tabdo bi sohha jayyida,*" Shiels adds.

Haroon takes the compliment in stride. "I eat well and

exercise when I can," he says, a line he's heard in the States.

Shiels smiles at that. *"Lakad mada waket tawil,"* he says.

"Ten years, at least," Haroon calculates. "Too long. *Ladayka awlad?"*

Shiels nods. "An eight-year-old boy, and my daughter's six."

Haroon smiles. It's hard to imagine Irving Shiels with a wife and children, but he is a long way from Pakistan, and maybe Haroon never knew the real man.

"This has to look like a suicide, Zulfi," says Shiels. "Everyone has to think Allison Pagone killed herself."

"Everyone will think she killed herself," Haroon says.

"When this is ending, you'll be stopped at the airport." Shiels looks at him. "There's nothing we can do about that. We've had to keep you on the 'watch' list to keep your cover."

"Understood."

"It will be one of my agents. Just be ready with the answers to the questions. She'll do a song and dance for the benefit of Customs, but she's been instructed to let you go."

"I am sure it will be a memorable experience," Haroon says.

Irv Shiels laughs, a forced effort, a brief smile that returns to stoicism almost immediately. Shiels was never particularly animated.

"Tawakka al hazar, sayyedee," Haroon says. Stay safe.

"You do the same." Shiels presses his hand in Haroon's. *"Al selem, lakan abadan lil istislam."*

Haroon leaves the vehicle and heads for the exit. *Peace,* Shiels said to him, *but never surrender.*

MONDAY, FEBRUARY 9

"Strange as it may seem, it's plausible." Paul Riley speaks in a hushed voice to Allison, though they are in a conference room with the door closed. "The likelihood of an acquittal is remote. So sooner or later, you'd fall into government hands. At that point, they would expect you to play whatever hand you could. Believe it or not, you're safer this way, Allison."

Allison starts, something like a nervous laugh.

"The timing is a bit concerning, I suppose," Paul adds.

"Very." Allison leaves her chair and paces around the long table. The contrast between this FBI office and the ones at Paul Riley's law firm is staggering. "I want to do it now. They're saying, ballpark, mid-May."

"They must have some reason." Paul sighs. "Not that they'll tell us."

Paul looks awful, out of sorts. He must be utterly exhausted. Since last night, when Allison reached him, and

through a long day today—it's close to eight in the evening—
Paul has probably only slept a handful of hours. About
twenty-four hours ago, he was probably dozing in front of a
television on a lazy Sunday, waiting for a busy week of court
appearances and meetings with clients. Instead, he has spent
nearly twenty hours straight digesting a very complicated situation and attempting to frame a solution.

"Let's go back in," Allison says.

J ane McCoy sits in one of the chairs in Special Agent-
in-Charge Irving Shiels's office. Harrick paces about
the room. Shiels is on his cell phone. United States
Attorney Mason Tremont is reading the news coverage of
Sam Dillon's murder.

"What a mess," Tremont says. This is the first time
McCoy has met Tremont. He's been U.S. attorney since the
new governor came in, about four years ago. He is the first
African American to hold the position. Word is, he was a
big fund-raiser for the governor, but the word also is that
he has done the office proud. He's not a bad-looking guy,
distinguished and fit in his mid-fifties, if a little too sober.

"She has to take this deal," Harrick says, lapping the
room. He's wearing a sportcoat and tie today, a step up
for him.

A knock on the door, and Allison Pagone enters with
her lawyer, Paul Riley. Riley used to be an AUSA, part of
the federal family, but he made his name prosecuting that
mass murderer, Terry Burgos, back when Jane McCoy was
in grad school.

Mason Tremont puts down his paper. Irv Shiels kills his
cell phone.

"We have a deal in principle," Riley announces. "We
have to see it all in writing, formally, of course."

"We'll have it done very soon," says Mason Tremont.
"Immunity letter for Mateo Pagone, affidavits, the works."

"Not just immunity," Allison says. "He doesn't even have to talk to you."

"I understand," says Tremont. "It's a clean deal, Mrs. Pagone. He walks and doesn't talk."

"Good." Allison claps her hands together. "So who's going to kill me?"

McCoy laughs at the bluntness of her comment. She removes a photo from a file and shows it to Allison. It is a photograph of Ramadaran Ali Haroon.

Allison recoils—not, McCoy assumes, because he's unsightly, because in truth Haroon is pretty handsome, but because he's from the Middle East. You can talk about political correctness all you want, but Allison and her lawyer are already probably thinking along these lines, and now they're surely suspecting that this operation involves international terrorism.

"The man in this photograph," McCoy says, "is working with us."

That will be the extent to which McCoy elaborates. This is all Allison Pagone needs to know. Ramadaran Ali Haroon is an undercover operative for the CIA, a non-official cover agent, but this is not something she would ever share with Allison. No, Allison Pagone cannot know Haroon's name or his specific occupation, or even his employer. All she needs to know is that this unidentified man in the photograph is a friend, a friend who will be dispatched by Larry Evans to kill her at some point down the road.

"This guy is some kind of undercover agent?" Allison asks, nodding at the photograph.

"He's working with Larry Evans, among others," McCoy answers, though it is not really an answer to the question posed. "He's calling the shots, Mrs. Pagone. He will insist that you be eliminated, and he will insist that he be the one who does it."

"He's supposed to kill me but make it look like a suicide."

"Yes," McCoy says. "The last thing they want anyone to think is that you were murdered. They want it to look like you were distraught, guilt-stricken, that kind of thing."

Allison looks skeptical. McCoy had thought this idea had already been accepted.

"You were in theater, right?" Harrick says to Allison, sensing her hesitation as well. "So this is playacting. This man in the photograph will come in and pretend to kill you and make it look like a suicide."

"I just—it seems so hard to believe that anyone would *believe* that."

"Who's 'anyone'?" McCoy shrugs. "All that Larry Evans will know is what he hears through his eavesdropping device. It's audio, not video. He'll hear a man he trusts"—McCoy shakes the photograph of Ram Haroon—"he'll hear this man enter your house, he'll hear you scream or whatever, he'll hear a struggle, he'll hear this man forcing you up to your bathroom, he'll hear a gun go off—a gun with blanks, of course, but he won't know that—and then he'll hear his trusted partner leave your house, and you just have to keep quiet for a few hours. Larry Evans will have no reason to think you *aren't* dead."

"I guess," Allison says.

"And then Agent Harrick and I, we'll come storming into your place early that next morning, and we'll find you 'dead,' and Larry Evans will still be listening. He'll hear me say, 'Allison's dead,' and he'll hear my partner say, 'Oh, yeah, she's dead, all right.' And we will come to the conclusion that you committed suicide. I will say, loud and clear for Larry Evans to hear, that this is all my fault, because I had been squeezing you for information on the bribery scandal, and because I threatened Mat. Poor me. Poor you."

Allison smiles sheepishly.

"Then we'll whisk you out of there, on a covered gurney, hopefully before any press or local officials get to the scene. Within the hour, you'll be sipping champagne in protective federal custody. Larry Evans will think he's home free—that you're dead with no questions asked—and he will complete his operation. And you will be totally safe."

"Mrs. Pagone," Harrick adds. "Larry Evans trusts the man in that photograph. He'll believe he is hearing a murder, staged to look like a suicide. And when we come in the next morning, we'll confirm it for him. There's no way he'll know the truth."

"It's not the first time we've staged a death," McCoy adds. "The fact that Larry Evans will be listening in only makes it easier. We can use his bugging device against him."

Allison raises her hands. "Fine. That's fine."

"So you're clear on how this works," McCoy asks.

Allison nods. "It's a five-step plan."

"Right. Step one?"

"Step one," Allison echoes. "You'll tell my lawyer, Paul, when it's time to begin. Paul will get in touch with me and he'll reference the murder weapon. That will tell me it's time to begin."

"Right." McCoy looks at Paul. "Just say something like, 'They still haven't found the murder weapon.' Something not too obvious."

Paul nods.

"Then we get to step two," Allison continues. "I will tell Mat, in my house, for Larry Evans to hear, precisely where I buried the murder weapon. Larry Evans will like that, because it adds something to the idea of my suicide. He will send that—that man in the photograph—to get the statuette, with the idea that he'll put it beside me after I 'kill myself.' It is tantamount to a suicide note, a confession."

"Exactly," McCoy says. "But what you're really doing is giving me the signal."

"Right," Allison agrees. "That's step three. You will be

watching the grocery store where I buried it. When you see that man in the photo retrieve the statuette from behind Countryside, you'll know it's time to work our plan."

"Good," McCoy says. "And step four?"

"Step four," Allison sighs, "you will come to my house and introduce yourself to me as if we had never met. We will have a conversation for Larry Evans to hear. You will say you are investigating the bribery scandal. You will say that you are going to take a deal to Mat, that if he confesses, you'll get the county attorney to spare me the death penalty."

"Yes."

"I will be distraught. Suicidal, I suppose. I will say things like, 'My daughter is already losing one parent.' And the obvious route for me to take—as someone who is looking at a surefire conviction and probably a death sentence—is just to take my own life, on my own terms."

"Which is perfect, from the perspective of Larry Evans," Harrick adds.

"And then," Allison continues, "step five, I can expect a visit from that man in the photograph."

McCoy brightens. "We'll stage your death/suicide and get you somewhere safe."

Paul Riley clears his throat. "There's one wrinkle, folks."

"A wrinkle," Irv Shiels repeats.

"There's a wrinkle?" McCoy asks.

"Yes," Paul says. "We want this to happen very soon. We would like it to happen now—tomorrow, the next day—or at the latest, after she is charged. Your target date of mid-May is not acceptable."

"It's the only way," McCoy says quickly. "We've told you that."

It's the only way because the scientist whom Larry Evans has compromised, Doctor Neil Lomas, apparently was extremely distraught about Sam Dillon's death and has told Evans that he will cease working on the formula if anyone else is killed. Paul Riley is right, in theory. They should stage Allison Pagone's "murder" very soon, a matter of days, and whisk her to safety. But reports of Allison's death would be big news in town, news that would not escape the attention of Doctor Neil Lomas, and the Bureau needs Doctor Lomas to complete his formula. Their intelligence tells them that Ram Haroon will likely deliver this formula to one of the high-ranking members of the Liberation Front, and they need that to happen. They need Doctor Lomas happy and productive.

Which means Allison Pagone can't "die" until the formula is completed, which is estimated at this point to be mid-May.

"We can't give on that," Irving Shiels says, standing in the corner in that military stance he so often assumes. "If we do this with Mrs. Pagone now, there's no point in doing it at all. It has to be when we say, and it looks like mid-May."

Allison Pagone looks at Paul Riley. McCoy expects them to leave the office and confer, but surely they've already discussed this. McCoy has never left any room for doubt on this point.

"Okay," Allison says to Irv Shiels. "I'll do mid-May, or whenever. Whenever you say. Whenever Paul comes to me with the talk about the 'murder weapon.'"

McCoy sits back in her chair, looks at her boss, Shiels, who stands with arms folded, scowling. Scowling, but content. They have their deal.

"Your ex-husband, Mat, obviously will know about this," Harrick says. "He will know about his immunity deal, and he will be the one who plays the partner in these staged conversations you will be having in your house for Larry Evans. You need someone to say these things to, and Mat makes sense. Your daughter, Jessica, remains in the dark."

"Yes." Allison shakes her head too eagerly. "She will not know the details."

A pause. Everyone looks at one another.

"We have a tentative agreement, then," Paul Riley says. "This is—I've only had today to digest an awful lot of information."

"Understood," Irv Shiels says. "But we don't have much time. We would assume that Mrs. Pagone will be questioned very, very soon. And things will start moving against her very quickly."

"You made sure of that," McCoy says to Allison.

"We'll get back to you tomorrow, when we see it in writing," Allison says. "But as long as you accept my terms, I'm in."

rv Shiels is fuming. The others have left, leaving McCoy and Harrick to bear the brunt of his frustration.

"This woman," Shiels says. "She's well known?"

"Yes, sir," McCoy says. "I read one of her novels. I think it was a bestseller."

"That's wonderful. Jesus H. So this will be a big story."

"Yes, sir."

"Sir." Harrick clears his throat. "Sir," he says, "we should bury this thing. Talk to the county attorney. Tell them to hold a press conference, say the murder of Sam Dillon is unsolved, and make Larry Evans feel safe. That makes more sense than going through with this whole charade."

Shiels looks at McCoy, not Harrick, holds a stare on her. McCoy figures it's one of two things. One, the boss is wondering what the hell Harrick is still doing in the room. Shiels is the SAC, and McCoy is running this operation. This isn't a roundtable discussion. But Harrick is McCoy's partner, and she's made him her right hand on this operation, too. Jane has been on the other side of this before and never appreciated being left out.

Or two, Shiels is insulted. *Don't you think that occurred to us, Agent Harrick?*

"That doesn't work." Shiels flicks a hand like he's swatting a fly. "One, we'd have to share a whole helluva lot with Elliot Raycroft to make him do that. This is an election year. A huge homicide in his jurisdiction, and he has a primary challenger, if you hadn't noticed. And he's a Republican, too, Agent Harrick, if you hadn't noticed that, either, so it's not exactly a waltz to reelection. He'll be crucified if this comes back 'unsolved.'"

Harrick nods, too enthusiastically.

"And at any rate, this thing would boil for a while no matter what. The county attorney has to investigate this somewhat—a lot—before he just walks up to a microphone and says, 'We have no idea what happened. We're folding up shop.' And this whole time, Larry Evans is watching Allison Pagone, and he's wondering, and if the CA is too eager in pronouncing this 'unsolved,' he'll wonder even more."

"Yes, sir."

"And you think"—Shiels's face is hot now—"you think our friends in Virginia are going to let us confide in a local prosecutor about this?"

"Understood, sir."

"To say nothing of Allison Pagone," Shiels adds. "She's in danger now, I think you'd agree, Agent?"

"Yes, sir."

"How do you think we are most effective keeping her safe, Agent? Do we whisk her away to federal protective custody right now?"

Harrick, licking his wounds from the scolding, struggles for the answer that will be least offensive.

"No, we can't do that," Shiels says, answering his own question, "because the operation dies if Allison Pagone dies—or if they think she dies. Doctor Lomas folds up

shop, and there's no formula, and there's no chance to catch
Muhsin al-Bakhari or whoever. So that's not acceptable.
You see that, Agent?"

"Yes, sir."

"So her being charged with murder is the best way to do
that. She's a big news item. Anything happens to her now,
it would receive tremendous scrutiny. Larry Evans is smart
enough to recognize that. And if he's not, Ram Haroon will
remind him. A spotlight shining on Allison Pagone is the best
way to keep her alive and help us do what we need to do."

Harrick, at this point, looks like one of those bobble-
head dolls, he's nodding so rapidly.

"So you see, Agent Harrick, where just telling Raycroft
that we're fighting an international terrorist operation, and
could he please take a pass on this high-profile murder,
maybe isn't such a hot idea."

"You made your point, sir," McCoy says, hoping to in-
terrupt the tantrum. "Several times over. It's been a long
day for everyone."

She waits a beat. On the scale of career moves, this one
didn't rate a perfect ten. No, this one would fall slightly
above kicking the boss in the balls.

"Okay." Shiels runs a hand over his face. "Right."

"We have to talk to Haroon, sir," McCoy says. "He has
to be clear on this."

"I know. We need clearance." Shiels sighs. "I have to call
the director."

"I'll meet with him, sir, if you'd like," she says. "I'll talk
to Haroon."

"No," says Shiels. "He's my guy. I'm the reason we have
this operation."

Normally, this operation would probably be handled by
CIA or the NSA, or some combination. But Shiels knows
Haroon, from way back—he's the reason Haroon pushed
for this city as a locale—so Shiels is the logical choice to
communicate with Haroon.

"God." Shiels shakes his head. "I haven't seen him for years."

"He doesn't know, does he?" McCoy asks. "He doesn't know everything?"

Shiels closes his eyes, makes a face. "He doesn't know, but he probably suspects."

That makes sense to McCoy. Haroon is basically the bagman. He gets the formula from Larry Evans, he pays Evans, and he delivers the formula for the poison to the Liberation Front. Surely, Haroon must suspect that if he delivers the formula directly to a high-ranking member of the Libbies, the U.S. Special Forces will be ready to pounce. And he must know that he could be caught in the crossfire. He must have known this the moment he was sent to this city by the Libbies, and he contacted the U.S. government to let them know he was coming.

"All Ram Haroon knows," says Shiels, "is that Doctor Lomas and Larry Evans will finish their formula, then give him a sample to verify the poison works. Haroon will pretend to sample it and will tell Evans that it's acceptable. Then he'll transfer the twenty-five million to an account that Evans specifies. Once the money transfer is made, Evans will deliver the formula for the poison to Haroon. Then Haroon will take the formula and modify it—change it, so that no matter what else happens, it's not really a formula for poison—and he'll deliver it to the Liberation Front. Haroon will be trusted enough to deliver it directly to one of the *shura majlis*. Directly to Muhsin al-Bakhari. We'll nail Evans and put him away for life, we'll catch Doctor Lomas, and we'll catch the brains and spirit behind the Liberation Front."

Shiels works the kinks out of his neck. "So yeah, Haroon is probably smart enough to know that this could end in an ambush. He knows he could be giving up his life for this. He already has instructions, if he's caught by U.S. Special Forces, to identify himself as 'Zulfikar,' his given name, so they know he's a friend. But in the midst of a gunfight to catch al-Bakhari, all bets are off. I'm sure he's figured that out."

"Haroon's good," McCoy says, more a request for confirmation than a statement.

"He's good."

"He'll fool Larry Evans, no question?"

"No question," says Shiels. "He's been fooling the Liberation Front for over a decade."

SUNDAY, FEBRUARY 8

12:44 A.M.

Jane McCoy, sitting in her car, looks at her watch. It is close to one in the morning, Sunday, only forty-five minutes into a new day, and she prays that it is not as eventful as the Saturday that just passed. Normally, she would be asleep now. Instead, she is parked one street over from the home where Sam Dillon lives—lived—and where he was murdered only several hours ago.

She closes her eyes as she listens to her instructions through her cell phone. She still can't believe that Dillon is dead. This is her fault. Her responsibility. She knew Dillon was at risk. She didn't expect *this*, though.

A fuck-up. A fuck-up times twelve. This thing has just gotten started, and already she's lost a civilian.

"I will, sir," she says into her cell phone to Irving Shiels. "You'll be the first. Okay."

She punches the cell phone off and looks at Harrick. "Jessica Pagone's still at her mother's house," McCoy says. "I assume she'll spend the night."

"So what do we do now?" Harrick asks.

McCoy shrugs. This is her operation, she has to make the calls.

"We wait," she tells her partner. "Somebody else is going to have to find Dillon's body."

"But what about Jessica?"

"We can't just drive over and chat with her, this time of night. Remember, he's got Allison's place wired up, too. It's one in the morning. We might as well raise a red flag if we go there now."

"No, you're right," Harrick agrees. "Tomorrow."

McCoy's phone rings again. "McCoy. What? Are you—what—hang on." She moves the phone from her mouth and turns to her partner. "Someone just left Allison's house," she says. "Not Jessica's car. Allison's."

"*Allison* Pagone? Jesus Christ." Harrick jumps in his seat. More action. What a night it's been. A good part of an FBI agent's job is watching, listening, waiting. Not so much this stuff, what they've seen tonight.

"Follow her," McCoy says into the phone. "But for God's sake, be invisible."

She clicks the phone off and turns to Harrick. "None of our people are in Dillon's house right now, right?"

"No, they're out," Harrick says. "I'll confirm that. Why?" He turns to her. "You think Allison is coming *here*?"

McCoy smiles. "Hell yes, she is."

1:06 A.M.

Allison brakes her Lexus SUV gently on Sam's driveway and checks her watch. It is just after one in the morning.

The front door was unlocked, Jessica said, so she should have no problem getting in.

The door is not even closed all the way. She pushes it open slowly, takes a breath, and walks in. With her shirt, she wipes the doorknob on both sides. Jessica swore that the doorknob was the only thing she touched.

She tells herself that she will not look at him—not directly—at least not until she is finished. But her instincts betray her, and she almost swoons as she sees him, lying motionless, face down, across the carpet. Her eyes move directly to the wound on the back of his head, to the stat-uette caked with blood and hair lying near him.

"Oh, Sam," she whispers, but hearing her voice snaps her to attention. *Do your job first.* She walks past his body stoically, searching the carpet, until she finds it. The single platinum earring. She places it in her jeans pocket.

There. She is done.

But she thinks of her daughter. She remembers the phone call that she forced Sam to make on Friday—Sam's call to Jessica, firing her from her position, shutting her out of his life, over an impersonal telephone line.

All I wanted to do was talk to him, Jessica told her, only hours ago.

Allison looks out the window. Most people don't live up here by the lake year-round. Sam did, loved the tranquillity. Maybe, what, three or four people live up here right now on this street.

Meaning three or four potential eyewitnesses, at a min-imum, who may have seen Jessica come here including the widower next door, whose light was on in the front room when she passed it driving up here.

And who *knows* who may have heard Jessica's reac-tion when she was at Dillon & Becker's offices in the city while Sam fired her from his office in the capital. Allison could hear, over the phone and sitting at a distance, Jessica's protests; did anyone at Dillon & Becker hear her?

Jessica was here, in this house, on the night of the murder. She was upset the day before, after a phone call from Sam. Not a good combination.

And all of this is Allison's fault.

Allison removes the single earring from her pocket and places it back near Sam's body. She yanks a strand of hair from her head and lets it fall to the carpet near Sam. She writes crime fiction; she knows that a strand of hair must have the follicle attached to provide DNA.

What else?

Allison grabs her finger, painted with red polish, and breaks off a substantial piece of her nail. She makes the motion in the air of swinging something, trying to figure where a fingernail might break off. Oh, who knows? She lets the fingernail drop to the carpet as well.

She can't be too obvious. It can't look staged. Maybe this is enough, to draw their attention to her.

What else?

Allison looks at the statuette, on the carpet near Sam's body. Plenty of blood on it, almost dried now. She touches it with her finger, thick like syrup now, and wipes a stain across her maroon sweatshirt. A trace of Sam's blood, on her sweatshirt.

What else?

The Alibi. She remembers it, from the novel she is writing. The novel she hates. *Best Served Cold.*

She knows where his computer is, upstairs. She takes the stairs carefully, lest she lose her balance and fall on her wobbly legs, and goes to his office.

She is lucky, she thinks, though *lucky* hardly seems the word, that Sam does not use a password to protect the screen saver on his computer. The screen is black with asteroids and stars moving about. With one push of the computer mouse, the screen returns to his e-mail's in-box. She hits the "compose" icon and pulls up a new mail message. She types in the words—murky, fuzzy words, that she comes up with off the top of her head—and addresses the message to her own web address, *allison@allison-pagone.com*:

> A:
> NEED TO DISCUSS FURTHER. GETTING WORRIED. MANY WOULD BE UNHAPPY WITH MY INFO. NEED ADVICE ASAP.
> S

She wipes down the keyboard and mouse after she sends the e-mail. She will wipe down the banister, too, and the front doorknob. No, she is not looking to guarantee herself a conviction. She is not going to write her name in blood on his bathroom mirror. What she has done is insurance, nothing more. They won't necessarily be able to make a case against Allison, or even suspect her. But after her work here, they certainly won't be able to make a case against Jessica, either, and that is her principal goal. If it ever gets close to Jessica, Allison will be able to hold herself out, plausibly, as the suspect. After her work here, her daughter will never be accused of this crime.

She checks her watch. It is close to twenty after one. Having sat down for even a minute, she feels intense exhaustion sweep over her. But she resists. Now is no time to get weary. She only has to get back home now.

She will retrieve that novel she's working on and delete it from her computer. If they come looking for her, they will undoubtedly seize the laptop. Another benefit of writing crime fiction—she knows, at least generally speaking, of the government's powers to retrieve deleted material from a computer's hard drive. They will find it. And they will find it very interesting that she deleted this document from her computer only minutes after returning from Sam's house.

Now for the hard part. She will see him one last time.
She thinks of what she wants to say. Yes, she knows it's
foolish, she knows he can't hear her now any more than he
would be able to hear her later, in the privacy of her home.

She comes back down the stairs and moves to Sam, gets
on her knees and begins to cry.

At this moment, she is sure that she loves him. At this
moment, her feelings for Sam have crystallized, have
moved from an intense passion, from a reawakening of
feelings dormant for so many years, to love.

"I love you," she says to him through a full throat. She
reaches for him but it seems inappropriate. Her hand is
only inches from his head. She wants him to see her one
more time, even if he can't. She wants to look into his eyes,
but she will not move him. His face is surprisingly peaceful, if defeated, his eyes closed but his mouth open ever so
slightly.

"I'm so very—Sam, I'm so sorry," she whispers.

But he is dead, and she has Jessica to protect. She rises
to her feet and heads to the kitchen, removes a freezer bag
from a drawer and grabs a paper towel off the roll. She returns to the living room and picks up the award from the
manufacturers' association, wipes it down as well as she
can, grips it firmly with her own hand, then puts it in the
freezer bag. She turns her head away as she does so, avoiding the blood and hair caked against the marble base, sti-
fling her tears because so much of the night remains.

1:31 A.M.

"Talk to me," McCoy says into her collar, as she keeps a
safe distance from Allison's SUV, heading south now, away
from Sam Dillon's house. McCoy left Harrick at Dillon's
house to work with the team, now that Allison is gone.

"I don't know," Harrick says through her earpiece. "I'm looking. What—hang on."

McCoy can hear muffled voices now. A team of federal agents are back in Dillon's home, trying to figure out what the hell Allison Pagone did while she was there.

Maybe, McCoy thinks, *she just came to say good-bye. To see for herself. But probably not.*

"The award is gone," Harrick says. "She took the fucking murder weapon!"

"The earring, too?" McCoy asks.

"Hang on." More muffled noise. "No, no, but it's closer to Dillon's body."

"Okay. Okay. You know what she's doing."

"Hang on," Harrick says. "There's gotta be more."

"Get back to me when you know everything. I'll see where she goes."

"She's going home, Jane."

"I'm not so sure," McCoy says. "Let's see."

1:47 A.M.

Yellow like lemon. She remembers it like it was yesterday, her utter relief when she found her five-year-old daughter outside the back of the Countryside Grocery Store, pointing at the yellow pole in the ground. She no longer shops at this store on Apple and Riordan; it was the place she shopped way back when, back when she and Mat lived around the corner. Now she lives several miles away, but she always smiles when she passes this particular store.

It's still here, the post, and still yellow. But her daughter is no longer five years old.

Allison has a shovel that she keeps in her SUV for snow removal, so it takes her little time to dig up the earth. She pushes the statuette into the ground. Now for the hard part, returning the earth to its previous form. She does the majority of the work with the shovel, but she is finally forced to bend down and use her hands to smooth the ground over. When she is finished, she wipes her forehead with her hands.

She gets up and turns to leave. A flashlight shines in her face. There is illumination out here but it's still relatively dark. The flashlight blinds her. She freezes. Her body goes cold. But if it has to start right here, so be it.

"I'm a federal agent, Mrs. Pagone. Please put down that shovel."

A federal agent?

"Mrs. Pagone, you didn't kill Sam Dillon with that trophy and I assume you won't try to kill me with that shovel. Now please, put down the shovel and back up ten steps."

Allison complies, dropping the shovel and backpedaling.

"I'm Special Agent Jane McCoy." The agent shines the flashlight on her credentials, which she holds out. "FBI."

"I don't understand what this is about," Allison says. "I don't understand what you mean about Sam Dillon."

"No?" McCoy asks. "And that trophy from the Midwest Manufacturers' Association you just buried? No idea what *that* is, either?"

"I don't know what you mean."

"Let me see your hands, please."

Allison raises her hands.

"Turn them around, palms facing you."

Allison reverses her hands.

"I wonder if that broken fingernail matches a nail my partner just found by Sam Dillon's body," McCoy says. "What other clues did you leave, Mrs. Pagone? A business card on the kitchen table?"

"Whoever you are, I don't know what you're talking about."

"I know about Jessica, Mrs. Pagone. I know what happened. I was there."

Allison closes her eyes. *They even know her name.*

"You broke a nail, you moved that earring next to Sam's body. You disposed of the murder weapon."

"She didn't mean to kill him," Allison says.

The federal agent is silent.

"Please," Allison says, realizing how ridiculous her plea must sound.

"Mrs. Pagone, we have a lot to talk about. We can help each other."

Allison's heart pounds. What is happening?

"We have a lot to discuss. Will you come with me to my car around the corner, so I don't freeze my butt off out here?"

Allison slowly moves toward the federal agent. The agent is trying to put her at ease. "What about the shovel?" she asks.

"I'll take it. Please walk past me and stop."

Allison passes the shovel, passes the federal agent, who moves well out of her way, and stops. She hears the agent pick up the shovel, iron scraping against pavement.

"Mrs. Pagone," the agent says, "I'm prepared to agree with you. I'm prepared to swear that your daughter didn't kill Sam Dillon. But I need your help."

2:57 A.M.

Allison drives around Jessica's two-door coupe parked on the driveway and parks her own car in the garage. She leaves the garage door open and stands next to her car.

She looks at her watch. It's almost three in the morning. She spent over an hour talking with Agent McCoy. Almost three in the morning, Jessica could very well have fallen asleep, overwhelmed emotionally.

Allison is hoping not.

She waits one, two minutes. Maybe Jessica did fall asleep. That will make this tougher.

The interior door from the garage opens. Jessica sticks her head out.

Allison brings a finger to her mouth, shakes her head slowly.

Jessica doesn't speak, which is the point here. She waits a moment, trying to understand.

Allison backs up onto the driveway and waves a cupped hand to Jessica.

Jessica slowly closes the door and walks out to her mother. She looks Allison over as she gets closer, her eyes slowly growing in horror.

"Mother—*what did you do*?" Jessica whispers.

"Everything's fine," Allison says, drawing close to her daughter but not touching her. "Something is going on that neither of us knew about. Something about Sam."

"I don't understand."

"I know, Jess, and you can't—"

"Tell me, Mother. Tell me what happened."

"This is what I can tell you. Nobody is going to connect you to this. Sam was—there was something we know nothing about. Sam was involved."

"Sam was involved in what? How do you know this?"

"Jess, I don't know, either, not the details. I just—you have to understand. I talked to somebody. Don't ask me who because I won't tell you. No one is going to say you killed him."

"I *didn't* kill him, Mother." Jessica stands back. "You don't believe me."

"Of course, I believe you."

Allison believes Jessica because she has to believe her. She cannot fathom not believing in Jessica's innocence. There is no other acceptable alternative.

"I'm prepared to have three federal agents swear, under oath, that Jessica didn't kill Sam Dillon," the agent, McCoy, told her an hour ago. *"We're prepared to say that this other man did it."*

Allison had been in no position to protest, because the federal agent was agreeing with her—Jessica didn't kill Sam. But her mind told her what her heart tried desperately to ignore: Jane McCoy wasn't *agreeing* with Allison, exactly. She was saying she was willing to agree, if Allison helped her.

"Of course I believe you," Allison repeats.

"Did you go to the house?" Jessica asks.

"Yes."

"Did you get the earring?"

"I left it there, Jess."

"You *left* it—"

"It's *my* earring, Jessica. *Mine*, not yours. And you have never, ever borrowed them. Okay?"

"I don't understand what you're doing, Mother. I don't understand who you talked to or what they told you. I don't understand why we're standing outside instead of going inside."

Yes, it is cold, very cold outside, and Jessica is only wearing a blouse.

"This is what you need to know," Allison says. "And this is *all* you can know, for now. Sam was involved in something else. He wasn't doing anything wrong, but he had some knowledge, or at least some people thought he did. And our government is interested in that other thing. They are willing to say that this is the reason he was killed. Nothing to do with you or me. They're going to say that. But I have to help them out."

"You're going to help them how?"

"Keep your voice down," Allison says. "They think my house might be bugged."

"What?" Jessica shivers, looks back at the house.

"Voice down, Jessica. It's okay. I'm going to be fine. I'm being protected."

"This is—this is related to what Sam knew about?"

"Yes. They're afraid that I might know, too. I don't. But that's why my house is bugged."

"This is *crazy*, Mother."

"It is what it is," she tells her daughter. "We deal with it." She reaches for her daughter's shoulders but pulls back, doesn't want to touch her with her dirty hands. "Jess, the police will probably think that I killed Sam."

"No."

"It's okay. I'm covered. It's all being worked out. But you have to understand what is going to happen. They're going to come to me, the police. They're probably going to charge me. People are going to think I'm a killer. It's going to be tough for you. But I'm going to be okay. I'm not going to prison. You'll have to trust me on that. It's going to be hard."

"Because you went to his house?" Jessica's face deteriorates into tears. "Mother," she manages, her voice breaking, "what did you do there?"

"It doesn't matter. I'm not going to tell you anything else. You can't know what's going on, Jess. You can't. You have to trust me. You trust me, don't you?"

"I—of course."

"Okay. Did you—have you spoken to anyone tonight? Make any calls or anything like—"

"No," she says. "I've been sitting here freaked out. You were gone so long."

"I know, baby. I'm sorry." She motions to the house. "We have to get back inside. Now, listen. I'm going to tell you inside, for the benefit of whoever's listening, that I killed Sam. Just refuse to believe it. That's fine. We'll talk for a few minutes, then you'll go to bed. Try to sleep, Jess. I promise you we're going to be fine. Then, in the morning, you have to leave. You have to leave and not come back to this house until this thing is over. You can't speak to your dad about this, either. I'm going to talk to him, okay? But you can't. When this is over, you'll understand why."

Jessica looks back at the house. "We have to go in," she says.

"Yes." Allison steers her daughter, whispers in her ear. "This is going to turn out fine, Jess," she promises.

SATURDAY, FEBRUARY 7

7:05 P.M.

ecrets. She lived with them for over a decade, maybe since the day she and Mat married, though she cannot rewind and know this. She did not love him. She did not love the man she spent over twenty years with, with whom she had a daughter.

Secrets never stay secret. She couldn't live with it forever, and once Jessica was in college, it seemed the time.

And secrets, now, with Sam. An *ethical dilemma*, he said twice over the phone during the last week, but he wouldn't elaborate. Wouldn't even discuss it with her face to face.

A secret. Sam wouldn't tell her.

And neither had she told him. A secret. Probably the same secret. She knows, too.

The FBI already seems to know. They have already seized Mat's bank records. Mat told her—in the way he does—over dinner, in January. They had promised to do it, to see each other, to keep in touch. Mat often drank too much but really overdid it on that occasion.

They think I bribed some senators, he said, spitting out the words as if they were poison.

It didn't take Einstein to fill in the gaps. It had been a big victory for Mat, when he got that bill out of the Senate last year, the prescription-drug bill. A big but controversial victory, involving a sudden vote change on the part of three different senators. That kind of behind-the-scenes arm-twisting might look bad to the public, but it makes legends out of lobbyists. Mat was a big winner in that deal.

Allison had noticed it when they were settling up on the divorce in December, a month earlier. Several large withdrawals from their bank account. About thirty thousand dollars, withdrawn in cash, over the last several months. She decided that she wouldn't care, wouldn't mention it. Maybe he had a mistress. Maybe he was trying to protect himself financially, stealing from the pot before it was divided up. She didn't know and she didn't care. She had plenty of her own money. If a peaceful resolution of the marriage cost her thirty thousand, it was the best money she had ever spent.

She didn't know Mat was putting the cash in the hands of state legislators.

An ethical dilemma, Sam told her, twice in the last week, over the phone. He wouldn't elaborate. A secret. He must have known.

She had the same secret, and neither of them wanted to tell the other because of who was involved.

Allison closes the book she's reading. She's hungry. It's just after seven in the evening and she hasn't eaten all day. Her stomach is in revolt.

Oh, she was so stupid, overreacting like a schoolgirl. Sam was admiring Jessica at the party, and she drives all the way down to the capital to make Sam fire her? Even accuses him of sleeping with Jess?

She had connected the three things like a paranoid, insecure child. Her daughter's comment, that she was interested in *a guy at work* and Allison *wouldn't approve*. Sam's mention of an ethical dilemma. And then Sam's look at Jessica at that party.

She covers her face with a hand. She wishes she could wipe yesterday off the calendar. Just remove Friday, February the sixth from the books, and explain to her daughter in a thoughtful, mature way that the man for whom she is carrying a torch is actually Mommy's boyfriend now.

She'll do it. She'll call Sam and apologize for her childish behavior.

She'll talk to Jessica and explain everything.

7:20 P.M.

Jane McCoy stands, silently, over the body of Sam Dillon. Owen Harrick walks out of the kitchen. "It's clean," he says. "We swept the whole place. The wire is gone."

"Positive?" McCoy whispers.

"Positive. It's clean, Jane."

Other agents, two men and a woman, emerge from other parts of the house, all standing around the body of Sam Dillon.

"So we're clean here," McCoy confirms.

Every agent nods.

"Okay," she says, her voice above a whisper for the first time—far above a whisper. "Then can someone tell me how the hell this happened?"

"Nobody thought he'd *kill* him," says Owen Harrick. "He never gave any indication. You saw Haroon's e-mail, Jane."

Yes, she did. Since he first arrived in the U.S., Ram Haroon has had an e-mail address set up—*pakistudent@interserver.com*. Whenever Haroon needed to communicate with the U.S. government, he sent an e-mail to himself, secure in the knowledge that the government was monitoring the site and reading the message, too. He would have to be careful with the text, in the incredibly unlikely event that the Liberation Front was hacking into the site, too, but he would be able to get his message across to the feds.

It had been through this e-mail address that Haroon informed the FBI, a few months ago, that he had made contact with a front man who was now calling himself Larry Evans. It was through this e-mail address that Haroon informed them, last week, that Larry Evans was carefully watching two people, Sam Dillon and Allison Pagone, because there was some fear that Dillon had become wise to the operation at Flanagan-Maxx and had told his girl-friend, Allison, about it.

"Haroon said Evans was going to watch and wait," Harrick agrees. "Not kill."

"You guys didn't see him come in?" McCoy asks, looking at the trio of agents assigned to watch the house.

"No. He slipped in when the food was delivered about six-twenty."

They know this now. The Bureau has been watching and monitoring, by video, the property surrounding Sam Dillon's house. Larry Evans was good. He snuck into the house when Sam Dillon was answering the front door. The problem is, Larry Evans not only escaped Sam Dillon's attention; he faked out three federal agents.

"We saw him leaving, which was when we called you," one of the agents says.

Yes, and then they went to the video and hit rewind, saw Larry Evans pick the lock through the back entrance at six-twenty—just as Sam Dillon was answering the front door—and saw him leave again about ten minutes after seven.

"I can't believe this," McCoy mumbles to herself. She looks at Harrick. "We're good on Allison Pagone?"

"Yeah. We've got her covered."

"Make sure of it, Owen. No one else is dying tonight."

"What do we do now?" Harrick asks.

McCoy walks around the room delicately. "We don't do anything, is what we do. We can't be seen here. We have to go."

"We leave this body here?" Agent Cline asks.

"Hell yes, we do. What do you suggest? We call the police? Maybe we should just call up Larry Evans and tell him we're interested in him."

"Okay, okay." Harrick waves his hands. "Let's get out of here, everyone."

McCoy is the first to walk out. A voice comes through her earpiece.

"Agent McCoy?" It's one of her team, watching the perimeter of the property.

"Yeah," McCoy says into her collar.

"Someone's driving down the street. A Mazda two-door coupe. I'll run the plates."

"How close?" McCoy asks.

"Very. You guys better clear out. Looks like it's stopping at Dillon's house."

7:24 P.M.

"*Jessica* Pagone?" McCoy says into her collar microphone. "The daughter?"

"Affirmative," the voice comes back through her earpiece. "Allison Pagone's daughter was just in his house. Less than three minutes. Just drove away."

McCoy looks at Harrick, who is also listening through an earpiece.

"Go back in there in one minute," McCoy says into her microphone. "Rear entry. Look around. Out."

"Out."

McCoy looks at her partner. "What the hell is *that* about?"

Harrick shakes his head. "Allison's daughter? She knows Dillon?"

"Shit, *I* don't know." McCoy's legs squirm in the car. McCoy and Harrick are parked the next street over from the street on which Sam Dillon lives, or *lived*, past tense.

"She was only there two minutes," Harrick says. "She saw him lying there on the carpet and flipped out, presumably. But where's she going now?"

"Who knows?"

"Do we do anything?" Harrick asks. "I'm not sure we do."

"There's nothing *to* do," McCoy agrees, trying to calm herself. "So she found him dead. Someone was going to. It's not like we're going to hand Larry Evans over to the police or anything."

"I wonder if Jessica called the cops." Harrick pats the steering wheel.

McCoy shrugs. "Probably. Who knows? I'm sending our team back in, just to look over the place. I doubt Jessica did anything in there. She didn't have the time. She probably saw him, wigged out, and got the hell out of Dodge."

"That's what *I'd* do," Harrick agrees.

"Let's just sit tight and wait a while. We'll keep our guys in position after they look the place over. Sooner or later, the police will be coming, and you and I will have to get out."

"We don't tell them anything?"

"There's nothing to tell them, Owen." The windows in their car are fogging up. McCoy recalls a time, years ago, when the windows fogged up for a much more enjoyable reason. "We can't let them in on this."

"They won't come up with Larry Evans as a suspect," Harrick says. "His prints aren't on any database, and I'm sure he was smart enough not to leave any, anyway."

"Yeah, he's smart. A clock? A trophy? This thing looks like anything *but* a professional hit."

"But what I'm wondering," Harrick says, "is whether the police will come up with someone *else* as a suspect."

"I don't know," says McCoy, her voice trailing off.

"We can't let someone else go down for this, Jane. Like Jessica Pagone, for one. She could have left ten different clues in there, pointing back to her."

McCoy pats her partner's arm. "Let's jump off that bridge when we come to it, okay?"

7:56 P.M.

Yes. She will call Jessica, Allison decides. She will meet with her and explain all of this. She will admit that it was she who demanded that Sam make that phone call and fire her. She will apologize for her misbehavior and use the apology as a segue, a bridge to fixing things between them. Telling Jessica about Sam will be a way of reintroducing herself as the same woman she's always been, the same mother who loves her daughter dearly, but who now is single and has a new man in her life.

Jessica's an adult now. She has to be ready for this. She has to accept that people—even her own mother and father—sometimes drift apart, and it's not one person's fault. It's not a question of fault at all.

She hears the doorknob rattling and pops out of her chair, moves into the hallway. This is a relatively safe part of the city, but it's still the city. And she lives alone now. The creaks and groans in the middle of the night take on a frighteningly new dimension, now that she doesn't have a former middle linebacker sleeping next to her. No, it's not exactly the middle of the night. It's only a little after eight in the evening—

She hears another noise—a key working the knob—and

the door opens. Jessica rushes in and closes the door behind her quickly. She turns and sees Allison. Jessica's face is washed-out, her mascara streaked down her cheeks. She is trembling, on the verge of collapse.

Allison reaches her in an instant, takes her in her arms and eases her to the floor.

"What happened?" Allison asks, holding Jessica's head, inventorying her body for injuries out of instinct. "God, sweetheart, what happened?"

8:04 P.M.

McCoy turns off her cell phone and plugs it into the charger, attached to the cigarette lighter in the car. The team that reentered Sam Dillon's home, after Jessica Pagone's unexpected visit, has just reported back.

"Well, at least she didn't mess with anything," McCoy says.

"But she didn't leave it clean, either," Harrick says. He is referring to the single platinum earring on the carpet near Sam's body.

"She probably bent over the body." McCoy shrugs. "Earrings fall off."

"We should retrieve it, Jane."

McCoy shakes her head. "I'm not going to have them tamper with a crime scene."

"It wouldn't be tampering, Jane. The crime scene didn't include an earring. And we know she didn't kill him. She came in afterward. Hell, we have Larry Evans on video."

McCoy looks at Harrick.

"I'm saying, this could put this girl in the soup," he says forcefully.

McCoy chews on her lip.

"That's a bad thing, by the way," Harrick adds.

"Maybe so, maybe not."

"Janey, listen to me. This has been a crazy night. I know that. Lot of things happening we didn't expect, a lot of on-the-spot decisions. But we can't let this girl get in trouble."

"Oh, we won't," she says absently.

"Then tell them to get back in there and remove the damn earring."

McCoy shakes her head slowly.

"Jane—"

"Jessica Pagone is Allison Pagone's daughter," she says. "And Allison Pagone may be a part of this now, like it or not."

"What are you thinking here, Agent?"

"Just thinking," she says. "Thinking that Larry Evans must have been pretty worried about Sam Dillon, right? Enough to kill him. He's got to be worried about Allison, too. He's already monitoring her, right? So he's worried about her, too."

"The point being," Harrick takes it, "that we might need her help."

"Yeah," McCoy mumbles, thinking it through.

Her cell phone rings. McCoy almost jumps out of her seat.

"McCoy. Okay? Okay." She looks at her partner. "Don't do anything. Just make sure that house is safe. Whatever it takes."

She punches off, raises her eyebrows. "Jessica just arrived at her mother's house."

"Allison's house." Harrick moans. "Okay. Jesus Christ, okay."

McCoy falls back in her seat.

"She's telling her mom that she just found Sam Dillon dead," Harrick envisions. "She's hysterical. Scared. Freaked out."

"All of those," McCoy agrees. "And Allison is worried."

"Worried?" Harrick seems doubtful. "Grief-stricken, maybe."

"No," McCoy says. "Worried."

Harrick touches Jane's arm. "You think she's wondering whether her daughter killed Dillon?"

McCoy's shoulders rise. "She can't be sure she *didn't* kill him."

"Jane, no," Harrick says. "You can't blackmail her."

"I'm not talking about blackmail, Agent." McCoy grinds her teeth, a nervous habit when she's thinking fast. "Allison Pagone is going to think what she thinks. Not putting her mind at ease is not the same thing as lying."

"She helps us out," Harrick says, perhaps warming to the deal, not that McCoy really cares, "and we make sure Jessica isn't implicated. And she's never the wiser about whether her daughter is a killer."

"Something like that," McCoy says. "Right about now, mother and daughter are probably discovering that Jessica left some evidence behind." She looks at Harrick. "Let's see what happens."

"Jane," Harrick says. "You'd really do that to this lady? Make her think her own daughter is a murderer?"

"*She'll* think it," McCoy says. "I won't say that to her."

"Jeez."

"Oh, lighten the hell up, Owen. You're in the big leagues now. I think what we're doing is worth it, don't you?" She waves at him. "When this is over, and everyone is safe and sound, I'll tell her the truth, okay? I'll give her a copy of the videotape of Larry Evans breaking into Dillon's house. But for now, we use whatever we have."

Harrick stares at McCoy.

"When this thing is all over," she repeats, annoyed, "I will make it very clear to Allison that her daughter did not kill Sam Dillon. But until then, we use what we have. Relax. You want to stop an international terrorist operation or not?"

8:38 P.M.

Allison sits next to her daughter, who is finally beginning to calm. Allison has put a blanket over Jessica's shoulders and given her some hot tea. They are sitting on the couch in the living room.

Jessica has been home for half an hour now. It took her the better part of ten minutes to even tell Allison what had happened. The next twenty minutes were spent with Allison confirming, absolutely, that she heard her daughter correctly.

Sam is dead.

"I just wanted to talk to him," she says. "I wanted to know why I was fired."

Sam is dead. She can't believe she is hearing the words. She can't believe it's true. Her first instinct is to rush out of her home and go there, or at least to call his house. That is her first reaction, her second, her third, but still she has not made a move. She is more concerned about someone else at the moment.

"Does anyone else at Dillon and Becker know he fired you?" Allison asks.

Jessica shakes her head. "No. I didn't talk to anyone. I was like a zombie. I just left. I didn't even pack my things."

"Good," Allison says. "Good."

Jessica's head whips around at Allison. "You think I might be blamed for this? Someone would think that *I*—"

"No, honey, of course not," Allison says quickly. "No one would think that."

"I was there," she says ominously.

"Yes, you were. Did anyone see you? Jess? Do you know if anyone saw you there tonight?"

"I don't—I don't know, Mother. How could I know that?"

Allison takes her daughter's hand, gets on her knees so she is face to face with Jessica.

"I'm not going to let anything happen to you," she says.

"I didn't—you think I killed him." Jessica pulls away from her mother, gets to her feet. "You think I killed Sam?"

"No, I don't." Allison follows, rising and moving to her daughter, who is backing away. "Of course I don't. I'm only saying, you were there. There might be questions. I'm not going to let anything happen to you."

"Oh, God." Jessica leans against the mantel over the fireplace for support.

"This is my fault, Jess. And I'll do anything to protect you from this."

Jessica's eyes slowly move to her mother. "What do you mean, it's your fault?"

Allison takes a breath. She was going to tell her anyway. There is some notion to not throwing fuel on a fire, but she thinks better of it. Full disclosure seems warranted right now.

"Sam and I have been seeing each other, Jess," she says.

Jessica's eyes widen. "You and—and *Sam*?"

"I know that you approached him a few months ago. He told me. You were interested in him. I can understand why."

"You and *Sam*, Mother?" She retreats from Allison.

"Yes," Allison says. "It happened after your father and I had split up. But yes."

Jessica's eyes cast about the room. This is overload. This, on top of everything else.

"This is my fault," Allison says. "I'm the reason you were there tonight."

"What does that mean?" She walks toward her mother, emboldened.

"You were fired," Allison says, "at the request of an insecure, jealous woman who wasn't thinking straight."

Jessica angles her face, looks hard at her mother. "You told him to fire me."

"I went down to the capital, yesterday, and made him call you."

"You told him—to *fire* me."

Allison nods. "I realized, today, how stupid I was. I was

going to call you and talk to you about it. I swear to you, I was. You were going to get your job back."

Jessica does not seem capable of a response, another emotional outburst. Where to put this, on the list of tonight's events? She tucks her hair behind her ear, a habit she formed during adolescence, a habit she got from Allison.

Allison sees, looking at her daughter's profile, the platinum earring on her ear, the earring she purchased not long ago. No big surprise. Allison had even noticed them absent from her jewelry box, over Christmas, and figured as much. Not the first time her daughter raided her jewelry or clothes. She always took a small pleasure in it, actually.

Jessica is well dressed, Allison now notices. A violet blouse, black skirt and boots, more makeup than usual, however smeared across her face it may be now. And the earrings. She was dressed up to see Sam. She sees with her own eyes now, for the first time, what Sam told her. Jessica was carrying a torch for him.

"I'm so sorry about this, honey."

Jessica continues to pace by the fireplace, fuming, the anger temporarily overcoming the horror.

She couldn't have done it, Allison says to herself. Not Jessica. She feels the heat burning in her chest, a moment of panic, however hard she tries to fight the logic working through her brain. *She wouldn't be so distraught that she'd kill him.*

They spend the remainder of the evening repeating this conversation. Allison interrogates Jessica on what, exactly, she did in the house, where she went, whether anyone saw her. She tries to cast aside the growing realization that Sam Dillon is dead, because she must focus on the young woman who might be charged with his murder.

Jessica decides to have some wine, the first time she has done so in front of her mother, the legal limits of a twenty-year-old drinking alcohol notwithstanding. It's a rebuke,

Allison realizes, but she will certainly not object under the circumstances.

Because either way, whether she killed him or she simply fears that she will be accused of doing so, Jessica needs to be calm now. A little wine won't hurt. And Allison sees, finally, that her interrogation is beginning to cause a panic in her daughter.

Oh, she is certainly behaving as if she were innocent. If she killed Sam, she is very talented at acting otherwise. So no, she couldn't have done it.

Right?

There is no remorse, not even a hint, which is what Allison would expect to see. It is horror, revulsion, but not remorse, or even fear.

So no, she couldn't have done it.

Jessica is wiped out by eleven-thirty, and a bit tipsy, after nearly three hours of conversation. They may go to the police together, tomorrow, they decide. Explain all of this. Allison is not so sure. She envisions a picture painted by local cops: a young, confused woman with a crush on a man; he dumps her; the woman goes to the house the next night and bludgeons him. There could be people, regardless of what Jessica thinks, who could attest to each and every one of these facts.

She is not so sure how this will look. She considers going to Sam's home now. She admits that in part it is because she wants to see him, to touch him again. To say good-bye.

But that is not the only reason. She wants to see how her daughter left things. She wants to see how things look before she marches her daughter into a police station to admit that she was there tonight.

Jessica goes off to bed. Allison watches her daughter take the stairs slowly. Jessica is utterly exhausted. Allison hopes that she will be able to sleep.

Allison returns to the living room and takes a bit of

wine for herself. Yes, she wants so much to see him again. It hasn't even registered yet. He is gone. Like something she has read about someone else, the anonymous victims in the news every day. Not Sam.

No, Jessica could not have killed him. No. Impossible.

"Oh, shit." She hears her daughter upstairs. *"Shit."*

Allison stands and moves to the hallway. Jessica rushes down the stairs and through the living room, scanning the carpet, overturning cushions, cursing as she goes along.

"What?" Allison asks in a panic. "What?"

Jessica continues her inventory, moving from the living room to the kitchen, running her hands over the countertops, even opening the refrigerator, then racing outside, leaving the front door wide open.

Allison follows, calling after her. Jessica runs to the driveway, jerks open her car door, and looks through the car even more thoroughly than the house.

"Jessica, for God's sake, what?" she asks. She sees the fear now, for the first time, on her daughter's face. She feels the fear in herself, too, followed immediately by a sense of calm. A mother's defense mechanism. She knows how much she loves the daughter who has felt betrayed by her. She knows that she would do anything for her.

"Tell me it's not at Sam's," Jessica mumbles urgently to herself, searching the floorboards of the car. "Please tell me I didn't leave it—"

"Jessica," Allison says calmly. "Tell me."

Jessica gets out of the car slowly and looks at Allison with tears in her eyes, searching her mother's face for some kind of comfort, no differently than she has looked at Allison so many times, for so many reasons, over the years.

"Mother," Jessica says, her throat full, "I'm missing one of my earrings."

ELEVEN
YEARS
EARLIER

Ram Haroon squints into the light of the room, after traveling blindfolded in a dark sedan, then up several flights of stairs. His father is next to him, patting his arm protectively.

"Everything is fine, Zulfi," he says to him.

"Not Zulfi," says the man behind the desk, an American speaking the native Pakistani language rather well. "Now it's Ram, I thought."

"Yes, Ram," says his father.

The man across the desk is wearing a light blue shirt and glasses. He is about Ram's father's age, but sun has damaged his Caucasian skin.

"Zulfi," the man says to Ram, "is a bit too, uh 'democratic,' let's say. Fine for Baluchistan, but here in Peshawar, not so good."

Ram—born Zulfikar Ali Haroon—was named after the first democratically elected prime minister of Pakistan, Zulfikar Ali Bhutto, who was ultimately overthrown by the first of several dictators who have controlled Pakistan since its birth. Ram's dead sister, Benazir, was named after Zulfikar's daughter, Benazir Bhutto, who later was elected to the same post herself.

"Your mother liked freedom," says the man.

Ram stares at the man.

The man nods. "Your mother worked for Central Intelligence for several years."

"I know that," Ram says defiantly. Ram has known this, to be precise, for all of forty-eight hours, after he confronted his father about what he had been doing in secret, all of the late-night business he had been conducting. He had figured that Father was running guns for the *mujahedin*, that he was probably connected to one of the militant groups, but he hadn't figured that Father was doing so at the request of American intelligence.

That was something that none of the militants knew, either.

"Your father is an undercover operative," says the man.

"I know that also."

"Good. So you know that if you ever released that information, he would be immediately killed. And so, probably, would you."

Ram feels the heat in his chest. Father places a hand on his arm.

"He knows that," Father says.

Ram sees his mother now with a renewed admiration. He is not, himself, political, and never has been. Such concerns are lost on this thirteen-year-old boy. His classmates who have lived in Peshawar their whole lives have experienced more of it, and have developed an anti-Western understanding of the world, but Ram is a child of Baluchistan, where this holy war means little more than a few hundred Afghan refugees spilling into their region. But Mother always preached about freedom, about America, about the bravery of Zulfikar Bhutto, who fought for freedom and spent the last years of his life tortured and neglected in prison, before he was summarily executed by one of the many dictators who have strangled Pakistan.

Your Pakistan will be a free Pakistan, she often told him.

"I want to join also, Mr. Shiels," Ram says in English.

"So your dad says." Shiels leans back in his chair, an easy smile on his face, but his eyes narrow.

Mr. Shiels will need convincing. Father, too, will need convincing. Father did not want this for Ram, but he probably realized that, in part, his son would want to be a part of this for the same reason that Father did, as a way of continuing a connection with Mother.

Father had reluctantly explained to Ram, after much prodding, that Ram would be treated differently in the CIA than Father. He was educated and had his mother's intelligence. He would probably continue in his education and become an asset, in the eyes of whatever Islamic militant organization he pretended to be a part of, someone who could plausibly travel overseas as a student and be engaged in a much more far-reaching operation than running guns.

And Father had repeated, so many times in the last two days, that Ram had a choice, at any time, to leave. *Preparing for an operation*, he told Ram, *is preparing to die.*

That meant Mother had been prepared to die, too, though she hadn't expected to die as a civilian casualty in a random bombing by the Soviets. And she hadn't anticipated that her four-year-old daughter would be sitting at the front of the class, playing dolls, when it happened.

The Soviets had killed Mother. Mother, who used to sing Ram to sleep at night, used to fill him with praise and hope for a better future. Mother, who used to tell him, before he did anything, to ask one question: *What would your parents do?*

"I want to join," Ram repeats.

The man comes from around his desk and sits on it, close to Ram. "We'll see about that," the man says. "We'll take it slow."

"I will do what you say," Ram says.

"Very good," the man says. "You'll be working with me for now. We'll see how things progress."

Ram nods and offers his hand. "My name is Ram Haroon."

"Call me Irv," Shiels says, shaking his hand.

ACKNOWLEDGMENTS

Writing a novel in reverse chronological order wasn't easy. It required the help of patient, generous friends, to whom I owe many thanks.

To Carole Baron, for supporting this ambitious project. To David Highfill, my editor, for taking a chance on a unique plotting concept and guiding me through it. To Marilyn Ducksworth, Michael Barson, and Megan Millenky, the best publicists in the business, who got stuck with the job of trying to make me look good (never an easy task). To Christine Zika, for all her hard work and enthusiasm. You guys are the best!

To Jeff Gerecke, my literary agent, for preserving my sanity through the drafting of the novel.

To Randy Kaplan, soon to be a household name in the book world, for his careful and thoughtful review of several drafts of the book. To Connie Stennes, my wife's drama teacher, in Montevideo, Minnesota, for offering her insights. To Todd (T.A.) Stone, a talented novelist himself, for his advice on how best to ambush a terrorist convoy. (Remind me never to get on your bad side, Todd.)

To Dr. Ronald Wright, a forensic pathologist in Florida, for once again volunteering his time to answer my technical questions. To Adam Tullier, for his critique of an earlier, rather different version of the novel. To Paul Johnson, for his translation of the Arabic language and for his sense of humor. To Drew Powers, for assisting on plot and characterization. If I can get it past Drew, I can get it past anyone.

A now redundant thank you to Jim Jann, a great friend with an incredible eye for nuance, characterization, and atmosphere in a novel. To Dan Collins, for lending an ear on plot and for answering my many questions regarding federal law enforcement.

Thanks to everyone at my law firm for their support and enthusiasm: David Williams, Doug Bax, Kerry Saltzman, Young Kim, Chris Covatta, Michelle Powers, Adam Tullier, and Grant Tullier.

To my wife, Susan, for spending countless hours listening to an obsessive writer ramble on about plot, character, and minor details, when that writer should be spending more time telling her how much he truly, madly loves her.

Edgar Award®-winning author
David Ellis

Jury of One
0-425-201457

Children's rights advocate Shelly Trotter is out of
her depth in criminal court, defending a teenager
accused of killing a cop. And when she discovers
that he may be her own son, nothing—not legal
ethics, not political pressure—will stop her from
keeping him off of death row.

"COMPELLING...ELLIS CREATES AN AUTHENTIC WORLD OF
CORRUPT COPS, AMBITIOUS POLITICIANS,
AND DOGGED P.I.S."
—*ENTERTAINMENT WEEKLY*

"TERRIFIC...A GRABBER FROM START TO FINISH."
—*TORONTO SUN*

Available wherever books are sold or at
penguin.com

Edgar Award®-winning author
David Ellis

Line of Vision
0-425-18376-9

"DON'T THINK YOU CAN PUT *LINE OF VISION*
DOWN—YOU CAN'T. ELLIS WON'T LET YOU GO, FROM THE
FIRST TANTALIZING PAGE TO THE FINAL DOUBLE TWIST."
—BARBARA PARKER

"THE BEST NOVEL I'VE READ IN A WHILE...SURPRISING."
—JAMES PATTERSON

Life Sentence
0-425-19480-9

"ELLIS SETS A NEW STANDARD WITH THIS SUPERB LEGAL
THRILLER...[A] STUNNING ENDING."
—*LIBRARY JOURNAL*

"CHILLING...A TALE COMBINING BETRAYAL, TENSE COURTROOM
DRAMA, FAMILY TRAGEDY AND A QUICK TWIST OF SURPRISE
AT THE END. IT WAS HARD TO PUT DOWN."
—*SAN ANTONIO EXPRESS NEWS*

Available wherever books are sold or at
penguin.com